CORNISH
HORRORS

CORNISH HORRORS

Tales from the Land's End

Edited by
JOAN PASSEY

This collection first published in 2021 by
The British Library
96 Euston Road
London NW1 2DB

Selection, introduction and notes © 2021 Joan Passey

'The Mask' © 1912 The Estate of F. Tennyson Jesse

Dates attributed to each story relate to first publication.

Cataloguing in Publication Data
A catalogue record for this publication is available from the British Library

ISBN 978 0 7123 5399 1
e-ISBN 978 0 7123 6758 5

Frontispiece illustration by Mauricio Villamayor with illustration by Sandra Gómez
Cover design by Mauricio Villamayor with illustration by Sandra Gómez
Text design and typesetting by Tetragon, London
Printed in England by CPI Group (UK) Ltd, Croydon, CR0 4YY

Contents

INTRODUCTION

When Sherlock Holmes and John Watson headed to Cornwall in 1910 it was for rest and recuperation. Being Holmes and Watson, their vacation was inevitably scuppered by the discovery that a crime was afoot. News of the horrible murders spreads across the newspapers and even reaches the far-flung city of London—"the Cornish horrors" captured the popular imagination, and Holmes himself claimed it was the "strangest case I had ever handled". In its own way, 'The Adventure of the Devil's Foot' is a travel narrative, responding to contemporary concerns about Cornwall, tourism, and mass media. Throughout the nineteenth century many people were visiting Cornwall for the first time and talking about it in increasingly strange and mystical ways. Like Holmes and Watson, many were attracted by the supposed health benefits of the sun and sea—Cornwall was thought to be Mediterranean in climate, and similarly foreign and mysterious in its culture and history. While Watson pleads with Holmes to rest, Holmes is more interested in the county's archaeology and anthropology, seeking arrow heads and ruins. Real nineteenth-century tourists, too, gravitated to Cornwall's history, and the sense that the past was somehow present in Cornwall—somehow living, tangible, visitable. Travelling to Cornwall was not just a long journey across land, but also seemingly through time.

It was easier to do this sort of time travelling than ever before. In 1859 Cornwall was the last English county to be connected to the national rail network with the construction of Isambard Kingdom Brunel's famous Royal Albert Bridge across the Tamar. New hotels were built along the railway line and guide books were produced in abundance, not just detailing Cornwall's lush scenery and best eateries, but its myths and legends, too. Alfred Lord Tennyson visited Cornwall in pursuit of the myth of King Arthur, and many followed in his footsteps, guided by the Cornish setting of his celebrated epic *Idylls of the King* (1859–1885). At the same time Cornwall's dominant industry, mining, was in decline, and its death was slow and painful. Mining did not just make up the bulk of Cornwall's economy, but its sense of culture, legend, and identity. Historically, Cornwall has considered itself to be both English and not-English, local and foreign, a county, a duchy, a nation of its own. Cornwall has a long and noble heritage of being both passionately royalist and rabidly resistant. Contrasts define the county, as it was also simultaneously conceived of as both technologically advanced, almost preternaturally so, and deeply primitive, a land of barbarous people and uncivilised behaviour. Cornish miners were seen as the best in the world and Cornwall's mining successes fuelled the industrial revolution. A lot of what makes the Victorians Victorian would not have been possible without Cornwall—while at the same time the Cornish were framed as somewhat antithetical to archetypal Victorian ideals of propriety, civilisation, and a thoroughly stiff upper lip. Instead the Cornish were "West barbary barbarians", ungovernable miners, fiery Celts, and potentially even smugglers, wreckers, and pirates. You would think this reputation would scare off any would-be tourists, but instead it had the opposite effect—tourists flocked to this strange, frightening land on England's own doorstep. At a time where rapidly expanding empire and imperialist energies led to a fascination with the other and the exotic, Cornwall offered all the novelty of foreign climes and a foreign people significantly closer to home. Robert Louis Stevenson, author of *Strange Case of Dr. Jekyll and Mr. Hyde,* turns his Gothic sights on Cornwall when he recalls the uncanny experience of meeting with Cornish miners abroad:

> A knot of Cornish miners who kept grimly by themselves... discussing privately the secrets of their old-world, mysterious race. Lady Hester Stanhope believed she could make something great of the Cornish; for my part, I can make nothing of them at all. A division of races, older and more original than that of Babel, keeps this close, esoteric family apart from neighbour-ing Englishmen. Not even a Red Indian seems more foreign in my eyes. This is one of the lessons of travel—that some of the strangest races dwell next door to you at home.[*]

This is an effective summary of attitudes towards Cornwall at the time as an ancient, distant, and separate place. Cornwall was seem-ingly conceptually "uncovered", a relic or artefact of the past dis-interred by tourists, filling the economic vacuum left in mining's wake. There was profound anxiety—from both within and without the county—that this influx of bodies and attention would corrode everything that made Cornwall attractive in the first place; that Cornwall's spectres and giants may be scared away by the visiting hordes. William Connor Sydney, writing in 1897, states

> [f]or lovers of the folk-lore and rapidly-vanishing popular superstitions few districts of England possess greater interest than Cornwall, though whether it will remain so much longer

---

[*] Robert Louis Stevenson, *Across the Plains* (London: Chatto & Windus, 1909), p. 55. Lady Stanhope (1776–1839) was a socialite, traveller, and adventurer.

may fairly be questioned. Railways, and the gradual assimilation of its people more and more into ordinary English society will have the effect, it is greatly to be feared, of banishing its huge array of witches and hobgoblins, giants and dwarfs, grim spectres, and haunted corridors to the limbo of things that had been.[*]

This goes some way to explaining the number of narratives in this collection that feature the county somewhat rejecting the unwary visitor. Yet, the visitors kept coming, both attracted and repulsed, seeking ghosts, but also inspiration. Some of the greatest literary minds in the world travelled to witness the county's wonders for themselves across the nineteenth century, including George Eliot, Charles Dickens, Thomas Hardy, Bram Stoker, and Mary Elizabeth Braddon, to name but a few. Their reports of and works on Cornwall then inspired and encouraged new travellers in turn—Dinah Craik went in pursuit of Tennyson's Arthur, as did celebrated ghost story author Vernon Lee. Wilkie Collins rushed to the county, eager to see it before it was changed by the railway. There was a need to capture something of old Cornwall before it was lost to the onslaught of modernity, a notion which appealed to a populace experiencing rapid change and fearing the consequences. It is difficult for us now to imagine the speed of changes to technologies, thought, politics, science, communication, and movement across the nineteenth century. Or maybe not, considering the ways in which the internet has changed our day to day lives so swiftly across our own century. The way people were talking to each other, experiencing reality,

---

[*]   William Connor Sydney, 'Superstition in Cornwall', *Belgravia* (Jan 1897), p. 45.

and conceiving of the size of the world was all in upheaval, and Cornwall became something of a microcosm for anxieties over the past colliding with the present and bearing the crushing weight of the future. This led to an outpouring of Gothic fiction set in the county. While Cornwall was newly interesting, however, it was far from new, and its ghosts were not nineteenth-century ghosts. John D. Sedding's 'A Ramble in West Cornwall' (1887) states that

> [o]n whatever side you like to take it, the historic, the pre-historic, the natural, architectural, geological, ornithological, or on the side of its folklore, Christian or heathen—the place teems with subject matter that is as curious as it is interesting. Cornwall is the nursery ground of the saints; the fabled land of Lyonesse; the home of the giants; the haunt of fairies, pixies, mermaids, demons, and spectres. To speak of its natural aspects, its wild seaboard, and frequent air of savagery, one is almost bound to use terms of fancy.[*]

Before Bram Stoker ever set foot in the county Cornwall had long been the home of piskies lurking in the mines, demanding the crusts of pasties in exchange for warning the miners of encroaching disasters. Tintagel was the seat of King Arthur and the setting for Tristan and Isolde, star-crossed lovers before even Romeo and Juliet. Even earlier than that it was theorised that Cornwall may have been the famous Cassiteride Isles written about by Herodotus, a place sought out by the ancient Phoenician people for its world class tin. These ancient bloodlines are referenced in 'The Mask' and 'The Coming

---

[*]   John D. Sedding, 'A Ramble in West Cornwall', *The British Architect* (1887), p. 443.

of Abel Behenna' in particular, with each narrative calling upon the racialisation of the Cornish as a seemingly foreign people, with this foreignness entrenched in Cornwall's global connections.

According to legend Joseph of Arimathea too came in search of tin—with the child Christ in tow. Perhaps, then, those are the "feet of ancient times" and Cornwall offers the "pastures green" of William Blake's *Jerusalem*. Despite this terrible bounty of history and legend Cornwall has always been somewhat occluded from national and literary histories. Hence, perhaps, why these stories have seldom been collected together before. When you start looking, Cornwall starts cropping up everywhere, a sort of haunting in its own right. And Cornwall's spectres did not stop their mischief in the nineteenth century, either. There is no doubt that this nineteenth-century Gothic energy inspired later authors like Daphne du Maurier and Winston Grahame and in 1960 the poet John Betjeman referred to Cornwall as a place laden with "imagined ghosts on unfrequented roads". A number of horror movies made use of the county's ample tempestuous coasts and barren moors, and more recently Wyl Menmuir's novel *The Many* (2019) and Mark Jenkin's film *Bait* (2019) have captured something of a haunted, isolated Cornwall. The legacies of these stories still imprint on the county today—in some quite literal ways. For example, Merlin's face has been carved into the rocks at Tintagel, and a statue of King Arthur stares down across the ruins. These features have not been popular with local people, who are as anxious about romanticising Cornwall as their ancestors. The associations of Cornwall with magic and mystery in some respects dislocated perceptions of the county from the lived reality of its people. The economic downturn of the nineteenth century is still felt, painfully, today, and Cornwall was named the second poorest region in Northern Europe in 2018.[*] The sense of particularism is still important to many, and the Cornish were granted minority status in 2014 in recognition of their distinct identity.[†] But thinking of Cornwall's rich lore, stories, and creative legacy, I hope, will serve to illuminate its realities rather than obscure them. Cornwall is not a fantasy land—it is real, and close, alternately viewed as the end of the land and its beginning. Surrounded on three sides by water, it can be a doorway to the world's oceans, and a site of vulnerability for this small island. This access to the sea provides opportunity for travel, expansion, and industry, but also exposes Cornwall to the elements and the wider world. It is both different and the same, strange and familiar, and always infused with the literary—and a touch of the macabre. I hope you think of this as a travel guide, in a way, both spatially and temporally. Carry it with you, as Vernon Lee and Thomas Hardy and Mary Elizabeth Braddon lugged Tennyson's *Idylls* across the rocks at Tintagel, and maybe you will encounter some Cornish ghosts of your very own.

—JOAN PASSEY

---

[*]   'Inequality Briefing: The poorest regions in the UK are the poorest in Northern Europe', Inequality Briefing (www.inequalitybriefing.org). Data produced by Eurostat, the data agency of the European Union.

[†]   'Press release: Cornish granted minority status within the UK: The government formally recognises the distinct identity of the Cornish people', www.gov.uk, 24 April 2014.

EDGAR ALLAN POE

Ligeia

Edgar Allan Poe (1809–1849) was a writer, critic, poet, and editor, and a pioneer of the American Gothic, perhaps most famous for Gothic staples like 'The Tell-Tale Heart' and 'The Cask of Amontillado'. His works were a huge influence on many subsequent authors and artists, including Arthur Conan Doyle, H. P. Lovecraft, and Alfred Hitchcock. He frequently drew upon an older European literary tradition and 'Ligeia' is set in mainland Europe. First published in 1838, it explores themes recurrent in Poe's wider body of work—tortured romantic love, monomaniacal fixations, metaphysical transformation, and dead women— which Poe declared the most poetical of subjects. While the tale does not reference Cornwall by name, the hero of 'Ligeia' does retire to "one of the wildest and least frequented portions of fair England" and "that remote and unsocial region of the country"—seemingly references to Cornwall's already burgeoning Gothic reputation. The woman he marries there is the Lady Rowena Trevanion, of Tremaine, a distinctly Cornish name drawing on the tradition of "Tre, Pol, and Pen" as common prefixes in the county. Trevanion is likely from Trevena, an old name for Tintagel, the legendary seat of King Arthur on the county's North coast. Arthurian legend was a topic of interest throughout Poe's career and his birthplace provides a fitting setting for a narrative of reanimation. The Gothic excesses of the short story have led to critics conceiving of it as a satire, and a fittingly excessive film adaptation was released in 1964 starring Peter Cushing and filmed on the Cornish coast.

And the will therein lieth, which dieth not. Who knoweth the mysteries of the will, with its vigour? For God is but a great will pervading all things by nature of its intentness. Man doth not yield himself to the angels, nor unto death utterly, save only through the weakness of his feeble will.

—JOSEPH GLANVILL

I cannot, for my soul, remember how, when, or even precisely where, I first became acquainted with the lady Ligeia. Long years have since elapsed, and my memory is feeble through much suffering. Or, perhaps, I cannot *now* bring these points to mind, because, in truth, the character of my beloved, her rare learning, her singular yet placid cast of beauty, and the thrilling and enthralling eloquence of her low musical language, made their way into my heart by paces so steadily and stealthily progressive that they have been unnoticed and unknown. Yet I believe that I met her first and most frequently in some large, old, decaying city near the Rhine. Of her family—I have surely heard her speak. That it is of a remotely ancient date cannot be doubted. Ligeia! Ligeia! Buried in studies of a nature more than all else adapted to deaden impressions of the outward world, it is by that sweet word alone—by Ligeia—that I bring before mine eyes in fancy the image of her who is no more. And now, while I write, a recollection flashes upon me that I have *never known* the paternal name of her who was my friend and my betrothed, and who became the partner of my studies, and finally the wife of my bosom. Was it a playful charge on the part of my Ligeia? or was it a test of my strength of affection, that I should institute no inquiries upon this point? or was it rather a caprice of my own—a wildly romantic offering on the shrine of the most passionate devotion? I but indistinctly recall the fact itself—what wonder that I have utterly forgotten the circumstances which originated or attended it? And, indeed, if ever that spirit which is entitled *Romance*—if ever she, the wan and the misty-winged *Ashtophet* of idolatrous Egypt, presided, as they tell, over marriages ill-omened, then most surely she presided over mine.

There is one dear topic, however, on which my memory fails me not. It is the *person* of Ligeia. In stature she was tall, somewhat slender, and, in her latter days, even emaciated. I would in vain attempt to portray the majesty, the quiet ease, of her demeanour, or the incomprehensible lightness and elasticity of her footfall. She came and departed as a shadow. I was never made aware of her entrance into my closed study save by the dear music of her low sweet voice, as she placed her marble hand upon my shoulder. In beauty of face no maiden ever equalled her. It was the radiance of an opium dream—an airy and spirit-lifting vision more wildly divine than the phantasies which hovered about the slumbering souls of the daughters of Delos. Yet her features were not of that regular mould which we have been falsely taught to worship in the classical labours of the heathen. "There is no exquisite beauty," says Bacon, Lord Verulam, speaking truly of all the forms and *genera* of beauty, "without some *strangeness* in the proportion." Yet, although I saw that the features of Ligeia were not of a classic regularity— although I perceived that her loveliness was indeed "exquisite," and felt that there was much of "strangeness" pervading it, yet I have tried in vain to detect the irregularity and to trace home my own perception of "the strange." I examined the contour of the lofty and pale forehead—it was faultless—how cold indeed that word when applied to a majesty so divine!—the skin rivalling the purest ivory, the commanding extent and repose, the gentle prominence of the regions above the temples; and then the raven-black, the glossy, the luxuriant and naturally-curling tresses, setting forth the full force of the Homeric epithet, "hyacinthine!" I looked at the delicate outlines of the nose—and nowhere but in the graceful medallions of the Hebrews had I beheld a similar perfection. There were the same luxurious smoothness of surface, the same scarcely perceptible tendency to the aquiline, the same harmoniously curved nostrils speaking the free spirit. I regarded the sweet mouth. Here was indeed the triumph of all things heavenly—the magnificent turn of the short upper lip—the soft, voluptuous slumber of the under—the dimples which sported, and the colour which spoke—the teeth glancing back, with a brilliancy almost startling, every ray of the holy light which fell upon them in her serene and placid, yet most exultingly radiant of all smiles. I scrutinised the formation of the chin—and here, too, I found the gentleness of breadth, the softness and the majesty, the fullness and the spirituality, of the Greek—the contour which the God Apollo revealed but in a dream, to Cleomenes, the son of the Athenian. And then I peered into the large eyes of Ligeia.

For eyes we have no models in the remotely antique. It might have been, too, that in these eyes of my beloved lay the secret to which Lord Verulam alludes. They were, I must believe, far larger than the ordinary eyes of our own race. They were even fuller than the fullest of the gazelle eyes of the tribe of the valley of Nourjahad. Yet it was only at intervals—in moments of intense excitement—that this peculiarity became more than slightly noticeable in Ligeia. And at such moments was her beauty—in my heated fancy thus it appeared perhaps—the beauty of beings either above or apart from the earth—the beauty of the fabulous Houri of the Turk. The hue of the orbs was the most brilliant of black, and, far over them, hung jetty lashes of great length. The brows, slightly irregular in outline, had the same tint. The "strangeness," however, which I found in the eyes, was of a nature distinct from the formation, or the colour, or the brilliancy of the features, and must, after all, be referred to the *expression*. Ah, word of no meaning! behind whose vast latitude of mere sound we intrench our ignorance of so much of the spiritual. The expression of the eyes of Ligeia! How for long hours have I pondered upon it! How have I, through the whole of a midsummer night, struggled to fathom it! What was it—that something more profound than the well of Democritus—which lay far within the pupils of my beloved? What *was* it? I was possessed with a passion to discover. Those eyes! those large, those shining, those divine orbs! they became to me twin stars of Leda, and I to them devoutest of astrologers.

There is no point, among the many incomprehensible anomalies of the science of mind, more thrillingly exciting than the fact—never, I believe, noticed in the schools—that, in our endeavours to recall to memory something long forgotten, we often find ourselves *upon the very verge* of remembrance, without being able, in the end, to remember. And thus how frequently, in my intense scrutiny of Ligeia's eyes, have I felt approaching the full knowledge of their expression—felt it approaching—yet not quite be mine—and so at length entirely depart! And (strange, oh strangest mystery of all!) I found, in the commonest objects of the universe, a circle of analogies to that expression. I mean to say that, subsequently to the period when Ligeia's beauty passed into my spirit, there dwelling as in a shrine, I derived, from many existences in the material world, a sentiment such as I felt always aroused within me by her large and luminous orbs. Yet not the more could I define that sentiment, or

analyse, or even steadily view it. I recognised it, let me repeat, sometimes in the survey of a rapidly-growing vine—in the contemplation
of a moth, a butterfly, a chrysalis, a stream of running water. I have
felt it in the ocean; in the falling of a meteor. I have felt it in the
glances of unusually aged people. And there are one or two stars in
heaven—(one especially, a star of the sixth magnitude, double and
changeable, to be found near the large star in Lyra) in a telescopic
scrutiny of which I have been made aware of the feeling. I have been
filled with it by certain sounds from stringed instruments, and not
unfrequently by passages from books. Among innumerable other
instances, I well remember something in a volume of Joseph Glanvill,
which (perhaps merely from its quaintness—who shall say?) never
failed to inspire me with the sentiment;—"And the will therein lieth,
which dieth not. Who knoweth the mysteries of the will, with its
vigour? For God is but a great will pervading all things by nature of
its intentness. Man doth not yield him to the angels, nor unto death
utterly, save only through the weakness of his feeble will."

Length of years, and subsequent reflection, have enabled me
to trace, indeed, some remote connection between this passage
in the English moralist and a portion of the character of Ligeia. An
intensity in thought, action, or speech, was possibly, in her, a result,
or at least an index, of that gigantic volition which, during our long
intercourse, failed to give other and more immediate evidence of
its existence. Of all the women whom I have ever known, she, the
outwardly calm, the ever-placid Ligeia, was the most violently a prey
to the tumultuous vultures of stern passion. And of such passion I
could form no estimate, save by the miraculous expansion of those
eyes which at once so delighted and appalled me—by the almost
magical melody, modulation, distinctness and placidity of her very
low voice—and by the fierce energy (rendered doubly effective

by contrast with her manner of utterance) of the wild words which she habitually uttered.

I have spoken of the learning of Ligeia: it was immense—such as I have never known in woman. In the classical tongues was she deeply proficient, and as far as my own acquaintance extended in regard to the modern dialects of Europe, I have never known her at fault. Indeed upon any theme of the most admired, because simply the most abstruse of the boasted erudition of the academy, have I *ever* found Ligeia at fault? How singularly—how thrillingly, this one point in the nature of my wife has forced itself, at this late period only, upon my attention! I said her knowledge was such as I have never known in woman—but where breathes the man who has traversed, and successfully, *all* the wide areas of moral, physical, and mathematical science? I saw not then what I now clearly perceive, that the acquisitions of Ligeia were gigantic, were astounding; yet I was sufficiently aware of her infinite supremacy to resign myself, with a child-like confidence, to her guidance through the chaotic world of metaphysical investigation at which I was most busily occupied during the earlier years of our marriage. With how vast a triumph—with how vivid a delight—with how much of all that is ethereal in hope—did I *feel*, as she bent over me in studies but little sought—but less known—that delicious vista by slow degrees expanding before me, down whose long, gorgeous, and all untrodden path, I might at length pass onward to the goal of a wisdom too divinely precious not to be forbidden!

How poignant, then, must have been the grief with which, after some years, I beheld my well-grounded expectations take wings to themselves and fly away! Without Ligeia I was but as a child groping benighted. Her presence, her readings alone, rendered vividly luminous the many mysteries of the transcendentalism in which we were immersed. Wanting the radiant lustre of her eyes, letters, lambent and golden, grew duller than Saturnian lead. And now those eyes shone less and less frequently upon the pages over which I pored. Ligeia grew ill. The wild eyes blazed with a too—too glorious effulgence; the pale fingers became of the transparent waxen hue of the grave, and the blue veins upon the lofty forehead swelled and sank impetuously with the tides of the most gentle emotion. I saw that she must die—and I struggled desperately in spirit with the grim Azrael. And the struggles of the passionate wife were, to my astonishment, even more energetic than my own. There had been much in her stern nature to impress me with the belief that, to her, death would have come without its terrors;—but not so. Words are impotent to convey any just idea of the fierceness of resistance with which she wrestled with the Shadow. I groaned in anguish at the pitiable spectacle. I would have soothed—I would have reasoned; but, in the intensity of her wild desire for life,—for life—*but* for life—solace and reason were alike the uttermost of folly. Yet not until the last instance, amid the most convulsive writhings of her fierce spirit, was shaken the external placidity of her demeanour. Her voice grew more gentle—grew more low—yet I would not wish to dwell upon the wild meaning of the quietly uttered words. My brain reeled as I hearkened entranced, to a melody more than mortal—to assumptions and aspirations which mortality had never before known.

That she loved me I should not have doubted; and I might have been easily aware that, in a bosom such as hers, love would have reigned no ordinary passion. But in death only, was I fully impressed with the strength of her affection. For long hours, detaining my hand, would she pour out before me the overflowing of a heart whose more than passionate devotion amounted to idolatry. How had I deserved to be so blessed by such confessions?—how had I deserved to be so cursed with the removal of my beloved in the hour of her making them? But upon this subject I cannot bear to dilate. Let me say only, that in Ligeia's more than womanly abandonment to a love, alas! all unmerited, all unworthily bestowed, I at length recognised the principle of her longing with so wildly earnest a desire for the life which was now fleeing so rapidly away. It is this wild longing—it is this eager vehemence of desire for life—*but* for life—that I have no power to portray—no utterance capable of expressing.

At high noon of the night in which she departed, beckoning me, peremptorily, to her side, she bade me repeat certain verses composed by herself not many days before. I obeyed her.—They were these:

> Lo! 'tis a gala night
>   Within the lonesome latter years!
> An angel throng, bewinged, bedight
>   In veils, and drowned in tears,
> Sit in a theatre, to see
>   A play of hopes and fears,
> While the orchestra breathes fitfully
>   The music of the spheres.
>
> Mimes, in the form of God on high,
>   Mutter and mumble low,
> And hither and thither fly—
>   Mere puppets they, who come and go
> At bidding of vast formless things
>   That shift the scenery to and fro,
> Flapping from out their Condor wings
>   Invisible Wo!

That motley drama!—oh, be sure
   It shall not be forgot!
With its Phantom chased forevermore,
   By a crowd that seize it not,
Through a circle that ever returneth in
   To the self-same spot,
And much of Madness and more of Sin,
   And Horror the soul of the plot.

But see, amid the mimic rout,
   A crawling shape intrude!
A blood-red thing that writhes from out
   The scenic solitude!
It writhes!—it writhes!—with mortal pangs
   The mimes become its food,
And the seraphs sob at vermin fangs
   In human gore imbued.

Out—out are the lights—out all!
   And over each quivering form,
The curtain, a funeral pall,
   Comes down with the rush of a storm,
And the angels, all pallid and wan,
   Uprising, unveiling, affirm
That the play is the tragedy, "Man,"
   And its hero the Conqueror Worm.

"O God!" half shrieked Ligeia, leaping to her feet and extending her arms aloft with a spasmodic movement, as I made an end of these lines—"O God! O Divine Father!—shall these things be undeviatingly so?—shall this Conqueror be not once conquered? Are we not part and parcel in Thee? Who—who knoweth the mysteries of the will with its vigour? Man doth not yield him to the angels, *nor unto death utterly*, save only through the weakness of his feeble will."

And now, as if exhausted with emotion, she suffered her white arms to fall, and returned solemnly to her bed of Death. And as she breathed her last sighs, there came mingled with them a low murmur from her lips. I bent to them my ear and distinguished, again, the concluding words of the passage in Glanvill—"*Man doth not yield him to the angels, nor unto death utterly, save only through the weakness of his feeble will.*"

She died;—and I, crushed into the very dust with sorrow, could no longer endure the lonely desolation of my dwelling in the dim and decaying city by the Rhine. I had no lack of what the world calls wealth. Ligeia had brought me far more, very far more than ordinarily falls to the lot of mortals. After a few months, therefore, of weary and aimless wandering, I purchased, and put in some repair, an abbey, which I shall not name, in one of the wildest and least frequented portions of fair England. The gloomy and dreary grandeur of the building, the almost savage aspect of the domain, the many melancholy and time-honoured memories connected with both, had much in unison with the feelings of utter abandonment which had driven me into that remote and unsocial region of the country. Yet although the external abbey, with its verdant decay hanging about it, suffered but little alteration, I gave way, with a child-like perversity, and perchance with a faint hope of alleviating my sorrows, to a display of more than regal magnificence within.—For such follies, even in childhood, I had imbibed a taste and now they came back to me as if in the dotage of grief. Alas, I feel how much even of incipient madness might have been discovered in the gorgeous and fantastic draperies, in the solemn carvings of Egypt, in the wild cornices and furniture, in the Bedlam patterns of the carpets of tufted gold! I had become a bounden slave in the trammels of opium, and my labours and my orders had taken a colouring from my dreams. But these absurdities I must not pause to detail. Let me speak only of that one chamber, ever accursed, whither in a moment of mental alienation, I led from the altar as my bride—as the successor of the unforgotten Ligeia—the fair-haired and blue-eyed Lady Rowena Trevanion, of Tremaine.

There is no individual portion of the architecture and decoration of that bridal chamber which is not now visibly before me. Where were the souls of the haughty family of the bride, when, through thirst of gold, they permitted to pass the threshold of an apartment *so* bedecked, a maiden and a daughter so beloved? I have said that I minutely remember the details of the chamber—yet I am sadly forgetful on topics of deep moment—and here there was no system, no keeping, in the fantastic display, to take hold upon the memory. The room lay in a high turret of the castellated abbey, was pentagonal in shape, and of capacious size. Occupying the whole southern face of the pentagon was the sole window—an immense sheet of unbroken glass from Venice—a single pane, and tinted of a leaden hue, so that the rays of either the sun or moon, passing through it, fell with a ghastly lustre on the objects within. Over the upper portion of this huge window, extended the trellis-work of an aged vine, which clambered up the massy walls of the turret. The ceiling, of gloomy-looking oak, was excessively lofty, vaulted, and elaborately fretted with the wildest and most grotesque specimens of a semi-Gothic, semi-Druidical device. From out the most central recess of this melancholy vaulting, depended, by a single chain of gold with long links, a huge censer of the same metal, Saracenic in pattern, and with many perforations so contrived that there writhed in and out of them, as if endued with a serpent vitality, a continual succession of parti-coloured fires.

Some few ottomans and golden candelabra, of Eastern figure, were in various stations about—and there was the couch, too—the bridal couch—of an Indian model, and low, and sculptured of solid ebony, with a pall-like canopy above. In each of the angles of the chamber stood on end a gigantic sarcophagus of black granite, from the tombs of the kings over against Luxor, with their aged lids full of immemorial sculpture. But in the draping of the apartment lay, alas! the chief phantasy of all. The lofty walls, gigantic in height—even unproportionably so—were hung from summit to foot, in vast folds, with a heavy and massive-looking tapestry—tapestry of a material which was found alike as a carpet on the floor, as a covering for the ottomans and the ebony bed, as a canopy for the bed, and as the gorgeous volutes of the curtains which partially shaded the window. The material was the richest cloth of gold. It was spotted all over, at irregular intervals, with arabesque figures, about a foot in diameter, and wrought upon the cloth in patterns of the most jetty black. But these figures partook of the true character of the arabesque only when regarded from a single point of view. By a contrivance now common, and indeed traceable to a very remote period of antiquity, they were made changeable in aspect. To one entering the room, they bore the appearance of simple monstrosities; but upon a farther advance, this appearance gradually departed; and step by step, as the visiter moved his station in the chamber, he saw himself surrounded by an endless succession of the ghastly forms which belong to the superstition of the Norman, or arise in the guilty slumbers of the monk. The phantasmagoric effect was vastly heightened by the artificial introduction of a strong continual current of wind behind the draperies—giving a hideous and uneasy animation to the whole.

In halls such as these—in a bridal chamber such as this—I passed, with the Lady of Tremaine, the unhallowed hours of the first month of our marriage—passed them with but little disquietude. That my wife dreaded the fierce moodiness of my temper—that she shunned me and loved me but little—I could not help perceiving; but it gave me rather pleasure than otherwise. I loathed her with a hatred belonging more to demon than to man. My memory flew back, (oh, with what intensity of regret!) to Ligeia, the beloved, the august, the beautiful, the entombed. I revelled in recollections of her purity, of her wisdom, of her lofty, her ethereal nature, of her passionate, her idolatrous love. Now, then, did my spirit fully and freely burn with more than all the fires of her own. In the excitement of my opium dreams (for I was habitually fettered in the shackles of the drug) I would call aloud upon her name, during the silence of the night, or among the sheltered recesses of the glens by day, as if, through the wild eagerness, the solemn passion, the consuming ardour of my longing for the departed, I could restore her to the pathway she had abandoned—ah, *could* it be forever?—upon the earth.

About the commencement of the second month of the marriage, the Lady Rowena was attacked with sudden illness, from which her recovery was slow. The fever which consumed her rendered her nights uneasy; and in her perturbed state of half-slumber, she spoke of sounds, and of motions, in and about the chamber of the turret, which I concluded had no origin save in the distemper of her fancy, or perhaps in the phantasmagoric influences of the chamber itself. She became at length convalescent—finally well. Yet but a brief period elapsed, ere a second more violent disorder again threw her upon a bed of suffering; and from this attack her frame, at all times feeble, never altogether recovered. Her illnesses were, after this epoch, of alarming character, and of more alarming recurrence, defying alike the knowledge and the great exertions of her physicians. With the increase of the chronic disease which had thus, apparently, taken too sure hold upon her constitution to be eradicated by human means, I could not fail to observe a similar increase in the nervous irritation of her temperament, and in her excitability by trivial causes of fear. She spoke again, and now more frequently and pertinaciously, of the sounds—of the slight sounds—and of the unusual motions among the tapestries, to which she had formerly alluded.

One night, near the closing in of September, she pressed this distressing subject with more than usual emphasis upon my attention. She had just awakened from an unquiet slumber, and I had been watching, with feelings half of anxiety, half of vague terror, the workings of her emaciated countenance. I sat by the side of her ebony bed, upon one of the ottomans of India. She partly arose, and spoke, in an earnest low whisper, of sounds which she *then* heard, but which I could not hear—of motions which she *then* saw, but which I could not perceive. The wind was rushing hurriedly behind the tapestries, and I wished to show her (what, let me confess it, I could not *all* believe) that those almost inarticulate breathings, and those very gentle variations of the figures upon the wall, were but the natural effects of that customary rushing of the wind. But a deadly pallor, overspreading her face, had proved to me that my exertions to reassure her would be fruitless. She appeared to be fainting, and no attendants were within call. I remembered where was deposited a decanter of light wine which had been ordered by her physicians, and hastened across the chamber to procure it. But, as I stepped beneath the light of the censer, two circumstances of a startling nature attracted my attention. I had felt that some palpable although invisible object had passed lightly by my person; and I saw that there lay upon the golden carpet, in the very middle of the rich lustre thrown from the censer, a shadow—a faint, indefinite shadow of angelic aspect—such as might be fancied for the shadow of a shade. But I was wild with the excitement of an immoderate dose of opium, and heeded these things but little, nor spoke of them to Rowena. Having found the wine, I recrossed the chamber, and poured out a goblet-ful, which I held to the lips of the fainting lady. She had now partially recovered, however, and took the vessel herself, while I sank upon an ottoman near me, with my eyes fastened upon her person. It was then that I became distinctly aware of a gentle footfall upon the carpet, and near the couch; and in a second thereafter, as Rowena was in the act of raising the wine to her lips, I saw, or may have dreamed that I saw, fall within the goblet, as if from some invisible spring in the atmosphere of the room, three or four large drops of a brilliant and ruby coloured fluid. If this I saw—not so Rowena. She swallowed the wine unhesitatingly, and I forbore to speak to her of a circumstance which must, after all, I considered, have been but the suggestion of a vivid imagination, rendered morbidly active by the terror of the lady, by the opium, and by the hour.

Yet I cannot conceal it from my own perception that, immediately subsequent to the fall of the ruby-drops, a rapid change for the worse took place in the disorder of my wife; so that, on the third subsequent night, the hands of her menials prepared her for the tomb, and on the fourth, I sat alone, with her shrouded body, in that fantastic chamber which had received her as my bride.—Wild visions, opium-engendered, flitted, shadow-like, before me. I gazed with unquiet eye upon the sarcophagi in the angles of the room, upon the varying figures of the drapery, and upon the writhing of the parti-coloured fires in the censer overhead. My eyes then fell, as I called to mind the circumstances of a former night, to the spot beneath the glare of the censer where I had seen the faint traces of the shadow. It was there, however, no longer; and breathing with greater freedom, I turned my glances to the pallid and rigid figure upon the bed. Then rushed upon me a thousand memories of Ligeia—and then came back upon my heart, with the turbulent violence of a flood, the whole of that unutterable wo with which I had regarded *her* thus enshrouded. The night waned; and still, with a bosom full of bitter thoughts of the one only and supremely beloved, I remained gazing upon the body of Rowena.

It might have been midnight, or perhaps earlier, or later, for I had taken no note of time, when a sob, low, gentle, but very distinct, startled me from my revery.—I *felt* that it came from the bed of ebony—the bed of death. I listened in an agony of superstitious terror—but there was no repetition of the sound. I strained my vision to detect any motion in the corpse—but there was not the slightest perceptible. Yet I could not have been deceived. I *had* heard the noise, however faint, and my soul was awakened within me. I resolutely and perseveringly kept my attention riveted upon the body. Many minutes elapsed before any circumstance occurred tending to throw light upon the mystery. At length it became evident that a slight, a very feeble, and barely noticeable tinge of colour had flushed up within the cheeks, and along the sunken small veins of the eyelids. Through a species of unutterable horror and awe, for which the language of mortality has no sufficiently energetic expression, I felt my heart cease to beat, my limbs grow rigid where I sat. Yet a sense of duty finally operated to restore my self-possession. I could no longer doubt that we had been precipitate in our preparations—that Rowena still lived. It was necessary that some immediate exertion be made; yet the turret was altogether apart from the portion of the abbey tenanted by the servants—there were none within call—I had no means of summoning them to my aid without leaving the room for many minutes—and this I could not venture to do. I therefore struggled alone in my endeavours to call back the spirit still hovering. In a short period it was certain, however, that a relapse had taken place; the colour disappeared from both eyelid and cheek, leaving a wanness even more than that of marble; the lips became doubly shrivelled and pinched up in the ghastly expression of death; a repulsive clamminess and coldness overspread rapidly the surface of the body; and all the usual rigorous stiffness immediately supervened. I fell back with a shudder upon the couch from which I had been so startlingly aroused, and again gave myself up to passionate waking visions of Ligeia.

An hour thus elapsed when (could it be possible?) I was a second time aware of some vague sound issuing from the region of the bed. I listened—in extremity of horror. The sound came again—it was a sigh. Rushing to the corpse, I saw—distinctly saw—a tremor upon the lips. In a minute afterward they relaxed, disclosing a bright line of the pearly teeth. Amazement now struggled in my bosom with the profound awe which had hitherto reigned there alone. I felt that my vision grew dim, that my reason wandered; and it was only by a violent effort that I at length succeeded in nerving myself to the task which duty thus once more had pointed out. There was now a partial glow upon the forehead and upon the cheek and throat; a perceptible warmth pervaded the whole frame; there was even a slight pulsation at the heart. The lady *lived;* and with redoubled ardour I betook myself to the task of restoration. I chafed and bathed the temples and the hands, and used every exertion which experience, and no little medical reading, could suggest. But in vain. Suddenly, the colour fled, the pulsation ceased, the lips resumed the expression of the dead, and, in an instant afterward, the whole body took upon itself the icy chilliness, the livid hue, the intense rigidity, the sunken outline, and all the loathsome peculiarities of that which has been, for many days, a tenant of the tomb.

And again I sunk into visions of Ligeia—and again, (what marvel that I shudder while I write?) *again* there reached my ears a low sob from the region of the ebony bed. But why shall I minutely detail the unspeakable horrors of that night? Why shall I pause to relate how, time after time, until near the period of the grey dawn, this hideous drama of revivification was repeated; how each terrific relapse was only into a sterner and apparently more irredeemable death; how each agony wore the aspect of a struggle with some invisible foe; and how each struggle was succeeded by I know not what of wild change in the personal appearance of the corpse? Let me hurry to a conclusion.

The greater part of the fearful night had worn away, and she who had been dead, once again stirred—and now more vigorously than hitherto, although arousing from a dissolution more appalling in its utter hopelessness than any. I had long ceased to struggle or to move, and remained sitting rigidly upon the ottoman, a helpless prey to a whirl of violent emotions, of which extreme awe was perhaps the least terrible, the least consuming. The corpse, I repeat, stirred, and now more vigorously than before. The hues of life flushed up with unwonted energy into the countenance—the limbs relaxed—and, save that the eyelids were yet pressed heavily together, and that the bandages and draperies of the grave still imparted their charnel character to the figure, I might have dreamed that Rowena had indeed shaken off, utterly, the fetters of Death. But if this idea was not, even then, altogether adopted, I could at least doubt no longer, when, arising from the bed, tottering, with feeble steps, with closed eyes, and with the manner of one bewildered in a dream, the thing that was enshrouded advanced bodily and palpably into the middle of the apartment.

I trembled not—I stirred not—for a crowd of unutterable fancies connected with the air, the stature, the demeanour of the figure, rushing hurriedly through my brain, had paralysed—had chilled me into stone. I stirred not—but gazed upon the apparition. There was a mad disorder in my thoughts—a tumult unappeasable. Could it, indeed, be the *living* Rowena who confronted me? Could it indeed be Rowena *at all*—the fair-haired, the blue-eyed Lady Rowena Trevanion of Tremaine? Why, *why* should I doubt it? The bandage lay heavily about the mouth—but then might it not be the mouth of the breathing Lady of Tremaine? And the cheeks—there were the roses as in her noon of life—yes, these might indeed be the fair cheeks of the living Lady of Tremaine. And the chin, with its dimples, as in health, might it not be hers?—but *had she then grown taller since her malady?* What inexpressible madness seized me with that thought? One bound, and I had reached her feet! Shrinking from my touch, she let fall from her head the ghastly cerements which had confined it, and there streamed forth, into the rushing atmosphere of the chamber, huge masses of long and dishevelled hair; *it was blacker than the wings of the midnight!* And now slowly opened *the eyes* of the figure which stood before me. "Here then, at least," I shrieked aloud, "can I never—can I never be mistaken—these are the full, and the black, and the wild eyes—of my lost love—of the lady—of the LADY LIGEIA!"

ANON.

My Father's Secret

Most articles and stories published in Victorian periodicals were done so anonymously. Periodicals were bountiful as printing was becoming increasingly cheap and accessible and literacy rates were on the rise throughout the nineteenth century. They varied wildly, targeting a broad range of demographics and covering the breadth of the political spectrum. Some were comical and satirical, some more literary, others dedicated to sporting, some geared specifically towards women, children, girls, and boys. This is one of many anonymous Cornish Gothic narratives published across the nineteenth century. I include it here as it is a great example of a werewolf story, popular at the time, and it was published in a hugely famous periodical—*All the Year Round*, edited by novelist Charles Dickens. Werewolf stories have their origins in Greek mythology and this particular version of the werewolf, the "Bisclavaret", is from medieval romances, likely dating back to one of the twelve lais (short narratives) of Marie de France in the twelfth century. Marie de France claims to have translated her "Bisclavret" from Breton. Brittany and Cornwall have historically enjoyed much cultural exchange. Cornouaille, a historic region of Western Brittany, is cognate with Cornwall, and was likely established by migrant Cornish royals. The Celtic language spoken would have differentiated into Cornish, Welsh, and Breton over time. Brittany would have been relatively easy to access from Cornwall by sea (especially compared to over land), and the two lands shared a common connection with fishing and seafaring life. The "Bisclavret" narrative emerging in Cornwall is demonstrative of the county's reputation as being both isolated and globally significant, with important international relationships and a blossoming Cornish diaspora across the nineteenth century, as miners migrated in huge numbers to build communities across Australia, the United States, and South America.

trange, how the merest trifles will sometimes call up, in the most vivid colours, a train of recollections we had fancied were so laid away in the lumber-room we all have in some back recess of our brains, that they have lost all distinct form and reality!

Tonight, a sound in the street at midnight, a cry, perhaps from some houseless wanderer, wakened in terror from her shivering, shelterless slumbers, thrilled through my very soul with the startled agony of fear such a sound excited in my childish mind—how many years ago? fifty, at least—and brought back to me, with a tumultuous rush, all the series of circumstances that then so oppressed my life with a vague, nameless, unspeakable horror; and when, in later life, these circumstances were explained, the explanation only substituted real for imaginary terrors.

An only child, my early days were spent in the old place that had been in our family for upwards of three centuries. It was situated in Cornwall, near the sea, far from any town of the least importance, and it and our lives—my father's and mine, for I was motherless— were so isolated that often months, nay, I may say years, passed, without our ever seeing a new face.

In those days of which I speak, my father must have been still a young and a handsome man; but children commonly have such incorrect ideas as to the ages and appearances of their elders, and of their parents especially, that the memory of my father always presents itself as that of a middle-aged, sombre, silent, not generally pleasing or attractive man.

I loved him less than I feared him; not that he was ever other than gentle and most kind to me; but somehow there was, I know not how, an uneasy feeling subsisting between us; we never were on the terms of fond protection on the one side, of clinging confidence on the other, that alone constitute the natural and healthy relations between father and child.

What above all caused this uneasy sensation on my part, was the consciousness—I cannot say when it first came, but come it did, gradually growing on me in a way whose oppression I cannot now recal without a return of its weight—that my father was constantly—furtively and secretly, but constantly—watching me. Watching me, too, with a sort of anxious, fearful expectancy, as if there was about me something alarming or unnatural, that should stamp me as a creature apart from the rest of my species.

From this thought came the yet more harassing one that such a feeling on his part might have a real foundation I knew not of. I can perfectly remember secretly studying my own face and figure in the large cheval-glass that stood in an unused dressing-room (my mother's, as I afterwards learnt), to discover if I had any personal peculiarity, or sign, or deformity, that might in any way account for this singular demeanour of my father's, and watching my own words, and habits, and behaviour, to test if in them lay the cause thereof. But I could myself discover nothing. The mirror only showed me a pale, large-eyed, delicate-looking boy, tall and slight beyond his years, with a particularly grave, reflective cast of countenance (these particulars, my recollection of my own image, rather than my then view of it, informs me), and loose, dark, curling hair, hanging over the forehead, and giving additional shade and solemnity to the eyes. And when I turned my thoughts inwards, to study, as well as I could, my moral characteristics, I could in them detect no incongruities calculated to justify uneasiness.

At last—never shall I forget the months of watchful terror that followed that supposed explanation of the mystery—I fancied I had found a clue to the awful secret.

Sometimes, weary with wandering about alone, I used to roam into the library, and, taking down a book by chance, try to find some amusement therein; few of the volumes were in any way calculated to suit the taste and comprehension of a child, being chiefly of a grave character, but at last I hit upon a collection of old legendary poems and ballads, and herein found ample food for interest. Among these was the Breton legend of Bisclavaret, the tale of the knight who, owing to some fearful but unexplained fatality, was compelled at certain times to assume the shape and nature of a wolf.

Could I be a Bisclavaret? was the question that instantly addressed itself to my mind. Did my father know that at some time I was destined to undergo this fearful transformation? Was he acquainted with the indications that announced the change? Had he yet perceived any of them?

Such were the questions that now haunted my waking thoughts and my nightly dreams, and as, no doubt, these terrible anxieties produced a visible effect on my looks and manner, my father, full of an uneasy terror whose nature I mistook, increased his painful surveillance, and, by it, my racking alarms.

I saw the moment when I should myself perceive the commencement of the transformation. I pictured the manner of it in fifty ways. Sometimes I fancied it would be gradual, and I should see and feel the slow blending of the human and bestial natures, till the former should be swallowed up in the latter, and I should become, for the time being, at all events, a real wolf. At others, I fancied the change would be instantaneous, that, from a boy, I should suddenly spring into a raging ravening monster, fall—who could tell?—on those around me?—my father, my nurse, my favourite animals, pony, dog, or bird, and then, with bloody fangs, rush howling, an object of hatred and terror to all, into the dark woods that extended for miles around the house, ending, perhaps, by falling into the black abyss of one of the worn-out mines that were not rare in the district.

Our house, which was a very large one, had been built and added to at different periods, and my father and I only occupied a comparatively small portion of one end of it. This portion was shut out from the rest by a door at the termination of a passage, which was kept so entirely closed up that I had never seen it opened, and the unused part of the house I had never once entered. Often, with intense curiosity, I had looked up at the shuttered windows, wondering what manner of rooms they were that daylight never visited, longing, yet half dreading, to explore them. Another object of curious and unsatisfied interest to me was a walled enclosure extending from the extreme end of the deserted part of the house, and covering a space of perhaps about half an acre. The wall was very high, much higher than an ordinary garden wall, and the door of it, which led into a dark shrubbery-walk, now almost blocked up with tangled undergrowth, was kept constantly locked, and, indeed, had no appearance of having been opened for any number of years. Why this was so I was never able to learn. I had asked the question of my nurse, a resident in the house since before my birth, but she had replied evasively that she supposed the key was lost, and at any rate there were gardens enough and to spare without using that one, adding an injunction to me not to go near there, as the shrubbery was damp and full of briars and nettles, and I should hurt myself and get my clothes torn. The result of her caution was, that the next day found me making my way through the tangled underwood in the direction of the closed door that so excited my curiosity. For some time the noise I made forcing a passage kept from me the knowledge that I was not alone in my progress. But pausing to take breath, I suddenly became aware of the fact, and, turning round, I found myself face to face with my father. In a voice of severity, very unusual when addressed to me, he asked me what I was doing there, adding a prohibition ever to return, as I should be sure to hurt myself, and he would not have it.

From that moment I became convinced that within the enclosure of those walls lay the secret of the mystery of our existence and of my father's strange watchfulness of me, and I resolved, come what might, to strive to solve it.

But two days later was commenced the erection of a high, strong paling round the shrubbery, and not being tall or strong enough to scale it, independent of the risk of being detected in the attempt to do so, I was baffled.

I was, I suppose, at this time, about seven or eight years old, but no notice ever being taken of my birthday, I did not then know what my age was, and now I can only guess approximatively what it might have been.

One thing I gained by this inkling of a discovery, and that was the dispersion of my terrors on the Bisclavaret grounds.

No; I felt assured that not in myself, alone and individually, lay the cause of my father's conduct towards me. There, behind that shrubbery, within those walls, was hidden the true explanation, and I only was an object of anxiety as being somehow connected with that impenetrable mystery.

That such was the fact, and how it was so, I had to learn later.

Months passed away, perhaps a year may have gone by, when one night I went to bed about my usual hour, half-past eight or nine o'clock.

It had been a hot summer's day, and a long ride had fatigued me, so that I slept unusually sound (I was, for a child, rather a light sleeper in general), when—I can describe the sensation in no other way than as that of being wrenched instantaneously from profound sleep into terrified waking—I was roused by a scream, so loud, so long, so agonised, that I sprang up shivering with a ghastly horror that made the cold sweat burst out over my quivering limbs.

In an instant, my father—I slept in a little room opening from his—rushed in, with a face I shall never forget, a look whose anxious terror was all directed to *me*—as if excited far less by that hideous sound, than by the fear of its influence on me.

Bursting into hysterical sobs, I stretched my arms to him, and almost for the first time I could remember, he took me to his breast, clasping me close, kissing, soothing, and reassuring me like a woman; yet, I had a consciousness, at the same time, dividing his attention to me with a restless intense anxiety as to the circumstance that had caused it, mingled with a dread of a recurrence of the alarm, an impatient desire to investigate the matter, of which, however, he attempted no explanation, being, I suppose, too shaken by his emotions to invent a plausible one.

While he still held me thus, my nurse entered. This seemed to relieve him. I observed that they exchanged looks of mutual intelligence, and my father, placing me in her arms, once more kissed me, telling me to fear nothing, and taking a light, he left my room by the opposite door from that by which he had entered it.

"What was it, nurse?" I whispered, when I had become a little reassured. She hesitated.

"It must have been Jane, frightened by a rat; or perhaps she had the nightmare. But it was nothing that could hurt *you*, dear."

I knew this was not the true explanation; but I also knew I was not likely to get another; so I was silent, and, I suppose, she thought, satisfied.

More than once, after that night, did the same harrowing sound disturb me, and sometimes the shrieks were not single, but iterated with fearful energy. On each occasion my father manifested the same intense disturbance and anxiety, though he endeavoured to conceal it from me, and invented some plausible explanation, which I was forced to appear to accept, though my life was rendered miserable by the terrors with which this state of things beset it.

One morning, after the shrieks had been more than usually terrific, my father, apparently driven into a desperate resolution, announced to me that we were going away for a time; that he would accompany me to our destination, and, leaving me with my nurse, he would come often to see me.

I had never been from home before, and the idea of the change—yet less for its own sake than for the escape it promised me from my terror-haunted life—afforded me unspeakable relief. Whether the evidence of this awakened in my father more pain or pleasure, I can hardly tell; certainly, the feelings were mingled.

In a week, it was fixed, we should go into Devonshire, where, in a village known to my nurse, we were to take up our abode, but for no specified time.

I counted the days with eager impatience, and already five of the seven had departed. At night I had gone to bed, and fallen asleep with a pleasant dreamy sense of approaching escape, and had slept, I suppose, several hours, when I suddenly awakened by the sound of the splashing of water in my room. Looking towards the washing-stand (a night-light, without which my terrors would not allow me to sleep, faintly lighted the chamber), I descried the figure of a woman, whose back was towards me, washing her hands.

I had never seen her before, of that I was quite certain, nor anything the least like her.

She was tall and thin, dressed in a loose, shapeless garment, and her hair, which was dark, was cropped close to her head.

Apparently unconscious of my presence, there she stood, washing her hands, but with an energy and intensity of purpose, curious in so ordinary an occupation; rubbing and wringing them, as if she would take the skin off, pausing to examine them, then with an exclamation of impatient disappointment—sometimes a sort of shudder—plunging them back into the water, splashing, rubbing, and wringing them again and again.

So extreme were my amazement and terror at this extraordinary apparition, that for some minutes I could neither speak nor move. As I lay, I heard the clock strike three, and as it was summer, I knew daylight was near: this was some slight relief. If I could only lie still till sunrise, I thought I might summon courage to address my wondrous visitor, or perhaps she might then retire. So I tried to regulate even my breathing so as not to attract her attention, and lay still, my eyes riveted on her with a fearful fascination, waiting for what might come.

For what *did* come I was little prepared. After long scouring and rubbing her hands, but apparently with no satisfactory result, she turned, and I saw her face.

Child as I was, I felt that it had in it a something that placed it out of the nature or order of all other faces. Not without traces of beauty, even in its haggard pallor and sunken eyes, it yet wore the stamp of something that seemed to me not to belong to humanity. There was a sort of mingled wildness and vacancy in the expression of the pale lips, of the troubled eyes, unnaturally yet gloomily bright in their dark and hollow orbits, like sullen fires in airless caves; and the thick, cropped, dark hair, coming in a ridge straight across the forehead, added not a little to the singular effect of the countenance.

At first her eye seemed to wander vacantly about the room, as if with a half-consciousness that it was unfamiliar to her. Then, after a while, it lighted on me.

She came quickly up to the bed, gazed at me with eager, startled scrutiny, then with hasty hand drawing down the bed-clothes a little way, she began feeling my throat.

Feeling it, not graspingly or clutchingly, or as though intending it any harm, but as if to satisfy some intense anxiety—to assure herself of some peculiarity respecting it.

What followed I cannot tell; for with her hand, deadly cold and wet on my throat, I became insensible.

A brain fever was the result of this night's adventure. And then came a dark period—I have never dared to inquire into the particulars of it, or even how long it lasted—of overshadowed consciousness, from which I awoke but gradually, and with occasional relapses.

That the period must have been considerable I know; for when I recovered I had arrived at another stage of growth, being no longer a child but a youth; and my father's hair was sprinkled with grey, and his face marked with lines I did not remember.

We were in France when I awoke from that long mental slumber, of whose very dreams I had no recollection; living in Brittany, in as retired a manner as we had lived at the old house in Cornwall.

Then we travelled for some years, and so I grew to manhood. Quite sane, and in full possession of my mental faculties, but always with a lingering sense of instability in their tenure, a dread of aught that might tend to shock or shake them, and a shy unwillingness to join in the society of those of my own age, or indeed to go forth at all into a world which had never been other than alien and unknown to me.

So I continued to the age of three-and-twenty, when my father died; died, taking with him the secret that had so terribly influenced my life. But years afterwards, when time and the necessity of action had brought with them their salutary results, and that living like other men, I had become as other men, my uncle, my father's only brother, revealed to me the mystery.

My father, at eight-and-twenty, had married my mother, then barely seventeen.

She was very pretty, very childish, fond of pleasure and the amusements of her age, and having been one of a large and happy, and well-united family, the change from her own gay home and circle to the lonely old house in Cornwall, and my father's grave, studious habits, fell heavily on her, and soon she pined in secret for what she had lost. My father saw it, and though deeply pained and disappointed, he was the first to propose what she was longing for, a visit to her family.

This was some three months before the expected period of my birth; he took her to her home, and it was settled that there he should leave her till her confinement should take place, at which period he was to rejoin her, and, in due time, to conduct her back to Cornwall.

But ere she had been more than a month away, news came to her that my father had been attacked with a pleurisy of the most dangerous kind, and she, smitten with grief and something like self-reproach, would listen to no persuasions that could keep her from him, and the next day, attended by her maid, set out, travelling post, to join him.

Early in the morning they had started, intending to sleep that night at a town of some importance on the way. But the roads were heavy, and the horses so jaded, that it was evident they could not reach their destination till far on in the night, even supposing it possible to achieve that much, and already fatigue and anxiety were beginning to tell strongly on my mother.

So there was nothing for it but to take the first tolerable shelter they could reach, and at ten o'clock they were glad to find themselves in a rural, but really not uncomfortable roadside inn.

Supper despatched, my mother was fain to retire to bed. The room, though small and poorly furnished, was clean, and the bed looked not uninviting, and the only serious drawback to its convenience was, that my mother's maid had to sleep in a room above, there being none other unoccupied on that floor. However, as Wilson's chamber was the one immediately over my mother's, and that she was a light sleeper, it would be easy, by tapping with the point of an umbrella on the low ceiling, at any moment to summon her, in case of there being occasion to do so.

And so, in a short time, my mother, worn out with all she had gone through in the long day, dropped into a profound sleep, and one by one the lights and the noises in the house sank into darkness and silence, and only the mice held their nightly orgies behind the old wainscoting.

Only in one room a light was still burning at two o'clock in the morning.

About that time my mother awoke; but in such ghastly terror and horror that it seemed not like waking from wholesome sleep, but like waking from death in the place of outer darkness—where are weeping and gnashing of teeth.

For *something* was clutching and tearing frantically at the bed-clothes, with a horrible gasping, gurgling sound unlike anything in or out of nature, and there was a struggling and writhing on the floor by the bedside, as if the *thing* was striving to clamber up on it. And so strong was my mother's impression that this was so, that though unable to scream, she put forth her hand, as if to repulse the thing, and felt it come in contact with something hot and wet, that clung stickily to her fingers.

Then she found breath to burst into wild ringing shrieks; and lights were brought; and lying by the bedside was a man in the agonies of death with his throat gashed, and the blood welling from it, and saturating the bed-clothes, and crimson on my mother's hand.

She never recovered her senses, and a few days after I was born.

My father, as soon as it was possible—much sooner than it was safe—for him to travel, came and took her and me, the one mad, the other apparently dying, to Cornwall. Two rooms on the ground floor of the house were arranged for her, opening on the enclosure that had so often excited my curiosity, so that she might, unseen, have air and exercise. There, attended only by her maid, an elderly woman, attached to her from her childhood, and by my father, she remained till the period of her death, which occurred but a few weeks after the night on which I had seen her for the first and last time. During the earlier years of her insanity she had, usually, been tolerably quiet; but some months before her death the infirmity took a new turn. She would be seized with sudden frenzies, uttering the shrieks that had occasionally reached my ears, going in imagination through the scene at the inn, constantly washing her hands to remove the blood with which her distracted fancy stained them, and examining the throats of my father, the doctor, and nurse, as she had examined mine.

And now was explained the meaning of the painful surveillance of me which, in my poor father, had so disturbed me. A constant dread was on him lest the condition of my mother's intellect at the period of my birth might exert an influence on mine. Day and night this terror haunted him; every word, look, and action of mine was weighed and studied with this idea; and little did he suspect how this very anxiety, or rather the unconscious evidence of it, tended towards producing a state of mind calculated to engender, under exciting circumstances, the very effect he dreaded. Above all things he trembled lest the truth of my mother's awful fate should, in any way, reach me; and thus arose the mystery which, I verily believe, might have been yet more dangerous to me than even some knowledge of the rightful fact.

My poor father! if error there were, it was wholly error of judgment, and I have no reason to blame him—to do other than regard his memory with pitying tenderness, to lament over a fate so undeserved and so terrible. He sleeps now under a monument I have erected in our parish churchyard, side by side with the wife from whom in life he was so cruelly divided.

The unfortunate cause of the calamity which thus overshadowed the lives of a family, proved to be a young gentleman, the son of Scottish parents, who, tired of the monotony of his quiet home life, had come south, fallen in with evil company, and, having disgraced the honest name he bore, resolved, in a moment of desperation, to end his life. No sooner, however, had his hand committed the fatal act, than, repentant and terrified, his only thought was to seek assistance.

Between his room and my mother's was a door of communication, which neither she nor Wilson had observed, and through this he, having heard voices on the other side, trailed himself, and, unable to speak, had sought to call my mother's attention in the way described.

But aid came too late, and in a few minutes later he expired, involving in his own fate those innocent sufferers.

ROBERT STEPHEN HAWKER

Cruel Coppinger

Robert Stephen Hawker (1803–1875) was a priest, writer, antiquarian, and poet. He famously wrote 'The Song of the Western Men', otherwise known as 'Trelawny' (1824), and considered to be a sort of 'national anthem' of Cornwall. It is sung at Cornish rugby matches and gatherings, such as celebrations of St. Piran's Day (5th March), Cornwall's patron saint's day. 'The Song of the Western Men' was published in Charles Dickens's magazine *Household Words* and Dickens himself had an interest in Cornwall and visited the county on multiple occasions throughout his life. Hawker published numerous stories in Dickens's magazines, many of which were Gothic in tone and set in Cornwall. He spent his honeymoon in Tintagel in 1823 and developed a fascination with the legends of King Arthur. He became such an established figure in Arthurian studies that Tennyson sought out his company and expertise upon his own visits to the county. Hawker was the vicar of Morwenstow, where he became horribly familiar with Cornwall's abundance of coastal disasters. He famously buried anonymous shipwreck victims in his own churchyard, paid for from his own pocket. He was regarded as somewhat of an eccentric in his lifetime, wearing brightly coloured clothes (he insisted mourners wore purple at his funeral), and supposedly enjoyed dressing up as a mermaid on the Cornish rocks. In another tale he excommunicated his cat for mousing on Sundays. These stories are likely part of a larger mythology of Hawker, perpetuated by a biography by fellow priest, antiquarian and writer of Gothic fiction, Sabine Baring-Gould. We do know for sure that Hawker built himself a hut from driftwood on the coast of Morwenstow for writing, and it is now the National Trust's smallest property.

Hawker had an immense influence on the popular perception of Cornwall through his antiquarian fiction. He played a key role in illuminating the importance of Cornish folklore and mythology and was a staunch proponent for King Arthur as a Cornish figure. Further, he demonstrates the ways in which the lines between fiction and folklore blur in Cornwall across the nineteenth century, feeding into and from each other in strange and productive ways. 'Cruel Coppinger' laid the groundwork for Sabine Baring-Gould's Cornish Gothic novel *In the Roar of the Sea* (1891) where the folk hero is reworked into a Byronic, Gothic antihero in the same vein as Rochester and Heathcliff.

record of the wild, strange, lawless characters that roamed along the north coast of Cornwall during the middle and latter years of the last century would be a volume full of interest for the student of local history and semi-barbarous life. Therein would be found depicted the rough sea-captain, half smuggler, half pirate, who ran his lugger by beacon-light into some rugged cove among the massive headlands of the shore, and was relieved of his freight by the active and diligent "countryside." This was the name allotted to that chosen troop of native sympathisers who were always ready to rescue and conceal the stores that had escaped the degradation of the gauger's brand. Men yet alive relate with glee how they used to rush, at some well-known signal, to the strand, their small active horses shaved from forelock to tail, smoother than any modern clip, well soaped or greased from head to foot, so as to slip easily out of any hostile grasp; and then, with a double keg or pack slung on to every nag by a single girth, away went the whole herd, led by some swift well-trained mare, to the inland cave or rocky hold, the shelter of their spoil. There was a famous dun mare—she lived to the age of thirty-seven, and died within legal memory—almost human in her craft and fidelity, who is said to have led a bevy of loaded pack-horses, unassisted by driver or guide, from Bossinney Haun to Rough-tor Point. But, beside these travellers by sea, there would be found, ever and anon, in some solitary farm-house inaccessible by wheels, and only to be approached by some treacherous footpath along bog and mire, a strange and nameless guest—often a foreigner in language and apparel—who had sought refuge with the native family, and who paid in strange but golden coins for his shelter and food; some political or private adventurer, perchance, to whom secrecy and concealment were safety and life, and who more than once lived and died in his solitary hiding-place on the moor.

There is a bedstead of carved oak still in existence at Trevotter—a farm among the midland hills—whereon for long years an unknown stranger slept. None ever knew his nation or name. He occupied a solitary room, and only emerged now and then for a walk in the evening air. An oaken chest of small size contained his personal possessions and gold of foreign coinage, which he paid into the hands of his host with the solemn charge to conceal it until he was gone thence or dead—a request which the simple-hearted people faithfully fulfilled. His linen was beautifully fine, and his garments richly embroidered. After some time he sickened and died, refusing firmly the visits of the local clergyman, and bequeathing to the farmer the contents of his chest. He wrote some words, they said, for his own tombstone, which, however, were not allowed to be engraved, but they were simply these: "H. De. R. Equees & Ecsul." The same sentence was found, after his death, carved on the ledge of his bed, and the letters are, or lately were, still traceable on the mouldering wood.

But among the legends of local renown a prominent place has always been allotted to a personage whose name has descended to our times inked to a weird and graphic epithet:—"Cruel Coppinger." There was a ballad in existence within human memory which was founded on the history of this singular man, but of which the first verse only can now be recovered. It runs:

Will you hear of the Cruel Coppinger?
He came from a foreign kind:

He was brought to us by the salt water,
He was carried away by the wind.

His arrival on the north coast of Cornwall was signalised by a terrific
hurricane. The storm came up Channel from the south-west. The
shore and the heights were dotted with watchers for wreck—those
daring gleaners of the harvest of the sea. It was just such a scene as
is sought for in the proverb of the West:

A savage sea and a shattering wind,
The cliffs before, and the gale behind.

As suddenly as if a phantom ship had loomed in the distance, a
strange vessel of foreign rig was discovered in fierce struggle with
the waves of Harty Race. She was deeply laden or waterlogged, and
rolled heavily in the trough of the sea, nearing the shore as she felt
the tide. Gradually the pale and dismayed faces of the crew became
visible, and among them one man of herculean height and mould,
who stood near the wheel with a speaking-trumpet in his hand. The
sails were blown to rags, and the rudder was apparently lashed for
running ashore. But the suck of the current and the set of the wind
were too strong for the vessel, and she appeared to have lost her
chance of reaching Harty Pool. It was seen that the tall seaman, who
was manifestly the skipper of the boat, had cast off his garments,
and stood prepared upon the deck to encounter a battle with the
surges for life and rescue. He plunged over the bulwarks, and arose
to sight buffeting the seas. With stalwart arm and powerful chest he
made his way through the surf, rode manfully from billow to billow,
until, with a bound, he stood at last upright upon the sand, a fine
stately semblance of one of the old Vikings of the northern seas.

A crowd of people had gathered from the land, on horseback and on foot, women as well as men, drawn together by the tidings of a probable wreck. Into their midst, and to their astonished dismay, rushed the dripping stranger; he snatched from a terrified old dame her red Welsh cloak, cast it loosely around him, and bounded suddenly upon the crupper of a young damsel who had ridden her father's horse down to the beach to see the sight. He grasped her bridle, and, shouting aloud in some foreign language, urged on the double-laden animal into full speed, and the horse naturally took his homeward way. Strange and wild were the outcries that greeted the rider, Miss Dinah Hamlyn, when, thus escorted, she reached her father's door, in the very embrace of a wild, rough, tall man, who announced himself by a name—never afterwards forgotten in those parts—as Coppinger, a Dane. He arrayed himself without the smallest scruple in the Sunday suit of his host. The long-skirted coat of purple velveteen with large buttons, the embroidered vest, and nether garments to match, became him well. So thought the lady of his sudden choice. She, no doubt, forgave his onslaught on her and on her horse for the compliment it conveyed. He took his immediate place at the family board, and on the settle by the hearth, as though he had been the most welcome and long-invited guest in the land. Strange to say, the vessel disappeared immediately he had left her deck, nor was she ever after traced by land or sea. At first, the stranger subdued all the fierce phases of his savage character, and appeared deeply grateful for all the kindness he received at the hands of his simple-hearted host. Certain letters which he addressed to persons of high name in Denmark were, or were alleged to be, duly answered, and remittances from his friends were supposed to be received. He announced himself as of a wealthy family and superior rank in his native country, and gave out that it was to avoid a marriage with a titled lady that he had left his father's house and gone to sea. All this recommended him to the unsuspecting Dinah, whose affections he completely won. Her father's sudden illness postponed their marriage. The good old man died to be spared much evil to come.

The Dane succeeded almost naturally to the management and control of the house, and the widow held only an apparent influence in domestic affairs. He soon persuaded the daughter to become his wife, and immediately afterwards his evil nature, so long smouldering, broke out like a wild beast uncaged. All at once the house became the den and refuge of every lawless character on the coast. All kinds of wild uproar and reckless revelry appalled the neighbourhood day and night. It was discovered that an organised band of desperadoes, smugglers, wreckers, and poachers, were embarked in a system of bold adventure, and that "Cruel Coppinger" was their captain. In those days, and in that unknown and far-away region, the peaceable inhabitants were totally unprotected. There was not a single resident gentleman of property or weight in the entire district: and the clergyman, quite insulated from associates of his own standing, was cowed into silence and submission. No revenue officer durst exercise vigilance west of the Tamar; and to put an end to all such surveillance at once, it was well known that one of the "Cruel" gang had chopped off a gauger's head on the gunwale of a boat, and carried the body off to sea.

Amid such scenes, Coppinger pursued his unlawful impulses without check or restraint. Strange vessels began to appear at regular intervals on the coast, and signals were duly flashed from the headlands to lead them into the safest creek or cove. If the ground-sea were too strong to allow them to run in, they anchored outside the surf, and boats prepared for that service were rowed or hauled to and fro, freighted with illegal spoil. Amongst these vessels, one, a full-rigged schooner, soon became ominously conspicuous. She bore the name of the Black Prince, and was the private property of the Dane, built to his own order in a dockyard of Denmark. She was for a long time the chief terror of the Cornish Channel. Once with Coppinger on board, when, under chase, she led a revenue cutter into an intricate channel near the Gull Rock, where, from knowledge of the bearings, the Black Prince escaped scathless, while the king's vessel perished with all on board. In those times, if any landsman became obnoxious to Coppinger's men, he was either seized by violence or by craft, and borne away, handcuffed, to the deck of the Black Prince; where, to save his life, he had to enrol himself, under fearful oaths, as one of the crew. In 1835, an old man of the age of ninety-seven related to the writer that, when a youth, he had been so abducted, and after two years' service had been ransomed by his friends with a large sum. "And all," said the old man, very simply, "because I happened to see one man kill another, and they thought I should mention it."

Amid such practices ill-gotten gold began to flow and ebb in the hands of Coppinger. At one time he chanced to hold enough money to purchase a freehold farm bordering on the sea. When the day of transfer arrived, he and one of his followers appeared before the astonished lawyer with bags filled with various kinds of foreign coin. Dollars and ducats, doubloons and pistoles, guineas—the coinage of every foreign country with a seaboard—were displayed on the table. The man of law at first demurred to such purchase-money; but, after some controversy, and an ominous oath or two of "that or none," the lawyer agreed to take it by weight. The document bearing Coppinger's name is still extant. His signature is traced in stern, bold, fierce characters, as if every letter had been stabbed upon the parchment with the point of a dirk. Underneath his autograph, also in his own writing, is the word "Thuro."

Long impunity increased Coppinger's daring. There were certain byways and bridle-roads along the fields over which he exercised exclusive control. Although every one had a perfect right by law to use these ways, he issued orders that no man was to pass over them by night, and accordingly from that hour none ever did. They were called "Coppinger's Tracks." They all converged at a headland which had the name of Steeple Brink. Here the cliff sheered off, and stood three hundred feet of perpendicular height, a precipice of smooth rock toward the beach, with an overhanging face one hundred feet down from the brow. There was a hollow entrance into the cliff, like a huge cathedral door, crowned and surrounded with natural Saxon arches, curved by the strata of native stone. Within was an arched and vaulted cave, vast and gloomy; it ran a long way into the heart of the land, and was as large and tall—so the country-people said—as Kilkhampton church. This stronghold was inaccessible by natural means, and could only be approached by a cable ladder lowered from above and made fast below on a projecting crag. It received the name of "Coppinger's Cave," and was long the scene of fierce and secret revelry, that would be utterly inconceivable to the educated mind of the nineteenth century. Here sheep were tethered to the rock, and fed on stolen hay and corn till their flesh was required for a feast; kegs of brandy and hollands were piled around; chests of tea; and iron-bound sea-chests contained the chattels and the revenues of the Coppinger royalty of the sea. No man ever essayed the perilous descent into the cavern except the captain's own troop; and their loyalty was secured not only by their participation in his crimes, but by a terrible oath.

The terror linked with Coppinger's name throughout the coast was so extreme that the people themselves, wild and lawless as they were, submitted to his sway as though he had been the lord of the soil and they his vassals. Such a household as Coppinger's, was, of course, far from happy or calm. Although when his wife's father died he had insensibly acquired possession of the stock and farm, there remained in the hands of the widow a considerable amount of money as her dower. This he obtained from the poor helpless woman by instalments; and when pretext and entreaty alike failed, he resorted to a novel mode of levy. He fastened his wife to the pillar of her oak bedstead, and called her mother into the room. He then explained that it was his purpose to flog Dinah with the sea-cat which he flourished in his hand until her mother had transferred to him such an amount as he required of her reserved property. This deed of atrocity he repeated until he had utterly exhausted the widow's store. He had a favourite mare, so fierce and indomitable that none but Coppinger himself could venture on her back, and so fleet and strong that he owed his escape from more than one menacing peril by her speed and endurance. The clergyman had spoken above his breath of the evil doings in the cave, and had thus aroused his wrath and vengeance. On a certain day he was jogging homeward on his parish cob, and had reached the middle of a wide and desolate heath. All at once he heard behind him the clattering of horse-hoofs and a yell such as might have burst from the throat of the visible demon when he hurled the battle on the ancient saint. It was Cruel Coppinger with his double-thonged whip, mounted on his terrible mare. Down came the fearful scourge on his victim's shuddering shoulders. Escape was impossible. The poor parson knew too well the difference between his own ambling galloway, that never essayed any swifter pace than a jog-trot, and that awful steed behind him with footsteps like the storm. Circling, doubling like a hare, twisting aside, crying aloud for mercy, all was vain. He arrived at last at his own house, striped like a zebra, and as he rushed in at the gate he heard the parting scoff of his assailant: "There, parson, I have paid my tithe in full; never mind the receipt."

It was on the self-same animal that Coppinger performed another freak. He had passed a festive evening at a farm-house, and was about to take his departure, when he spied at the corner of the hearth a little old tailor of the countryside, who went from house to house to exercise his calling. He was a half-witted, harmless old fellow, and answered to the name of Uncle Tom Tape.

"Ha! Uncle Tom," cried Coppinger, "we both travel the same road, and I don't mind giving thee a hoist behind me on the mare."

The old man cowered in the settle. He would not encumber the gentleman; was unaccustomed to ride such a spirited horse. But all his excuses were overborne. The other guests, entering into the joke, assisted the trembling old man to mount the crupper of the capering mare. Off she bounded, and Uncle Tom, with his arms cast with the strong gripe of terror around his bulky companion, held on like grim death. Unbuckling his belt, Coppinger passed it around Uncle Tom's thin haggard body, and buckled it on his own front. When he had firmly secured his victim, he loosened his reins, and urged the mare with thong and spur into a furious gallop. Onward they rushed, till they fled past the tailor's own door at the roadside, where his startled wife, who was on the watch, afterwards declared "she caught sight of her husband clinging on to a rainbow." Loud and piteous were the outcries of Tailor Tom, and earnest his shrieks of entreaty that he might be told where he was to be carried that night, and for what doom he had been buckled on. At last, in a relaxation of their pace going up a steep hill, Coppinger made him a confidential communication.

"I have been," he said, "under a long promise to the devil, that I would bring him a tailor to make and mend for him, poor man; and as sure as I breathe, Uncle Tom, I mean to keep my word tonight!"

The agony of terror produced by this revelation produced such convulsive spasms, that at last the belt gave way, and the tailor fell off like a log among the gorse at the roadside. There he was found next morning in a semi-delirious state, muttering at intervals, "No, no; I never will. Let him mend his breeches with his own drag-chain, as the saying is. I will never so much as thread a needle for Coppinger nor for his friend."

One boy was the only fruit of poor Dinah's marriage with the Dane. But his birth brought neither gladness nor solace to his mother's miserable hearth. He was fair and golden-haired, and had his father's fierce, flashing eyes. But though perfectly well-formed and healthful, he was born deaf and dumb. He was mischievous and ungovernable from his birth. His cruelty to animals, birds, and to other children, was intense. Any living thing that he could torture appeared to yield him delight. With savage gestures and jabbering moans he haunted the rocks along the shore, and seemed like some uncouth creature cast up by the sea. When he was only six years old, he was found one day upon the brink of a tall cliff, bounding with joy, and pointing downward towards the beach with convulsions of delight. There, mangled by the fall, and dead, they found the body of a neighbour's child of his own age, who was his frequent companion, and whom, as it was inferred, he had drawn towards the steep precipice, and urged over by stratagem or force. The spot where this occurred was ever afterwards his favourite haunt. He would draw the notice of any passer-by to the place, and then point downward where the murdered child was found with fierce exultant mockery. It was a saying evermore in the district, that, as a judgment on his father's cruelty, his child had been born without a human soul. He lived to be the pestilent scourge of the neighbourhood.

But the end arrived. Money had become scarce, and the resources of the cave began to fail. More than one armed king's cutter were seen day and night hovering off the land. Foreigners visited the house with tidings of peril. So he, "who came with the water, went with the wind." His disappearance, like his arrival, was commemorated by a turbulent storm. A wrecker, who had gone to watch the shore, saw, as the sun went down, a full-rigged vessel standing off and on. By-and-by a rocket hissed up from the Gull Rock, a small islet with a creek on the landward side which had been the scene of many a run of smuggled cargo. A gun from the ship answered it, and again both signals were exchanged. At last a well-known and burly form stood on the topmost crag of the island rock. He waved his sword, and the light flashed back from the steel. A boat put off from the vessel, with two hands at every oar; for the tide runs with double violence through Harty Race. They neared the rocks, rode daringly through the surf, and were steered by some practised coxswain into the Gull Creek. There they found their man. Coppinger leaped on board the boat, and assumed the command. They made with strong efforts for their ship. It was a path of peril through that boiling surf. Still, bending at the oar like chained giants, the man watched them till they forced their way through the battling waters. Once, as they drew off the shore, one of the rowers, either from ebbing strength or loss of courage, drooped at his oar. In a moment a cutlass gleamed over his head, and a fierce stern stroke cut him down. It was the last blow of Cruel Coppinger. He and his boat's crew boarded the vessel, and she was out of sight in a moment, like a spectre or a ghost. Thunder, lightning, and hail ensued. Trees were rent up by the roots around the pirate's abode. Poor Dinah watched, and held in her shuddering arms her idiot-boy, and, strange to say, a meteoric stone, called in that country a storm-bolt, fell through the roof into the room, at the very feet of Cruel Coppinger's vacant chair.

MARY ELIZABETH BRADDON

Colonel Benyon's Entanglement

Mary Elizabeth Braddon (1835–1915) was a popular novelist of the nineteenth century, best known for the sensation novel *Lady Audley's Secret* (1862). Sensation fiction arose in the nineteenth century and was largely preoccupied with sensory effects, nervous bodies, and excess of feeling—all closely aligned with the Gothic. She was a prolific author, producing over 80 novels, and many of her works were concerned with the supernatural. Her work was popular at its publication and sustained interest into the twentieth century, when her short stories were anthologised by figures like Montague Summers, an early collector of Gothic works in the 1930s. 'Colonel Benyon's Entanglement' includes themes Braddon explores in her wider oeuvre, such as global travel and globalisation, changing attitudes towards domesticity, and anxieties surrounding gender and class. This was not her only work set in Cornwall—her novel *Mount Royal* (1882) is a modernisation of the Cornish myth of Tristan and Isolde. One of Cornwall's oldest legends, the story centres on star-crossed lovers and confused heritage. Like the legend, *Mount Royal* offers villainy and vengeance. 'Colonel Benyon's Engagement' is less on the villainous side but does demonstrate a tendency for Cornwall to be represented as a place of sanctuary and recuperation. In the nineteenth century it was often promoted as a site of healing due to its seemingly warm weather and pure waters; Cornwall's effects on the body could be imagined as healthful, as well as fatal.

I

"Thou see'st, we are not all alone unhappy:
This wide and universal theatre
Presents more woful pageants than the scene
Wherein we play in."

t was late in July when Herbert Benyon, colonel of a Bengal cavalry regiment, landed at Southampton from one of the P. and O. steamers, home from India on sick-leave. The Colonel had been very ill indeed with jungle fever; very close to the shadowy boundary which divides us from that unknown country, whither we are all journeying with steady footsteps on the separate roads of life. The fresh sea-breezes and idle steamboat life had done a good deal for him, but he still bore the traces of that desperate sickness. The sunburnt face was wan and haggard, and there were lines of premature age about the mouth and dark shadows under the large lustrous grey eyes. Those eyes of Colonel Benyon's had been wont to strike terror to the souls of defaulting soldiers, conscious of a deficiency in the way of pipeclay or a laxity as to drill; the grey seemed to change to black when the Colonel was angry, and at such times his men were apt to say that their commanding officer looked a very devil. He was not exactly a martinet either, and was known to be as particular about the comfort and well-being of his soldiers as he was about their appearance on parade; but he was a hard master, and his men feared him.

The Colonel gave a sigh, that was the next thing to a groan, as the express from Southampton slackened its pace at Waterloo. He had a first-class carriage all to himself, and had littered all the seats with an accumulation of newspapers, despatch-boxes, dressing-bags, and such light luggage. He had tramped to and fro the narrow space, like some restless lion in its den, during that rapid journey; had taken up one newspaper after another, and tossed it aside again with an air of weariness nigh unto death. And now, at the end of his journey, during which he had seemed devoured by impatience, he groaned aloud from very heaviness of spirit.

He was nine-and-thirty years of age, something over six feet in height, broad-shouldered, strong-limbed, and, if not exactly handsome, at least distinguished-looking; his military career had been one continued success, and the men who knew him best prophesied for him distinction in the future. He had been eleven years away from England, and had passed through the fiery furnace of the Indian Mutiny, reaping a harvest of laurels from that most bloody field. And now he came home with two years' furlough, a handsome balance at his English bankers', and not a creature in the world with a claim upon his purse or his care.

A more thoroughly independent man than Herbert Benyon never landed upon British soil. He had escaped the rocks and shoals of matrimony by what his brother officers called a fluke. In plain words, he had been jilted at the outset of his career by a high-born and penniless flirt, who had thrown him over at the last moment in favour of a wealthier suitor. In all outward seeming he had borne his disappointment gaily enough; but from that hour he became as a man hewn out of granite in relation to all womanly fascinations. The prettiest girls in Calcutta, the most dangerous young matrons in the Indian military world, had flashed their brightest glances upon him with no more effect than the rising sun has nowadays upon the head of Memnon. He was one of the best waltzers in English India, and was wont to declare that waltzing was an intellectual exercise; but in all the giddy mazes of a dozen seasons, Colonel Benyon had never been known to entangle himself. There were women who were said to have been, in the graceful phraseology of the junior officers, "down any amount of a pit," or "up no end of a tree," on the subject of the Colonel; but the Colonel himself had never been known to smile upon a woman with anything warmer than the conventional smile demanded of him by society, since the hour when Lady Julia Dursay had written to tell him that she had looked into her own heart, and found that it was better for both of them that they should break an engagement which could never result in happiness to either.

He had taken life pleasantly enough withal, and was eminently popular among his brother officers: a great billiard-player, a most implacable and inscrutable opponent at the whist-table; and a mighty hunter of those larger animals which enliven the jungle by their existence. He had sent home innumerable tiger-claws mounted in silver, as labels for his English friends' decanters, and had more skins of wild-beasts than he knew what to do with.

Indeed, Herbert Benyon excelled in all those accomplishments which win a man the respect of his fellow-men, and the admiration of the softer sex.

He was rich as well as successful. A bachelor-uncle had died during his absence in the East, leaving him a considerable fortune, and a fine old place in the north of Scotland. It would have seemed as if a man could scarcely desire more good things than had fallen to the lot of Herbert Benyon; and yet the man was not happy. Coming home to familiar scenes after those eleven years of exile awoke no thrill of rapture in his heart. He had perhaps no enthusiastic affection for the country of his birth; in any case his return brought him no pleasure, only a gloomy sense of his own isolation.

Near relatives he had none; neither sister nor brother would smile a welcome upon him: his father and mother had been dead twenty years. He had some distant kindred of course—men and women who bore his name, and professed a certain amount of affection for him; and he had friends by the score—the people to whom he had sent tiger-claws, and wonderful inlaid boxes lined with sandalwood, and cashmere shawls, and embroidered muslins, and all those treasures of Ind wherewith the wanderer is wont to gratify his acquaintance: but that was all. Amongst all the men he knew there was only one to whose friendly smile and welcoming grasp of the hand he looked forward with any ray of real pleasure.

This was a man of about his own age, a comrade at Eton and Cambridge, a certain Frederick Hammersley, who had begun life as a country curate, and had been spoiled for the church by the inheritance of a comfortable fortune, and the development of views in which his diocesan, a bishop of evangelical tendencies, had recognised a leaning towards Romanism.

Mr. Hammersley had not gone over to Rome, however; he had contented himself with writing several theological pamphlets setting forth his principles, which were of the most advanced Anglican school, and with doing much good in his immediate neighbourhood. If he were no longer an accredited shepherd, he had not forgotten the divine precept, "Feed my sheep."

The last that Colonel Benyon had heard of this friend was the announcement of his marriage. They did not maintain friendship by an interchange of long letters, like a couple of school-girls. Each in his way was fully occupied by the business of life; and each felt secure of the other's friendship. There was no need of pen-and-ink protestations between men of this stamp.

Yes, there was some pleasure for the Colonel in the thought of meeting Fred Hammersley. He deposited his goods and chattels at the British, in Cockspur-street, and went straight to his friend's club, the respectable Athenæum. The London season was over, and passers-by stared a little at the Colonel's tall figure, with its unmistakable military air. There were some changes in the aspect of things even at this end of the town since those days before the Indian Mutiny, but the Colonel did not take the trouble to notice them; the Corinthian pillars of a renovated club-house, or a new shop-front here and there, seemed trivial objects to a man fresh from the natural splendours of Cashmere; or it may be that Herbert Benyon was uninterested in these things for lack of any personal association that went home to his heart. When he came to the Athenæum, where he had eaten many a pleasant dinner with his old friend, the familiar look of the hall stirred something in his breast that was almost emotion.

He was doomed to encounter a disappointment here. "Mr. Hammersley was abroad," the porter told him, "on the Continent." The porter could not tell where; "but he had been absent for a long time; ever since—ever since—last spring was a twelvemonth," the porter said, pulling himself up, as if he had been about to say something else.

"And his letters," asked the Colonel—"what becomes of them?"

"We don't get many," answered the man; "but any that do come here for him are sent to Coutts's. He's always on the move, they say, and nobody but his bankers knows where to find him."

There was something in the man's face that impressed Colonel Benyon with the idea that he could say more, if he pleased. He lingered on the threshold of the strangers' room with a dubious meditative air, and slipped half a sovereign into the porter's hand, almost as if from pure absence of mind.

"Thank you, sir; you're very kind, sir. I'm sure I'm sorry enough Mr. Hammersley has left us. It was always a pleasure to do anything for him. Not that he ever gave any trouble—wanting hansoms fetched when it's raining cats and dogs, or anything of that kind. He was always quiet in his ways and affable in his manners. I wish there was more like him. And it do seem a hard thing that he should have to turn his back upon his country like that."

The Colonel stared at the speaker.

"But he travels for his own pleasure, I suppose?" he exclaimed. "He had no particular reason for leaving England?"

"Well, yes, sir; there was unpleasant circumstances connected with his going away. Of course at the West-end those things get talked of, and a person in my position can't shut his ears to such reports. I should be the last in the world to talk, but there's nothing going that don't come to my hearing somehow."

Colonel Benyon stared aghast. What did it mean? Had Frederick Hammersley, that most conscientious and devoted of Anglicans, committed forgery? What was the meaning of this enforced exile? Then a light suddenly flashed on the Colonel's mind.

"His wife is with him, I suppose?" he said interrogatively.

"No, sir; Mrs. Hammersley is not with her husband. In fact his going abroad arose from circumstances connected with that party. She turned out a bad lot, sir. I should be the last to speak disrespectuously of a lady, and of a lady connected with ourselves, as I may say; but I have heard our gentleman say that Mrs. Hammersley's conduct was very bad."

"She left him, I suppose?"

"Yes, sir; ran away from him, after they'd been married little better than six months, with a gentleman they say she was engaged to before she kept company with Mr. Hammersley. The marriage was her father's doing, so I've heard; and when this gentleman, who was a captain in the army, came home from India, she ran away with him. They went to Orstend and suchlike places together, and two months afterwards the captain was found dead early one September morning, shot through the heart, on the sands at Blankenburg. There was a great piece of work. Every one thought it was a duel, and that Mr. Hammersley had killed him; but he was supposed to be in London at the time, no one had seen him or heard of him in Belgium, and they never tried to bring it home to him. The matter dropped after a little while. Mr. Hammersley got a divorce soon after, and left England directly his case was decided."

"And what became of the lady?" asked the Colonel, curious to know the fate of a creature so lost.

"I've never heard, sir. She made no defence in the Divorce Court. It would go rather hard with her, I should think, the captain being dead, unless her friends took her back, which don't seem likely."

"Poor wretch! Do you remember the man's name?"

"What, the captain, sir? I've heard it times and often. He was a Junior-United gentleman. Let me see—was it Chandos? No. Champney—Captain Champney."

Colonel Benyon remembered the name, but not the man; he was in a line regiment, altogether an obscure person compared with the dashing colonel of Bengal cavalry. He had not even heard of the scandal connected with the poor fellow's death. He had never been an eager devourer of English newspapers, unless they had some bearing on the politics of martial India; so whatever mention there had been of Champney's death and Hammersley's divorce had escaped him.

He left the Athenæum and strolled into his own club, the Senior United Service, very much cast down. He ordered his dinner; it was growing dusk by this time; and the coffee-room had an empty and even sepulchral look, with lamps glimmering here and there in the twilight, like the religious gloom of some Egyptian temple. Modern architects have a knack of giving an air of Carthage or Babylon to their public dining-rooms.

After dinner the Colonel wrote to his old friend an honest straight-forward epistle, touching lightly upon Frederick Hammersley's trouble, but withal full of manly sympathy; not such a flowery mis-sive as the Orestes of a French novel would have addressed to his Pylades under the like circumstances, but a thorough English letter. If Hammersley were within any accessible distance, the Colonel pro-posed to join him as soon as he was strong enough for the journey.

"I am on leave for my health, and for that alone," he wrote; "and I do not see why I should not get well as fast, or perhaps faster abroad than I should in England. I have scarcely an association in this country that I care to renew. I am not even eager to visit that stern old Scottish barrack where you and I once hunted the Caledonian boar or stag, in an autumnal holiday, and which now belongs to me. In short, I have outlived most of the illusions of life, and have nothing left, save a belief in friendship where you are concerned. Let me come, my dear Hammersley, unless solitude is your fixed humour; but do not say yes if inclination says no."

Colonel Benyon addressed this letter to his friend under cover to Messrs. Coutts; and having done this, he felt almost as if he had no more to do until the wanderer's reply came. The waiters at the United Service told him that London was empty—in a fashionable sense a veritable desert. Yet no doubt there were people he knew to be found in the great city, and there were theatres enough open for his amusement had he cared to visit them; but he had lost his relish for the modern drama fifteen years before; so he went home to the British, read the papers, and drank the weakest decoction of soda-and-brandy until an hour or so after midnight.

He had a little business to transact with his army agent next day, and an interview with a stockbroker in Warnford-court, to whom he intrusted the investment of those moneys which had accumulated during his absence. On the day after he made a round of calls at the houses of his old acquaintances; and had reason to acknowledge the truth of the waiter's assertion as to the barrenness of civilised London. Every one best worth seeing was away. There were two or three business men, who professed themselves the most miserable drudges in the great mill which is always grinding everything into money; here and there in that obscurer region beyond Eaton-square he found a homely matron who lamented her inability to take the dear children to the seaside until Edwin or Augustus should be able to leave that tiresome office in the City, and who seemed unaffectedly rejoiced to see the Colonel; but the choicer spirits among his old circle—the *dessus du panier*—were away yachting off Cowes, or gambling in Germany. Altogether the day was a dreary one. Colonel Benyon was glad to return to the solitude of his hotel and the intellectual refreshment of the evening papers. After this he idled away a week in revisiting such familiar haunts of his early manhood as he cared to see again. The contemplation of them gave him very little pleasure; that one brief letter of Julia Dursay's seemed to have taken all the sunshine out of his nature. There was a settled bitterness in his mind—a sense that outside his profession there was nothing in the world worth living for.

Nearly a fortnight went by before there came any answer from Mr. Hammersley; and the Colonel felt that he could shape no plan for his holiday till he received his friend's reply. The letter came at last—a letter that went to Herbert Benyon's heart; for it told him in a few words how dire a death blow had shattered his friend's life.

"No, my dear Benyon," wrote the exile, whose letter was dated from a small town in Norway; "you must not join me. The day may come, God only knows when, in which I may be fitter for a friend's companionship; but at present I am too miserable a creature to inflict my society upon any one I care for. I have been roughing it in this country for the last six months, and like the fishing, the primitive life, and simple friendly people; but I doubt if such an existence in such a climate as this would suit an Anglo-Indian valetudinarian, even supposing I were decent company. I write in all candour, you see, my dear Benyon, and I do not think you will doubt my regard for you because, under the bitter influence of an affliction which happily few men can measure, I shrink even from your companionship.

"And now I have a proposition to make to you. You are home on sick-leave, you tell me, and really in need of perfect rest. I have a house in the extreme west of Cornwall—a cottage in a garden of roses, within sight of the sea—which I think would suit you to a nicety, if I can persuade you to make your home there for the next few months. The place is full of bitter associations for me, and I doubt if there is another living creature to whom I would offer it; but I shall be heartily glad if you will inhabit a spot that was once very dear to me. The climate is almost equal to Madeira; and if you have any inclination left for that kind of thing, there is plenty of shooting and hunting to be had in the neighbourhood. I have a couple of old servants in charge of the place, to whom I shall write by this post, telling them to hold themselves ready for your reception; so you will have nothing to do but put yourself into the train at Paddington any morning you please, and go straight through to

Penjudah, from which station a seven-mile drive will carry you to Trewardell, by which barbarous name my place is known. If you would drop a line to Andrew Johns, Trewardell, near Penjudah, beforehand, to announce your coming, he would meet you at the station with a dog-cart. There are a couple of good hacks in the stable, and a hunter I used to ride two years ago, which is, I fancy, about up to your weight."

The offer was a tempting one, and after some hesitation the Colonel decided upon accepting it. Cornwall was a new country to him—a remote semi-barbarous land, he fancied, still pervaded by the Phœnicians and King Arthur; a land that had been more civilised two thousand years ago than today; a land with which Solomon had had trading relations in the way of metal; a land where, at some unknown period, the children of Israel had worked as slaves in the mines; a land of which one might believe anything and everything, in fact. There was some smack of adventure in the idea of going to take possession of his absent friend's house, some faint flavour of romance in the whole business. It would be dull, of course; but the Colonel liked solitude, and found himself year by year less inclined for the kind of life most people consider pleasant. He might have spent his autumn in half a dozen fine old country houses, and received unlimited petting from their fair inhabitants, if he had desired that kind of thing; but he did not. He only wanted to recover his old health and vigour, and then to go back to India.

He wrote to Mr. Andrew Johns, informing that worthy of the probable time of his arrival; and three days afterwards turned his back upon the great city, and sped away westwards across the fields, where the newly-cut stubble was still bright and yellow, onward through a region where the land was red, then away skirting the edge of the bright blue water, across Isambard Brunel's wonderful bridge at Saltash, and then along a narrow line that flies over deep gorges in the woodland, through a fair and lonely landscape to the little station of Penjudah.

It was dusk in the late summer evening when the traveller heard the barbarous name of the place called out with the unfamiliar Cornish accent by a stalwart Cornish porter. The train, which had been about a quarter of a mile long when it left Paddington, had dwindled to a few carriages, and those were for the most part empty. Penjudah seemed the very end of the world. The perfect quiet of the place almost startled the Colonel as he stood upon the platform, looking round about him in the faint grey evening light. He found himself deep in the heart of a wooded valley, with no sign of human life within sight except the two officials who made up the staff of Penjudah station. There was a balmy odour of pines, and a subdued rustle of leaves lightly stirred by the warm west wind. Among the Indian hills he could scarcely remember a scene more lonely. A rabbit ran down a wooded bank and scudded across the line while he was looking about him. The guard told him afterwards that scores of these vermin might be seen playing about the line at odd times. The trains were not frequent enough to scare them.

Outside the station the Colonel found an elderly man-servant, out of livery, with a smart dog-cart and a capital horse.

This was Andrew Johns. He handed the reins to the traveller, and took his seat behind in charge of Colonel Benyon's portmanteaus; and a few minutes afterwards the Colonel was driving up a hilly road that wound across the twilit woods. That seven miles' drive to Trewardell was all up and down hill. The Colonel had rarely encountered a stiffer road even in the East, but the landscape, dimly seen in that dubious light, seemed to him very beautiful; and he was glad that he had accepted his friend's offer. From the top of one of the hills he caught a glimpse of the distant sea; on the summit of another there was a stretch of commonland, and a tall obelisk that served as a beacon for all the countryside, a monumental tribute to a great Indian soldier.

Something over half an hour brought them into a valley, where there was a church with a square tower surmounted with stone pinnacles, a church of some pretension for a parish which consisted of about half a dozen houses. Close to the church were the gates of Trewardell. They stood open to receive the stranger; and after a winding drive through a shrubbery, the Colonel saw the lighted windows of a long low white-walled cottage half smothered in foliage and flowers.

Mrs. Johns and a fat-faced housemaid were waiting in the hall, and a male hanger-on in corduroy and a stable-jacket was in attendance to receive the horse. Everything within looked bright and homelike; one might have fancied the house in full occupation. The hall was low and wide, with panelled walls painted white, and hung with water-coloured sketches prettily framed. The dining-room was a comfortable square apartment, with light oak furniture of the modern mediæval order, and dark-blue silk hangings. The drawing-room opened out of it, and was more of a boudoir or lady's morning-room than an actual drawing-room. Everywhere, in the dining-room, and even in the entrance-hall, there were books, from ponderous folios (choice editions on elephant-paper) to the daintiest duodecimos in white-vellum binding. There was a brightness and prettiness about everything which the Colonel never remembered to have noticed in any house before. It looked like a home that had been made beautiful by the hands of a lover preparing a bower for his bride.

"A woman must have been hard to please who could not make herself happy here, and with so good a fellow as Fred Hammersley," he said to himself.

An excellent dinner had been prepared for him, at which repast the versatile Mr. Johns waited, and proved himself an admirable butler. The Colonel asked him a good many questions about the neighbourhood in the course of the meal, to all of which Mr. Johns replied with considerable intelligence; but he uttered no word about his absent master, or of the kind of existence that he had led there in the brief period of his wedded life.

It was ten o'clock when Colonel Benyon had finished dinner, a warm moonlit night; so he went out to explore the gardens and enjoy his evening smoke. It might be very long before any feminine presence would lend its grace to those bright-looking rooms; but Herbert Benyon would as soon have thought of committing sacrilege as of desecrating his friend's house with the odour of tobacco. A woman had left the impress of her individuality upon everything. Those water-coloured sketches in the hall were signed by a woman's hand; in the drawing-room there were caskets and writing-cases, work-baskets and photographic albums—innumerable trifles that were unmistakably a woman's belongings. It seemed as if every-thing had been religiously preserved exactly as the traitress had left it. Colonel Benyon could fancy her last look round this room, or fancied that he could fancy it. There was a low armchair on one side of the fireplace, with a gem of a work-table beside it—her seat, of course. How often had she sat there meditating treason, with her husband sitting opposite to her perhaps, watching her fondly all the while, and thanking God for having given him so sweet a wife!

"Confound the woman!" muttered the Colonel impatiently; "I can't get her out of my mind."

It did indeed seem to him tonight as if that false wife had left an evil influence upon the scene of her iniquity. He could not feel at ease in the house; he could not help wondering and speculating about that lost creature.

"Where is she now?" he asked himself; and then there arose before him an image of her sitting alone in some sordid continental lodging, poor, friendless, desolate; or worse, flaunting on a Parisian boulevard, in the livery of sin. Do what he would, he could not help thinking of her.

"It will wear off in time, I suppose," he said to himself; "but upon my word, if I were her husband, I could scarcely worry myself more about her."

He went out into the gardens, and roamed about amongst the flower-beds, and in the darksome shrubbery-paths, smoking and communing with himself for more than an hour. The grounds of Trewardell were spacious and lovely, quite out of proportion with the humble pretensions of the house. There was a lake on one side of the lawn, on the other a group of fine old plane-trees; beyond these a short avenue of elms leading to a meadow that looked almost a park. The soft night air was heavy with the perfume of myrtle and magnolia.

"The place is a perfect Eden," said the Colonel; "but I wish I had not been told the history of Eve and the Serpent."

II

"Name her not now, sir; she's a deadly theme."

For the first fortnight of his sojourn at Trewardell, Colonel Benyon's Cornish experiences were altogether agreeable. The weather was brilliant; and in a county much given to moisture he was not

inconvenienced by a single shower. There was plenty for him to
see within a day's ride: here a ruined castle, there a nobleman's
seat renowned amongst the show places of the west; and during
those first two weeks the Colonel spent the greater part of every
day in the saddle; or on foot, tramping over sunburnt hills high
above a broad sweep of sea, while his horse rested at some solitary
rustic inn. He was somewhat inclined to forget how short a time
had gone by since he was lying in his Indian bungalow, well-nigh
given over by the regimental doctors. Perhaps in that first fortnight
of genuine enjoyment he sowed the seeds of a mischief which
was to overtake him by and by. The third week brought him into
September, and he had a good time of it among the partridges,
with Andrew Johns for his guide and counsellor. For three con-
secutive mornings the two men set out at daybreak when the dew
was heavy upon the ground, and tramped over miles of stubble
and turnip-field before breakfast. On the fourth day the Colonel
suddenly knocked under, and told Mr. Johns that he had had
enough, just for the present. Partridge-shooting was all very well
in its way; but there were shooting-pains in the Colonel's limbs,
and a dull perpetual aching in the Colonel's shoulders which a
man of forty rarely cares to cultivate. There was a drizzling rain,
too, upon that fourth day of September; and Colonel Benyon was
very glad to find a blazing fire in the bright-looking drawing-room,
wherein he had a knack of painting imaginary scenes—scenes
out of that tragical drama of which Flora Hammersley had been
the heroine.

In his enforced idleness today, the thought of his friend's sorrow,
and this woman's sin, haunted him more vividly than ever. That
young soldier lying dead in the chill autumn sunrise on the sands
near Blankenburg, slain by a hand that had never before been

lifted to do a cruel thing—the hand of a generous single-minded man. As to the fact of Fred Hammersley's share in this transaction, Colonel Benyon felt no doubt. His friend had killed the seducer. It was the thing he would have done himself, unhesitatingly, under like circumstances. He walked up and down the room. He had read yesterday's *Times* and *Globe*, *Standard* and *Telegraph*, and there was no more mental pabulum for him till a post came in—per special messenger on pony from the nearest post-town—at five o'clock P.M. At another time Mr. Hammersley's splendid library might have afforded him ample entertainment; but today he was in no humour for books; he had opened half a dozen or so, and after skimming a page or two absently, had put each volume back on its particular shelf. He could not fasten his mind upon any subject.

The rain came down in a monotonous hopeless way; even the standard roses on the lawn outside had a dreary look. The Colonel longed, like Horace Walpole, to bring them indoors and put them by the fire. Sometimes Colonel Benyon stood staring out at the deluged garden; sometimes he threw himself into a low armchair by the fire, and amused himself by a savage demolition of the coals; anon he paced the room again, pausing now and then, in an idle way, to examine some one of those womanly trifles whose presence reminded him of the lost mistress of Trewardell.

The day seemed interminable. He was glad when it grew dark; still more glad of the slight distraction afforded by his seven-o'clock dinner, though he had no appetite—an utter distaste for food, indeed—and a burning thirst.

"I feel very much as I used to feel at the beginning of my fever," he said to himself, a little alarmed by these symptoms, and by the heaviness and aching of his limbs. "God forbid that I should have another spell of it!"

Andrew Johns had gone to the market-town on business connected with the victualling of the small household; and Mrs. Johns had put on a black-silk gown and her best cap to wait upon the Colonel, not caring to trust that delicate office to the fat-faced rustic handmaiden.

"The girls we get hereabouts are so rough," she said; "and this one has never been used to much out of the dairy. We had a houseful of servants when Mr. Hammersley lived here; but since he's gone abroad there's been scarcely enough work for me and a girl."

The dame gave a profound sigh. Colonel Benyon perceived that she was garrulously given, and perceived that if he had a mind to hear about his friend's history in this house, it would not require any great effort to set Mrs. Johns discoursing thereupon.

"Do try one of those red mullet, sir; I dressed them with my own hands. It's a sauce that Mr. Hammersley was fond of—poor dear gentleman!"

Here came another profound sigh; and the dame lingered, trifling absently with the arrangements of the sideboard, as if willing to be questioned.

"You seem to have been very fond of your master," said the Colonel.

"We shouldn't be much account if we weren't fond of him," replied Mrs. Johns. "He was as good a master as ever lived. We'd known him from a boy, too. He used to come down to Penrose Abbey for his holidays in the old Squire's time—Mr. Penrose; you've heard tell of him, I daresay, sir. Andrew and me were butler and cook at Penrose for twenty years. Mr. Hammersley was only a distant relation to the Squire, you see, sir, and nobody thought that he'd come in for all the property; but he did. I suppose Mr. Penrose took a fancy to him when he was a boy; but there were plenty more young nephews and cousins on the look-out for his money, I can tell you."

"Did Mr. Penrose ever live here?"

"No, sir. Trewardell was his mother's place, and it was shut up after her death. But since Mr. Hammersley came into the estate, the abbey has been kept as a show house. He didn't care to live there: it was cold and gloomy, he said; and he took a fancy to this place, and had it done up against his marriage—a power of money he spent upon it, to be sure. But, dear me, sir, you haven't eat a mouthful of that mullet. Perhaps you don't like the sauce?"

"It's excellent, my dear Mrs. Johns, but I really have no appetite this evening."

"And there's a boiled fowl with stewed artichokes, and a brace of those birds you shot the day before yesterday. I hope you'll eat something, sir."

"I'm sorry to do injustice to such good cooking; but upon my word, I can't eat a morsel. If you'll make me a stiffish glass of brandy-and-water, as hot as you can make it, I think perhaps it might do me some good. I had a bad fever in India, and seem to have a touch of my old enemy tonight."

"Wouldn't you like Andrew to ride back for the doctor, as soon as he comes in? or I could send one of the men at once, sir."

"On no account. Pray don't make an invalid of me. I walked a little too far after the partridges yesterday; I daresay I've knocked myself up, that's all. Even if I should feel worse, which I don't expect, I've some medicine in my dressing-case."

Mrs. Johns mixed the brandy-and-water with an anxious face, and watched the Colonel while he drank it. Then she persuaded him to return to the drawing-room, where she ensconced him luxuriously in an easy-chair by the fire, with a tiger-skin carriage-rug over his knees.

"Don't hurry away, Mrs. Johns," he said, after duly acknowledging her attention. "I like to hear you talk of my poor friend Hammersley; sit down by the fire, do, there's a good soul. That's right; it looks quite comfortable and homelike to see you sitting there. I could almost fancy I'd discovered some treasure in the way of an aunt. I can't tell you how dreary I've felt all day. My mind has been running perpetually upon poor Hammersley and his wife. It's no use speaking of them to your husband; if I do, he tightens up his lips in a most impenetrable way, and is dumb immediately."

"Yes, sir, that's just like Andrew," replied the dame, smoothing her white-muslin apron and settling herself comfortably in the chair opposite the Colonel's; "I think he'd lie down on the ground for his master to walk over him; but you can never get him to talk about him, nor of her either, poor soul!"

"She behaved so badly, and worked such ruin, that I almost wonder you can find it in your heart to pity her," said the Colonel.

The good woman sighed again, and shook her head dubiously.

"You see, I knew her, sir," she replied; "and it isn't likely I could bring myself to think as hardly of her as the rest of the world. She was such a noble generous creature, no one could ever have thought she would do such a wicked thing. She hadn't been here very long before I found out that the love was all on one side in that marriage. She was very gentle and winning in all her ways towards her husband; but she didn't care for him, and never had cared for him, and never would; that was plain enough to me. And she wasn't happy; do what he would to please her, he couldn't make her happy. There was a look in her face of missing something—a sort of blank look; and whenever her husband was away—though goodness knows that was not often—she would roam about the house in a restless way that gave one the dismals only to watch her."

"Did he see that she was unhappy, do you think?" asked the Colonel.

"No, sir, I don't think he did; and that's why it came upon him like a thunderclap when she ran away. He was so bent upon making her happy, that I think he believed she was so. He was so proud of her too. Everybody admired her. She was the loveliest woman in the county, they said, though the west is famous for pretty women; and she was so clever—such a sweet singer. It was she who painted all the pictures in this room and in the hall. It was Mr. Hammersley's fancy to have none but what she had painted."

"Did she belong to this part of the country?"

"O dear no, sir. Her family were Suffolk people, I've heard say; her father was a colonel in the Indian army, and there was a very large family of them—not too well off, I believe; so of course it was a very good match for her. I suppose she married to please her friends; such things seem common enough nowadays. She was always very sweet-spoken and affable with me. One day when I was talking to her of a son of mine—my only child, that died young—she said, 'Ah, Mrs. Johns, I have my dead too!' and I fancied she was speaking of some sweetheart very like that she'd had in time past."

"Did Captain Champney come here as Hammersley's friend?"

"No, sir; he never came to this house at all; she must have met him out of doors. It was summer time, midsummer, and very sultry weather. Mr. Hammersley was up in London on business connected with his estate. He was to be away a week at most, and he had wanted her to go with him; but she wouldn't, not being over well or strong at the time. She'd had a low nervous fever in the spring, that had pulled her down a good deal. It was the morning after her husband left—I remember it all as well as if it was yesterday—she had been out in the village and round about the lanes visiting the poor—she was a rare hand at that always—and she came in at one of those windows while I was dusting the china in this room. I never shall forget her. Her face was as white as a sheet, and she walked in a strange tottering way, with her eyes fixed, until she came right up against me. Then she gave a start, and dropped into the nearest chair, half fainting. I brought her a glass of water, and asked her what had happened. 'O, Mrs. Johns,' she said, 'I've seen a ghost!' I couldn't get her to say more than this; all the rest of the day she was shut up in her room. The next day there came a messenger with a letter for her, and late in the afternoon the same man came again with another letter. They were both from the Captain, of course; but all that day she never stirred outside the doors, not so much as to go into the gardens, though it was a splendid summer day. Early the next morning there came another letter, and in the afternoon she went out. She wore her garden-hat and a light muslin dress, and she took nothing with her. I could lay my life that when she left the house that afternoon she had no thought of going away; but she never came back."

"Were the two seen together in this neighbourhood?"

"Yes; a lad met Mrs. Hammersley and a strange gentleman in Farmer Goldman's field—there's a short cut across that way to the Penjudah-road—she had her hands clasped over her face, and was sobbing as if her heart would break, the boy said, and the gentleman was talking to her very earnestly. The boy turned and watched them. They loitered about, talking for half an hour or so, Mrs. Hammersley crying almost all the time; and then the boy saw them get into a close carriage that had been waiting in the Penjudah-road, and heard the gentleman tell the man to drive to the station. This was about four o'clock in the afternoon, and the Plymouth train leaves Penjudah at a quarter to five. It came out afterwards that Captain Champney had been staying at the Rose and Crown at Penjudah, and had hired a close fly on that day. The driver could tell all the rest—how he had waited above an hour in the road near Trewardell, and picked up a lady there."

"How soon did Hammersley learn what had happened?"

"My husband telegraphed to him that night, and he was back early the next evening. He was very quiet. I never saw any one take a great blow so quietly. He didn't bluster or rave, as some gentlemen would have done; but he sat in the library for one whole day, writing letters and seeing every one who had anything to tell him, while Andrew was about making inquiries quietly in every direction. There was no fuss or talk, considering, and it was only a few people knew anything of what had happened. As soon as Mr. Hammersley had heard all he could hear in this place he started off—after those two, I suppose; and that's the last we ever saw of him. He wrote to Andrew soon after, telling him how the house was to be kept up, and so on; and that was all."

"You heard of Captain Champney's death, I suppose?" said the Colonel.

"Yes," Mrs. Johns replied, with a doubtful air, "we did hear that he was dead."

"And you heard the strange manner of his death, no doubt?"

"We saw something in the papers, but didn't take much heed of it," replied Mrs. Johns, with an air of not caring to pursue this subject.

The Colonel did not press it. There was no doubt in his own mind as to the hand that had slain Captain Champney, and he fancied that Mrs. Johns shared his conviction upon that subject.

"Have you ever heard what became of Mrs. Hammersley?" he asked presently.

"Not a word, sir. That's what makes me pity her sometimes, in spite of myself. It's a hard thing for her to be left like that, without a soul to care for her—him that she sinned for dead and gone. She may be starving somewhere, poor misguided creature! without a roof to cover her perhaps, and these empty rooms looking as if they were waiting for her all the while, with all the pretty things she was so fond of just as she left them. It always gives me the heartache to think of her, or to touch any of the things that belonged to her."

"Was it Hammersley's wish that the place should be kept just as she left it?"

"Yes, sir, that was one of his orders in the letter of instruction that he wrote to my husband before he left England."

"Is there no portrait of her anywhere about the house?"

"No, sir. There was a likeness of her, painted by some great artist in London, but I never saw that after the day when Mr. Hammersley came back and found her gone. Whether he destroyed it in secret that day, or put it away somewhere under lock and key, I can't tell. I only know that when I came into this room next morning the picture was gone. There's the blank space where it hung just above your head."

The Colonel looked up. Yes, there was the empty panel. On the opposite side of the fireplace there was a portrait of his friend, little more than a head, against a dark background, bold and truthful, by the hand of John Philip. He had made a shrewd guess why the companion picture was missing.

He had been so much interested in the housekeeper's talk as almost to forget his pain and weariness; but by this time the stimulating effect of his dose of brandy-and-water had worn off, and he felt really ill, quite as ill as when the first warning of his fever came upon him up the country.

"I'm afraid I'm in for it, Mrs. Johns," he said, with a faint groan; "I'm afraid I'm going to be very ill. Rather hard upon you and your husband, isn't it, and not in the bond? My friend lent me his house to get well in; he didn't bargain for my falling ill in it."

Mrs. Johns did her best to console and cheer him with assurances that his symptoms indicated nothing more than a cold and a little over-fatigue.

"A cold's a hazardous thing for a man in my condition, my good soul," said the Colonel, "and I was a fool to overdo it with those long tramps over the damp stubble. The doctor who sent me home gave me all manner of solemn warnings as to what I might and might not do, and I'm afraid I've paid very little attention to any of them. However, I'll go to bed at once, take a dose of the fellow's medicine, and wrap myself in a blanket. Perhaps I may be all right in the morning. But if I should be worse, you'd better telegraph to Plymouth for one of the best medical men there. Don't put me in the hands of a local doctor."

Mrs. Johns promised to obey these instructions, still protesting that the Colonel would be better in the morning; and then hurried off to see that there was a blazing fire made in his bedroom, and to provide one of her thickest blankets in which to envelop him.

III

> *"Ah, homeless as the leaf that winds have blown*
> *To earth—in this wide world I stand alone."*

The Colonel's dismal prophecy was but too faithfully realised. The next morning found him in a raging fever, with a furred tongue, bloodshot eyes, a galloping pulse, and racking pains in his limbs.

It was no case of infection, no village epidemic. The Colonel had simply, in his own language, overdone it.

Mrs. Johns opined that this was the beginning of a rheumatic fever; but she still kept up her cheery tone to the patient, looking anxiously all the while for the advent of the Plymouth doctor.

He did not come till sunset, by which time the Colonel was worse. After making a careful examination of his patient, and questioning Mrs. Johns closely as to the Colonel's antecedents, the physician sat down to write a prescription.

"It is not so much a question of physic as of care," he said. "You have not called in any one from the neighbourhood yet, I suppose?"

"No, sir. Colonel Benyon begged me not to call in any one of that kind, or else I should have sent at once for Mr. Borlase."

"Never mind what the Colonel says. Let your husband call for Mr. Borlase, and get this prescription made up. He can ask Mr. Borlase to come back with him and see me. Or, let me see, there'll scarcely be time for that. I can call on Borlase as I drive back to the station, and explain matters. Mr. Borlase will watch the case for me."

"But you'll come to see him again, sir?"

"Most decidedly. This is Friday. I shall come again on Monday by the same train. The case is rather a critical one."

"You don't think there's any danger, sir?"

"Not immediate danger; but the man's constitution has been undermined by hard work and illness in India, and he's not a good subject for rheumatic fever. However, I shall be able to say more on Monday. In the mean time, the grand question is good nursing. I think I had better send you a professional nurse."

Mrs. Johns protested her ability to nurse the Colonel herself; but the physician shook his head.

"My good creature, you have your house to look after," he said, "and that poor fellow will want constant watching. We must expect delirium in such a case. You and your husband must contrive to look after him tonight, and I will send you a reliable person early tomorrow morning."

Having made this promise, the doctor got into the fly from the Rose and Crown, and drove back to Penjudah, where he had a brief interview with Mr. Borlase, who came out of his trim-looking stone house and stood upon the pavement before his door, while the great man talked to him out of the fly.

"I shall send a nurse from Plymouth tomorrow morning," said the physician. "There's no one about here, I suppose, that one could depend upon for such a case?"

"I don't know about that," replied Mr. Borlase. "There's a person I've had a good deal to do with lately amongst my very poor patients, and if you could only get her, you'd find her a treasure; but whether she would attend a wealthy person as a paid servant is a question I can't answer. She has only nursed the poor hereabouts, and evidently does it as a pious duty. I fancy, from her dress and manner, that she belongs to some religious community—not exactly Roman Catholic perhaps, but very near it."

"Who is she?"

"A Mrs. Chapman—a widow; poor herself, I suppose, for she occupies very humble lodgings in Bolter's-row, at the other end of the town. She never takes payment from any one; indeed she only attends a class that are quite unable to pay. She is a young woman, fragile-looking, and very pretty; but she is the best nurse I ever met with."

"I don't think the Colonel will object to her youth and good looks," said the doctor, laughing. "That kind of thing is much pleasanter in a sick-room than some gorgon of the Gamp species. Have you known this Mrs. Chapman long?"

"Not long. She has only been here three months; but I have seen a great deal of her in that time; and I can answer for her patience and devotion."

"I've half an hour to spare before my train starts. I'll go down to Bolter's-row, and have a look at this paragon of yours."

"I'm sure you'll be pleased with her; but I very much doubt your being able to get her to do what we want," said Mr. Borlase.

"We'll see about that," answered the physician, who had some confidence in his own powers of persuasion. "You say the woman is poor. She'll scarcely care to decline an advantageous offer, I should think. Good-night, Borlase. Be sure you go to Trewardell the first thing tomorrow."

With this injunction the doctor drove away down the little hilly High-street to the outskirts of Penjudah, where he alighted, and groped his way along a narrow alley of queer old-fashioned cottages, so crooked that they seemed scarcely able to support themselves in a standing position.

Upon inquiring for Mrs. Chapman, he was directed to the last house in Bolter's-row, and here he was ushered into a tiny sitting-room, daintily neat, and with an air of freshness and prettiness that struck him as something beyond the common graces of poverty. The room was dimly lighted by one candle, beside which a woman sat reading; a slim fragile creature in a black gown and a white-muslin cap of some peculiar fashion, a cap which concealed almost every vestige of her hair, and gave a nunlike aspect to her pale thin face.

The doctor felt at once that this was no vulgar sick-nurse. This was not a woman to whom he could broadly offer money as an inducement to her to depart from her established round of duty.

He told her his errand, told her what he had heard from Mr. Borlase, and how anxious he was to secure her services for a gentleman lying dangerously ill.

"It is quite impossible," she said, in a sweet firm voice. "I nurse only the very poor."

"You belong to some sisterhood, I suppose?" said the physician.

"No; I belong to no sisterhood," she answered, with something that was half bitterness, half sorrow in her tone; "I stand quite alone in the world."

"Pray pardon me; I thought by your dress you might be a member of one of those communities so numerous nowadays."

"No, sir. It is a simple dress, and suits my circumstances; that is my only reason for wearing it. I have made my own line of duty, and try to follow it."

"I wonder you should have chosen so obscure a place as Penjudah as a field for your charitable work. Do you belong to this part of the country?"

"No. The place is quiet, and I can live cheaply here. Up to this time I have always found plenty of work."

"The duty you have chosen is a very noble one, and the sacrifice most admirable in so young a woman."

"It is no sacrifice for me," she answered decisively; and the doctor felt he had no right to ask any more questions.

He pressed his request very warmly, however; so much so, that at last Mrs. Chapman seemed almost inclined to yield.

"You have owned that you have no pressing duties in Penjudah just now," he said, when they had been talking together for some time; "and I do assure you that you will be performing a real act of charity in looking after this poor fellow at Trewardell."

It was the first time he had mentioned the name of the place.

"At Trewardell, did you say?" asked Mrs. Chapman.

"Yes. It's a gentleman's house, seven miles from here; a charming place. This Colonel Benyon is a friend of the owner, who has lived abroad for some years. Pray, now, consider the case, and extend your charity to this poor man, Mrs. Chapman. Remember it's not as if he were in the bosom of his family. He's quite alone, with no one in the house but servants, and a stranger in the land, as one may say. Of course I might send a nurse from Plymouth, as I intended in the first case; but after what Mr. Borlase told me, I set my heart upon having you."

"Mr. Borlase is very good. I will come."

He had expected to conquer in the end, but had not expected her to yield so suddenly.

"You will! That's capital; and allow me to say that, as far as remuneration goes, you will be quite at liberty to name your own terms."

"Pray do not mention that. I could not possibly take payment for my services. I shall come to Colonel Benyon as I should to the poorest patient in Penjudah."

"Do just what you please, only come; and the sooner the better."

"I can come immediately—tonight, if you please."

"I should be very glad if you will do so. I am just off to the station, and will send my fly to take you back to Trewardell."

"Back to Trewardell!" Mrs. Chapman repeated those three last words as if there were something strange in them.

The doctor was too hurried to notice anything peculiar in her tone. As it was, he ran some risk of losing his train. He wished her good-night, and went back to the fly.

IV

"There are some things hard to understand:
O, help me, my God, to trust in Thee;
But I never shall forget her soft white hand,
And her eyes when she looked at me."

Colonel Benyon had a hard time of it. Again, as in his Indian bungalow, grim death claimed him for his own, and was only to be kept at bay by prodigies of care and skill; again the lamp of life flickered low, and for a while the sick man lay in a land where all was darkness, knowing no one, remembering nothing, and suffering the unspeakable agonies of a mind distraught. There is no need to describe the variations of the fever, the changes from bad to worse, the faint improvement, the threatened relapse. Through all that month of September Mr. Borlase came twice a day, and the Plymouth physician twice a week to Trewardell. They both declared themselves proud of their victory when Herbert Benyon could be fairly pronounced out of danger. They both acknowledged that they owed that victory, under Providence, to Mrs. Chapman.

She had been indefatigable, working and watching by day and night with a quiet patience that knew no limit. No other hand than hers had ever administered the Colonel's medicine, or smoothed his pillow, since she came to Trewardell; no eyes but hers had watched him in the dead of the night. It was quite in vain that Mr. Borlase and Mrs. Johns had urged her to accept assistance, to let some one relieve her of her night watch now and then. Upon this point she was inexorable. If she ever slept at all, she so planned her slumbers that they should not interfere with her duties. Sometimes in the dusk of the evening, when it was very nearly dark even out

99

of doors, she would take a solitary walk in the gardens for half an hour or so. That was her only relaxation. Sweet and gentle as she was in her manners, she was rather an unapproachable person, and she contrived to keep Mrs. Johns at a distance; which was somewhat galling to that matron, who had never been able to beguile her into a little friendly gossip since she entered the house.

"She's as proud as Lucifer, I do believe, in spite of her meek quiet ways," Mrs. Johns declared to her husband, with an aggrieved expression of countenance. "Why, I've scarcely heard her voice half-a-dozen times since she's been here; and I can't say that I've seen her face properly yet, that black hood she wears overshadows it so. I hate such popish ways."

This hood which Mrs. Johns objected to had certainly a somewhat conventional aspect, and served to hide the nurse's pale sweet face much more than the cap in which Dr. Matson had first seen her. The physician perceived the change of headgear when he came to Trewardell, but considered it only a part of that harmless eccentricity which might be permitted to this lay sister of charity.

The time came at last when Herbert Benyon awoke from that long night of suffering and delirium to some faint interest in external things. He had not been unconscious all this time; on the contrary, for long afterwards he had a keen remembrance of every detail of his illness; but mixed up with all the realities of his life had been the dreams and delusions of fever. He knew that throughout his illness by day and night a slender black-robed figure had sat by his bedside, or flitted lightly about his room; he knew that a woman's soft hand had administered to his comforts day after day, without change or weariness; he knew that a very sweet sad face had looked down upon him in the dim lamplight with ineffable pity; but he had cherished strange fancies about this gentle watcher. Sometimes she was a sister he had loved very dearly, and lost in his early youth; sometimes she was Lady Julia Dursay. That she resembled neither of them mattered little to his wandering mind.

But this was all over now. He knew that he was at Trewardell, and that this black-robed woman was a stranger to him.

It was upon a Sunday, a mild October day, towards sunset, that he felt himself for the first time able to speak to his patient nurse. A broad bay-window in his room looked westward, and he saw the evening sky with a warm rosy light in it, and heard the rooks cawing in the avenue, and the church-bells ringing for evening service.

Mrs. Chapman was sitting by the window reading, with her hood thrown back, and her dark-brown hair only shrouded by her muslin cap. She did not wear the hood always, though Mrs. Johns had never happened to see her without it. She had a habit of throwing it off at times.

The Colonel lay quite motionless, looking at the sky and at that quiet figure by the window, wondering dreamily who this woman was. Her profile was clearly defined against the soft light, as she sat there, unconscious that he was watching her; and Herbert Benyon thought that he had never seen a lovelier face.

It was a spiritualized beauty, sublimated by some great sorrow, the Colonel fancied. The glory and bloom of youth were gone, though the woman was evidently young; but with the loss of these she had gained in the charm of expression. It was a face that went to one's heart.

She turned from the window presently, hearing her patient stir, and came towards the bed. He saw that her eyes were grey, large, and dark, with a plaintive look in them.

"I did not know that you were awake," she said gently. "Let me alter your pillows a little, and then I will bring you some tea."

It was the voice that had been with him in all his foolish dreams. It seemed as if he had come back to life out of a living grave, bringing only this memory with him. She bent over him, arranging the pillow, which had slipped to a position of torture on the edge of the bed. The dexterous hands made all comfortable in a few moments, while the lovely face looked down upon him.

"How good you have been to me all this time!" he said. He had uttered protestations of gratitude and regard many times during his delirium, but these were the first thoroughly sensible words he had spoken to her.

The surprise overcame her a little. Sudden tears started to her eyes, and she turned her head aside to hide them.

"Thank God!" she exclaimed earnestly; "thank God!"

"For what?" asked the Colonel.

"That you are so much better."

"I have been very ill, then, I suppose?"

"You have been very ill."

"Off my head, haven't I? Yes, I know I thought myself up the country; and that I could hear the jackals screaming outside. And I am really in Cornwall, down at Hammersley's place—poor Hammersley!—and you have been nursing me for I don't know how long! You see I am quite rational now. I thought once you were my sister—a girl who died nearly twenty years ago."

"Yes, you are much better; but pray do not talk. You are very weak still, and the doctors would be angry with me for letting you talk so much."

"Very well. I will be as quiet as a lamb; indeed I don't feel capable of disobeying you. But there is one question that I must ask."

"I do not mind answering one question, if I can."

"To what beneficent influence do I owe your care of me? what freak of fortune brought such a ministering angel to my sick-bed?"

"I am here to perform a work of charity, that is all," she answered quietly; "I am a nurse by profession."

"But you are a lady!" he exclaimed, surprised.

"That does not prevent my nursing the sick."

"Then you do not mean that you are a hospital nurse—a person to be engaged by any one who needs your services?"

"You are asking more than one question. No; I am not a hospital nurse, nor do I take payment for my services."

"I thought not," murmured the Colonel, with a faint sigh of relief.

It would have shocked him, somehow, to discover that the patient watcher whom he had mistaken now for his lost sister— anon for his false love—was only a hireling after all.

"I wished to perform some duty in the world, being quite alone, and I chose that of attendance on the sick poor. I have never wearied of it yet."

"And have you been long engaged in this good work?"

"Not very long; but you must not talk any more. I must positively forbid that."

The Colonel submitted very reluctantly. He was so eager to know all about this woman—this ministering angel, as he called her in his own mind. He repeated Scott's familiar lines in a low voice as she moved softly about the room making preparations for his evening meal.

Betsy Jane, the fat-faced housemaid, brought the tea-tray.

Mrs. Johns had avoided all actual attendance on the sickroom of late, offended by the nurse's stand-offishness. The Colonel did not want her, she said. He had that fine lady with her popish headgear.

Mrs. Chapman arranged the tea-things on the table by the bed—the small home-baked loaf, the tiny rolls of rich yellow butter, and a noble block of honeycomb on a glass dish. There was a nosegay of autumnal flowers, too, for the embellishment of the table; and altogether Herbert Benyon fancied that innocent repast the most tempting banquet that had ever been spread before him.

"Please sit there and pour out my tea," he said in his weak voice. "But see, you have forgotten your own cup and saucer," he added, looking at the table.

"I will drink my tea presently."

"You must drink it now with me, or I will drink none."

She complied; it was not worth while arguing with him about such a trifle. She brought the second cup and saucer, and sat where he ordered her. He looked at her very often as he sipped the tea she had poured out for him, and ate bread and honey, like the queen in the famous nursery rhyme. He looked at her, wondering what her life had been, with an intense curiosity only possible to a prisoner in a sick-room. He would have given the world to question her farther; but that was forbidden, to say nothing of the impertinence of such a proceeding. He was fain to lie there, and look at her with fixed dreamy eyes, speculating idly about her and her history.

The patient had taken a turn, and the doctors rejoiced exceedingly; but his progress even now was very slow. He lay for four long weeks almost as helpless as a child, attended upon day and night by Mrs. Chapman and a young man out of the stables, a handy young fellow, whose genius had been developed by the exigencies of the case, and who made a very decent amateur valet. How he should have endured this dreary time without Mrs. Chapman's care and companionship, Herbert Benyon could not imagine. She brightened the dismal monotony of the sick-room, and lightened his burden for him more than words could tell; and yet she was by no means what any one would call a lively person. Indeed, after that close companionship of many weeks, Colonel Benyon could not remember ever having seen her smile. But her presence had an influence upon him that was better than commonplace cheerfulness. She read to him, and the low sweet voice was like music. She talked to him, and every word helped to reveal the wealth of a highly-cultivated mind. With such a companion life could not be irksome, even in a sick-room.

Before the fourth week of that first stage of his convalescence was ended, Colonel Benyon had made many efforts to learn his nurse's history; but had failed utterly in the endeavour.

"My story is common enough," she told him once, when he said that he was convinced there was some romance in her life.

"I have lost all that I ever loved, and am obliged to interest myself in strangers."

"You are very young to be a widow," said the Colonel. "Had you been long married when Mr. Chapman died?"

A sudden look of pain came into her face.

"Not very long. Please do not ask me to recall my past life. My history is the history of the dead."

After this he could not push his curiosity farther; but he was not a little tormented by his desire to know more. In the dead of the night he lay awake saying to himself, "Who the deuce could this Chapman have been to leave his wife in such a desolate position?

and what has become of her own relations? I would stake my chances of promotion that she is a lady by birth; but how comes a lady to be left to carry out such a quixotic scheme as this sick-nursing business?" For to the Colonel's mundane mind the nursing of the sick poor seemed an eccentric, an abnormal employment for a well-bred young woman—above all, for a beautiful woman like this widow, with the classic profile and luminous grey eyes.

As soon as the Colonel was strong enough to totter from his bed to a sofa, Dr. Matson suggested a change of quarters.

"You must get nearer the sea," he said; "this flowery dell is all very well in its way; and you certainly do get a sniff of the Atlantic mixed with the perfume of your roses. But I should like to plant you somewhere on the very edge of the ocean. There is a decent inn at Penjudah, now, directly facing the sea, built almost upon the beach; a homely place enough, but where you would get very good treatment. I think we might move you there with advantage."

The Colonel groaned.

"I don't feel strong enough to be moved from one room to another," he said.

"I daresay not. There's a good deal of prostration still, no doubt; but the change would do you a world of good. We must manage it somehow—contrive some kind of ambulance, and carry you in a recumbent position. Mrs. Chapman will go with you, of course."

The Colonel's face brightened at this suggestion.

"Would you go?" he asked, looking at his nurse.

"Of course she would. She's not done with you yet, by any means. You are not going to slip out of our hands for some little time, I assure you, Colonel Benyon," said Dr. Matson, with professional jocosity.

"I do not wish; I am quite content to remain an invalid," replied the Colonel, looking at his nurse and not at his doctor.

The physician saw the look.

"Bless my soul," he said to himself, "is that the way the cat jumps? The Colonel's friends won't thank me for getting him such a good nurse, if he winds up by marrying her. That look was very suspicious."

The doctor had his way. The chief inn at Penjudah was quite empty at this late period of the year; and the best rooms, old-fashioned capacious chambers facing the sea, were at the patient's disposal. So one fine morning in the beginning of November, while the reddened leaves in this mild western country still lingered on the trees, Colonel Benyon left Trewardell, which had been a somewhat unlucky shelter, it seemed.

Even on that last morning busy Mrs. Johns scarcely caught so much as a glimpse of the nurse's face; but just at the final moment, when the Colonel had been made comfortable in the carriage, wrapped up to the eyes in woollen rugs and tiger-skins, Mrs. Chapman turned and held out her hand to the housekeeper. She had her veil down, a thick black veil, and she wore a close black bonnet of a somewhat by-gone fashion.

"Good-bye, Mrs. Johns," she said in her low plaintive voice. "This is the last time I shall ever see Trewardell. Please shake hands before I go away."

There was something that seemed almost humility in her tone. The housekeeper drew herself up rather stiffly, quite taken by surprise; and then, in the next moment, her good nature got the better of her resentment, and she took the proffered hand,

What a slender little hand it seemed in the grasp of Sarah Johns' stout fingers!

"I am sure I bear you no malice, mum," she said, "though you have kept yourself so much to yourself, as if other folks weren't good enough for you; and if you like to walk over from Penjudah any fine afternoon to take a cup of tea with me and my husband, you'll be heartily welcome. There's always a bit of cold meat and an apple-pasty in the house."

"You are very kind; but I feel somehow that I shall never see Trewardell again. May I gather one of those late roses? Thanks; I should like to take one away."

She went to one of the standard rose-trees on the lawn, and gathered one solitary tea-rose—a pale primrose-coloured flower—a melancholy-looking blossom, the Colonel thought, when she took her seat in the carriage with this rose in her hand.

"I don't like to see you with that pale yellow flower," he said; "it reminds me of asphodel, and seems symbolical of death. I should like to do away with that ugly black bonnet, and crown you with a garland of bright red roses, the emblems of renewed youth and hope."

She looked at him with sad earnest eyes.

"I have done with youth," she said, "and with hope, except—"

"Except what?" he asked eagerly.

"Except a hope that I do not care to talk about—the hope of something beyond this earth."

After this the Colonel was silent. There was something in those grave words that sounded like a reproof.

Mrs. Johns stood in the porch watching the carriage drive away, with a thoughtful countenance. "What was in her voice just now that gave me the shivers?" she said to herself, perplexed in spirit.

V

"So may one read his weird, and reason,
And with vain drugs assuage no pain;
For each man in his loving season
Fools and is fooled of these in vain.

Charms that allay not any longing,
Spells that appease not any grief,
Time brings us all by handfuls, wronging
All hurts with nothing of relief."

Colonel Benyon was in love. That rigid disciplinarian, that battered soldier, who had boasted for the last fifteen years of his freedom from anything approaching what he called "an entanglement," now awoke to the consciousness that he was the veriest fool in the universe, and that unless he could win this woman, of whose antecedents he knew nothing, for his wife, he was a lost man. That he could return to the outer world, that he could go back to India and begin life again without her, seemed to him impossible. His world had narrowed itself into the sick-chamber where she ministered to him. All the voices of this earth seemed to have melted into that one low tender voice that read to him or talked with him in the long tranquil evenings. Until now he had scarcely known the meaning of a woman's companionship. Never had he lived in such close intimacy with any one, not even a masculine friend. But now he looked back at his hard commonplace life, the conventional society, the stereotyped pleasures, and wondered how he had endured so many years of such a barren existence. He loved her. For a long time—his idle weeks in that sick-room had seemed so long, giving him so much leisure for thought—he had struggled against this folly, if folly it were; but he had struggled in vain. He loved her. Her, and none other, would he have for his wife; and he told himself that it was, after all, no great sacrifice which he contemplated making. That she was a lady he had never doubted from the first hour when, restored to his sober senses, he had looked at her face and heard her voice. It was just possible that she was born of a less noble race than his own, though he could scarcely bring himself to believe even this; it was more than probable that she was very poor. The Colonel was glad of this last fact. It pleased him to think that his wealth might give her a new and brighter life, surrounding her with all those luxuries and elegancies which seemed the natural attributes of her beauty.

Was there any hope for him? Well, yes, he was inclined to believe his case far from desperate. There was a subtle something in her looks and tones at times that made him fancy he was not quite indifferent to her, that he was more than the mere object of her charity. Nothing could be more vague than these signs and tokens, for she was the most reserved of women—the proudest he sometimes thought—and he felt convinced that she was herself unconscious of them. But, slight as they were, they were sufficient to kindle hope in Herbert Benyon's breast, and he fancied that he had only to wait the fulness of time for the hour of his confession and the certainty of his happiness.

He was not eager to speak. There was time enough. This tranquil daily intercourse was so sweet to him, that he almost feared to end it by assuming a new relation to his gentle nurse. He did not want to scare her away just yet, even if she left him only to come back to him later as his wife. He wanted to have her all to himself a little longer in this easy undisturbed companionship.

So the days and weeks went on. The Colonel grew so much

stronger, that Dr. Matson bade him good-bye, and even Mr. Borlase began to talk of releasing him. He was able to take a short stroll in the sunniest hour of the autumn day, leaning on his cane, and occasionally getting a little help from his nurse's supporting arm. He was very fond of Penjudah; the scattered houses on the sea-shore—the curious old-fashioned High-street straggling up a hill—the sheltered nook upon the grassy hillside, that served as a burial-ground for the population of Penjudah—the rustic lanes, from which one looked right out upon the broad Atlantic—all these things grew very dear to the Colonel, and it seems to him that he could be content to live in this remote western haven for ever with this one woman for his companion.

It was very nearly the end of November, but the weather was wonderfully mild in this region, the days bright and balmy, the evenings clear and calm. The Colonel stopped to rest sometimes in the burial-ground, seated on a moss-grown granite tomb, with his face towards the sea, and Mrs. Chapman by his side.

He had told her all the story of his past life, even that ignominious episode of Lady Julia Dursay's ill-treatment. It was his delight to talk to her. He confided in her as he had never done in any one else. He had such unbounded faith in her integrity, such a fixed belief in her good sense. He had talked to her of his friend Hammersley, and had told her the story of the guilty mistress of Trewardell.

"Strange that we should both have come to grief about a woman, isn't it?" he asked; and Mrs. Chapman owned that it was very strange.

"You'd heard the story before, I daresay," remarked the Colonel. "I suppose all the gossips of Penjudah know it by heart?"

"Yes," she answered, "everybody in Cornwall knows it."

It was the last day of November. Mr. Borlase had again talked about taking leave of his patient, and the Colonel was sitting on his favourite tomb, the memorial of some race whose grandeur was a memory of the past. He began to think the time was drawing near when he must make his confession and hear his fate. He was no coxcomb, yet he had no fear of the result; indeed, he was certain that she loved him. While he was meditating this in a dreamy way, in no hurry to speak, and quite satisfied with the happiness of having the woman he loved by his side, Mrs. Chapman suddenly broke the silence.

"You are so much better, Colonel Benyon," she began—"almost well, indeed, Mr. Borlase says—that I think you can afford to spare me now. I have stayed with you already much longer than I felt to be really necessary, only"—she hesitated just for a moment, and then went rapidly on—"only yours was a critical case, and I did not wish to leave you while there was the faintest chance of relapse. There is no fear of that now, and I am wanted elsewhere. There is a little boy in one of the cottages up the hill dying of consumption. His mother came to the hotel to speak to me last night, and I have promised her to go to him this evening."

"This evening!" cried the Colonel aghast. "You mean to leave me this evening!"

"To go to a dying child, yes, Colonel Benyon," the nurse answered reproachfully. "There is so little that I can do for you now—for I suppose you may be trusted to take your medicines regularly—you really do not want me any longer."

"I do not want you any longer!" repeated the Colonel, "I want you all my life. I want you for my wife!" he went on, laying his hand upon her shoulder. "I cannot live without you. You must stay with me, dearest, or only leave me to come back to me as my wife. We have no need of a long courtship. I think we know each other thoroughly as it is."

"You think you know me thoroughly as it is!" the woman echoed, shrinking away from him, and standing with her face turned towards the sea, only the profile visible to the Colonel, and upon that the impress of a misery that struck him to the soul.

"My dear love, what is this?" he asked. "Have I distressed you so much by my avowal? Am I so utterly repugnant to you?"

"Your wife," she murmured, as if she had scarcely heard his last words, "your wife!"

"Yes, dearest, my beloved and honoured wife. I did not believe it was in my nature to love any one as I love you."

"That any man upon this earth should care for me!" she murmured; "you, above all other men!" And then turning to him with a calmer face, she said decisively, "That can never be, Colonel Benyon. You and I can never be more to one another than we have been. The wisest thing you can do is to wish me good-bye, here where we stand, and forget that you have ever known me."

"That is just the last thing possible to me," he answered impetuously. "There is nothing upon this earth I care to live for, if I cannot have you for my wife. You must have known that I loved you. You had no right to stay with me so long; you had no right to let me love you, if you meant to treat me like this at the last. But you do not mean to be so cruel; you are only trying me; you are only playing with your victim. O my darling, for pity's sake, tell me that I am not quite indifferent to you!"

"That is not the question," the woman replied quietly. "Have you thought of what you are doing, Colonel Benyon? Have you counted the cost? Have you thought what it is to intrust your name and your honour to the keeping of a woman of whom you know nothing?"

"I know that you are an angel," he said, putting his arm round the slender figure, trying to draw her to his breast.

Again she shrank from him—this time with a gesture so repellent, that he drew back involuntarily, chilled to the heart. "Do not touch me," she said. "You do not know who and what I am."

"I ask to know nothing," he cried vehemently. "If there is any secret in your past life that might divide us, hide it from me. Do you think I am going to bring the scrutiny of a detective to bear upon the antecedents of the woman I love? Blindly I give my happiness and my honour into your keeping. I see you, and love you for what you are—not for what evil fortune may have made you in the past."

"You do not know the weight of your words," she answered sadly. "I thank you with all my heart for your confidence, for your love; but that which you think you wish can never be. It is best for us to part this very day, this very moment. Let us shake hands, Colonel Benyon, and say farewell."

"Not till you have told me your reasons," the Colonel cried imperiously. "I may know those, at least."

"I do not recognise your right to question me. I cannot explain my reasons."

"But I will know them," he cried, seizing her wrist. "I have been fooled by one woman; I will not be trifled with by another. I will know why you refuse to be my wife. Is it because you hate or despise me?"

"No, no, no; you *know* that it is not that!"

She looked at him piteously, with a look that said as plainly as any words she could have spoken, "You know that I love you."

"Is it from any mistaken notion of fidelity to the dead?"

"No, it is not that. Yet, heaven knows, I have reason to be faithful to the dead."

"What is it, then? You must and shall tell me."

"For pity's sake, spare me. You are torturing me, Colonel Benyon."

"Give me your promise to be my wife, then, and I will not ask a question. There can be no strong reason enough to divide us, if you love me; and I think you do."

"Heaven help me!" she sobbed, clasping her hands with a piteous gesture.

To Herbert Benyon those three words sounded like a confession. He was sure that she loved him, sure that his will must conquer hers in the end.

"Yes," she cried passionately, "I do love you. Nothing could excuse such an admission from my lips but the knowledge that in this hour we part for ever. I do love you, Colonel Benyon; but there is nothing in this world that would induce me to become your wife, even if you knew the worst I can tell and were yet willing to take me, which you would not be."

"You are wrong," he exclaimed with an oath. "There is nothing you can tell me that can change my resolution, or diminish my love."

"Do not promise so rashly," she answered, ashy pale, and with tremulous lips.

He drew her to the old granite tomb, and persuaded her to sit down beside him, seeing that she was nearly fainting.

"My love, I do not wish to be cruel," he said, tenderly. "I do not seek to lift the veil of the past. I am content to love you blindly, foolishly, if you like. I will do anything to prove my devotion, will shape the whole course of my future life for your happiness. There is nothing in the world I would not sacrifice for your sake. Be generous, for your part, dearest Say that you will be my wife, or give me some adequate reason for your denial."

She did not answer him immediately. There was a silence of some moments, and then she said in a low voice:

"You have a friend to whom you are very much attached, Colonel Benyon, a friend who is almost as dear to you as a brother. I have heard you say that."

"What, Hammersley? Yes, certainly; Hammersley is a dear good fellow; but what has he to do with my marrying as I please? I should not consult him about *that*."

"You were talking the other night of that guilty creature—his wife."

"Yes, I have spoken to you about his wife."

"You have—in terms of reprobation which were well deserved. Have pity upon me, Colonel Benyon—I am that wretched woman!"

She had slipped from the tombstone to the turf beside it, and remained there, half crouching, half kneeling, in her utter abasement, with her face hidden.

"You!" exclaimed the Colonel, in a thick voice. "You!"

The blow seemed almost to crush him. He felt for the moment stupefied, stunned. He had been prepared for anything but this.

"I am that wretched woman. I do not know if there is the shadow of excuse for my sin in the story of my life; but, at any rate, it is best that you should know it. George Champney and I were engaged to be married long before I saw Mr. Hammersley; and when he went to India, we were pledged to wait till he should come back and make me his wife. We had known each other from childhood; and I cannot tell you how dearly I loved him. It means a mockery now to speak of this when I have not even been faithful to his memory; but I did love him. I have mourned him as truly as ever any man was lamented upon this earth. From the first my father was opposed to our engagement, and my stepmother, a very worldly woman, set her face against it most resolutely. But we braved their displeasure, and held our own in spite of them.

It was only when George was gone that their persecution became almost unendurable to me. I need not enter into details. Captain Champney had been away more than two years when I first met Mr. Hammersley. We were forbidden to write to each other; and I had suffered unspeakable anxiety about him in that time. It was only in some indirect manner that I ever had news of him. When Mr. Hammersley first proposed to me, I refused him decisively; but then followed a weary time in which I was tormented by my stepmother, and even by my father, who was influenced by her in this business. I do not think any man can understand the kind of domestic persecution which women are subject to—the daily reproach, the incessant worry. But I went through this ordeal. It was only when my father brought home a newspaper containing the announcement of George Champney's death that my courage gave way. They let me alone for some time after this, let me indulge my grief unmolested; and then, one day, the old arguments, the familiar reproaches, began again; and in an hour of fatal weakness, worn out in body and mind—for I had been very ill for a long time after that bitter blow—I yielded."

She paused for a little; but the Colonel did not speak. He sat upon the granite tomb, looking seaward with haggard eyes, motionless as a statue, the living image of despair. He could have borne anything but this.

"You know the rest. No, you can never know how I suffered. The false announcement in the paper nad been an error, common enough in those days, Captain Champney told me, when he came upon me one summer morning near Trewardell like a ghost. He had heard of the report in India, and had written to a common friend of ours, entreating her to let me know the truth; whether she had attempted to do so, and had been in some manner prevented by my father or my stepmother, I cannot tell. Another Champney had been killed. The mistake was only the insertion of the wrong initials; but it was a fatal error for us two. He came to me to remind me of my promise; came determined to take me away from my husband. I cannot speak of the events that came afterwards. There was no such thing as happiness possible for either of us. We were not wicked enough to be happy in spite of our sin. You know how they found George Champney lying dead on the sands at Blankenburg one bright September morning. After that I had a dangerous illness, during which I was taken to a Belgian convent, by my husband's influence, I believe, where I was tenderly nursed till I recovered. They knew my story, those spotless nuns, and yet were kind to me. I stayed with them as a boarder for a year after—after Mr. Hammersley obtained his divorce; and it was there I learned to nurse the sick. I was not destitute; a sister of my mother's, knowing my position, settled a small annuity upon me; and on that I have lived ever since. Six months ago I was seized with a yearning to see the place where the most tranquil days of my life had been spent. I knew that Mr. Hammersley was living abroad; and I fancied that I ran no risk of recognition in returning to this neighbourhood. I knew how much misery and illness had changed me since I left Trewardell. It was a foolish fancy, no doubt; but I, who had nothing human left to love, may be forgiven for a weak attachment to familiar places. I came to Penjudah, thinking that I should find plenty of work here of the kind I wanted. I had no intention of coming any nearer to Trewardell, where I must, of course, run considerable risk of being recognised; but when Dr. Matson urged me to come to you the temptation was too strong for me, and I came to see the dear old place once more. That is the end of my story; and now, Colonel Benyon, I have but one word more to say— Farewell!"

She rose from the ground, and was going to leave him; but he detained her.

"You have almost broken my heart," he said; "but there is nothing in this world can change my love for you. I still ask you to be my wife. I promise to cherish you with a love that shall blot out the memory of your past."

She shook her head sadly.

"It can never be," she answered; "I am not vile enough to trade upon your weakness or your generosity. Let me be faithful to the dead, and loyal to you. Once more, good-bye."

"Will nothing I can say prevail with you?"

"Nothing. I shall always honour and revere you as the most generous of men; but you and I must never meet after today."

He pleaded with her a little longer, trying by every possible argument to vanquish her resolution; but his endeavours were all in vain. He knew that she loved him; he felt that he was doomed to lose her.

And so at last she left him, sitting in the quiet burial-ground, in the pale winter sunshine, with all the glory of the Atlantic before him, and the stillness of a desert round about. Even after she had left him he determined upon making one more attempt to win her. He found out the place where she lived, and went to that humble alley in the early dusk, bent upon seeing her once more, upon pleading his cause more calmly, more logically, than it had been possible for him to do in the first heat of has passion. He found the house, and a very civil good-natured woman, who told him that Mrs. Chapman had left Penjudah two hours before, for good. She had gone abroad, the woman said.

"To Belgium, I suppose."

"Yes, sir, that was the name of the place."

As soon as he was strong enough Colonel Benyon went to Belgium, where he spent a couple of months searching for Flora Hammersley in all the convents. It was a long wearisome search; but he went through with it patiently to the end, persevering until he found a quiet little conventual retreat six miles from Louvain, where boarders were admitted. It was the place where she had been. His search was ended; and the woman he loved had been buried in the tiny convent cemetery just a week before he came there. After this there was nothing left for the Colonel but to go back to India to the old familiar life. It was only his closest friends who ever perceived the change in him; but, although he never spoke of his trouble, those who did thoroughly know him, knew that he had suffered some recent heart-wound, and that the stroke had been a heavy one.

M. H.

The Phantom Hare

This is a particularly frightening example of the ways in which
Cornish folklore influenced Cornish Gothic fiction across the
nineteenth century. This story comes from the legend of the White
Hare of Looe, which has variants across other Celtic regions. In this
legend, a woman betrayed by the man she loves wholly returns to
haunt him in the form of a white hare. She will follow him unre-
lentingly, even warning him of danger to ensure he lives a long
(and guilty) life. In Looe in particular the white hare also warns of
a storm at sea and is specifically feared by fishermen and sailors.
Versions of this story were collected by antiquarians of Cornwall
throughout the long nineteenth century, including a rather milder,
less gory version by Enys Tregarthen in *The Piskey-Purse: Legends
and Tales of North Cornwall* (1905). The version included here, by
the mysterious "M. H.", relies more on body horror to convey its
message, and incorporates the mythology of the preserved "bog
body". Bog bodies are cadavers mummified by peat bogs and have
been found all over the world. They received renewed attention
in the nineteenth century with the rise in popular archaeology
and anthropology, where antiquarians began connecting them to
ancient cultures, whereas previously they were considered to be
more recent murder victims. This sense of preservation and disin-
terment has metaphorical weight in this Gothic tale, representing
the inevitable return of secrets, and the continued presence of

the betrayed—as spectral hare or preserved corpse. The bog also says something, perhaps, about Cornwall being both of the land and the sea.

essy, did you ever see a white hare?"

"A white hare! No, never. Why do you ask it?"

Susan Stanhope did not say why she asked it. She seemed to have come home in a kind of excitement. I saw her fly up the broad garden path between the beds, crowded with sweet and homely flowers, as though she were in a hurry to escape from some danger. Her light footfall ran up the stairs to our bedroom, where I sat sewing, and she burst in upon me with the above question.

"Do not you Cornish people attach some superstition to the appearance of a white hare, Bessy?" she continued. "I think I once heard mamma say so."

"Well, I fancy we do, now you speak of it. But I don't know what the superstition is."

Susan folded the mantle she had taken off, put her bonnet up, and sat down in a chair on the opposite side of the open window. I had drawn my little work-table as close to the window as possible, being anxious to finish mending Janey's frock, which she had torn at the brook stile; and the twilight was already upon us. In September— we were in the earlier days of it—the evenings draw in quickly.

We lived at the Mount Farm, a large estate belonging to the Bertrams, situated near Penryn, in Cornwall. My father, Roger Trenathy, had been born in the parish; his people had rented it for several generations. He was what is called a substantial man, and was superior in cultivation to some farmers; but he lived in a homely style, and we, his children, had to work, as (*he* said) all farmer's daughters ought. Roger was his only son, already as busy on the land as he was. I was the eldest of all; Eunice was next to Roger, and seventeen this summer; little Jane was ten only, and went, day-boarder, to Mrs. Pollock's school. A great deal lay upon me, both of work and care. Our two maids were light-headed things, and Eunice was lighter-headed than they were.

Our mother was dead. She had been a clergyman's daughter, and was a true gentlewoman. It was to her training and companionship that I owed all the culture I possessed. Roger was like her: he had her pleasant eyes and her sweet smile. Her only sister had married a clergyman—the Reverend Philip Stanhope. He and his wife had both died, leaving one child, Susan—this same Susan now visiting us. Susan had had a first-rate education, but she had not much fortune: just one thousand pounds in the Three per Cents. When she left school, some eighteen months ago, my father had said she must make her home with us: but she preferred to be independent, and went out as a governess. Moreover, she wrote us word, in a cordial but half-jesting manner, that she should not care to live always in a farm-house. This was the first holiday she had had—seven weeks long it was to be—and she had come to spend it with us, arriving two days ago.

"You found your way readily to Dame Mellon's, Susan?" I asked her, as I stitched away. For she and I were both to have gone to the widow Mellon's cottage after tea, to take the old woman some wool for knitting. For years she had knitted my father's winter stockings—as she did those of many other people around. It was the only work she could do, being blind, and we all liked to employ her. And, by the way, though I have called her *old*, she was not yet fifty. Care and illness had served to wrinkle her brow and to bend her back: and we young people are apt to think everybody else old if they have left forty years behind them. But Janey came home with this dreadful rent in her new frock—and the rent went more ways than one. I was angry with her, and had to mend it; and Susan said she would take the wool. So I let her take it, adding a little basket of things from our plentiful larder, and directing her which way to go.

"Oh yes! I found it quite well," answered Susan. "It is a picturesque little cottage, resting in that shady dell."

"What made you ask me about a white hare, Susan?"

"Because I have just seen one. I have had an adventure, Bessy."

"Indeed! What was it?"

"You were talking yesterday about Miss Bertram," she said, after a pause, never answering my question—"that she was to marry Mr. Arlegh. It was just, you know, as she passed the gate yonder in her pony carriage, drawing an old lady."

"Her aunt. Well?"

"*Is* she to marry Mr. Arlegh?"

"Why, of course she is. They are to be married in November. He is her cousin. Not a first cousin; a second or third. When her father, Sir William, died, thirteen months ago now, the title lapsed, but the Hall and all the large estates were left to Miss Bertram. Upon that, Hubert Arlegh (as is said) hastened to make her an offer, and after a time, but not at first, she accepted him."

Susan lifted her blue eyes quickly. "His name is Hubert, is it? What sort of a looking man is he?"

"A very handsome one."

"Tall and dark?"

"Tall, and rather dark. He is very good-looking indeed."

"Then I don't think him so, Bessy," she returned, in a contradictory, positive tone. "He may be what many people call handsome, as to features and colouring, but he has a most disagreeable expression; and—"

"Why Susan!" I interrupted, "What has taken you? Has Mr. Arlegh offended you?"

"Offended *me*! Oh dear, no."

"You spoke like it. Where have you seen him?"

"I will tell you, Bessy. I said I had had an adventure. In coming from Dame Mellon's cottage, through that dark, shady lane that leads from it—I don't know its name—"

"The park lane," I interrupted. "It belongs to Miss Bertram's park, but we have the liberty of passing through it."

"Well, I was coming quickly along, for it seemed to be getting quite dusk there under the trees, swinging the little straw basket in my hand, and doing it so carelessly that it swung off and went ever so many yards beyond me, just as a lady and gentleman turned the corner. I knew her for Miss Bertram—and a nice face I must say she has, and a charming manner. He stooped to pick up the basket, and she said a few pleasant words to me—something to the effect that she could see I had been to Mrs. Mellon's cottage, no doubt to take her some good cheer. I did not quite catch them; they were over in a moment, and Mr. Arlegh—for I am sure by your description it was he—"

"Yes, yes; no one would be walking with Miss Rose but he: and, for the matter of that, he is the only visitor staying at the Hall. Go on, Susan."

"At the very moment that he was holding out the basket to me, a beautiful white hare suddenly sprang out of the edge, bounded directly over his feet, and was lost in the opposite bushes. At least, I don't know where else it could have sprung from," broke off Susan, thoughtfully. "It seemed to startle him so much that he dropped the basket, and leaped back with a smothered cry. Miss Bertram did not appear to have seen it; she turned her head, and asked what was the matter. 'Oh, nothing,' he answered lightly, save that he had been careless enough to drop the young lady's basket: but I saw that his face had turned of a ghastly whiteness. As I stooped for the basket, for I was quicker than he, the same white hare reappeared from the bushes, crossed the lane as before, passing over his feet, and was lost to sight in the hedge. Bessy, he shuddered from head to foot like a man in dreadful fear: it is as true as that I am telling it to you."

"Fear of what?"

"How should I know? Miss Bertram looked about her as though some unseen danger were near, turning her head from side to side. Such was the idea that struck me; but still I do not think she saw the hare. They walked on, wishing me good evening, and I came running all the way home."

"It must have been a white rabbit, Susan."

"I assure you it was a hare: I could not mistake it. The question is—Why should it have frightened Mr. Arlegh?"

"Another question is," I said, passing over that, for in truth I saw no solution to it, and thought Susan must be fanciful—"Why this should have made you take a prejudice against Mr. Arlegh?"

"It did not make me. It had nothing to do with it. One reason why I do not like him is, that he—"

"That he what, Susan?"

"Well I hardly know how to express it. But he looked at me in so free and ugly a manner. As if really, Bessy, it was just as if I were a 'lass o'lightness.'"

I was silent. One or two disagreeable stories had gone about to Mr. Arlegh's discredit, and people wondered whether they had been quite kept from Miss Bertram. Possibly so; for they were not connected with our immediate neighbourhood, but with his own.

He lived near St. Huth, a village seven miles off, upon the small property that had been his father's. Rose Bertram's riches, apart from her own sweet self, must have presented a temptation to him. He passed his time chiefly in London before being engaged to Miss Bertram, and made debts there.

"You give that as one reason for taking a dislike to him, Susan, though possibly you were mistaken. What is the other?"

"The other is a private reason of my own, Bessy. I cannot tell it."

She sat on at the window in deep thought, her blue eyes strangely serious as they gazed outwardly on the gathering gloom, her right hand pushing back unconsciously her fine golden hair. At length, just as it got too dark to see, I made a finish of my work, and we went down to the parlour. Eunice was helping Patience to lay the cloth for supper; father and Roger were coming in for it. Janey had been in bed long ago.

The last thing we did at night was to sing the evening hymn, I or Eunice playing it. Susan offered to play tonight. She was a skilful musician, as compared with us, and her soft touch was of itself melody.

It was Susan's custom to read the psalms for the evening to herself after we got into my bedroom, which she shared with me. On this evening she sat down as usual, but almost immediately closed the prayer-book.

"No, I *cannot* read tonight; it is of no use," she cried, almost passionately. "My wandering thoughts will not let me."

I turned round from the glass, unpinning my collar, and looked at her. Her cheeks were flushed, her eyes wore a troubled light.

"Bessy, will you let me tell you a tale?"

"Certainly I will, dear?"

"Then let us put out the light and sit at the window."

She clapped the extinguisher on the candle herself, and we sat down at the window—closed now. It was a fine night; the moonlight flooding hill and dale, the bare cornfields, the pasture lands, and the houses, large and small, scattered among them.

"You know, Bessy, that when mamma died, I was placed at school at Walborough for two years, to complete my education. It was a notedly good school, not a large one, Miss Robertson, the governess, being very indulgent to us. I took a fancy at once to one of the girls, Agnes Garth. She was about my own age, which was sixteen then, and one of the sweetest, best, loveliest girls I ever saw—"

"Lovelier than you?" I interrupted.

"How silly you are!" she exclaimed, laughing and blushing. "Of course I know that I am—not ugly; but I could not be compared with her. Not but that the girls thought us a little alike, in as much as that we were both fair, with bright complexions and the same coloured hair. They had given her a name, Beauty, and generally called her by it—Beauty Garth. I cannot tell you how I loved that girl: my father and mother were gone, and it seemed that all the love within me was concentrated upon her. She was so gentle, so kind, so good; a very angel."

I laughed.

"Ah well, it was so, Bessy. Miss Robertson used to say Agnes had no stability, that she might be swayed any way by those she loved; but it was an amiable weakness. We were like sisters all the two years we passed together. She never could think ill of anyone: she put trust in all the world. A sort of cloud hung over her—"

"A cloud?"

"Well, we never could find out who she was. The rest of us talked freely of our home and friends, of our past life; but she was silent as to hers, even to me. An impression obtained in the school—I know not whence derived—that her mother was an actress at a theatre in London. Her father she had never known—that much Agnes did tell us. Miss Robertson never spoke upon the subject: Agnes was treated just as the rest of us were, and we knew nothing."

"Did she go home for the holidays?"

"No; she passed them at school—as I usually did: and perhaps that served to draw us closer together. My two years were nearly up, when one day, when we were with the German master, Miss Robertson sent in for Agnes; and when the class was over and we got back to the ordinary school-room, we heard that Agnes had gone to London, in answer to some message received by the governess. She came back in a month's time in deep mourning, and told us her mother was dead. But, though her frank spirit was subdued and sad-dened by the loss, there was evidently some deeper joy within her that had not existed before. I found out what it was—Beauty was in love. She had met a gentleman in London, and was already secretly engaged to him. She would not tell me his name or who he was, though I asked it over and over again. 'There will be no necessity for me to be a governess now,' she said to me one day—for that's what she was to have been, as her mother left her little, if any, fortune."

"How old was she, Susan?"

"Eighteen then, just as I was. This was last year, in the earlier part of it. I left the school at Easter, you may remember."

"Yes."

"The week previous to it I was invited to spend the evening with some people in the town who were kind to me, they having formerly lived near papa's rectory. Beauty was also invited out elsewhere the same evening. It chanced in returning home that we both reached the door together; an old maid-servant was my escort, Beauty's was a tall, handsome young man. She held his arm, and I divined, as by instinct, that her lover had come to Walborough. I had a good look at him; the gas-lamp shone right upon his face. He wished her good-night abruptly, and was turning away when Agnes stopped him. 'This is Miss Stanhope, of whom you have so often heard me speak,' she said: and of course politeness compelled him to stop and say a few words to me. Not many: before the door was opened to us, he had lifted his hat, and was gone. 'Don't tell of me, Susan,' Beauty entreatingly whispered; 'Miss Robertson might not like it?'"

"And did you tell?"

"Why, of course not, Bessy. Would we tell tales of one another? Besides, there was no harm, that I saw, in his just walking home with her. I supposed the friends she had been with sanctioned it."

"Go on."

"The next week I left school, and entered on the situation Miss Robertson had procured for me at Lady Leslie's. It was a long, long way from Walborough; about midway, you know, between that place and this, Penryn; Beauty and I could not expect to meet often, but we promised each other, amid our farewell tears and kisses, to correspond constantly. Bessy, I never got but two letters from her."

I felt surprised at Susan's tone more than at the words.

"But two letters. One of them was written from school; the other, only a week later, from London. She had left Walborough, she told me, and was staying with some friends in London until her marriage, which was to take place immediately, and she only wished I could go up to be her bridesmaid—which of course was not to be thought of. After that, I never heard from her."

"And have you never heard yet?"

"Listen. A few months later, at the close of August, I think, or beginning of September—I know it was a warm, hazy day—I was in the school-room, correcting exercises, my pupils being out walking with their French maid, when one of the servants came to say that a young lady was asking for me, and showed her in. It was Agnes: and, as the door closed, she fell into my arms with a sort of moan. How terribly the girl had changed in the five or six months since we parted I cannot express to you, Bessy; her once lovely face had become thin and drawn, her once pretty, rounded shoulders sharp. I could not speak for dismay; I saw something was wrong. She clung to me sobbing and shivering. 'I was obliged to come to you on my journey, Susan, as this place lay in my way,' she gasped out; 'some power that I could not resist compelled me. It is only for a few minutes, Susan; only just to see you, Susan; and then I shall be gone again.' 'Are you married, dear Agnes?' I whispered, kissing her tenderly. 'I *thought* I was, Susan,' she said; 'I thought it all that while, though he would not let me tell you, or anyone:' and, with that, she sat down, poor weary girl, and laid her face, moaning, against the long desk. 'You speak of a journey, dear,' I said, 'where are you going?' But she did not answer. There was a faint bluish tinge about her lips that I did not like; evidently she needed both food and rest. The thought came over me to beg of Lady Leslie to allow her to stay a day or two with me. I felt sure she would, being a kind, motherly woman. 'Stay here a few moments, dear,' I whispered, kissing her wan cheek. 'I am going to bring you a glass of wine and a biscuit.' Lady Leslie, I found, was with friends in the drawing-room; I hardly knew what to do, not liking to call her out, or to speak before them. While I was hesitating they came out to depart, and then I spoke to Lady Leslie, telling a little of Beauty's history, and hinting at my fears that something was wrong. 'By all means, let Miss Garth stay for a few days,' Lady Leslie warmly said; 'if she is in distress or any kind of trouble, all the more need that her friends should see after her:' the children might have holiday, and I could devote myself entirely to her. I was so pleased and grateful, Bessy, that I burst into tears. Then I ran to get a glass of wine from the butler, and returned to the school-room. It was empty. Beauty was gone."

"Gone?"

"Quite gone. She must have left the school-room almost as soon as I: one of the servants met her in the hall and opened the door for her. Lady Leslie had enquiries made, and we found that Agnes had hastened back to the railway-station and taken the train onwards."

"To London?"

"No, she had come from London. It was to Cornwall. There was some trouble about her ticket—a through ticket—because she had left the train. The railway clerk said it was made out for St. Huth. Bessy, I have never seen or heard of her from that day to this."

"St. Huth is a small place about seven miles off beyond this."

"I know. I traced it out upon the map and in 'Bradshaw.' But now—why do you suppose I have told you this story?"

Leaning forward to me as she put the question, I could not fail to see that Susan was agitated; her soft colour went and came; her beautiful blue eyes were strangely bright.

"That man, Hubert Arlegh, who is to marry Miss Bertram, over whose feet the white hare passed and repassed tonight, startling him to terror, was the lover of Agnes Garth."

I uttered an exclamation of dismay.

"I knew him instantly, Bessy. Though I had seen him but once before, and then by gas-light, I recognised both himself and his voice, as he stood before me in the park lane tonight. It is a very peculiar voice: deep and gruff, as if it lay in his throat. You say Mr. Arlegh's name is Hubert. *His* name was Hubert. Agnes never called him anything else. And what I want to know is this: if he is going to marry Miss Bertram, where is Agnes?"

I could not answer. Thought upon thought crowded my mind, each more unwelcome than the last. All in a moment, *another* thought—or, rather, a recollection—came up; and it was the worst of all.

"When do you say this was, Susan?—that she came into Cornwall?"

"Just about a year ago."

Why yes, that was the very time. It was about a year ago now, so far as I could remember, that a young lady, weary, anxious, footsore, found her way to the Widow Mellon's cottage. She lay ill there for two days, and then disappeared. They could not tell what became of her; nobody else could tell. Minnie Mellon told a curious tale—but, as people said, she was only a child. Nothing of this did I disclose to Susan, though the description of this young lady, given to me by Mrs. Mellon's sister, who was then at the cottage, was exactly like the one Susan gave of Agnes Garth. It would not do for us Trenathys to bring up ought against Mr. Arlegh. Once his marriage with Miss Bertram had taken place he would be our landlord to all intents and purposes—and my father would want his lease renewed the year after next.

We got to bed at last: but I could not speak for thinking of it all.—of the story told by Susan, of Miss Bertram's ill-luck to be engaged to such a man, of the uncertain fate of poor Agnes Garth, and last, though not least, of the white hare that had run over Mr. Arlegh's feet. I must have a spice of romance in my composition, I take it, for that white hare kept pushing itself into my thoughts above all the rest of the perplexity.

There had been some trouble lately with our poultry, especially the geese; many had sickened, and died; and in the morning, as soon as my various duties were over, I put on my sun-bonnet to run down to Michael Hart's, who was gamekeeper to Miss Bertram, to consult his wife, for she was learned in poultry. Mary Hart was not at home. However, Michael, smoking his after-dinner pipe at the cottage door, said she had stepped over towards the swamp-land, with a bit of stewed rabbit for old Widow Loam, who was ill—thought to be dying. I hardly knew whether to wait for Mary Hart or not; it was nearly one o'clock, our dinner-hour. Michael thought she would not be long; so down I sat upon the bench outside the kitchen-window and talked to him.

"Are there any white hares about, Michael?"

"White hares!" he exclaimed in his slow way, turning his head to look at me. "Why no, Miss Bessy, we've no game o' that sort."

"My cousin, Miss Stanhope, thought she saw a white hare cross the park lane yesterday evening."

"Must ha' been a rabbit," said Michael—just as I had said to Susan. "Folks don't like the white hares in this country," he added, changing his pipe from one hand to the other. "They bode no good when seen."

"But how can they be seen if there are none, Michael?"

"Well, it's thought they white hares are not real hares, but spirits, Miss Bessy; apparitions. I never saw a white hare but once, and don't want to see one again."

"You have seen one, then?"

"I saw that one, Miss Bessy. It's a matter o' ten years ago. Do you remember as fur back as that?"

"Of course I do, Michael. I am twenty-two."

"In that red house over yonder—you can see its chimbleys above the trees—lived old Trehern and his wife and son. Young Trehern was a bit wild, and gave 'em some trouble—but you'd know naught about that. One autumn day, when I was out with Sir William and a party and the guns and dogs, young Trehern, who made one o' the gentlemen, lagged behind the rest, telling me of a dog of his that had been sick; when, just as we were crossing the five-cornered coppice, a white hare—as it looked—ran out o' the brushwood right over his feet. Right over his feet, Miss Bessy; I never saw such a thing afore. Young Trehern didn't much like it; I could see that; and he jumped aside ever so far. He thought of the superstition, I suppose, but he made light of it to me. 'What thing was that, Hart?' says he, swearing a bit and shaking his feet, as if he'd shake off the touch the thing had left on his boot. 'It looked uncommon like a hare, sir,' says I, 'but 'twas gone so quick there's no telling.' We went on then, and no more passed. Nine days after that young Trehern died. He was throwed out of his gig coming home from a dinner, and was killed on the spot."

"And now, Michael, what is the superstition?"

Michael smoked for a full minute in his slow way before attempting to answer.

"It's not much the sort o' thing to tell to young ladies, Miss Bessy."

"But I want to know it. I have a very particular reason for wishing to know it. I am a woman grown, remember, Michael; not a child."

"Well, as to young Trehern, he had talked and laughed too much with Patty, the Widow Loam's daughter—her, by token, that Mary's gone to take the bit o' rabbit to—and then turned round and laughed at her for it. A pretty young thing she was; and 'twas told that the widow cursed him. I did not know how that might have been. Any way, Patty died of it."

"But the superstition, Michael?"

"That *is* the superstition, Miss Bessy. When a young girl gets treated in that way and dies of it, she comes back in the form of a white hare, whenever his own death shall be nigh at hand; comes back in love to give him warning of it."

A slight shiver took me at the words. Could Mr. Arlegh's death be near at hand? What a foolish thought! I mentally said, and threw off the shiver and superstition together. That we Cornish people hold to many ridiculous fancies I know, but surely not to one so ridiculous as this.

"Your wife does not seem to return, Michael," I said, rising from the bench; "so I will not wait longer. Perhaps she can come up to the farm; I should like her to see the geese."

"She'll come safe enough, Miss Bessy."

But, do what I would, I could not get these matters out of my mind. Not the superstition; that did not linger in it much; but the story Susan had told of Agnes Garth, and the curious likeness that seemed to exist between her and the girl who had gone to Mrs. Mellon's, and the coincidence as regarded the time.

That afternoon we had tea unusually early; four o'clock, to accommodate my father, who was going out. I contrived to run down alone to Mrs. Mellon's afterwards: I wanted to question her. Susan was busy over some strips of beautiful old pillow lace that had been her mother's, and which had got yellow with lying by. It had been washed that afternoon and Susan was pulling it out preparatory to spreading it on the grass to bleach. It served as an excuse for my leaving her.

"What was the young lady like who came here about a year ago, Miss Bessy?" repeated Mrs. Mellon, in answer to me. "Well, you know, miss, I couldn't see her myself; but my sister Ann, who was over here just then, couldn't talk enough about her beauty and her wan looks and her dreadful sadness."

"Very fair, was she not?—with blue eyes?"

"Oh very fair, and her eyes the bluest and sweetest and saddest, and her hair a bright golden colour. Minnie here was talking of her only last night, miss: she said that the young lady who came here from your house with the wool had just the same beautiful golden hair."

It seemed to me like a confirmation, and I drew a long breath. "Will you tell me the particulars of her coming, and of her stay here?" I asked.

"It is a matter of a year ago, Miss Bessy. We were having our tea at this round table one afternoon, Ann, and me, and the child, when we heard a sort of stir outside, and Ann went to the door. There stood at it a young girl dressed in black, pale and weary, as if she had travelled far, with a wan, lovely face. Would we allow her to sit down for a few minutes, she asked, and give her a drink of water, for she felt faint. Ann brought her in, and she fainted right off in the chair as she sat down. Well, Miss Bessy, we undressed her and put her into Minnie's bed, for she was a great deal too ill and weak to go away that night. And in that bed she stayed nigh upon three days, not strong enough to get out of it, and crying a'most all the time, and—"

"Did she tell you her name?" I interrupted.

"She never told her name, nor where she belonged to, nor anything else about herself. But she did say she had walked over from St. Huth early that morning. We thought she must have been waiting about here all the day since, as if waiting for somebody, for two or three people saw her; and Michael Hart he said—but he told me afterwards I had better not speak of that," broke off Mrs. Mellon, "so I'll let it alone. On the third day she got up, Miss Bessy, and I remember well as she sat here with me after our bit of dinner—Ann was gone—she asked me many questions about Miss Bertram and the marriage it was said she was going to make with Mr. Arlegh—just as if she had knowed Miss Rosy afore. Leastways it struck me so, and I put the question to her plain. No, she had never seen Miss Bertram in her life, she answered, but she had heard of her. After that, I heard her stirring about, and it seemed that she was putting her bonnet and mantle on to leave. I asked her whether she was sure she was strong enough, and whether she had far to go. 'Not far, only a very little way,' she answered me, and she felt quite strong. With that, she took off a locket that she had worn on her neck, fastened to some blue ribbon, and put it upon Minnie's neck. 'Keep it, my dear,' she said to her; 'it is all I have to give you, and I shall not want it where I am going.' Upon that she wished me good-bye very hastily, and was gone from the door afore I could say a word, leaving (as I found afterwards) a gold sovereign wrapped in a bit o' paper on the table at my elbow. 'Run, Minnie,' I says, 'and see which way she goes, and watch her a bit,' for I thought it likely she might faint again, besides feeling anxious about her. So Minnie ran, and watched her ever so far—down to the swamp-land, wasn't it child?"

"Yes, mother," replied Minnie, an elfish-looking child of ten, who had been listening with both her ears. "I kept behind her all the way, watching her till I couldn't see her no longer. She went down the lane to the swamp-land, and she never came out again."

"Never came out again," I exclaimed, the phrase striking me as an odd one. "How do you mean, Minnie?"

"She never did come out," replied Minnie. "I stood watching for her ever so long."

"The child means that she never saw her come out," put in the mother. "She didn't like to follow her too close, for fear of being seen."

"Did you follow her down the lane, Minnie?"

"After a bit I did. I saw her under they willows that edges the swamp on this side, and I stopped by the trees half way down the land to see where she went to. When I didn't see her come back nor nothing, I went on to they willows too, but she was gone."

"But where could she go to?" I cried, something like a panic seizing my heart. "She could not walk over the swamp to gain the road: she would sink into it."

"I'm sure she never came back down the lane," repeated Minnie. "I never see her come."

"She must have managed to get round the swamp by they dwarf stumps o' trees, Miss Bessy, and so gained the high road that way," put in Mrs. Mellon, her quiet, matter-of-fact tone proving that no worse thought had ever occurred to her.

"You do not think she could have—have got *into* the swamp?" I asked, scarcely above my breath.

The woman turned her sightless face to me in surprise. Minnie stared with wondering eyes. The idea to them seemed very far-fetched.

"Why no, Miss Bessy, there was no fear o' that kind. There wouldn't be. Had the poor young lady lost her footing and fell in, which was not likely, she'd naturally ha' cried out; and there was Minnie at hand to hear her."

The conviction that, had she put herself in purposely she would *not* have cried out, ran through my mind like a flash of lightning: and then I mentally called myself a wicked girl for thinking it. "Would you let me see the locket she gave Minnie?" I asked aloud.

Dame Mellon took a small key from her pocket, felt her way to the dresser, and unlocked a tea-caddy that stood on it. "I keep it locked up for fear Minnie should lose it," she remarked, placing it in my hands; "they small things is so easy dropped, and children be so careless."

Ah! no need to take a second look. The golden locket had a lock of golden hair inside it—Susan's hair beyond all doubt—and it bore the inscription "Susan to Agnes."

"I should like to show this to my cousin: it is very pretty," I said impulsively. "Will you let me take it home, Mrs. Mellon? You shall have it back tomorrow."

Ready permission was given, and I was desired not to be in a hurry to return the locket. The old woman took her stick, and walked with me, talking, to the little bridge. Some children were playing at the entrance to the park lane, and Minnie ran off to them.

"I wish you would tell me one thing," I said in a low tone—"what it was that Michael Hart told you. You may trust me, you know."

"Dear, yes, I may, Miss Bessy. Well, Michael saw the young lady that same afternoon, talking with Mr. Arlegh in the coppice. He was coming home from shooting, and she darted out from the coppice, as if she had put herself there to wait for him, and laid her hand upon his arm. Mr. Arlegh shook her hand off, and swore at her; asking where she had sprung from, and what she wanted: Michael heard that much, as he walked onwards with the dogs. Half an hour later he came by again and they were there still. She was crying and moaning bitterly; and he was calling her a tramp, in harsh tones, and threatening to give her into custody for molesting him, unless she went back at once to 'whence she came.' Michael didn't know how the quarrel ended; except that Mr. Arlegh must have left her there, for he presently saw him cross the park lane on his way to the Hall. It wasn't a thing to talk about, you see, Miss Bessy, and that's why he wanted me to be silent."

All sorts of troubles were worrying my brain as I went home. It was poor Agnes Garth safe enough. But what could I do in it? And where was she?

Very much to my surprise, when I came within sight of our gate, I saw Mr. Arlegh's horse fastened to it, and himself on the grass-plat with Susan. She had her hands folded before her, and her face, as she spoke to him, wore a cold, haughty expression. Suddenly he wheeled round on his heel, came out, mounted his horse and rode past me, not vouchsafing me any notice by word or look. Susan explained to me what had happened.

She was spreading her lace on the grass, putting a stone at the ends of each piece to secure it, when Mr. Arlegh rode by. Seeing Susan, he checked his horse suddenly, dismounted, and came in.

"So you are one of Farmer Trenathy's daughters, my dear," he began, in a free tone that Susan did not like at all. "And where have you been hiding yourself pray, that I never saw you before last night?"

"Mr. Trenathy is my uncle," replied Susan, turning from the lace to face him.

"Have you come to live here?"

"No."

"To stay for a time, at any rate, I conclude. I am very glad. It is not often we get such beauty as yours in this out-of-the-world place."

"Mr. Arlegh," began Susan, "you have taken upon yourself to ask me questions. In return, may I put one or two to you?"

"Fifty if you like, my dear. The more the better."

"When you were quite a lad, were you not placed for three or four years with the Reverend Philip Stanhope, of Grassmere? That lad's name was, I know, Hubert Arlegh."

"Just so. Mr. Stanhope was my tutor."

"You respected and liked him, I believe."

"Liked and respected Stanhope! I just did. What next?"

"I am his daughter—Miss Stanhope—and a gentlewoman, Mr. Arlegh."

He seemed quite taken to, and his face flushed, Susan said. But he had the grace to change his manner to one of respect, offered his hand, and said he was glad to see her.

"There is another question I wish to ask you, and it is a painful one," Susan went on; "one very painful to me to put. Can you tell me where Agnes Garth is?"

He stared at her for a moment, his countenance visibly changing. "Agnes Garth!" he presently rejoined, breaking the silence. "I do not know any one of the name."

"I think you did know her, Mr. Arlegh. She was my best friend, dear to me as a sister: we were at school together at Walborough. For this past twelvemonth I have been anxiously waiting for news from her, watching for it daily: and it never comes."

"I protest I cannot understand why you should say this to me, Miss Stanhope," he replied, his manner cold, his tone repellant. "I never heard of the person you mention. Allow me to wish you good evening." And, with that, he turned quickly, as I had seen him turn, and took his departure.

Susan told me this as we sat side by side on the bench under the large pear-tree, the horse's hoofs dying away in our ears as they grew more distant. I held out the gold locket on my glove.

"Do you know this, Susan?"

She caught hold of it, gave one look, and burst into tears. "Oh Bessy, where did you get this? It was the keepsake I gave to Agnes when I left school. She gave me that pretty cross that I wear, in exchange."

I told her all—even my doubts and fears about the swamp. It is true I had not meant to say so much: but tales, at such moments, expand in the telling. "But, Susan dear," I added, in conclusion, "you must keep all this strictly quiet. It would not do to stir in it for my father's sake."

"*I* keep it quiet!" she retorted, turning her tearful eyes upon me. "Why, Bessy, do you imagine this is a thing we mortals can control? If my poor Agnes does indeed lie in that swamp-land, rely upon it that a Higher Power holds its elucidation in His hands."

The stars were beginning to twinkle in the sky, the moon was rising, the scent of the closing flowers was almost lost on the cool air; and still we sat on. Out came Eunice, wondering why we stayed there when we must know the early supper was ready.

"You will take me to look at this swamp-land tomorrow, Bessy," whispered Susan, as we rose. "I cannot rest until I see it." And I promised.

But, like many another promise, it was not fated to be performed. Some friends, not expected, came over from St. Huth in the morning to spend the day with us, and the next day it was raining, pouring cats and dogs—as Janey said when she had to go through it to school; aye, and the next day also. Altogether, the following week had come in when we went.

The sun, glowing and red, and nearing its setting, was shining on this marsh land as we gazed upon it. It was a curious looking spot— half water, half earth, wholly black mud—as it seemed to Susan. In Sir William's time he would not have had this bay touched—it would be valuable sometime, he said, but *he* should not trouble himself to make it so. It lay about as far from our house, on that side, as the Hall did on the other. The willows, spoken of by Mrs. Mellon, drooped over the edge of a portion of it, then came a crowd of rushes, then the dwarf trees, some of them only stumps.

"You see, Susan," I observed, "she could have crept round by the rushes and stumps, and so gained the road."

"Yes, I see," replied Susan; "it would have been possible, I suppose. On the other hand, she may have thrown herself in, to escape her troubled life."

"*Don't* think it, Susan, for heaven's sake!"

As we regained the road, which was narrow just there, not much better, indeed, than a lane, Miss Bertram drove up in her pretty low carriage, drawn by its cream-coloured pony, Mr. Arlegh sitting beside her. She pulled up to speak to me, and he raised his hat.

Suddenly, as if it sprang out of the ground, for I'm sure I saw not where else it could have come from, a white hare was disporting itself under the pony's feet. Whether it was a real hare or a phantom, the pony became curiously terrified, his eyes glaring, his mouth foaming. The hare disappeared almost instantly, but the animal continued to rear and plunge. Miss Bertram was a remarkably timid girl, although she did drive this hitherto quiet pony: she dropped the reins, and would have leaped out. Mr. Arlegh prevented her, jumped out himself, and went to the pony's head. He had not, I am sure, seen the hare.

But he saw now. The hare—and this seemed to me the strangest part of it—the hare, which had certainly disappeared, was back again, running over *his* feet. With a sort of suppressed yell, Mr. Arlegh jumped back and loosed his hold of the pony. Again the hare had disappeared; he re-caught the pony's head, and Miss Bertram jumped out.

"Selim, what can be the matter with you?" she cried, addressing the pretty and trembling cream-coloured animal. "Did you see anything frighten him?" she added to me. "Did you, Hubert?"

But what could I answer? Nothing. Mr. Arlegh was now leading the pony forward, and when he seemed quiet, they got in and drove off, Mr. Arlegh taking the reins.

Once more, but this time we only knew of it by hearsay, Mr. Arlegh was frightened by the white hare. It was on the following Sunday. He was walking across the churchyard with our clergyman, Mr. Chasnel, they having stayed in the vestry after service to discuss some parish business, when, just as they were going by old Mrs. Barton's high tomb, a white hare ran across Mr. Arlegh's feet; seemed to *stand* on them for a moment.

"Why that looked just like a hare!" cried the clergyman. "Where's it gone to? Has it startled you?" he added to Mr. Arlegh, seeing that his face had turned whiter than death.

"I—don't know what it was," replied Mr. Arlegh, as they looked about. But the hare was gone.

The Reverend Charles Chasnel talked of this—that's how it came to be known. He told people that he had seen a white hare. Being a stranger in Cornwall, just appointed to the living, he had never heard of the superstition.

"What news do you think I have got?" cried Roger, coming in to breakfast on the Tuesday morning. "That old bog is going to be redeemed. Drained, and—"

"I'll believe it when I see it," interrupted father. "Sir William was always talking of that, but he never did it, and the fields around are nothing but a marsh. It has long been the shame of the place."

"It is really going to be done now," said Roger, smiling at his father's vehemence. Some gentlemen are coming to the Hall today about it; scientific men from London; and the work is to be begun immediately. The bailiff himself told me. They say," and here Roger laughed outright, "that there's great value in that swamp, as it now is."

Father looked at him quite angrily. "*Value* in it?"

"In the mud—or the water—or both combined. They talk of its chemical properties? It is Mr. Arlegh who has set all this in motion, Stone says, and has persuaded Miss Bertram to have it done."

"Time it was," grunted father. That swamp had always been a sore point with him.

Not that day, but the next, during the afternoon, we saw several gentlemen, followed by some rough workmen—not our ordinary country labourers—go down the road on their way to the swamp. Mr. Arlegh was first and foremost of them. He looked wonderfully handsome, was talking eagerly and laughing gaily, just as though he had forgotten the white hare.

But—it is the sad truth—before the sun had well set that night he was carried back past our gate, cold and dead.

That excursion to the swamp was a fatal one. I cannot tell you precisely what happened, or how; nor is it necessary. For some purpose or other, the workmen began dragging the swamp near the willows—perhaps to see what sort of mud it really was. The first thing they got up, apart from mud, was a black bonnet; the second looked like a rake full of golden hair. That made them drag on again with a purpose: and they drew up a young lady.

It was poor Agnes Garth. And her face presented the most wonderfully-preserved appearance. Hubert Arlegh could not fail to recognise her. Those around him told afterwards how he turned cold and sick.

But, in the excitement of this finding, they had been neglecting proper precautions, and had ventured too far over the swamp, standing on the pieces of wood that jutted out from the old fence. The wood had become porous and rotten, and it broke: and one of them fell down into the swamp, uttering a shrill and bitter cry. It was Mr. Arlegh.

He had sunk utterly; was gone clean out of sight; and he did not rise again. As soon as the apparatus could be disentangled from what it had already brought up, it was sent down again in search of him. He was quite dead; choked probably by the poisonous mud: and, do what they would, they could not restore life to him.

Many a year has gone by since then. My father is at rest in the church-yard, and I am Bessy Trenathy still. I am at the old home with Roger and his delicate wife, who whispers to me that she hopes I shall never leave it—for what would the children do without Aunt Bessy?

Susan married Charles Chasnel. He did not long remain in Cornwall; he had good connections and interest, got better and better preferment, and is now Dean of W. She meets Lady Calloway—formerly Miss Bertram—sometimes in society, and they rarely fail to exchange a word about the old place, Penryn. But there's one topic Susan never talks about, save to me, and perhaps once in a way to her husband, and that is the sad history of the past: of the ill-fated Agnes and of Hubert Arlegh and the warning of the phantom hare.

CLARA VENN

Christmas Eve at a Cornish Manor House

Cornwall was an excellent place for a ghost hunt, as demonstrated by Clara Venn's 'Christmas Eve at a Cornish Manor-house' (1878), where twin sisters travel to Cornwall with the express purpose of confronting its ghosts and living an "uncivilised" life of a different time. The people they are visiting reject "every modern convenience", which only proves more attractive—the sisters "having never done without modern conveniences in [their] lives, of course" made up their "minds that it would be charming to do so now". They are in pursuit of a very particular, romanticised Cornwall—a place where one can encounter spectres of the past and past ways of living. Their journey is less than comfortable, however. While Cornwall was easier to access than before, it still was not easy—and, arguably, is still a long and arduous trip today! The difficult journey exaggerates Cornwall's distance and perceived "primitivity". Ultimately their quest is frustrated—this is not a ghost story that features ghosts, but a ghost story about looking for ghosts. In this way it expresses a very Victorian interest in hunting down the paranormal and understanding the unexplainable. Psychical researchers and paranormal investigators (like Elliott O'Donnell, featured in this collection) sought to apply rational, empiricist methods to the seemingly supernatural world. Ghosts were all the rage across the century, and Christmas ghost stories in particular were popular. Christmas was becoming more of a consumerist, commodified celebration at this time, alongside the rise of industrial capitalism, and perhaps Christmas ghosts acted as a reminder of the holiday's more spiritual roots. There is a possibility that Cornwall features in one of the most well-known Christmas ghost stories—in Charles Dickens's 'A Christmas Carol' (1843) the Spirit leads Scrooge to "[a] place where Miners live", "a bleak and desert moor, where monstrous masses of rude stone were cast about, as though it were the burial-place of giants". Cornwall has, in myth and legend, been seen as a place where giants once roamed, evidenced by the rocky landscape.

t was a bleak, stormy afternoon, two or three years ago, on which my twin-sister, Alice, and I, found ourselves, for the first time, in a wild corner of the west of England.

"Come and spend Christmas in an uncivilised fashion with us, in our old Manor—built four hundred years ago," wrote a school-friend; "we cannot boast of 'every modern convenience' in our surroundings—that would be an anachronism,—but if you can spend a merry Christmas amongst Bohemians, we will give you a hearty welcome."

We readily accepted the invitation, and having never done without modern conveniences in our lives, of course, we made up our minds that it would be charming to do so now—to spend Christmas after the fashion of four hundred years ago, if we could discover how it *was* spent then, and, in short, that the season would be much merrier than usual, without nineteenth century conventionality. Perhaps it was; but certainly our first experience of the ancient customs was rather a rude shock to us both, and I am afraid we felt a decided preference for later ones.

We made part of our journey from Clifton by rail, and at the last point we could reach in that way, procured a travelling carriage, which we shared with a friend, who was going some distance further than we, and would leave us at the little town of Laresminster, where Mr. Bellew was to meet us, in his carriage, When we reached our halting-place it was late, and a cold mist from the sea was driving over the hills, making us shiver as we stepped out of the close carriage at the door of the little inn, where we expected to find what our friend called his "trap." Nothing was visible, and we hastened to ask whether any one was awaiting us within.

"If he has forgotten us," said Alice, calmly, "of course we can get a carriage here and go on. I think Emmie over-coloured her description—you see there is an inn even in Bohemia."

We were extremely glad to enter it and get out of the fog for a few minutes, earnestly hoping that the carriage sent for us might not be an open one. None had yet arrived; we waited several minutes listening for the sound of approaching wheels; it was half an hour past the time we had named, and still none came.

"Very strange," said Alice, at last. "They would get our letter this morning, fixing the time for our coming."

A sudden and very unpleasant idea crossed my brain. "What time do they get letters in Nectansham?" I asked our hostess. "Is it once or twice a-day?"

"Oh, only once a-day, ma'am," she answered, lifting her eyebrows in a little surprise. "About three o'clock in the afternoon; but they'm late today; didn't go away from here above an hour afore you come. They didn't use to send the letters round to the house there, but they was going to begin last week; leastways, so I've heard tell."

My sister and I looked at each other. Was a postal delivery among the "modern conveniences" that our friends could not boast of?

"Oh, never mind," said Alice, determined to make the best of the matter. "I am afraid they won't get the letter in time to send for us; but you will be able to find us a carriage, will you not?" turning to the landlady. "A close one, please, as it is so cold tonight."

"I am very sorry, ma'm," was the answer. "We don't keep no post-horses here. If you could put up with a cart, and wasn't afraid to trust yourselves with a young horse, my husband would drive you over."

"Oh, a dog-cart," I said. "Yes, we don't at all mind that, if we must have an open vehicle."

"Well, ma'am, p'raps that's what you call it," said she. "We calls it here a spring-cart. It'll take you over in a little more than an hour."

"Thank you," we said; "please let us have it as soon as you can."

We had already refreshed ourselves with some tea, so Alice suggested that we should go and look at the church, which was close by, while the dog-cart was being prepared. Lights were burning as we entered it; feeling rather ashamed of ourselves, because Evensong was just over, instead of about to begin, and we seemed to have avoided the service. We saw a fine, old church, with three aisles running parallel to the east end the chancel enclosed by wooden screens, whose rare carving delighted us both. Rows of tall granite pillars supported the roof, where there was more carving on the rafters, and splendid bosses fixed where they crossed. The seats were low, oaken benches, black with age, and immensely thick: carved with curious arabesques, and some with more significant designs. Looking round the walls, we saw that the church, unfortunately, possessed friends in the last century, who had left unmistakable traces of the time when ideas of church furnishing were a medley of coats-of-arms, skulls, cross-bones, and sheep-pens. The end of one aisle was a mortuary chapel; there the windows were filled with portraits, *In Memoriam*. The chancel was reverently closed; but we stood at the gate to admire the beauty within, and, after a few quiet minutes, left the church, wondering that we had not been summoned before to continue our journey. We found, however, that we had still some time to wait.

"All ready, ladies," said the landlord, appearing at last, whip in hand. And we went out of the inn parlour, to behold an unmistakable market-cart, and to experience the pleasure of a journey therein for the first time in our lives.

"How do you get into it?" said Alice to me. "I wish we had not to begin Bohemianism before we get to Waddonscombe Manor."

At last we were settled. Alice and the driver on the front seat. I at the back, having very little room for my feet, as I soon found—for our trunk took up nearly all the space at the bottom. The sea-fog came round us denser than ever, and Alice put up her umbrella.

"It's raining fast," said she.

"Oh, no! ma'am," said our companion. "This isn't to say raining; it's what you may call a sea-mist—that's all."

"But I'm quite wet—look here!" she protested, brushing the drops off her cloak.

"Yes, to be sure, ma'am; that's the way of it," he answered, so contentedly, that I was quite exasperated; for I slipped off my seat periodically, and could hardly keep the railway-rug over my knees, far less hold up an umbrella; while Alice's gave me continual pokes in the back of my neck.

Presently we turned down a steep hill.

"This here's called the unlucky road," said the driver. "Somebody's always comin' to grief on it, and this is a young horse, so I'm sure I don't know what he'll do. I hope you're not nervous, ladies?"

I assured him that we were not, and so burdened my conscience with a falsehood.

"After we get down this hill, and up the next one, I don't rightly know my way," he continued; "but I suppose we shall get somewhere at last."

It was so dark by this time that we could not see the horse's head; but after, as it seemed to me, creeping slowly down the side of a house, we began to ascend still more slowly on the opposite side. A light gleamed at the top of the hill, and, as it was the only thing we could see, our man stopped, and shouted at it. In two or three minutes we heard footsteps, and a little boy stood beside us.

"Tell us the way to Waddonscombe, can 'ee," said the driver.

"Yes," was the welcome answer.

"Would 'ee like a ride?"

And actually that misguided child did consent to climb up beside us in the darkness and be brought home to his enraged mother, dripping with the sea-mist, for the pleasure of being jolted for two miles in a spring-cart. We were devoutly thankful when at length two immense gate-posts seemed to rise out of the blackness before us and the child-guide cried, "Here's Waddonscombe!"

We drove through the gate and stopped at a door in the wall within. A thundering knock brought out a servant, holding a lantern in her hand, which lighted up her figure and the low granite archway in which she stood. We jumped out of the cart, leaving our luggage and the driver to her care, crossed a little court, and, passing through another door, entered the old dining-hall of the Manor-house, feeling much the same desire for light and warmth that induces moths to commit suicide in their efforts to reach it.

The table was spread for tea, a huge fire crackled on the hearth, and our host was marching, in an irritated fashion, up and down the room, while Emmie stood by the fire with a newly-arrived post-bag on the ground at her feet, out of which she had just taken the letter which we supposed would arrive early in the morning.

"Walter, what can we do?—this is dreadful," we heard her say, as the door was opened for us; but a surprised shout from her husband made her turn suddenly as we entered.

"My dear Fanny, my dear Alice!" she exclaimed, rushing to meet us, "what must you have thought of me? I have only just got your letter saying you would arrive at Laresminster today, and all yesterday we expected to hear. Why didn't you write before?"

"Oh, we thought you'd get the letter this morning," said I. "However, never mind now, Emmie. It was our own fault, and after all we have managed to reach you, in spite of the sea-fog and by means of a Bohemian conveyance called a spring-cart."

"No, you don't say so," said her husband. "You didn't come all the way in a spring-cart."

"From Laresminster; yes, we did," answered Alice. "Thank goodness that's over."

"I thought you might find Nectansham a little wild, but I never dreamt of your having such an experience as this," he answered. "However it's cruel to laugh, and really I'm extremely sorry for you, for you must be wretched. Is Miss Cary's room ready, Emmie?"

"Oh, yes," said she. "Come upstairs and get warm, you poor, dear things."

She took us up a curious wooden staircase to an equally curious bedroom, where, through a little loop-hole in the wall, we could see the dining-hall below.

"That is the Lady Châtelaine's peep," said Emmie. "It was made that she might see her husband feasting. Let me help you unpack," and she took possession of my keys and made us sit by the fire; then after we had got rid of wet cloaks, hats, and boots, she took us down to the "high tea" which was awaiting us, and we discussed our adventures, after which we were glad to go to bed early.

Next day was Christmas Eve. We unpacked; we helped our hostess stir her Christmas pudding, "a time-honoured custom" this, as she declared, and as such we were bound to observe it; then we went off to the church, which was to be decorated for the following day's service. Emmie's children accompanied us, a boy of about seven and a sweet, little golden-haired girl, a most irrepressible chatterbox, whose Christian name was quite superseded by the soubriquet, "Princess."

At the church we met Emmie's nearest neighbour, Mrs. Danvers, with her little girl, a most motherly little being, in charge of a rather obstreperous younger brother. Their mother kept a watchful eye on both children, but we thought Norah would have been quite equal to her duty as nurse if it had been left to her alone. The church was old and very picturesque, built at different periods, as the union of Norman, Early English, and Tudor architecture shewed; but all the more interesting on this account, though sadly out of repair. It was nearly dark when our work was over, and we were all glad to return to Waddonscombe, Mrs. Danvers and her little girl coming also for a cup of tea, before they continued their road home.

"No one would believe what gruesome work church decoration is," said Mrs. Danvers, as we all made our toilet upstairs, preparatory to kettledrum.

"*Gruesome*," said Alice, laughing; "is that another word from the Nectansham dictionary? I have heard a great many new terms today."

"My dear good lady," was the reply, "you'll both be infected with our vulgarity before you leave Cornwall. 'Gruesome' is not Cornish, though—it's a Lincolnshire word for dirty."

The drawing-room at Waddonscombe was panelled with oak, very dark and polished; its doors opened with iron latches, and not even its modern furniture could redeem it from the Middle Ages, to which it belonged of right, but the fire had been let out, so we went at once into the dining-hall, where we had been welcomed the night before.

A large fire burnt on the wide, open, hearth. Two great logs, upheld by high brass dogs, were the *piéce de résistance* supplemented by coal and various smaller branches. Tea was brought in, and Emmie would have ordered the lamp; but we begged her to leave us to the firelight, which was quite bright enough, and shone in red gleams on the white walls, revealing curious pictures, and little shields bearing the arms of former inhabitants long ago departed. The warm glow found out the rafters of the high vaulted roof, leaving in deep shadow the minstrel gallery at the lower end of the hall.

The living inmates of the place harmonised better than could have been expected with its old world character. Emmie's evening dress was a black velveteen; the open bodice trimmed with old point that might have been worn by any ancestress, and Alice and I wore some old-fashioned brocades; the children were always prettily dressed in a quaint, fanciful, style, that kept their mother's brains busy devising new costumes, and was in harmony with their quaint surroundings.

"Now, Emmie, if you presided over a wassail bowl instead of a tea-set, we might imagine that the sun-dial had gone back four hundred years," said Alice.

"It would be easy to imagine, instead, that there is a ghostly company of men and women of that time in the darkness of the minstrel gallery," said I. "Have you a ghost here, Emmie?"

"No," she answered; "is it not strange? There is a vague idea amongst us that it would be fit and proper to have one, but no authentic story of any apparition."

"I think all the old inhabitants must have been very exemplary people," said my sister, "or surely one unquiet spirit would haunt the scene of its former ill-deeds."

"I don't think they were," said Mrs. Danvers. "They say murder has been done here, and there is a secret chamber in the drawing-room chimney, so that one quite expects a ghost story at

Waddonscombe, and it is most extraordinary not to hear one. Now, Westdown, which is not nearly such an old house, had a ghost."

"*Had* a ghost," I said. "Surely you have not lost such a possession!"

"It was laid," she replied.

"Oh! do tell us the story!" exclaimed Alice and I together.

"Well," said she, "soon after we took the house we were told it was haunted, but we never heard or saw anything of the ghost for some time. At last, one Sunday afternoon, I was left alone in the house as usual, for I always let the servants go to church, and stayed at home with Norah, who was then a baby. Jack had walked up to the village to see if there were any letters for us, because they used to be left there, and we had to send for them. I was just going to put Norah to bed, when down came Mr. and Mrs. Land, who lived at Sanctuary. I asked if they had not seen Jack, who was just gone up the road. However, they had not seen him, so I wanted them to come in, but Mr. Land preferred walking about the garden with a cigar, while his wife came up to the nursery with me. Presently we heard heavy steps in the passage, and thought it must be Mr. Land, so we called to him to come up to us, and as he did not appear, or answer, she looked over the bannisters."

"'It's very odd,' she said, 'there's no one there. Can it be Captain Danvers trying to play us a trick?'

"But I told her if it was Jack, he would not stay down stairs by himself. Presently Mr. Land did come up, and we told him our story, but he was positive that no one had entered the house, for he had been watching for Jack's return.

"'It must be the ghost,' I said. Just then we heard the steps again, right through the hall, as if they were coming up stairs.

"'Ghost or no ghost, I'll be even with it now,' said Mr. Land, springing up and dashing down stairs. But he saw no more than his wife, and soon came back again. A few minutes later Jack arrived.

"'I say, Danvers,' said Mr. Land, 'you know its no use your coming to play ghost on us.'

"'What do you mean?' he said, quite surprised.

"'Why, you know you've been in before?'

"'No, I've only just come back, honour bright,' he answered. So they told him the story, saying, 'it must have been a ghost'; and then if you believe it, actually took him away with them, and left me alone in the house. Wasn't it too bad?"

"Yes, indeed," I replied. "Well, was that all you heard of the ghost?"

"No," said she. "About a month afterwards, Jack had gone to dine at Sanctuary, and I intended to sit up for him. Now I'd an old cook, that we had known for years; she had been my nurse when Norah was born, and then thought she'd like to stay with me. She was a very good cook, only the other servants used to say that she had the cooks' weakness for something stronger than water. At ten o'clock that night, the old lady came into the drawing-room, and said: 'If you please ma'am, we'd like to go to bed if you don't want anything more, and we have put Master's slippers and things all ready for him?'"

"'Oh, certainly,' I said, 'Go to bed, all of you. He can let himself in, indeed, if he's not very late, I'll sit up for him.'

"So off she went, and I'm sure she had nothing to drink that night. I waited a few minutes, trimming the baby's dress, until at last I got so frightened, sitting up by myself, that I couldn't stay any longer; so I went upstairs, and got into bed as fast as I could. It was not long before I heard steps in the hall, and thought they must be Jack's, only it was wonderful for him to come home so early; but then, whoever it was, went into the kitchen and made a great noise, opening and shutting doors, and I thought, What can he be looking for down there? Then the steps came out of the kitchen, right up the stairs, past the door of my room. I was sure now it could not be Jack, for he would have come straight in, and then they went down stairs, and I heard no more. You may imagine I did not go to sleep very soon. Jack came home about two o'clock. I said, 'Have you been in long?' but he answered, 'No, I've only just come back,' so I said no more, thinking I'd better keep my ghost story quiet.

"Next day the old cook said to me, 'If you please, ma'am, did you hear a noise last night about half-past ten or eleven?'

"'A noise,' I said, 'What do you mean?'

"'Oh, steps in the passage, ma'am, and some one opening the kitchen cupboards.'

"I was obliged to say, 'Yes.'

"'Well ma'am,' she said, 'It's very strange that we both heard it. Last night, after we was all in bed, I heard some one coming through the passage, and I thought, Master's home wonderfully early; and then the thing came into the kitchen, opening and shutting the cupboards, as if 'twas looking for something; so I says to myself, Drat them girls, they didn't put his slippers ready for him! and I throws on my dress to run down stairs. When first I went into the kitchen, I could see nothing; but presently, whew—w! something flies past me like the wind, and I followed it into the dining-room, and it rushed past again through the door—something white it was. I was dreadfully frightened, and stood still where it had been, but I didn't see or hear anything more; and after a bit, I went through the passage and the kitchen to look, but there was nothing, and then I went back to bed, but never to sleep, till I heard Master come in this morning.'

"I thought it very odd that she and I should have heard exactly the same thing; so next time I saw Mr. Falconer, our old Vicar, I told him, and he promised to come over to Westdown, and hear all about it. My old lady told him her story, and he made her shew him the exact spots in the kitchen and in the dining-room, where the ghost passed her, and then took out a book and said some Latin prayers in each place. Then he said to me.

"'I suppose you'll all be in church next Sunday?'

"I said, 'yes, of course, unless we were ill.'

"'You must also stay for the Holy Communion,' said he; 'and I do not think that spirit will ever trouble you again, for I have read that if prayers are said in a place where an unquiet spirit wanders, and the heads of the family it troubles receive the Holy Communion on the next opportunity afterwards, it will leave them in peace.'

"We went to Church as he bade us, and, do you know, from that day to this, the ghost has never been heard."

"What an interesting ghost story," said Alice; "it is the first I have ever heard from an eye-witness; or, in your case, one ought to say, an *ear*-witness."

"And fancy the laying of the ghost," put in Emmie.

"Mr. Falconer repeating his Latin prayers!"

"He was a dear old man," said Mrs. Danvers. "I wish you could have seen him. He was very good to the children, and they were so fond of him."

"Have you got a cup of tea for me, Emmie?" asked a voice from the shadow under the minstrel gallery. And Mr. Bellew, in shooting costume, walked into the midst of our fireside circle.

"You home, Mr. Bellew," said Mrs. Danvers, springing up. "Here have I been telling ghost stories by the fire; quite forgetting that hungry mortals were coming home to supper. Come, Norah, we must run all the way, or papa will be tired of waiting for us."

"And the singers, mother," said the little girl. "We shall hear the carols tonight!"

So they left us, and the quaint tapestry curtains were drawn over the windows, and the old hall was lighted for the evening. After supper, the children began to ask when the singing would begin, and Princess insisted on retiring behind the tapestry, to peer through the window, that she might watch for the coming of the singers. Her little brother had a sudden inspiration.

"Oh, mama! do let me take pussy to the window; because you said she could find mice in the dark, and I'm sure she can see the people."

In due time their patience was rewarded. There was a faint stir in the court outside, and then the following carol, in excellent time and tune—a good specimen of the musical genius of Cornwall.

> Hark, the music of the cherubs,
> Sweetly bursting from on high,
> And the choir of flaming seraphs,
> Telling wonders from the sky.
>
> See the frighted shepherds gazing
> On the bright celestial train,
> While each dazzling glory blazing,
> Raise each manful, wakeful strain.
>
> Cease your fears, the joyful story,
> "Unto you is born a child;
> Through His name, the Lord of glory,
> God to men is reconciled.

Now He leaves His blissful station,
Now descends with men to dwell,
Robes himself with incarnation,
And subdues the powers of hell.

Glory be to God the Father,
Glory be to God the Son,
Glory to the Lamb for ever,
The eternal Three in One.

At the last verse Mr. Bellew threw open the hall door, and invited
the musicians to enter. Two or three women, wrapped up in picturesque shawls, and about a dozen men, some singing, some playing
various instruments.

"A merry Christmas to you, ladies and gentlemen," said the oldest
among them, and we echoed the cordial wish.

A chair was brought for the leader of the party—a man of many
callings, for he played a violincello, sang bass, and gave out the first
line of every verse, as a word of command to his little company.

They lent us a book of words, and Alice and I found many
an old friend, in an older dress than we had known, amongst the
carols it contained. Grammar and orthography were alike traditional
throughout the collection. One with a Latin chorus, "*Venite adoremus
dominum*," filled us with wonder, and in an interval, allowed for the
enjoyment of ale and cakes, we asked that it might be sung.

"We don't sing that very often, ma'am," was the answer, "for
those that don't understand it laugh at the words."

"The laughing should be on the other side," said I. "You understand it, and they don't. Do sing it to us, for we shouldn't think of
laughing."

There was something sympathetic in the Christmas music sung in that old hall by the group of village musicians under the minstrel gallery; some of the faces bore an unmistakable stamp of old ancestry; it was no surprise to hear that their names could be traced back three hundred years in the parish records, and they answered us with a real courtesy, not often surpassed, and very often unequalled amongst those of gentle birth.

"Your Cornish people have the most wonderful manners," said Alice to our host.

"Haven't they?" said he. "Emmie was lost in admiration when we came down here first."

We were very sorry when the farewell verse brought our Christmas Eve pleasure to a close.

> My song is done, I must be gone,
> Come stay no longer here,
> God bless you all, both great and small,
> And send you a joyful year.

MARY E. PENN

In the Mist

Very little is known about author Mary E. Penn. A number of her short stories were collected into *In the Dark: And Other Ghost Stories* (1999) by Richard Dalby as the second volume of his *Mistresses of the Macabre* series. Dalby was an editor and collector of ghost stories, responsible for elevating and re-releasing many significant tales from nineteenth-century periodicals. Fellow collector, Alastair Gunn, posits that Mary E. Penn could have been the pseudonym of Ellen Wood (1814–1887). Ellen Wood was a prolific author of fiction and the owner of the magazine the *Argosy*, where this story was originally published (alongside others in this collection). Wood wrote much of the magazine's contents until her death in 1887, though many other celebrated women of the time contributed, including figures such as Christina Rossetti, Julia Kavanagh, and Hesba Stretton. Gunn's argument is largely based upon Wood's bountiful content for the magazine and tendency towards using pseudonyms, as well as the mystery surrounding Penn. The majority of Penn's publications appeared in the *Argosy*, and her name is associated with at least eight ghost stories and nineteen other chilling tales. Her last publication was 'The Secret of Lyston Hall' in 1897. 'In the Mist' is reliant upon Cornwall's mining history and its reputation as a hollowed landmass, riddled with subterranean crypts and crevices. Parallels are drawn between being lost in the mines and being buried alive. In many narratives Cornwall's mines are aligned with cemeteries, and even with the bowels of hell. This subterranean space in particular is a smuggler's hideaway, tapping into Cornwall's reputation for criminality. Cornwall's vast stretches of coast and networks of caves and hiding spaces made it an ideal locale for smuggling. It was a significant distance from major administrative centres and its waters were difficult to navigate, for even the most experienced of seamen. Cornwall's smuggling habits may have offered economic reprieve in desperate times, and the smuggler's tunnels become a sanctuary for our protagonist.

" es, Winnie, I say it, and I mean it—you are a cruel coquette. You know that I love you more than life itself, and yet you take a pleasure in tormenting me."

"It is you who torment me with your jealous suspicions, Noel, and your temper is simply unbearable. I warn you that you may try me too far."

This fragment of dialogue reached my ears one autumn afternoon as I—the Vicar of Penravon—was returning home across the heights after a long round of parochial visits.

The speakers stood facing each other, on the dusty, sunburnt turf at the edge of the cliff, too much absorbed in their quarrel to notice my approach. Not that my presence would have greatly disconcerted them had they been aware of it. I had known both Winnifred Carlyon and Noel Tremaine from childhood; had christened them, and should probably have the pleasant task of marrying them, if all went well—though the course of their true love did not seem to be running very smoothly at this moment.

It must be admitted that there was some ground for their mutual reproaches. Tremaine, who was a clever young mining engineer, had the quick temper which often goes with a warm heart, and the very strength of his affection made him jealous and exacting. As for Winnifred, her best friends could not deny that she was somewhat wayward and capricious, though so thoroughly lovable withal that those little failings, which time would certainly correct, might well be forgiven. She was the orphan granddaughter and spoilt darling of the wealthiest man for miles round Penravon—old Michael Carlyon, the shipowner—and was, besides, as pretty a girl as you would meet in a summer day; with a complexion like a May rose, and eyes of the wonderful blue that seems peculiar to Cornwall—the deep, limpid, changeful hue of the western sea; whilst she never smiled but to reveal a set of teeth dazzlingly white and even.

Noel's stalwart form, and handsome, vivacious, olive-tinted face, made a picturesque contrast to her delicate beauty: a better matched young couple could not have been found in the Duchy.

Just now, however, neither of my favourites appeared to advantage. The girl was flushed and defiant, her companion white with anger. Hitherto their disagreements had merely been the "renewing of love," but in this there appeared to be something more serious.

"What, quarrelling again!" I exclaimed, looking at them severely over my spectacles. "When will you two learn to agree?"

They started and turned, both looking rather guilty.

"Noel has insulted me, Mr. Glynn!" Winnie declared, hotly.

"I have not—unless truth is an insult," asserted Noel. "I said that you—"

"There's no need to repeat it," interposed Winnie.

"Excuse me," he returned. "As you have appealed to Mr. Glynn, it is only fair he should know what has passed. I said it was scandalous that you should encourage other men's attentions when you are my betrothed wife."

Winnie laughed provokingly, though her fingers trembled as she trifled with a spray of heather at her breast. "Is no one else even to look at me without your permission?" she asked.

"No one shall make love to you if I know it," he answered between his teeth.

"And pray who has done so?"

Tremaine hesitated a moment. "Walter Borlace, for one," he said at length.

Winnifred raised her pretty brows in affected astonishment. "Walter Borlace! why—I have known him all my life. We are almost like brother and sister."

"'A little less than kin and more than kind,'" quoted Noel, with an angry laugh. "You know well enough that he is in love with you."

"I—" Winnie began, then stopped short, colouring to her temples. "At any rate he has never told me so," she finished proudly.

"But you know it well enough, I repeat, and you encourage him."

"It is false!" she interrupted. "I have never encouraged him."

"It is *true*," returned Noel. "I have watched you, and I know it. I am not blind."

An angry retort rose to her lips, but she controlled herself.

"Yes, Noel, you *are* blind," she said, more gently. "You are blinded by jealousy, or you would know that, whatever my faults may be, I am not untrue or false-hearted. But you can think so if you choose," she concluded, raising her head proudly. "I will be indifferent to your opinion."

"You would not say that if you really cared for me," returned Noel, "but you don't. I have long thought your love is given elsewhere, and now I am sure of it."

Her lip quivered, but she said nothing, looking away from him across the calm, sunlit sea. Noel gazed into her face as if he were trying to read her heart in it.

"Is it so?" he questioned, with fierce anxiety. "Have I lost your heart, Winnie?"

Her breath came quickly; she raised her eyes to his with a look which ought to have convinced him to the contrary; but meeting his angry, suspicious gaze, her face froze again.

"You have not taken much trouble to keep it," was her reply.

He drew a quick breath and stepped back from her. "I see—it is as I thought," he muttered, with an expression in his eyes that almost marred the beauty of his face. "As such is the case," he resumed, speaking slowly and with difficulty, "I release you from your promise. I will not wed a woman whose heart is elsewhere. But listen"—he caught her wrist, bending his angry face close to hers—"if you will not be my wife you shall be no other man's. I will kill you first."

She drew back with a faint cry, turning suddenly pale.

"Tremaine, you forget yourself!" I interposed. "Your temper betrays you into conduct that you will blush for later. Threats and violence—for shame!" And, to do him justice, he looked ashamed already of his outburst.

"Come, come," I continued paternally, "you are both wrong. Temper on one side, pride on the other. Forgive and forget, both of you, and resolve that this shall be your last quarrel."

"That it certainly shall be," Winnie said quickly, but in a tone of resolution that was new to her. Her young face had a hard, resentful look that altered it strangely.

"You have given me my freedom," she continued, turning to Noel; "I accept it. Here is your ring. Henceforth you and I are strangers."

She held it out to him, and as he made no movement to take it, threw it at his feet, and went her way, with a firm step and erect figure, taking the road over the moor towards Borlace Court, as the old-fashioned manor-house was called.

Tremaine mechanically picked up the ring, and stood, looking after her, with a blank, incredulous expression, as if he hardly realised what had happened. The tempest of passion had passed as quickly as it rose, leaving pain and remorse behind.

"Do you think she is in earnest, Mr. Glynn?" he asked at last, in a tone of dismay.

"It looks very like it," I answered dryly.

"You think she really intends to take me at my word, and— But, good heavens, I did not mean it! I was so maddened with jealousy I hardly knew what I said."

"You must have been mad indeed to believe for a moment that Walter Borlace had taken your place in her heart," I said.

"She did not contradict me," he muttered.

"Pride sealed her lips, but her face spoke for her, if you had had eyes to see."

He was silent a moment, looking down. His colour came and went; his face was troubled and remorseful.

"I have acted like a fool!" he burst out at last. "I know that she is true at heart, in spite of her little coquetries, and I have driven her from me—perhaps for ever! What shall I do? Do you think she will forgive me? I will ask her pardon on my knees—"

"I hope you will do nothing so ridiculous," I interrupted. "It will be better policy to keep away for a few days, until she has had time to think it over, and then—"

"And then, perhaps, I shall find that she has engaged herself to that fellow"—he nodded towards Borlace woods—"in a fit of pique. No; I will not eat or sleep till my ring is on her finger again. She is gone to the Court to tea; I shall wait here till she returns, and it will be strange if I can't win her pardon for a few hasty words. She knows that my temper, and not my heart, was to blame."

"You must learn to control that temper of yours," I said gravely, as we shook hands, "or I fear it will lead you into terrible trouble some day."

I little thought when I uttered that prediction how soon it was destined to be fulfilled.

He turned from me without replying, and I left him standing with folded arms on Penravon Cliff, while I went on my way home, pondering, with a bachelor's amused perplexity, on the strange inconsistencies of "the passion called love."

Five minutes' walk brought me to the Vicarage—a low, square house of grey stone, facing the sea, while its back windows looked out over the broad purple moor. Between the house and the cliffs stood the church, a quaint, weather-stained granite building, said to be of sixteenth century architecture. In stormy weather its walls were ofter wet with spray, and in its crowded graveyard many a humble stone bore witness to the perils of those that "go down to the sea in ships." The most striking object in the view from my windows was the ancient Martello Tower on Penravon Cliff, locally known as the "Smugglers' Keep." The vaults beneath had once been used as a storing-place for contraband goods, and it was said that a subterranean passage connected them with the beach, but the entrance in the face of the cliff had probably long ago been blocked up by falls of rock. These slips were of constant occurrence, sometimes only consisting of loose stones and sand; but often great masses of rock, detached from the overhanging edge, went crashing and thundering to the beach.

The narrow footpath, passing the churchyard gate, wound along Penravon Cliff, and dipped abruptly into the wooded hollow which sheltered the village—one of the most picturesque on the Cornish coast. Its steep, zigzag main street went straggling down to the water's edge, where it terminated in a little jetty of rough boulders and dark beams dripping with seaweed. The houses were, for the most part, low stone cottages, with deep doorways and slated roofs, and gardens where myrtle and fuchsia flourished luxuriantly; but on the wooded slope above were dotted not a few white-walled villas, among which the shipowner's house, substantial and sturdy-looking like himself, showed conspicuously.

A couple of hours later, having dined and rested, I strolled out through my garden into the humble "God's acre" which adjoined it, and sat down on the low stone wall, under a twisted old thorn-tree. The glory of the evening had departed, and twilight was gathering over land and sea—a chill grey twilight, with something melancholy in its utter stillness. The sun had set in a hazy horizon, and now the cold sea mist was drifting inland like a ghostly veil, gradually blotting out the familiar outlines of the scene.

As I sat, smoking meditatively, and watching old Dan Tregellas, the sexton, who was digging a grave not far off, two figures approached along the path, looming suddenly out of the mist—Winnifred Carlyon and Walter Borlace.

The latter was a slight, rather effeminate-looking young fellow of two or three-and-twenty, with pale grey eyes and thin lips—as great a contrast to Tremaine in person as in character. There had always been a latent antagonism between the two men, which only needed a pretext to break into open enmity.

His expression, as he looked down into his companion's face, left little doubt as to his feelings for her. But Winnie did not seem to observe it; her eyes were bent on the ground with a downcast, troubled look. Neither of them noticed me, though they passed so closely to where I sat that I could not help overhearing a part of their conversation.

"Why do you look so sorrowful?" were the first words I heard, in Walter Borlace's soft, drawling voice. It seems to me that you ought to congratulate yourself on your escape. What chance of happiness would you have had with Tremaine—a violent, danger-ous fellow, who—"

"He is nothing of the sort," she interrupted quickly. "You were always prejudiced against him, and for no earthly reason."

"And yet you told me just now that he had threatened your life!" exclaimed Borlace.

"He said some wild words in the heat of passion," replied Winnie; "but of course they meant nothing. I am very sorry I repeated them. I was the most to blame; I ought not to have pro-voked him to anger."

He glanced at her with an unpleasant smile. "I see—it is the old story. You have quarrelled just for the pleasure of making it up again."

She shook her head. "Not this time; it has gone too far," she said gravely.

"Are you sure of that?" he asked, taking her hand, and speaking for once without affectation. "Are you really free? Then, Winnie, I may say to you at last what has been on my lips many a time before, though you would never let me speak. I think you know what it is. You must know that I—"

Winnie coloured, and drew her hand away.

"Walter, please say no more," she interrupted. "I am not in the mood to listen just now."

His thin lips tightened. "Will you ever be in the mood?" he questioned.

"Some other time I may be—I don't know; but certainly not now." She put out her hand as she spoke. "Don't trouble to come any further," she added abruptly. "Good-bye."

"Are you offended with me?" he asked, bending to look into her face.

"No, but—but I would rather be alone."

"How white you are," he exclaimed, as they shook hands; "and you are shivering. Are you cold?"

She laughed uneasily. "No, it was only a nervous tremor. Someone is walking on my grave, as the country people say."

He lingered a moment, twisting his neat little blonde moustache as he looked after her; then, with a slight shrug, turned and walked slowly away in the opposite direction.

I watched the girl's retreating figure till the mist hid it from view, wondering if Noel was still waiting on Penravon Cliff, and whether there would be another angry scene when they met.

As the thought crossed my mind I was conscious of a strange, uncomfortable feeling, such as I have experienced sometimes in a troubled dream; a vague dread; a presentiment of some impending calamity which I was powerless to avert. I tried to shake it off, but it clung to me, assuming every moment a more definite shape.

At length, yielding to an impulse I could not understand, I swung myself over the low wall, and followed her.

The mist was now so dense that I was obliged to proceed cautiously lest I should stray from the path, which at some points is dangerously near to the edge of the precipitous cliff.

I had passed the spot where I parted from Tremaine, and was approaching the old tower, when a confused sound of voices reached me; voices I recognised, though the speakers were as yet invisible.

"Winnie, don't madden me! You know that I didn't mean what I said. Take back the ring."

"After you have insulted and threatened me? Never! No, you shall not force it on me; let go my hand—how dare you!"

"I dare anything rather than lose you."

"This is not the way to win me back. Let go my hand—you hurt me! Ah, take care, Noel! you will—"

The words broke off in a scream—a cry so wild and terrible that it went through my nerves like an electric shock. In another moment I was on the spot.

Tremaine was standing, rigid and motionless as a figure carved in stone, on the extreme verge of the cliff, gazing blankly into the depth below, where there was nothing to be seen but the drifting mist; nothing to be heard but the wash of the incoming waves upon the rocks.

Where was Winnifred?

When I put the question in a faltering voice, and laid my hand upon his arm, he slowly turned his head and looked at me.

I trust I may never again see on a human face the expression his wore at that moment—the speechless horror and despair which seemed to petrify every feature. He tried to answer, but no sound came from his white lips. He mutely pointed down to the beach.

"Great heaven!" I gasped, "you do not mean that you—that she has fallen over?" He inclined his head.

"We were standing on the path close to the edge," he began, in a low hoarse whisper. "I tried to force the ring upon her; she resisted and struggled to get her hand away. I loosed it suddenly—so suddenly that she staggered backwards, and—and before I could prevent it, she—"

His voice broke; a shudder ran through him from head to foot. He threw up his hands with a wild despairing gesture.

"I have killed her—I that would have died for her! I have killed her—my love, my darling! Well, it is but a step to join her."

In another moment he would, in the frenzy of despair and remorse, have thrown himself over the cliff, but I seized his arm and dragged him back by main force.

As I did so, young Borlace came hurrying up, out of breath.

"What has happened?" he panted. "I heard a cry—"

"There has been a terrible accident," I began, and in a few hurried words told him all.

He stared at me with an expression of incredulous horror, then turned his eyes on Noel Tremaine. "An accident?" he repeated slowly. "*Was* it an accident?"

Tremaine started, and raised his head. Their eyes met, and for a moment they looked at each other as if under a spell.

"Good heavens—you cannot believe that I intended—" Noel began, but reading the other's dark suspicion only too plainly in his face, he left the sentence unfinished, and turned abruptly away.

"That is a shameful insinuation," I cried warmly. "You know that Tremaine loved her too well to—"

"I know that he threatened her life this afternoon," interrupted Borlace; "let him deny it if he can."

Noel looked round. His face had frozen into a strange quietude. "I do not deny it. It is true."

"And a moment ago I heard you say that you had killed her."

"But not intentionally!" I exclaimed; "it was an accident. Tremaine—speak! defend yourself from this shocking accusation. Do not let it be supposed that you are—a murderer!"

He shuddered, and covered his eyes with his hand. "I feel like one," he groaned. "But for me this would never have happened. Her death lies at my door—"

"We do not yet know that she is dead," I returned, hastily. "While we are loitering here she may be lying insensible on the beach."

The suggestion—improbable as I felt it to be—had the effect of rousing him from his despairing apathy. The words had hardly left my lips when he turned from us, and hurried away, soon disappearing in the mist.

"If she has survived such a fall it is little short of a miracle," Walter Borlace remarked, as we followed.

"And you forget, Mr. Glynn, that the tide is at the flood. It will take us more than an hour to reach Penravon Rocks; by that time the waves will have carried her away."

I made no answer; I knew only too well that he was right, and my heart sank as I thought of all the misery that was to come.

The nearest way to the beach was through the village, where Noel had arrived before us. The news spread like wild-fire through the place (though none dared to carry it to Michael Carlyon), and half the population turned out to accompany us. There was some delay while the boats were put out, and lanterns and torches provided, and it seemed hours to our impatience before we reached the spot.

A light breeze had sprung up, dispersing the mist, and the moon and stars looked forth as serenely as if there were no death in the world, no sin or sorrow. The pale, pure light gleamed on Penravon Rocks, from which the tide had retreated, leaving them wet and bare; sparkled on the shallow pools between the boulders, showed every crevice and projection of the rugged cliff—but it did not show us the figure we hoped, yet dreaded, to see.

Noticing that there had been a recent fall of turf and soil from the edge of the cliff, some of the men set to work to remove the débris, while the others gathered round, hardly daring to think what piteous sight might be revealed. But they found nothing.

Hoping against hope we continued the search for hours, sometimes mistaking a patch of moonlight for a fair dead face, or a floating tangle of seaweed for "a drowned maiden's hair,"—all in vain. Of Winnifred Carlyon, dead or living, there was no trace.

At length we prepared to return, but without Noel, who refused to leave the spot.

"I shall find her yet—something tells me that I shall," he muttered, casting a haggard glance round him. "Go—all the rest of you; I would rather be alone."

Walter Borlace gave him a curious look from his pale grey eyes, and seemed about to speak, but checked himself, and followed the others in silence.

"Who'll break the news to old Carlyon?" the men whispered among themselves, glancing furtively at me.

I knew that the sorrowful task would be mine, though I would have given much to avoid it. I dared not think of the grief and desolation the tidings would bring into the home which the sweet girl's presence had brightened.

II

Nothing travels so swiftly as ill-tidings, and nothing is more infectious than suspicion. Before another day had dawned the tragedy was known far and wide, and as the news spread, a vague shadow of doubt and distrust gathered round Noel's name. No accusation had yet been uttered, but on every side I heard the echo of Walter Borlace's doubting question—

"*Was* it an accident?"

Tremaine himself seemed unconscious of the whispered suspicion; unconscious of everything except his despair. All day long he was wandering on the heights, or by the margin of the "cruel, crawling foam," as if in the wild hope that the waves would give back what they had taken.

There had been a sudden change in the weather. A strong northwesterly gale was rising, and as I sat in my study at the vicarage that evening I felt the sturdy old house vibrate beneath the gust, while the rain beat against the panes as if it would drive them in. I was endeavouring, not very successfully, to concentrate my mind on the sermon I had begun when there was a tap at the door, and old Dan Tregellas, the sexton, entered, looking scared and startled.

"What is it?" I enquired. "You look as if you had seen a ghost."

"Something like one, sir. Coming up from the village just now I met young Tremaine, and it gave me quite a turn."

"Where was he?"

"On Penravon Cliff, just about where the accident happened. He was walking fast, talking to himself. I spoke to him, but he didn't hear me; didn't even see me, though he passed close to me. He was staring straight before him like a sleep-walker, and his face was as white as this"—laying his finger on my writing-paper. "I doubt his mind's giving way, sir, and he'll do himself a mischief if he's not prevented."

I threw down my pen and rose.

"In which direction was he going?"

"Straight towards the Keep."

I drew aside the curtain and looked out. Dusk was deepening into night; a wild stormy night of hurrying clouds and driving rain. Enough light remained to show me the massive form of the tower, standing sentinel above the angry sea.

"Surely he doesn't mean to spend the night in that dismal place?" old Dan muttered at my elbow.

"He must not be allowed to do so. Fetch me a lantern and help me on with my overcoat; I shall go after him at once."

Five minutes later I sallied forth into the rain and darkness.

The moment I emerged from the house the wind swooped down upon me with a rush that nearly took me off my feet, half blinding me as it drove the sharp sleet into my eyes. I struggled on, however, fighting my way along, with bent head, and at length, out of breath and dripping with rain, I reached the tower.

In the days when it was used for contraband purposes, the lower part of the building had been roughly restored; the breaches in the wall stopped up, the windows barred across, and a massive door added, which now hung awry on its rusty hinges. The place had an uncanny sort of reputation in the neighbourhood, and nothing would have induced the superstitious fishermen to enter it after dark.

I pushed open the door and looked in, holding the lantern above my head. Its light showed me the figure of Noel Tremaine, standing motionless in the middle of the floor, as if he had stopped short in the act of crossing it. His face was turned towards the door, but he did not appear to see me. He stood in a listening attitude, his lips apart, his eyes fixed and dilated, every line of his face expressing strained and anxious attention.

What was it he heard? No sound reached my own ears but the roar of the wind and the murmur of the sea. A vague, half-superstitious fear crept over me as I watched him, but I shook it off and entered, closing the door loudly to attract his attention. But though the sound echoed through the place, it did not break the strange spell that held him. It was not until I touched his arm that he seemed conscious of my presence. Then he started violently, and looked at me with a wild, haggard stare, but expressed no surprise at my sudden appearance, and for a moment seemed hardly to recognise me. At length he drew a deep breath, as if waking from a dream, and laid his hand on my wrist.

"Do you hear it?" he asked, in a breathless whisper.

"I hear nothing but the wind and the sea."

"Not that—the sound is within the tower. Hark!"

I listened intently a moment, then shook my head. "It was the cry of a seagull."

"I tell you it is here, close to us, seeming to come from the ground beneath our feet," he persisted excitedly.

"What is the sound?"

His answer fairly took my breath away.

"Winnie's voice."

I looked at him compassionately. "You are dreaming, Noel! grief and excitement have unnerved you. Come out of this gloomy place; come home with me, and—"

He shook his head impatiently.

"No, I dare not leave this spot. Something—an attraction I can't explain—drew me to it in spite of myself, and just now, before you came, I thought I heard— There again!" he broke off, seizing my shoulder. "Good heavens! is it possible you don't hear it too?"

Was I infected by his delusion, or did I indeed hear a faint muffled cry, seeming, as he had said, to come from the ground beneath our feet?

He had watched my face, and his own lighted up with a wild triumph.

"Do you believe me now, or are we both dreaming?" he cried; then, relinquishing my arm, he threw himself on the floor, beating the stones as if he would have torn them up with his bare hands.

"Winnie—Winnie! Speak to me—where are you?"

It was no delusion this time: no trick of excited fancy. A voice—not the "wail of a soul in pain," but the voice of a living woman, answered: "I am here, in the vault! Help—come to me!"

Noel sprang to his feet, with a cry that rang through the place. "Ah, I understand! Dolt that I was not to think of it before! Mr. Glynn—the subterranean passage—"

I started, and looked back at him with a face as excited as his own. "But—but how could she—" I began.

"I don't know. It is all mystery at present," he interrupted; "but one thing is certain. By some strange chance she must have discovered the opening in the cliff, and made her way to the vault. The entrance is somewhere in the floor. Give me the lantern—quick!"

I handed it to him, and we anxiously examined the pavement, which was of square stone slabs, worn and uneven with age. In one of them, which appeared newer than the rest, was embedded a rusty iron ring. My companion pointed to it without a word, and set down the light.

The stone had become firmly fixed in its position, and it required the utmost exertion of our united strength to raise it. When, at length, we succeeded in removing it, a breath of damp cold air, charged with an earthy odour, came rushing up from the vault beneath.

Noel bent over the opening, gazing down anxiously as he swung the lantern to and fro. Its rays fell on what looked like a heap of light drapery, huddled together at the further end of the vault.

"She is there!" he breathed; "but—but she does not speak or stir. Suppose—suppose we are too late?"

I took the lantern while he let himself drop into the vault, then handed it down to him, and watched him as he approached the motionless figure.

He bent over it, raised the drooping head, and turned the white face to the light. Then, with an inarticulate sound of mingled pain and rapture, he lifted the slight form and bore it towards the opening where I was waiting to receive it.

We took off our coats and laid her down upon them. I supported her head on my knee while he tenderly chafed her hands.

"Are we too late?" he faltered, looking up at me with a face hardly less white than hers.

"No, she has only fainted. Look, she is reviving already."

Even as I spoke she stirred uneasily, drew a deep breath, and unclosed her eyes. They wandered round the unfamiliar place, then rested on her lover, who knelt at her side, watching her with breathless anxiety.

The change in her face was something to remember. Light, life and colour rushed back to it in a sudden tide of joy that transfigured every feature.

"Noel, Noel!"

The next moment his strong arms were round her, and his lips pressed to hers.

"My love—my darling!" he whispered between his passionate kisses. "How can I thank heaven enough for its mercy in giving you back to me almost from the grave!"

"It would indeed have been my grave, but for you," Winnie faltered.

His face darkened with a look of pain and remorse. "If you knew what I have suffered since yesterday! the agony of self-reproach."

"My poor Noel, your face speaks for you," she interrupted, with a faint smile. "But you need not have reproached yourself; it was a pure accident."

"Are you badly hurt, my darling?" he asked anxiously.

"I am a little bruised and stiff—nothing more."

"You escaped without injury from that terrible fall," I exclaimed. "It seems a miracle."

"It was indeed little short of one," she answered gravely. "Let me try to tell you how it happened. After I fell from the cliff—was it only yesterday? it seems *so* long ago—I must have been unconscious for some time. When I recovered I found myself lying on a projecting ledge of rock, my dress entangled in a straggling brier. Though not injured I was terribly bruised and shaken, and the ledge was so narrow that I dared not stir for fear of falling again. I cried for help, but my voice was drowned in the noise of the breakers, and the mist hid me from your sight. As I looked up despairingly, thinking every moment would be my last, I noticed a hollow in the cliff just above me, like the mouth of a natural cavern, half-hidden by brambles and furze-bushes. The thought flashed across me that it must be the entrance to the old 'Smugglers' Passage,' and that if I could creep into it I should be safe till you found me. With some difficulty, for the opening was only just large enough to admit me, I succeeded, disturbing a whole colony of seagulls who had built their nests inside. But another danger threatened me, which I could not foresee. I was beginning to get accustomed to my position, and to feel thankful for my merciful escape, when I heard a curious sound in the cliff above me—a cracking, rending noise. A quantity of loose stones and gravel came rushing down before the opening, half blinding me, and almost at the same moment I found myself in total darkness. A mass of rock and earth falling from the upper part of the cliff had blocked up the entrance, making me a prisoner. At first I hardly realised what had happened, but when I found that I was actually walled up in the cliff a dreadful fear seized me. Still I did not yet despair. I resolved to make my way along the passage, hoping to find another outlet in the tower. It was a steep incline, with rough steps at intervals, and it brought me, as I expected, to a vault. But, to my horror, I could find no outlet of any sort. I groped round the damp stone walls again and again before I could believe it, then sank down, as if stunned. I pictured you all seeking for me in vain; poor grandpapa's grief—Noel's despair. I thought what my fate would be, dying of slow starvation in the dreadful darkness of that living tomb."

She broke off, shuddering; then, after a moment's pause, went on again.

"The time dragged by till, from sheer exhaustion, I fell into a deep dreamless sleep, which must have lasted many hours. At length I woke with a start, thrilling in every nerve with a strange conviction that Noel was somewhere near me. I sat up, stretching out my arms in the darkness, calling to him, imploring him to come to me. When at last he replied, the sudden joy and relief overcame me, and I fainted."

"Never while I live shall I forget what I felt when I heard your voice," said Noel, in a low tone of deep emotion. "And yet it was scarcely surprise. I, too, had the same instinctive conviction that you were near me. My spirit was conscious of yours—"

They clasped hands and were silent a moment; a silence I would not interrupt, for I saw they were blissfully oblivious of my presence.

"Noel," Winnifred whispered after a pause, in a tone half playful, half serious, and wholly tender; "when you offer me the ring again I shall not refuse it. I think you believe now that I love you—a little?"

"I was mad ever to doubt it, as Mr. Glynn told me. But you need not fear, Winnie," he added with a smile, "the 'green-eyed monster' will never come between us again. I have learnt a lesson in self-control that I shall remember all my life."

"Thus, out of evil comes good," I put in sententiously. "But listen; I hear footsteps outside."

There was a moment's pause—a sound of whispering voices, then the heavy door suddenly swung open, and Walter Borlace appeared on the threshold, followed by the old shipowner and two men, whom I recognised as police-constables.

Hastily signing to Tremaine to place himself so that Winnie's figure was hidden, I advanced towards the intruders, who seemed not a little astonished at my presence.

"What does this mean?" I enquired, looking from one to the other.

"It means, Mr. Glynn, that these men have a warrant for the arrest of Noel Tremaine," young Borlace answered. "We tracked him here, and—"

"May I ask of what I am accused?" Noel interrupted, with a coolness which seemed to take them all by surprise.

Before the other could reply, Michael Carlyon stepped forward. He was a tall, stately old man, with silver hair, and a handsome weather-beaten face, pale and haggard just now.

"Noel," he began, in an agitated voice, "they tell me that—that you killed my darling in a fit of jealousy—" (there was a smothered exclamation from the background, which passed unnoticed)—"but now I look you in the face I can't believe it. It was an accident; you did not—you could not have intended to—"

"Heaven knows I did not, Mr. Carlyon," the young man answered earnestly; "but I don't ask you to take my word for it. Here is a witness who will speak for me."

He stepped back, and showed—Winnifred, who rose hastily to her feet, and quickly sought the shelter of her grandfather's arms.

I shall not attempt to describe the scene which followed; old Carlyon's joy, Walter Borlace's amazement, and the bewilderment of the two police-constables, who suddenly found themselves de trop.

When the first excitement had subsided, Winnie, after describing how the accident occurred, repeated what has already been told—often interrupted by the questions and exclamations of her hearers. When she had concluded, she turned to Walter Borlace.

"Was it you, Walter, who first suggested that monstrous accusation?" she asked, in a tone which brought the blood to his cheek. He hung his head, muttering something inaudible. After a moment's struggle with himself, however, he turned to his rival.

"Tremaine, I don't know whether you can ever forgive me," he began, awkwardly enough, but with evident sincerity. "I feel heartily ashamed of my unjust suspicion, and—"

"Let us shake hands and say no more about it," Noel interrupted, suiting the action to the word. "Even if I were disposed to resent it, my heart is too full of thankfulness just now to have room for any other feeling."

"Well spoken," said the old shipowner heartily; "you can afford to be generous, my boy. And now," he added, "the sooner we get home the better for this young lady, who is looking like a little ghost."

"You must please to consider the Vicarage your home, for tonight at least," I put in.

"Thank you, Mr. Glynn, that's kind. Can you manage to walk so far, my dear, or shall Noel carry you?"

Winnie essayed a few steps, then paused, looking white and faint.

"I think I shall have to trust myself to Noel," she said shyly, blushing as she looked up at him.

He stepped forward, nothing loth, lifting her as easily as if she had been a child.

"Yes, you may trust yourself to me, my darling," I heard him whisper as he passed out. "These arms shall guard and serve you faithfully all your life to come."

Winnie made no verbal reply, but the sigh of rest and contentment with which she let her head sink on his shoulder was an answer more eloquent than words.

MRS. H. L. COX

The Baronet's Craze

'The Baronet's Craze' was published in *Tinsleys' Magazine* in 1889. It features a young man falling in love with a beautiful Cornish woman only to seemingly lose her to a gruesome fate. This narrative is specifically dependent on Cornwall's distance from the rest of the mainland and the still relatively new improved railway network. It is part of a longer tradition of Cornish Gothic stories that conspicuously rely upon bodies being transported by train. The most famous example of this is likely Thomas Hardy's 1873 novel *A Pair of Blue Eyes*, featuring two potential suitors bickering over the hand of the fair Elfride. They rush to Cornwall on the next train out of Paddington to compete for her love—both of them oblivious to the fact her coffin is in the very same train. In *Jewel of the Seven Stars* (1903) Bram Stoker imagines a mummified body being transported into Cornwall on a train, and in 'Dr. Wygram's Son' (1887) by G. M. McCrie a man transports his son's eternally preserved, catatonic body in and out of the county. Throughout the nineteenth century trains became a key emblem of the rapid, terrifying progress being achieved at the time. Alfred Tennyson famously warned "Let the great world spin for down the ringing grooves of change", founded on a misunderstanding that trains ran on grooves rather than rails. These Gothic short stories arose contemporaneously to railway developments. It was difficult to read on a horse and cart but reading on a train was easier and book shops opened in rail stations, including the first branches of W. H. Smith's. The books sold in these shops were usually cheap, short, disposable, and designed to be read on a journey. It is impossible to extricate the rise of popular fiction from the development of the railway, and here the railway is used to tremendous effect as a factor complicating the experience of reality.

he London season was at its height. I had at the commencement entered into its pleasures with the greatest zest, having previously been absent from England for some time.

My wanderings had extended to distant lands, where civilisation in many parts was unknown, and a white face but seldom seen. Hence the return to all the blandishments of beauty, and the elegances and refinements of life, gave me unfeigned pleasure; until suddenly I began to tire of the gaieties into which I had plunged, for the face and form I had watched with so much interest,—in fact, which so entirely fascinated me,—suddenly disappeared, and my enjoyment in the gay world vanished also. I will not attempt to disguise the fact that *I*, Hugh Bertram, at twenty-six years of age, was for the first time really in love.

Miss Gertrude Sinclair, the young lady to whose charms I had succumbed, was staying with her maternal aunt, Lady Bohun. She was an old family friend, and as such soon favoured me with an introduction to her niece; and this was her first visit to town.

There was a refined loveliness in Miss Sinclair's appearance and movements far beyond mere beauty; and yet her beauty was of the highest order: apparently she was unconscious of it. At times her face wore a look of pensive sadness that was deeply touching, and I could not but think she had passed through some sorrow that had left its mark on her.

From the first I was singularly attracted; her sweet voice and conversation, with the ring of truth and sincerity in it, in addition to her other fascinations, quickly brought me to that happy or unhappy state, as the case may be, when my every thought and feeling was centred in her. I met her frequently at different houses, but more especially at Lady Bohun's. One morning I called to inquire how it was I had not met her the evening before at a house to which I knew they intended going; to my great disappointment I heard that a telegram had arrived the previous evening summoning Miss Sinclair to return home immediately, and she had set off that day by an early train. I expressed the deepest regret that I had not been able to take leave of her. Lady Bohun, seeing how it was with me, and how much I was disappointed, determined to impart to me, in strict confidence, certain circumstances that affected the life and character of Gertrude's father, Sir James Sinclair.

"Several years ago," said she, "when he was residing on his estate near Edinburgh, his wife (my only sister) died. He felt the loss so severely that he left home, and travelled in various places for some time, leaving his two daughters under my care and that of an excellent governess. Gertrude's sister Alice was two years older than herself, and at the time of their father's return they were aged respectively nineteen and seventeen years. Both girls were beautiful and attractive. During the time he was absent they had emerged from childhood into womanhood.

"On his return the companionship of his daughters soon endeared them to him so much that although he never ceased to regret the loss of his wife, his spirits so much revived in their society that he again appeared to be a happy and contented man. Both were dear to him, but his love for his eldest daughter, Alice, almost amounted to idolatry. But this state of things was, alas! comparatively of short duration, for a year only had passed away when Alice formed the most romantic attachment to a man altogether unworthy of her. His birth and position were equal to her own, and to all outward seeming he was a gentleman of good character. He had come on a visit to some friends living near Sir James, but nothing was known to them of the wild and reckless life he had lived in Paris previously. He was a handsome man, and his manner especially fascinating. He apparently fell in love with Miss Sinclair from the first, and ere long proposed, and was accepted.

"At the end of a few months the day was named for the marriage, and everything between the respective families had been arranged. The trousseau was packed, the wedding breakfast prepared, the invited guests had arrived, when at the last moment, the morning of the wedding, the expected bridegroom was missing. Upon inquiry, it was found he had that morning departed by train, and had eloped with a young school-girl from Edinburgh, supposed to be an heiress. They were traced to Dover, but there all further clue to their movements was lost.

"The engagement and contemplated marriage of his beloved daughter had been a severe trial to her father. In the first instance he had done all in his power to oppose it, but, finding her heart was set upon it, and that she loved the young man deeply, he had felt constrained to give his consent, although reluctantly. The effect of thus being jilted by the man to whom she had given her whole heart, and the revelation of the utter baseness and heartlessness of his conduct, so preyed upon and undermined the poor girl's health, that she faded away day by day,—in fact, it broke her heart, and before three months were over, she was no more.

"The loss of his daughter was almost a death blow to her father also: he was never seen to smile; the light of his life seemed to have departed, for, alas! he had not the comfort of religion to support him in his dire distress. The moment matters were arranged he left his Scotch home, never to return to it, and having, after much research, heard of a solitary 'castle' to be let on the coast of Cornwall, took up his abode there with his daughter Gertrude, growing day by day more silent and misanthropical.

"They led perfectly secluded lives.

"Sir James would enter into no society; and for the past three years, until Gertrude's visit to town, the latter had been quite alone with her ever-mourning father, who was attended only by four old servants who had accompanied him to Cornwall.

"I have a great affection for my niece," continued Lady Bohun; "and it was only after my most earnest entreaty that her father consented to spare her to me for a few weeks, but with the most solemn charge that no especial attention was to be permitted from any gentleman, and should such be the case, her return home must be immediate. I was on the point of cautioning you not to make your admiration of her so apparent, when, unfortunately, it was too late. Some one had been commissioned by Sir James to warn him if there were any signs of danger, and the warning was given. Hence his daughter's recall."

Lady Bohun was kind enough to add that she lamented for my sake (as well as that of her niece) the extraordinary resolve, or delusion, that had taken possession of her brother-in-law; but ever since the death of his eldest daughter his one fixed idea was, that any one who sought Gertrude in marriage would turn out to be a villain like the other, and probably break her heart in a similar manner.

This was undoubtedly a species of monomania. Lady Bohun had tried to reason him out of it, but it was of no use. This craze of his had not been made known to Gertrude.

After expressing to Lady Bohun how grateful I felt for her kindness in acquainting me with all this, I asked if she would be so kind as to entrust me with Sir James Sinclair's address.

"That is just what I can't do," she replied, "for I was strictly forbidden to reveal it. But, my dear Mr. Bertram," she added, "there are ways and means of finding out, but pray be cautious."

II

I had not gone many steps from the door after this encouragement without having come to the conclusion that nothing would be so desirable as a walking tour on the Cornish coast, in the secret hope that in that way I might again meet Gertrude, and eventually make her father's acquaintance, remove his suspicions, and in time win his peerless daughter for my wife.

I was an only son, was rich, of good family, and would inherit a title from my bachelor-uncle, and I knew that I bore the character of an honourable man. Thus, if Gertrude could only return my love, and I could gain her father's consent, I had nothing to fear.

The next morning I announced my intention of leaving town for awhile, for a visit to Cornwall. Upon arriving at Falmouth I made all preparations for my ramble along the coast, and after consulting a local map, I found the name of a small castle (as it was called), situated within a quarter of a mile of the cliff, midway between a well-known harbour and fishing village and the town of Penzance to the west.

So, shouldering my knapsack, I passed Pendennis Castle and walked down to the celebrated Kynance Cove. Its great beauty has often been described, and cannot be exaggerated; but I could not enjoy the wonderful phenomena of nature to be met with there as

I otherwise should, for my thoughts dwelt upon, and my heart was in, the little castle I was bent upon discovering.

In the evening of my second days' tramp, I arrived at a coast-guard station in the immediate neighbourhood of the castle named in the map.

Upon meeting a coastguardsman pacing up and down, telescope in hand, on the look-out, I began my inquiry:—

"Can you tell me," I said, "who lives in the castle not far from here?"

"Yes, sir," replied the man; "the place you mean is called 'Beacon Castle.' The gentleman is a 'baronite,' and an uncommon queer sort of man he is. All the county gentry called at the castle when he fust came there, nearly three years agone, but he wouldn't see none of them; his man-servant sayin' his master wishes to live quite private, and wouldn't make friends with any one, not even the parson of the parish church, who lives about two miles off; it made a good bit of talk at the time."

"And does he live quite alone?"

"Oh, no, sir; a young lady, his daughter, lives there; and people say it is very hard upon the lady to keep her shut up like that. We did hear she went away for a short time; but I see her walking down to the Cove yesterday. She is very good to the poor fishermen and their families here about; but this is a lonesome place, and not fit for the likes of her.

Suppressing all appearance of the rapture I felt at being so near the one I loved best on earth, I continued my questions.

"Do you know," I said, "if there is any place near here on the coast where I could get a room or two for a short time? There must be a good bathing cove near?"

"That there is, sir," he answered; "about half a mile yonder a steep path over the cliff and rocks takes you down to a sandy cove quite sheltered like; there are two caverns there; the place is lonely, and not much known, but just round the point a very respectable man and his wife let lodgings, and good ones too, and, in the summer time, ladies, and sometimes artists, lodge there."

I cordially thanked him for his information, and very soon settled into the lodgings, to my entire satisfaction.

The next morning I saw Miss Sinclair pass the house on her way to the cliff over the caverns. She was accompanied by a little spaniel, who frisked about, apparently wild with delight. I hastened after her, and, as soon as she passed round the point, I approached nearer; the dog gave a sudden bark, and she turned to see what had excited him. I was at her side in a moment, and, as I raised my hat, she looked at me with the utmost surprise. The next moment we exchanged the friendliest greetings. With difficulty I retained my self-possession; she looked, in her simple morning dress, lovelier than ever.

"I had no idea, Mr. Bertram, when we last met that you contemplated a visit to Cornwall; you did not mention it."

"No," I replied, "I had no intention at that time; it was a sudden idea."

We sauntered on, talking of all sorts of things,—reminiscences of our life in town, the suddenness of her return home, and so on; but I said nothing of my interview with her aunt except that, not having met them the evening I expected, I had called and heard from Lady Bohun that she had left for home.

We walked on until we reached a reef of rocks that extended a long way out, and was of considerable height, forming a very prominent point from whence we could overlook the bay, with its brilliant colouring and sparkling waters, which washed over and around the time-worn crags. Many sea-birds rested on them, now in, now out of the water; while numbers, flapping their wings and stalking about on solitary rocks, made the air resound with their peculiar cry, but were so far below that the noise was not disturbing.

Several fishing-boats and vessels were in sight, and altogether the scene, with the grand old Mount in the distance, was both picturesque and beautiful.

Miss Sinclair had brought her sketch-book, and, seated on the moss-covered boulders, sheltered by high projecting rocks, was soon busy with her sketch. I had a small volume of Tennyson with me, and, at her request, read aloud, choosing, I must confess, the most sentimental portions, in harmony with my own feelings. I think the two hours we spent there were the happiest I had ever known.

For several days we met in the same way, our solitude being perfectly undisturbed, and I believe we got to know more of each other during that time than if we had continued our acquaintance in the ordinary way for a twelvemonth.

I now felt it would be impossible to longer forbear expressing the love that filled and engrossed my whole being; and by that lone sea-shore, just when twilight was advancing, and the setting sun's rays gilded and beautified the clouds with roseate splendour, I told Gertrude all that was in my heart of my deep love, and hope that she would be mine. My darling confessed her affection also, and our happiness seemed perfect.

On our way home I told her that I must call upon her father the next morning, for notwithstanding I had heard he did not receive visitors, it was imperatively necessary I should see him without delay.

"Papa has never allowed any one to call since we have been here," said Gertrude, now looking anxious and perplexed. "I don't know how we shall manage about it."

"I will make the attempt," I replied, "and if that fails, must write; for surely there can be nothing urged by him to prevent our union."

"My dear father is very strange," faltered Gertrude, "and ever since the death of my sister, is perfectly altered. He seems to have quite a horror of my knowing any gentlemen; but Aunt Bohun wrote to him of you so kindly that perhaps with you he may be different. We must hope and trust, dear Hugh, it will be so."

We were nearing her home, and I thought upon this occasion of accompanying her to the door, but she begged me not to do so, adding, "For Papa must first hear from you when alone of our acquaintance and attachment." We were now standing in a sheltered walk near the entrance gates of the grounds, and here I was to take my leave. My beautiful Gertrude and I parted in the most loving manner, with the fond hope that we should meet happily on the morrow; and as I pressed my last kiss on her sweet lips, I could by no possibility have contemplated or imagined the bitter grief that would befall me.

III

The next morning, with a beating heart and alternations of hope and misgiving, I presented myself at the door of the castle. An elderly man-servant opened it, and, looking at me suspiciously, asked my business.

I offered him my card, and at the same time inquired if Sir James Sinclair was at home, and could see me.

"Yes, sir," replied the man; "but my master never receives visitors, and forbids me to take in any cards."

"I am not an ordinary visitor," I said; "my business is important, *most* important, and you really must take my card, and request him to grant me an interview." At the same time, when again offering the card, I put a sovereign in his hand as well.

"What is this for?" asked the old servitor, dropping the card, and extending his open hand with the gold lying on it.

"It is for you, if you will accept it."

"Is it a bribe?" asked the man, looking at me steadily. "We don't take bribes here; put it back, sir, put it back in your purse."

"Very well," I said, feeling considerably crestfallen, and dropping it into the nearest pocket.

"This is perplexing," I thought. "What can I do or say now?" for I was determined to make one more effort to gain admittance. The man was about to shut the door.

"Will you be good enough to tell your master that I am a gentleman from London, a great friend of Lady Bohun's, and also am acquainted with Miss Sinclair?"

"I will see, sir," he replied, taking up my card, "but I don't expect Master will see you."

I was left outside for about ten minutes. He at length returned and invited me to enter. I was conducted to the library, and there stood Sir James awaiting me. I bowed low. He waved me to a chair, but as he did not sit down, I stood also. I was struck at once with his very sad expression of face blended as it was with one of anger and annoyance.

"What is the nature of your business, sir?" he sternly, asked, "and in what way can it concern Lady Bohun or Miss Sinclair?"

Thinking that perfect candour and plain speaking would answer best, without preface or apology, I at once replied:—

"I met Miss Sinclair several times in town, Sir James, at various places; I visited at her aunt's house; I have met her a few times in her walks in this neighbourhood, and renewed my acquaintance; and the result is, I am deeply attached to her. I have reason to believe she returns my affection, and my hope is, that after you have made every necessary inquiry respecting me, you will see no reason to do otherwise than ratify our engagement."

"And pray, sir, am I to understand" (and he spoke in the haughtiest and most frigid tones) "that you have *dared* to address my daughter unknown to me?"

"I certainly have; I proposed to her only yesterday, and was accepted, and have lost no time in making you acquainted with the matter, trusting you will bestow upon us your sanction and blessing."

"You have made a very great mistake, young sir. I recalled my daughter from London upon hearing that her affections were likely to be beguiled or entrapped by a man calling himself a gentleman. *You* are the man! You have also had the audacity to follow her to this place, and would, if possible, condemn her to misery. And now hear my unalterable and fixed decision."

Upon this I interrupted him.

"First allow me to assure you," I said (with as much calmness as I could command after what I considered his abominable impertinence), "that I am no adventurer. I possess a large fortune; my family is equal to your own, and well known to Lady Bohun; and my antecedents will bear the strictest examination. I cannot therefore admit there has been any audacity in my conduct!"

"Stop!" he thundered forth, "Your asseverations make no difference to me; my final resolve is, that I *will not* receive you here, that my daughter shall never be your wife, that she shall *not* meet you again, and I command you to give up all intercourse with her by word or letter, and I require you to pledge your word of honour that you obey me."

"I utterly and entirely refuse to give any such promise; and I tell you, sir, that you have no authority, human or divine, to exact it! You have vouchsafed no reason whatever for your refusal, which I can but regard as an act of tyranny to your daughter, and an endeavour, not only to blast the happiness of my life, but to destroy hers also for no possible reason."

"My secret motives," he replied, "are locked up in my own breast, and I will not reveal them. Go, sir! You will see my daughter no more!"

The last sentence he spoke with the greatest solemnity. He rang the bell. The same servant appeared directly.

"Show this gentleman out," he quietly said. And thus ended my interview with Sir James Sinclair.

I thought the old servant looked at me almost with tears in his eyes: he had evidently heard all that had passed, although he said nothing, but his manner evinced marked respect and good feeling.

"So this," I thought, as I strode away, burning with anger and indignation, "is the father, guardian, and only companion of my dearest Gertrude; his sorrow at the loss of his daughter has evidently, on one point, altogether turned his brain. After one more interview with my darling I must hasten to town, and consult with Lady Bohun as to what steps ought to be taken. It is certain the present state of things cannot be allowed to go on."

Miserable and heartsick, I wandered about during the remainder of that day, and also the following one, hoping I should meet Gertrude; but there was no sign of her. I could bear the suspense no longer, and on the third morning proceeded to the Castle, and was about to enter the gate, when I was met by the old gardener, who informed me that I could come no farther; such were his master's orders.

"Can you tell me if Miss Sinclair is well, for I have not seen her out for the last two or three days?"

"Why, sir, Robert did tell me that our young miss warn't very well, and mayhap would keep her room for a few days."

"And who attends upon her?" I inquired.

"Why, Mary does, sir; she has tended upon her and nussed her ever since she was a baby. We old servants loves her as if she were our own, if I may make so bold as to say so."

This assurance gave me some comfort in the midst of my anxiety about her.

"Will you give Mary a letter for her young lady," I said, "if I bring one presently?"

"I dusn't dare, sir; for master told us if we carried or brought any letters except to him, either one of us should be turned off."

I wrote to her by post, but received no answer, and felt certain her father had intercepted the letter.

I lingered on in the hope she would soon be able to come out again, walking two or three times a day to the places where we had met, but all to no purpose. Each evening I wandered round the grounds of the Castle, but could see no one. My restlessness and anxiety increased day by day; I could scarcely eat or sleep: she neither came nor wrote. Ten days had now gone by. I would on the morrow return to town and see Lady Bohun. That night an indescribable foreboding of ill took possession of me.

IV

About an hour after midnight I felt I must again take a look at the house in which, perhaps, my Gertrude was immured, and, if possible, enter the grounds. The gates, I knew, were always locked at nightfall; but I had observed a gap in the bank, or hedge, near a small plantation of firs, and almost in front of the Castle, although hidden by the trees. I easily got through, and was at once attracted by seeing a bright light shining through the blinds of a solitary room situated in the turret. Shadows as of several people moved rapidly across it; something particular evidently was going on! Could it in any way be connected with Gertrude? I stood riveted to the spot under shelter of a large tree, and where the faint beams of the moon did not penetrate. Ere long the hall door was opened, and I could just discern four persons carrying out a huge case, apparently very heavy; it was borne on slings, not more than a foot from the ground. After taking a few steps the people set it down and rested for a minute or two; this they did several times.

As they advanced I recognised the old man-servant and gardener; the other two were women, dressed in long cloaks and hoods. Very soon the procession was joined by Sir James Sinclair, who, as he left the door, turned and locked it, then slowly walked behind within a yard of the others.

Ere long they entered the plantation, placed the case down, and two torches were lighted. The glare from them made objects near at hand distinctly visible; the faces of the party as they stood formed a picture worthy the pencil of a Rembrandt, as the flickering light played over their intent and solemn faces. Beside where the case was placed I observed a long and deep hole capable of receiving it. "It must be a quantity of plate and valuables they are going to bury," I thought, "and no doubt Sir James is about to leave and take his daughter away"; and I remembered the words he had spoken, "You will see my daughter *no more!*" The men raised the lid of the case, and oh, horror! it contained a coffin!!—a coffin of polished oak, partly covered with silver ornaments. My feelings I will not attempt to describe; I stood as if petrified. After taking a long look at the coffin, Sir James placed the lid of the case on again, and, assisted by the others, lowered it with difficulty into the grave prepared for it. He then took a Prayer-book from his pocket and commenced reading the service for the burial of the dead.

Tears were streaming down his haggard and much-aged face; the women were weeping, and tears stood also in the eyes of the two old men.

Sir James was so deeply affected that he could scarcely proceed. Just when he came to the words, "Earth to earth, ashes to ashes, dust to dust," the gardener stooped down, took up a handful of earth, and sprinkled it on the coffin. The dull thud of the earth as it fell, gave me such a thrill of horror that involuntarily I cried out, as I made a step forward,—

"Whom are you burying?"

The entire party looked up with amazement and saw me. Sir James approached to where I stood.

"Come no further," he said, in the most solemn tones, raising his hand on high, "nor dare to interfere with or interrupt this most sacred rite; retire, and leave me in peace to bury my beloved daughter, and never reveal what you have seen."

I staggered as if I had received a blow, then turned and fled. I felt as if I should go mad. Horror-struck as I had been, my heart filled with dread, in the midst of all a vague hope had hitherto sustained me that some aged relative of whom I had not heard might have passed away, and, with the extraordinary eccentricity or madness that possessed him, Sir James had decided the burial should take place here. But now all hope was over. What more terrible words could I hear than those he had so solemnly and mournfully uttered! *"Leave me in peace to bury my beloved daughter."*

The despair I felt unmanned me. I wandered I know not where. I pictured the beloved and chosen one of my heart in a hundred different ways; not a look or expression was forgotten. I seemed to again take her in my arms and imprint warm kisses on her lips. And then the agonising thought would come over me, that she was for ever hidden from sight: her smile would no more be seen; the sweet voice I loved so well to hear, now, yes *now*, silent evermore; her body lying in an unhallowed grave, in a solitary spot on a lone and wild coast.

Of her lovely Christian character I had no doubt, nor yet that her pure spirit had winged its flight to happiness above; but alas! so weak was my faith, so selfish was I in my grief, so wanting in Christian resignation, that all I could feel was,—"she is lost to me!"

"At last, when morning had fully dawned, I wandered back to the spot where she was laid. All that I saw was some newly-turned and flattened earth (the superfluous mould taken from the grave, piled up a short way off), so that before long, when the grass grew over the spot, but little trace would be visible that it was the resting-place of the sainted dead. My landlady was shocked at my appearance upon my return, and both she and the kind old sailor, her husband, implored me to go to bed, as I must be ill to look as I did.

"I have seen it coming on for several days past," exclaimed my hostess.

My exhaustion at length was so great that I yielded to their wishes, and threw myself on my bed; and, strong man as I usually was, I lay there for a considerable time, prostrate. The good souls gave me something to drink, and at length, notwithstanding my mental distress, tired nature asserted itself, and I fell asleep for some hours, for it was long since I had done so.

After awhile I roused myself with the thought that I had work to do; my sorrow must no longer master me. I felt I could not in my present state of mind appear before Lady Bohun, and suddenly alarm her by the terrible news I had to relate, but must nerve myself to write of all that had taken place, and break the news of her beloved niece's death as gently as possible, begging her to come to the castle at once and investigate all that had happened. I filled page after page with an account of everything, even to the bitter end.

That night my packet was despatched to the post.

V

For the next two days I eagerly intercepted the man who brought the letters, but there were none for me. Lady Bohun had sent no reply. I felt I should lose my senses were I to remain longer in this place where every sight, that had formerly given me so much pleasure when with my lost love, now seemed to, if possible, intensify my grief. The dull thunder of the waves as they broke on the shore sounded in my ears as a funeral dirge.

I therefore packed up, and took the first train from Marazion for London, leaving no address behind me.

In my present mood I seemed to have done with the world. I longed to break away from all association with it, and be as lost to my former friends as if they had never existed, so resolved to get away as far as I could from human beings, compatibly with the retention of some sort of civilisation.

A man who is heavy with grief loses all energy; I felt that I could not go on hunting or shooting expeditions in the solitude of the far West, as formerly I had done; all I wanted was opportunity for indulging my sorrow away from the eyes of my acquaintances and friends. I at once made my way to Weymouth, took the steamer to Guernsey, and, crossing over to Sark on the first opportunity, there established myself in one of the fishermen's squalid cottages in the rudest portion of Little Sark.

Looking back, I cannot but think that I must at that time have to a certain extent gloried in discomfort, when I recall the miserable room I slept in, the badly cooked, scanty meals I shared in common with the fisherman, his coarse untidy wife, and his ragged children.

I felt a certain pride sometimes in the fact that I had gone without my dinner from sheer inability to eat the untempting food, for I thought that this proved how entirely all my mind was given up to memory of the past. I have no doubt I was very foolish, but I was a young man, and I could feel deeply.

I spent my time wandering about this beautiful and desolate island, the world lost to me, and I to the world. I never even saw a newspaper, and all tourists I scrupulously avoided.

Weeks passed by. I kept no account of time. Whether I scrambled over the jagged rocks, or listened to the melancholy sea resounding in the great caverns, or wandered over the headlands, there was always one name on my lips and in my heart,—Gertrude.

The clergyman of Great Sark had called on me, but I saw him coming and went out; neither did I return his visit. But one day, when standing in the centre of the Coupé and involuntarily admiring the chasms below, the Seigneur of the island came up and spoke to me. Without positive rudeness I could not refuse to enter into conversation with him.

"Why do you not stay at the hotel?" he asked, after a time, "You would be infinitely more comfortable than at that hovel where you are living. They are moderate in their charges," he added kindly, possibly thinking economy influenced me.

I replied that I was completely indifferent to outward circumstances. He looked at me curiously, and, after a few courteous words, went away. During the two or three weeks that ensued I met him frequently, and he invited me to visit him at the Seigneurie and inspect his beautiful gardens. Against my will I consented, but the companionship of this pleasant, genial young man did me good, and I began to wonder if I had done well in trying to escape the world. When he left the island soon after, I felt I had lost my only friend.

It was now autumn; the weather became colder, the trees lost their leaves, the days shortened greatly. One day I was walking on the shore, heedless of the spray that drenched me and the chill wind that pierced through my thick coat; for my mind was intently fixed on the circumstances that had transpired during my short stay in Cornwall: more than ever they seemed to take hold on me this day, I could not shake them off even when nightfall came.

I sat up, smoking with my host in his desolate little cabin, until eleven o'clock, saying not a word. He was accustomed to my taciturnity, and I knew the inhabitants looked on me as a species of Diogenes. At twelve o'clock I went to bed, but what with the intensity of my thoughts on what had happened at the castle, and the roaring of the wind and the surf, it was long before I could sleep.

After a while I woke, as it seemed to me, with a start. I was no longer in the poor, untidy bedroom, but in a lofty room furnished as a study. I recognised it at once as Sir James Sinclair's. There were the same oak panels and wainscotings, the same heavy antique furniture and fittings.

Gradually two figures made themselves plain to my eyes, those of Sir James and his daughter, my beloved Gertrude. I had no power to join in the conversation, but I heard distinctly some of their words. He reproached her with having encouraged me and suffered me to address her; she, on her part, avowed her love to me, and determination to be my wife. Confused talking followed; Gertrude appeared to be firm in her expressions of attachment, the Baronet angry and excited. The figures became shadowy and indistinct. It changed to night: a small lamp was lit which illumined a portion of the study, but there were great shadows in the corners amongst which I lurked.

"You shall *not* marry him," said Sir James, in sepulchral tones. "Come with me as you are so rash, and learn what will be your fate if you persist!"

He took up the lamp and led the way up winding stairs, through dark corridors and galleries, until we came to what appeared to be the turret room. I could hear Gertrude's heart beat with fear. I had followed them, but was powerless to speak to her. The wind was wailing round the turret; everything looked ghastly and fearful. He opened the door of the lonely chamber and bade her look in. What she saw I know not. She gave a piercing shriek and fell down outside; the door had closed. Her father took something from his pocket, poured some liquid into a cup, and forced her to drink it. She rallied for a moment and stood up, then, giving a long sigh, again fell motionless. All then seemed indistinct. I heard the tramp of feet, some of the old servants came, cries and reproaches were mingled with the sound of a raging tempest. The scene changed. I saw the funeral enacted in all its miserable details, and then everything became a blank.

VI

It was broad daylight when I found myself in my bed in the fisherman's hut. The wind was blowing furiously. Soon I knew it had been a dream that I had seen Gertrude and her father face to face. But what did it mean? When the gale had somewhat moderated I rambled over the island for several hours, asking myself the question, but I could find no satisfactory answer. Vague fears haunted me; I stayed out till late at night, going to bed utterly exhausted; sleep I had none. I rose at daybreak, and heard the waves booming on the shore; their voices seemed to say, "What does it mean?"

Suddenly the thought came over me with overwhelming force, "Why have I left the place where my beloved Gertrude died and was buried, without investigating the case, and learning, with Lady Bohun's assistance, every particular? Have I not acted a craven's part in running away without first doing so? Have I been mesmerised, or has my mind been under the influence of Sir James Sinclair, that in my grief for his youngest daughter I should have adopted the same misanthropical character and conduct that he has displayed ever since the loss of his eldest one? Did I not despise his weakness in yielding so completely to despair, and nursing his grief in selfishness until his mind could receive no other ideas than those connected with his bereavement? and what am *I* doing?—I, a young man in the very prime of life and strength, giving myself up entirely to wretchedness, without making one effort to restrain or alleviate it! If this goes on I shall, by-and-by, become little better than a drivelling idiot! Fool that I have been in thinking I was honouring the dead! What would my Gertrude think if she could look down and witness the useless and inane life I live, and have lived, since she was taken away? Would she think I was honouring her memory by occasioning the greatest anxiety to my mother and family, who, for aught I know, may believe me dead? Have I no duties in life? No friendships? No human being but myself to consider? Would she thus wish me to act? *No!* a thousand times *No!* My conduct, on the contrary, is dishonouring to her memory, to all I am connected with, and to myself."

I felt like one who had awakened from a nightmare. I should never cease to regret the loss of my first, my only love; but, God helping me, I would hallow and sanctify her memory by doing good and caring for others.

That night the dream was repeated in all essential details; and oh! dreadful thought! what signification could the dream have, but that in a fit of frenzy Sir James had *murdered* his daughter! I was no longer undecided. I would go to England at once: all should be investigated and discovered.

This interpretation of the twice-repeated dream produced such a tumult in my thoughts that it was difficult to form any settled plan; my mind was in a chaos of bewilderment.

That Sir James loved his daughter I was sure; had I not witnessed his deep grief at the funeral. Was his mind so far unhinged that he was not responsible for his actions? Did the old servants know of all that had happened? if so, and her life had been sacrificed by him, had they, loving her as they did, connived at what he had done? Or was it possible that the dreams were altogether owing to my own disordered imagination! Any way, before denouncing that old man, or throwing a shadow of suspicion on him, I would find out what really had taken place, and insist upon the servants confessing why their young mistress had been buried with so much secrecy and mystery.

I packed up immediately. The steamer from Guernsey came in that day, and I left without a shadow of regret the beautiful island where I had spent so long a time.

The delay in embarking seemed to me intolerable. I noted, as though I saw not, the picturesque fishermen in their red caps, conveying passengers to and from the vessel, chattering the while in their peculiar *patois*. But at last we started, and, after our enforced delay at St. Peter's Port, I was fairly on my way to England.

It was a beautiful afternoon at the end of autumn when I once more revisited the little cove where my short-lived happiness had been experienced; where the greatest sorrow I had ever known had been met,—a sorrow now aggravated by an awful dread of what the next few days might bring to light. Before seeking my former lodgings I walked on the beach. But I started when in front of me I saw the figure of Sir James, old, bent, and worn. At sight of him I could not believe him guilty. Even if he were, could I expose that old man to the obloquy of the world, perhaps consign him to the doom of the scaffold? Knowing that parental love had been the cause, the undisciplined cause, of the craze that had proved (it might be) so fatal, I felt I could not. The vengeance that had burned in my heart seemed to fall to the ground as I thought, "Could my Gertrude impart her wishes, would they not be 'Spare and protect my father?'"

He turned and passed close by without seeing me. His face was haggard and careworn, and his hair—but partially grey when I saw him on the morning of my interview—was now of silvery whiteness.

Without heeding whither my footsteps led me I ascended towards the road leading to the castle grounds, and, still thinking deeply, entered the gate, and at once went to the secluded spot near the grave. No change had taken place there except that the ground was strewn with the fallen leaves. I walked beneath the bare branches of the trees, lost in sorrowful meditation.

The sun had set, leaving a red wintry glow amongst the grey clouds. I found myself at length in front of the castle; its dark turret rose against the crimson sky.

Was I *mad*?...

Whose was the face I saw for a moment at one of the windows? Who is this who comes flying towards me in the twilight? Whose arms are those that close, soft and warm, round my neck, while my name is murmured in tones of love? A footstep on the gravel-walk draws near; a hand is extended to mine and warmly clasped.

Sir James, in deeply feeling tones, exclaims, "I give her to you, Mr. Bertram. Make her as happy as she deserves to be, and may God bless you both."

Then, with one loving kiss to his daughter, he left us. I will not attempt to describe the bewildering and overpowering joy and deep thankfulness I felt as I held my darling in my arms while she sobbed upon my breast tears of happiness at our reunion. My own emotion was also too deep for words, for was she not restored to me, as it seemed, as one from the grave. After a while we entered the castle, and I was met in the most affectionate way by Lady Bohun; and ere I retired for the night, Sir James again gave us his formal sanction and blessing.

And so all our sorrow, all our poignant suffering, the mistakes of the last few months, with the fearful idea that had in my mind connected my darling's father with a dreadful crime,—all this had vanished and would be explained hereafter, while nought remained but happiness, too deep for utterance.

Here ends my personal narrative. What happened with respect to Gertrude after my interview with her father, and I had left Cornwall for Sark, the following pages will reveal.

VII

On the morning of Hugh Bertram's interview with Sir James, Gertrude expected to be summoned by her father to meet him, and was surprised when she saw him from her window leaving the house. Directly after, she was informed by Robert that her father desired her presence in the library, and as he followed her downstairs she was startled to hear him say quietly,—

"Don't you fear, Miss; we old servants will stand by you!"

This was ominous, but she made no reply, and a moment after entered the room: the door was closed.

"I am much displeased with you, Gertrude," said her father; "you have distressed me beyond expression. A Mr. Bertram has been here,—I fain would hope without your permission,—who told me that you,—yes, *you*,—had given him sufficient encouragement to request your hand in marriage! What have you to say to that?"

"It is quite true, papa; we hope for your consent to our engagement. When you know him, you will see he is everything you could wish."

"Has not the past, my daughter, had any warning for you? Do you forget your beloved sister's fate, and how her death was occasioned by the conduct of a villain?"

"But Mr. Bertram is not a villain," replied Gertrude with spirit; "there is no truer gentleman than he is; my aunt, and all who know him, think highly of him!"

"Enough, my child! enough! I have dismissed him. Never again will I allow you and him to meet."

"Papa! We love each other! You cannot be so cruel as to wish to part us!"

"My dear daughter, what now appears to you cruelty is, believe me, a proof of my strongest love and kindness. I cannot, I *will* not, see you doomed to wretchedness as your sister was."

"Father," urged poor Gertrude, "the cases are not similar; much as I loved my sister, and deeply as I have mourned for her, I cannot submit to be sacrificed on account of what was a most unfortunate attachment on her part. I am twenty-one years of age; I have been almost excluded from society; and now I am loved by one I can love in return. I cannot give him up. It is *you* who are dooming me to wretchedness—"

Here Gertrude's tears flowed fast, and throwing her arms around her father's neck, she besought him, in faltering tones, not to embitter her life by a refusal.

Much more she tremblingly said to the same purport, but all was of no use; his will was as adamant.

Sir James, looking powerfully agitated, bade her stand up.

"Girl," said he, "but one alternative remains: follow me!"

Wonderingly, and with an indefinable dread, Gertrude did so. They went upstairs until they came to a staircase she had never ascended; it was shut off by a wide door at the bottom. Sir James took a key from his pocket and unlocked it, then led the way upstairs to the turret-room, the door of which he also unlocked, and, throwing it open, exclaimed in a voice of passionate emotion: "Behold, rash girl, the victim of man's perfidy!"

The sight that met Gertrude's eyes was a small room, hung in black, and decorated with funeral symbols. In the centre, on an elevated platform, covered with a pall of velvet and white silk, stood a coffin, richly ornamented with silver. A cross of silver stood on it, surmounted by a crown, on which was carved in raised letters the word *Alice*. This Gertrude saw at the first glance, then gave one long piercing shriek and fell down senseless.

The old servant Mary was in her mistress's room, and although some distance off, heard the dreadful cry, as also did Robert, for the door of the staircase had not been shut. They rushed up to see what had happened, and found Gertrude lying in a dead faint, while Sir James, kneeling on the floor, was trying to pour some brandy down her throat from a flask. He was trembling in every limb. The servants were horrified.

"Take her to her room," said Sir James, wringing his hands. "Get everything you can to bring her to! Great God!" he wildly cried, "is she dead also?"

The utmost excitement prevailed. Gertrude was borne to her room and placed on the bed; every restorative they could think of was applied, but it was long before there was any apparent return to life.

"Leave the room, sir," entreated Mary, for the sight of you, after where you have taken our precious young lady, might kill her, should she ever recover consciousness. Oh, my poor dear lamb," groaned Mary, "I never thought this would happen."

"We were fools," said Robert, "not to foresee that one day something of this sort would occur. Come, sir," he exclaimed sternly to his master, who was getting more and more excited. When he got him to his room, Robert gave him one of his occasional sleeping draughts, and induced him to lie down, for Sir James was so overcome with grief and remorse that he appeared quite dazed; soon, however, the draught took effect, and he fell into a state of sleep or stupor.

VIII

The next morning Robert, and Andrew the gardener, presented themselves very early at their master's door.

"How is my beloved daughter?" Sir James gasped forth. "Come in and tell me."

"Bad, sir, very bad; you a'most killed her."

Sir James's look of misery was pitiable to behold.

"We have come to speak our minds, sir," he continued. "We have acted like idjets to do your bidding as we have done, and now it has very likely killed our dear young missus. We had no right, sir, to give way to your mad folly in keeping of our poor Miss Alice above ground; it warn't neither right nor Christian-like. You told us if we didn't want to be turned off, arter thirty years' service, we must do what you asked of us; so we did it. I feel now as if we a'most deserved to be hanged, the whole on us. But Andrew and me don't mean to stand it no longer; and tomorrow one of us is goin' to the nearest magistrate to give information that a unburied corpse has been in this house for three years, unless, sir, you now promise faithful, on your word of honour as a gentleman, that the poor young lady shall be buried as soon as things can be made ready, for we don't mean that Miss Gertrude shall ever again see the sight she did yesterday."

"Yes, sir," said old Andrew, now speaking for the first time, "we won't have such fearsome doings here no more."

"What do you wish me to do?" asked the master, in terrified tones.

"Well, sir, poor Miss Alice must be buried at once. Besides the mischief done to Miss Gertrude,—and there's no telling the harm it may have done her, poor dear young lady,—it have been the ruin of you. Hasn't it made you a most unnatural father? Don't we know that great part of every day, and sometimes of a night, you are up in that there room a workin' yourself up, and rebellin' again the Lord's will, and so muddlin' your brain that you can't see no difference atween good and bad, right and wrong! Isn't it spilin' the life of every one you come near? See what a character we have got in this place and all the country round! Didn't you send off that fine young gentleman, and turn him away like as if he was a low snob, 'cause he came askin' your leave to court our Miss Gertrude?"

"P'raps he's drowned himself by this time!" put in Andrew.

"Don't talk like a fool, Andrew," said Robert. "And now, sir, if you don't consent directly, off I goes to the magistrate!"

Poor Sir James was now thoroughly cowed: the fright of his daughter's illness had altogether unnerved him.

"I see I was wrong," he moaned. "I promise to do as you wish; but remember this, it is upon one condition only—that my child is buried in the plantation here, that no one is told of it, and that it is done in the dead of night."

When the men left the room after their conversation with Sir James, Andrew remarked:—

"We give it to old master hot and strong; I was a'most feared he'd shy summat at our heads."

"*You* give it him!" said Robert; "you scarce opened you mouth."

"But I did feel sorry to have to speak so rough to poor old master: only I knowed that if we didn't scare him to get the job done now, there Miss Alice would stay."

It may be as well to state here that all the arrangements were made immediately, Andrew agreeing to dig the grave. It took him nearly a week, but as the spot was quite sheltered from observation, the work went on unnoticed.

IX

The shock to Gertrude had been so great that she remained very unwell and weak for several days. At first the servants thought of sending for a doctor, though anxious to avoid such a step, if possible, so that no risk might be incurred of scandal ensuing; but Gertrude, the moment she was able to speak, entreated them not to do so. Ten days passed away before Sir James was well enough to do what he had promised; the funeral then took place, by night, in the manner witnessed by Hugh Bertram. The following day, Gertrude, who was now much better, wrote an account of all that had happened to

Lady Bohun, begging her to come to the castle as soon as possible. Hugh's letter arrived by the same post. The contents of both amazed and horrified her, and she set off to get to her niece at once. After a brief consultation with Gertrude, who was deeply distressed to learn how Hugh had suffered, Lady Bohun despatched a note by the gardener to Hugh's lodgings, but it was brought back; he had gone away that morning, leaving no address. Every effort was made to find out where he was, but without effect. Advertisements were inserted in the newspapers, but as he never saw them they were useless.

All that was heard of him was that he had telegraphed a line to his mother, merely saying he was about to leave England for a few months. Gertrude's illness and continued anxiety so alarmed her father that after hearing what Lady Bohun had to say respecting her lover, Sir James gave his unqualified consent to the engagement, and full authority to his daughter and her aunt to act in every way they thought best.

As weeks went by and no tidings were heard of Hugh, Gertrude's anxiety increased day by day, and had it not been for Lady Bohun's companionship and cheering society, the poor girl would have sunk altogether. Often her aunt would console her by saying, "You know, my dear, that after a time, when he has recovered from the first grief of his supposed loss, he will return, or let his family hear where he is; but the blow has been a dreadful one to him, as you may gather from his letter to me." Yet at times Gertrude's hope seemed almost gone. Latterly, she had frequently taken to wander alone in all the places where they had met. She would sit down on the rocks near the caverns, or pace up and down on the cliffs above, thinking of him, praying for him, that he might in some way be restored to her. On the night when Hugh had the remarkable dream that induced him to return to Cornwall, she had poured out her whole heart in an agony of supplication that soon they might see each other again. How far this concentrated earnestness at a particular time on the part of both, produced such an effect, we are not permitted to know, but similar coincidences, as they are called, have many times been known to take place. In the evening, as twilight approached, Gertrude sat at the window watching, with what result has been already related.

As, after the night of the funeral, Sir James could no longer shut himself up with his beloved dead, feeding his morbid imagination and perpetually brooding over all the harrowing details of the past, his mind ere long recovered its balance, Lady Bohun never allowing him to be long alone. He had even sanctioned the visits of the clergyman of the parish, and in all respects a vast mental improvement had taken place,—in fact, his *craze* seemed altogether gone. His chief feeling was one of deep sorrow for having occasioned his daughter so much suffering. Thankfully would he receive Hugh Bertram whenever he might appear.

The account given by the servants was, that at the time of Alice's death, her body was secretly embalmed, and then placed in the usual shell and lead coffin, with an outer one of oak. The burial service was read in the presence of many friends in the little chapel attached to the ancestral home; afterwards the coffin was lowered into the family vault underneath, Sir James taking charge of the ponderous key of the door leading to it. He had resolved, not only to leave Scotland, but to remove to a place sufficiently solitary to enable him to indulge his morbid feelings unmolested, and keep his dead, as well as his living daughter, under the same roof with himself. With much difficulty he at last prevailed upon four of his oldest and most trustworthy servants to assist him in carrying out this plan; but in what way it is unnecessary to particularise.

Gertrude had remained in Scotland until after the removal of the coffin, and all was arranged without any knowledge on her part as to what had been done.

But little now remains to be told.

Two or three weeks of perfect happiness soon restored the bloom to Gertrude's cheek and brightness to her eyes; while great would be the surprise of the old Sark fisherman if he could see and hear his former moody lodger. Sir James, now like another man, not only agreed, at the unanimous request of those around them, to leave the lonely castle on the Cornish coast, but also consented that poor Alice's remains should be disinterred and once more consigned to the family vault in Scotland as their final resting-place.

Hugh Bertram, who owned a house and estate not far from town, was soon busily engaged in making alterations and preparations for his expected bride; and as a suitable residence was for sale in the immediate neighbourhood, Sir James became its purchaser, the marriage being celebrated a few months after the removal from Cornwall.

In course of time, when little feet pattered about, and childish voices were heard, the happiness of their grandfather was complete.

Known and respected in the neighbourhood for his unostentatious worth, and as the friend of the poor, the sick, and the afflicted, Sir James had found rest and true peace at last.

No one who saw him now could realise that aught connected with him had ever borne the appellation of "The Baronet's Craze."

BRAM STOKER

The Coming of cAbel Behenna

Abraham "Bram" Stoker (1847–1912) was an author and theatre manager best known for the canonical Gothic novel *Dracula* (1897). Born in Dublin, Ireland, he attended Trinity College, Dublin, before starting a long career in theatre. He began as a theatre critic for the *Dublin Evening Mail,* then co-owned by fellow Irish Gothic author Sheridan Le Fanu. Following a rave review of Henry Irving's *Hamlet* the celebrated actor invited Stoker for dinner, beginning a lifelong partnership. Stoker became the manager of Irving's Lyceum Theatre in London and married Florence Balcombe, a former beau of Oscar Wilde. While in London Stoker wrote and socialised in writerly circles, becoming friends with his distant relative Sir Arthur Conan Doyle, whose work also appears in this collection. It is possible that his interest in Cornwall was inspired by Irving's own experiences in the county. While Irving was born in Somerset he was raised by his aunt in Cornwall, an experience he spoke and wrote about extensively. It is possible that the dashing, bewitching, and charming Irving served as an inspiration for Stoker's Count. It is known that a further source for Stoker's *Dracula* was Sabine Baring-Gould's *The Book of Werewolves* (1865), which described the history and folklore of lycanthropes—fanged, clawed creatures with transformative abilities. Baring-Gould himself was an antiquarian of Cornish folklore and wrote Gothic tales set in Cornwall. While *Dracula* is Stoker's most famous work he wrote a number of reviews, novels, and short stories in his lifetime, including the mummy novel *Jewel of the Seven Stars* (1903), which was set in Cornwall. In this novel an eccentric Egyptologist must find a foreign, mysterious space in which to reanimate an ancient mummy—and Cornwall fits the bill. In 'The Coming of Abel Behenna' Stoker draws upon the recurrent trope of re-emergent histories inevitably washed up upon Cornish shores, later seen in arguably the most well-known Cornish Gothic text—Daphne du Maurier's *Rebecca* (1938).

he little Cornish port of Pencastle was bright in the early April, when the sun had seemingly come to stay after a long and bitter winter. Boldly and blackly the rock stood out against a background of shaded blue, where the sky fading into mist met the far horizon. The sea was of true Cornish hue—sapphire, save where it became deep emerald green in the fathomless depths under the cliffs, where the seal caves opened their grim jaws. On the slopes the grass was parched and brown. The spikes of furze bushes were ashy grey, but the golden yellow of their flowers streamed along the hillside, dipping out in lines as the rock cropped up, and lessening into patches and dots till finally it died away altogether where the sea winds swept round the jutting cliffs and cut short the vegetation as though with an ever-working aerial shears. The whole hillside, with its body of brown and flashes of yellow, was just like a colossal yellow-hammer.

The little harbour opened from the sea between towering cliffs, and behind a lonely rock, pierced with many caves and blow-holes through which the sea in storm time sent its thunderous voice, together with a fountain of drifting spume. Hence, it wound west-wards in a serpentine course, guarded at its entrance by two little curving piers to left and right. These were roughly built of dark slates placed endways and held together with great beams bound with iron bands. Thence, it flowed up the rocky bed of the stream whose winter torrents had of old cut out its way amongst the hills. This stream was deep at first, with here and there, where it widened, patches of broken rock exposed at low water, full of holes where crabs and lobsters were to be found at the ebb of the tide. From amongst the rocks rose sturdy posts, used for warping in the little coasting vessels which frequented the port. Higher up, the stream still flowed deeply, for the tide ran far inland, but always calmly for all the force of the wildest storm was broken below. Some quarter mile inland the stream was deep at high water, but at low tide there were at each side patches of the same broken rock as lower down, through the chinks of which the sweet water of the natural stream trickled and murmured after the tide had ebbed away. Here, too, rose mooring posts for the fishermen's boats. At either side of the river was a row of cottages down almost on the level of high tide. They were pretty cottages, strongly and snugly built, with trim narrow gardens in front, full of old-fashioned plants, flowering currants, coloured primroses, wallflower, and stonecrop. Over the fronts of many of them climbed clematis and wisteria. The window sides and door posts of all were as white as snow, and the little pathway to each was paved with light coloured stones. At some of the doors were tiny porches, whilst at others were rustic seats cut from tree trunks or from old barrels; in nearly every case the window ledges were filled with boxes or pots of flowers or foliage plants.

Two men lived in cottages exactly opposite each other across the stream. Two men, both young, both good-looking, both prosperous, and who had been companions and rivals from their boyhood. Abel Behenna was dark with the gypsy darkness which the Phœnician mining wanderers left in their track; Eric Sanson—which the local antiquarian said was a corruption of Sagamanson—was fair, with the ruddy hue which marked the path of the wild Norseman. These two seemed to have singled out each other from the very beginning to work and strive together, to fight for each other and to stand back to back in all endeavours. They had now put the coping-stone on their Temple of Unity by falling in love with the same girl. Sarah Trefusis was certainly the prettiest girl in Pencastle, and there was many a young man who would gladly have tried his fortune with her, but that there were two to contend against, and each of these the strongest and most resolute man in the port—except the other. The average young man thought that this was very hard, and on account of it bore no good will to either of the three principals: whilst the average young woman who had, lest worse should befall, to put up with the grumbling of her sweetheart, and the sense of being only second best which it implied, did not either, be sure, regard Sarah with friendly eye. Thus it came, in the course of a year or so, for rustic courtship is a slow process, that the two men and woman found themselves thrown much together. They were all satisfied, so it did not matter, and Sarah, who was vain and something frivolous, took care to have her revenge on both men and women in a quiet way. When a young woman in her "walking out" can only boast one not-quite-satisfied young man, it is no particular pleasure to her to see her escort cast sheep's eyes at a better-looking girl supported by two devoted swains.

At length there came a time which Sarah dreaded, and which she had tried to keep distant—the time when she had to make her choice between the two men. She liked them both, and, indeed, either of them might have satisfied the ideas of even a more exacting girl. But her mind was so constituted that she thought more of what she might lose than of what she might gain; and whenever she thought she had made up her mind she became instantly assailed with doubts as to the wisdom of her choice. Always the man whom she had presumably lost became endowed afresh with a newer and more bountiful crop of advantages than had ever arisen from the possibility of his acceptance. She promised each man that on her birthday she would give him his answer, and that day, the 11th of April, had now arrived. The promises had been given singly and confidentially, but each was given to a man who was not likely to forget. Early in the morning she found both men hovering round her door. Neither had taken the other into his confidence, and each was simply seeking an early opportunity of getting his answer, and advancing his suit if necessary. Damon, as a rule, does not take Pythias with him when making a proposal; and in the heart of each man his own affairs had a claim far above any requirements of friendship. So, throughout the day, they kept seeing each other out. The position was doubtless somewhat embarrassing to Sarah, and though the satisfaction of her vanity that she should be thus adored was very pleasing, yet there were moments when she was annoyed with both men for being so persistent. Her only consolation at such moments was that she saw, through the elaborate smiles of the other girls when in passing they noticed her door thus doubly guarded, the jealousy which filled their hearts. Sarah's mother was a person of commonplace and sordid ideas, and, seeing all along the state of affairs, her one intention, persistently expressed to her daughter in the plainest words, was to so arrange matters that Sarah should get all that was possible out of both men. With this purpose she had cunningly kept herself as far as possible in the background in the matter of her daughter's wooings, and watched in silence. At first Sarah had been indignant with her for her sordid views; but, as usual, her weak nature gave way before persistence, and she had now got to the stage of acceptance. She was not surprised when her mother whispered to her in the little yard behind the house:

"Go up the hillside for a while; I want to talk to these two. They're both red-hot for ye, and now's the time to get things fixed!" Sarah began a feeble remonstrance, but her mother cut her short.

"I tell ye, girl, that my mind is made up! Both these men want ye, and only one can have ye, but before ye choose it'll be so arranged that ye'll have all that both have got! Don't argy, child! Go up the hillside, and when ye come back I'll have it fixed—I see a way quite easy!" So Sarah went up the hillside through the narrow paths between the golden furze, and Mrs. Trefusis joined the two men in the living-room of the little house.

She opened the attack with the desperate courage which is in all mothers when they think for their children, howsoever mean the thoughts may be.

"Ye two men, ye're both in love with my Sarah!"

Their bashful silence gave consent to the barefaced proposition. She went on.

"Neither of ye has much!" Again they tacitly acquiesced in the soft impeachment.

"I don't know that either of ye could keep a wife!" Though neither said a word their looks and bearing expressed distinct dissent. Mrs. Trefusis went on:

"But if ye'd put what ye both have together ye'd make a comfortable home for one of ye—and Sarah!" She eyed the men keenly, with her cunning eyes half shut, as she spoke; then satisfied from her scrutiny that the idea was accepted she went on quickly, as if to prevent argument:

"The girl likes ye both, and mayhap it's hard for her to choose. Why don't ye toss up for her? First put your money together—ye've each got a bit put by, I know. Let the lucky man take the lot and trade with it a bit, and then come home and marry her. Neither of ye's afraid, I suppose! And neither of ye'll say that he won't do that much for the girl that ye both say ye love!"

Abel broke the silence:

"It don't seem the square thing to toss for the girl! She wouldn't like it herself, and it doesn't seem—seem respectful like to her—" Eric interrupted. He was conscious that his chance was not so good as Abel's in case Sarah should wish to choose between them:

"Are ye afraid of the hazard?"

"Not me!" said Abel, boldly. Mrs. Trefusis, seeing that her idea was beginning to work, followed up the advantage.

"It is settled that ye put yer money together to make a home for her, whether ye toss for her or leave it for her to choose?"

"Yes," said Eric quickly, and Abel agreed with equal sturdiness. Mrs. Trefusis' little cunning eyes twinkled. She heard Sarah's step in the yard, and said:

"Well! here she comes, and I leave it to her." And she went out.

During her brief walk on the hillside Sarah had been trying to make up her mind. She was feeling almost angry with both men for being the cause of her difficulty, and as she came into the room said shortly:

"I want to have a word with you both—come to the Flagstaff Rock, where we can be alone." She took her hat and went out of the house up the winding path to the steep rock crowned with a high flagstaff, where once the wreckers' fire basket used to burn. This was the rock which formed the northern jaw of the little harbour. There was only room on the path for two abreast, and it marked the state of things pretty well when, by a sort of implied arrangement, Sarah went first, and the two men followed, walking abreast and keeping step. By this time, each man's heart was boiling with jealousy. When they came to the top of the rock, Sarah stood against the flagstaff, and the two young men stood opposite her. She had chosen her position with knowledge and intention, for there was no room for anyone to stand beside her. They were all silent for a while; then Sarah began to laugh and said:

"I promised the both of you to give you an answer today. I've been thinking and thinking and thinking, till I began to get angry with you both for plaguing me so; and even now I don't seem any nearer than ever I was to making up my mind." Eric said suddenly:

"Let us toss for it, lass!" Sarah showed no indignation whatever at the proposition; her mother's eternal suggestion had schooled her to the acceptance of something of the kind, and her weak nature made it easy to her to grasp at any way out of the difficulty. She stood with downcast eyes idly picking at the sleeve of her dress, seeming to have tacitly acquiesced in the proposal. Both men instinctively realising this, pulled each a coin from his pocket, spun it in the air, and dropped his other hand over the palm on which it lay. For a few seconds they remained thus, all silent; then Abel, who was the more thoughtful of the men, spoke:

"Sarah! is this good?" As he spoke he removed the upper hand from the coin and placed the latter back in his pocket. Sarah was nettled.

"Good or bad, it's good enough for me! Take it or leave it as you like," she said, to which he replied quickly:

"Nay lass! Aught that concerns you is good enow for me. I did but think of you lest you might have pain or disappointment hereafter. If you love Eric better nor me, in God's name say so, and I think I'm man enow to stand aside. Likewise, if I'm the one, don't make us both miserable for life!" Face to face with a difficulty, Sarah's weak nature proclaimed itself; she put her hands before her face and began to cry, saying—

"It was my mother! She keeps telling me!" The silence which followed was broken by Eric, who said hotly to Abel:

"Let the lass alone, can't you? If she wants to choose this way, let her. It's good enough for me—and for you, too! She's said it now, and must abide by it!" Hereupon Sarah turned upon him in sudden fury, and cried:

"Hold your tongue! what is it to you, at any rate?" and she resumed her crying. Eric was so flabbergasted that he had not a word to say, but stood looking particularly foolish, with his mouth open and his hands held out with the coin still between them. All were silent till Sarah, taking her hands from her face, laughed hysterically and said:

"As you two can't make up your minds, I'm going home!" and she turned to go.

"Stop," said Abel, in an authoritative voice. "Eric, you hold the coin, and I'll cry. Now, before we settle it, let us clearly understand: the man who wins takes all the money that we both have got, brings it to Bristol and ships on a voyage and trades with it. Then he comes back and marries Sarah, and they two keep all, whatever there may be, as the result of the trading. Is this what we understand?"

"Yes," said Eric.

"I'll marry him on my next birthday," said Sarah. Having said it the intolerably mercenary spirit of her action seemed to strike her, and impulsively she turned away with a bright blush. Fire seemed to sparkle in the eyes of both men. Said Eric: "A year so be! The man that wins is to have one year."

"Toss!" cried Abel, and the coin spun in the air. Eric caught it, and again held it between his outstretched hands.

"Heads!" cried Abel, a pallor sweeping over his face as he spoke. As he leaned forward to look Sarah leaned forward too, and their heads almost touched. He could feel her hair blowing on his cheek, and it thrilled through him like fire. Eric lifted his upper hand; the

234

coin lay with its head up. Abel stepped forward and took Sarah in his arms. With a curse Eric hurled the coin far into the sea. Then he leaned against the flagstaff, and scowled at the others with his hands thrust deep into his pockets. Abel whispered wild words of passion and delight into Sarah's ears, and as she listened she began to believe that fortune had rightly interpreted the wishes of her secret heart, and that she loved Abel best.

Presently Abel looked up and caught sight of Eric's face as the last ray of sunset struck it. The red light intensified the natural ruddiness of his complexion, and he looked as though he were steeped in blood. Abel did not mind his scowl, for now that his own heart was at rest he could feel unalloyed pity for his friend. He stepped over meaning to comfort him, and held out his hand, saying:

"It was my chance, old lad. Don't grudge it me. I'll try to make Sarah a happy woman, and you shall be a brother to us both!"

"Brother be damned!" was all the answer Eric made, as he turned away. When he had gone a few steps down the rocky path he turned and came back. Standing before Abel and Sarah, who had their arms round each other, he said:

"You have a year. Make the most of it! And be sure you're in time to claim your wife! Be back to have your banns up in time to be married on the 11th April. If you're not, I tell you I shall have my banns up, and you may get back too late."

"What do you mean, Eric? You are mad!"

"No more mad than you are, Abel Behenna. You go, that's your chance! I stay, that's mine! I don't mean to let the grass grow under my feet. Sarah cared no more for you than for me five minutes ago, and she may come back to that five minutes after you're gone! You won by a point only—the game may change."

"The game won't change!" said Abel shortly. "Sarah, you'll be true to me? You won't marry till I return?"

"For a year!" added Eric, quickly, "that's the bargain."

"I promise for the year," said Sarah. A dark look came over Abel's face, and he was about to speak, but he mastered himself and smiled.

"I mustn't be too hard or get angry tonight! Come, Eric! we played and fought together. I won fairly. I played fairly all the game of our wooing! You know that as well as I do; and now when I am going away, I shall look to my old and true comrade to help me when I am gone!"

"I'll help you none," said Eric, "so help me God!"

"It was God helped me," said Abel simply.

"Then let Him go on helping you," said Eric angrily. "The Devil is good enough for me!" and without another word he rushed down the steep path and disappeared behind the rocks.

When he had gone Abel hoped for some tender passage with Sarah, but the first remark she made chilled him.

"How lonely it all seems without Eric!" and this note sounded till he had left her at home—and after.

Early on the next morning Abel heard a noise at his door, and on going out saw Eric walking rapidly away: a small canvas bag full of gold and silver lay on the threshold; on a small slip of paper pinned to it was written:

"Take the money and go. I stay. God for you! The Devil for me! Remember the 11th of April.—ERIC SANSON." That afternoon Abel went off to Bristol, and a week later sailed on the *Star of the Sea* bound for Pahang. His money—including that which had been Eric's—was on board in the shape of a venture of cheap toys. He had been advised by a shrewd old mariner of Bristol whom he knew, and who knew the ways of the Chersonese, who predicted that every penny invested would be returned with a shilling to boot.

As the year wore on Sarah became more and more disturbed in her mind. Eric was always at hand to make love to her in his own persistent, masterful manner, and to this she did not object. Only one letter came from Abel, to say that his venture had proved successful, and that he had sent some two hundred pounds to the bank at Bristol, and was trading with fifty pounds still remaining in goods for China, whither the *Star of the Sea* was bound, and whence she would return to Bristol. He suggested that Eric's share of the venture should be returned to him with his share of the profits. This proposition was treated with anger by Eric, and as simply childish by Sarah's mother.

More than six months had since then elapsed, but no other letter had come, and Eric's hopes, which had been dashed down by the letter from Pahang, began to rise again. He perpetually assailed Sarah with an "if!" If Abel did not return, would she then marry him? If the 11th April went by without Abel being in the port, would she give him over? If Abel had taken his fortune, and married another girl on the head of it, would she marry him, Eric, as soon as the truth were known? And so on in an endless variety of possibilities. The power of the strong will and the determined purpose over the woman's weaker nature became in time manifest. Sarah began to lose her faith in Abel and to regard Eric as a possible husband; and a possible husband is in a woman's eye different to all other men. A new affection for him began to arise in her breast, and the daily familiarities of permitted courtship furthered the growing affection. Sarah began to regard Abel as rather a rock in the road of her life, and had it not been for her mother's constantly remind-ing her of the good fortune already laid by in the Bristol bank she would have tried to have shut her eyes altogether to the fact of Abel's existence.

The 11th April was Saturday, so that in order to have the marriage on that day it would be necessary that the banns should be called on Sunday, 22nd March. From the beginning of that month Eric kept perpetually on the subject of Abel's absence, and his outspoken opinion that the latter was either dead or married began to become a reality to the woman's mind. As the first half of the month wore on Eric became more jubilant, and after church on the 15th he took Sarah for a walk to the Flagstaff Rock. There he asserted himself strongly:

"I told Abel, and you too, that if he was not here to put up his banns in time for the eleventh, I would put up mine for the twelfth. Now the time has come when I mean to do it. He hasn't kept his word"—here Sarah struck in out of her weakness and indecision:

"He hasn't broken it yet!" Eric ground his teeth with anger.

"If you mean to stick up for him," he said, as he smote his hands savagely on the flagstaff, which sent forth a shivering murmur, "well and good. I'll keep my part of the bargain. On Sunday I shall give notice of the banns, and you can deny them in the church if you will. If Abel is in Pencastle on the eleventh, he can have them cancelled, and his own put up; but till then, I take my course, and woe to anyone who stands in my way!" With that he flung himself down the rocky pathway, and Sarah could not but admire his Viking strength and spirit, as, crossing the hill, he strode away along the cliffs towards Bude.

During the week no news was heard of Abel, and on Saturday Eric gave notice of the banns of marriage between himself and Sarah Trefusis. The clergyman would have remonstrated with him, for although nothing formal had been told to the neighbours, it had been understood since Abel's departure that on his return he was to marry Sarah; but Eric would not discuss the question.

"It is a painful subject, sir," he said with a firmness which the parson, who was a very young man, could not but be swayed by. "Surely there is nothing against Sarah or me. Why should there be any bones made about the matter?" The parson said no more, and on the next day he read out the banns for the first time amidst an audible buzz from the congregation. Sarah was present, contrary to custom, and though she blushed furiously enjoyed her triumph over the other girls whose banns had not yet come. Before the week was over she began to make her wedding dress. Eric used to come and look at her at work and the sight thrilled through him. He used to say all sorts of pretty things to her at such times, and there were to both delicious moments of love-making.

The banns were read a second time on the 29th, and Eric's hope grew more and more fixed though there were to him moments of acute despair when he realised that the cup of happiness might be dashed from his lips at any moment, right up to the last. At such times he was full of passion—desperate and remorseless—and he ground his teeth and clenched his hands in a wild way as though some taint of the old Berserker fury of his ancestors still lingered in his blood. On the Thursday of that week he looked in on Sarah and found her, amid a flood of sunshine, putting finishing touches to her white wedding gown. His own heart was full of gaiety, and the sight of the woman who was so soon to be his own so occupied, filled him with a joy unspeakable, and he felt faint with languorous ecstasy. Bending over he kissed Sarah on the mouth, and then whispered in her rosy ear—

"Your wedding dress, Sarah! And for me!" As he drew back to admire her she looked up saucily, and said to him—

239

"Perhaps not for you. There is more than a week yet for Abel!" and then cried out in dismay, for with a wild gesture and a fierce oath Eric dashed out of the house, banging the door behind him. The incident disturbed Sarah more than she could have thought possible, for it awoke all her fears and doubts and indecision afresh. She cried a little, and put by her dress, and to soothe herself went out to sit for a while on the summit of the Flagstaff Rock. When she arrived she found there a little group anxiously discussing the weather. The sea was calm and the sun bright, but across the sea were strange lines of darkness and light, and close in to shore the rocks were fringed with foam, which spread out in great white curves and circles as the currents drifted. The wind had backed, and came in sharp, cold puffs. The blow-hole, which ran under the Flagstaff Rock, from the rocky bay without to the harbour within, was booming at intervals, and the seagulls were screaming ceaselessly as they wheeled about the entrance of the port.

"It looks bad," she heard an old fisherman say to the coast-guard. "I seen it just like this once before, when the East Indiaman *Coromandel* went to pieces in Dizzard Bay!" Sarah did not wait to hear more. She was of a timid nature where danger was concerned, and could not bear to hear of wrecks and disasters. She went home and resumed the completion of her dress, secretly determined to appease Eric when she should meet him with a sweet apology—and to take the earliest opportunity of being even with him after her marriage. The old fisherman's weather prophecy was justified. That night at dusk a wild storm came on. The sea rose and lashed the western coasts from Skye to Scilly and left a tale of disaster everywhere. The sailors and fishermen of Pencastle all turned out on the rocks and cliffs and watched eagerly. Presently, by a flash of lightning, a "ketch" was seen drifting under only a jib about half-a-mile outside the port. All eyes and all glasses were concentrated on her, waiting for the next flash, and when it came a chorus went up that it was the *Lovely Alice*, trading between Bristol and Penzance, and touching at all the little ports between. "God help them!" said the harbour-master, "for nothing in this world can save them when they are between Bude and Tintagel and the wind on shore!" The coastguards exerted themselves, and, aided by brave hearts and willing hands, they brought the rocket apparatus up on the summit of the Flagstaff Rock. Then they burned blue lights so that those on board might see the harbour opening in case they could make any effort to reach it. They worked gallantly enough on board; but no skill or strength of man could avail. Before many minutes were over the *Lovely Alice* rushed to her doom on the great island rock that guarded the mouth of the port. The screams of those on board were faintly borne on the tempest as they flung themselves into the sea in a last chance for life. The blue lights were kept burning, and eager eyes peered into the depths of the waters in case any face could be seen; and ropes were held ready to fling out in aid. But never a face was seen, and the willing arms rested idle. Eric was there amongst his fellows. His old Icelandic origin was never more apparent than in that wild hour. He took a rope, and shouted in the ear of the harbour-master:

"I shall go down on the rock over the seal cave. The tide is running up, and someone may drift in there!"

"Keep back, man!" came the answer. "Are you mad? One slip on that rock and you are lost: and no man could keep his feet in the dark on such a place in such a tempest!"

"Not a bit," came the reply. "You remember how Abel Behenna saved me there on a night like this when my boat went on the Gull Rock. He dragged me up from the deep water in the seal cave, and now someone may drift in there again as I did," and he was gone into the darkness. The projecting rock hid the light on the Flagstaff Rock, but he knew his way too well to miss it. His boldness and sureness of foot standing to him, he shortly stood on the great round-topped rock cut away beneath by the action of the waves over the entrance of the seal cave, where the water was fathomless. There he stood in comparative safety, for the concave shape of the rock beat back the waves with their own force, and though the water below him seemed to boil like a seething cauldron, just beyond the spot there was a space of almost calm. The rock, too, seemed here to shut off the sound of the gale, and he listened as well as watched. As he stood there ready, with his coil of rope poised to throw, he thought he heard below him, just beyond the whirl of the water, a faint, despairing cry. He echoed it with a shout that rang into the night. Then he waited for the flash of lightning, and as it passed flung his rope out into the darkness where he had seen a face rising through the swirl of the foam. The rope was caught, for he felt a pull on it, and he shouted again in his mighty voice:

"Tie it round your waist, and I shall pull you up." Then when he felt that it was fast he moved along the rock to the far side of the sea cave, where the deep water was something stiller, and where he could get foothold secure enough to drag the rescued man on the overhanging rock. He began to pull, and shortly he knew from the rope taken in that the man he was now rescuing must soon be close to the top of the rock. He steadied himself for a moment, and drew a long breath, that he might at the next effort complete the rescue. He had just bent his back to the work when a flash of lightning revealed to each other the two men—the rescuer and the rescued.

Eric Sanson and Abel Behenna were face to face—and none knew of the meeting save themselves; and God.

On the instant a wave of passion swept through Eric's heart. All his hopes were shattered, and with the hatred of Cain his eyes looked out. He saw in the instant of recognition the joy in Abel's face that his was the hand to succour him, and this intensified his hate. Whilst the passion was on him he started back, and the rope ran out between his hands. His moment of hate was followed by an impulse of his better manhood, but it was too late.

Before he could recover himself, Abel encumbered with the rope that should have aided him, was plunged with a despairing cry back into the darkness of the devouring sea.

Then, feeling all the madness and the doom of Cain upon him, Eric rushed back over the rocks, heedless of the danger and eager only for one thing—to be amongst other people whose living noises would shut out that last cry which seemed to ring still in his ears. When he regained the Flagstaff Rock the men surrounded him, and through the fury of the storm he heard the harbour-master say:

"We feared you were lost when we heard a cry! How white you are! Where is your rope? Was there anyone drifted in?"

"No one," he shouted in answer, for he felt that he could never explain that he had let his old comrade slip back into the sea, and at the very place and under the very circumstances in which that comrade had saved his own life. He hoped by one bold lie to set the matter at rest for ever. There was no one to bear witness—and if he should have to carry that still white face in his eyes and that despairing cry in his ears for evermore—at least none should know of it. "No one," he cried, more loudly still. "I slipped on the rock, and the rope fell into the sea!" So saying he left them, and, rushing down the steep path, gained his own cottage and locked himself within.

The remainder of that night he passed lying on his bed—dressed and motionless—staring upwards, and seeming to see through the darkness a pale face gleaming wet in the lightning, with its glad recognition turning to ghastly despair, and to hear a cry which never ceased to echo in his soul.

In the morning the storm was over and all was smiling again, except that the sea was still boisterous with its unspent fury. Great pieces of wreck drifted into the port, and the sea around the island rock was strewn with others. Two bodies also drifted into the harbour—one the master of the wrecked ketch, the other a strange seaman whom no one knew.

Sarah saw nothing of Eric till the evening, and then he only looked in for a minute. He did not come into the house, but simply put his head in through the open window.

"Well, Sarah," he called out in a loud voice, though to her it did not ring truly, "is the wedding dress done? Sunday week, mind! Sunday week!"

Sarah was glad to have the reconciliation so easy; but, womanlike, when she saw the storm was over and her own fears groundless, she at once repeated the cause of offence.

"Sunday so be it," she said without looking up, "if Abel isn't there on Saturday!" Then she looked up saucily, though her heart was full of fear of another outburst on the part of her impetuous lover. But the window was empty; Eric had taken himself off, and with a pout she resumed her work. She saw Eric no more till Sunday afternoon, after the banns had been called the third time, when he came up to her before all the people with an air of proprietorship which half-pleased and half-annoyed her.

"Not yet, mister!" she said, pushing him away, as the other girls giggled. "Wait till Sunday next, if you please—the day after Saturday!" she added, looking at him saucily. The girls giggled again, and the young men guffawed. They thought it was the snub that touched him so that he became as white as a sheet as he turned away. But Sarah, who knew more than they did, laughed, for she saw triumph through the spasm of pain that overspread his face.

The week passed uneventfully; however, as Saturday drew nigh Sarah had occasional moments of anxiety, and as to Eric he went about at night-time like a man possessed. He restrained himself when others were by, but now and again he went down amongst the rocks and caves and shouted aloud. This seemed to relieve him somewhat, and he was better able to restrain himself for some time after. All Saturday he stayed in his own house and never left it. As he was to be married on the morrow, the neighbours thought it was shyness on his part, and did not trouble or notice him. Only once was he disturbed, and that was when the chief boatman came to him and sat down, and after a pause said:

"Eric, I was over in Bristol yesterday. I was in the ropemaker's getting a coil to replace the one you lost the night of the storm, and there I saw Michael Heavens of this place, who is a salesman there. He told me that Abel Behenna had come home the week ere last on the *Star of the Sea* from Canton, and that he had lodged a sight of money in the Bristol bank in the name of Sarah Behenna. He told Michael so himself—and that he had taken passage on the *Lovely Alice* to Pencastle. Bear up, man," for Eric had with a groan dropped his head on his knees, with his face between his hands. "He was your old comrade, I know, but you couldn't help him. He must have gone down with the rest that awful night. I thought I'd better tell you, lest it might come some other way, and you might keep Sarah Trefusis from being frightened. They were good friends once, and women take these things to heart. It would not do to let her be pained with such a thing on her wedding day!" Then he rose and went away, leaving Eric still sitting disconsolately with his head on his knees.

"Poor fellow!" murmured the chief boatman to himself; "he takes it to heart. Well, well! right enough! They were true comrades once, and Abel saved him!"

The afternoon of that day, when the children had left school, they strayed as usual on half-holidays along the quay and the paths by the cliffs. Presently some of them came running in a state of great excitement to the harbour, where a few men were unloading a coal ketch, and a great many were superintending the operation. One of the children called out:

"There is a porpoise in the harbour mouth! We saw it come through the blow-hole! It had a long tail, and was deep under the water!"

"It was no porpoise," said another; "it was a seal; but it had a long tail! It came out of the seal cave!" The other children bore various testimony, but on two points they were unanimous—it, whatever "it" was, had come through the blow-hole deep under the water, and had a long, thin tail—a tail so long that they could not see the end of it. There was much unmerciful chaffing of the children by the men on this point, but as it was evident that they had seen *something*, quite a number of persons, young and old, male and female, went along the high paths on either side of the harbour mouth to catch a glimpse of this new addition to the fauna of the sea, a long-tailed porpoise or seal. The tide was now coming in. There was a slight breeze, and the surface of the water was rippled so that it was only at moments that anyone could see clearly into the deep water. After a spell of watching a woman called out that she saw something moving up the channel, just below where she was standing. There was a stampede to the spot, but by the time the crowd had gathered the breeze had freshened, and it was impossible to see with any distinctness below the surface of the water. On being questioned the woman described what she had seen, but in such an incoherent way that the whole thing was put down as an effect of imagination; had it not been for the children's report she would not have been credited at all. Her semi-hysterical statement that what she saw was "like a pig with the entrails out" was only thought anything of by an old coastguard, who shook his head but did not make any remark. For the remainder of the daylight this man was seen always on the bank, looking into the water, but always with disappointment manifest on his face.

Eric arose early on the next morning—he had not slept all night, and it was a relief to him to move about in the light. He shaved himself with a hand that did not tremble, and dressed himself in his wedding clothes. There was a haggard look on his face, and he seemed as though he had grown years older in the last few days. Still there was a wild, uneasy light of triumph in his eyes, and he kept murmuring to himself over and over again:

"This is my wedding-day! Abel cannot claim her now—living, or dead!—living or dead! Living or dead!" He sat in his armchair, waiting with an uncanny quietness for the church hour to arrive. When the bell began to ring he arose and passed out of his house, closing the door behind him. He looked at the river and saw the tide had just turned. In the church he sat with Sarah and her mother, holding Sarah's hand tightly in his all the time, as though he feared to lose her. When the service was over they stood up together, and were married in the presence of the entire congregation; for no one left the church. Both made the responses clearly—Eric's being even on the defiant side. When the wedding was over Sarah took her husband's arm, and they walked away together, the boys and younger girls being cuffed by their elders into a decorous behaviour, for they would fain have followed close behind their heels.

The way from the church led down to the back of Eric's cottage, a narrow passage being between it and that of his next neighbour. When the bridal couple had passed through this the remainder of the congregation, who had followed them at a little distance, were startled by a long, shrill scream from the bride. They rushed through the passage and found her on the bank with wild eyes, pointing to the river bed opposite Eric Sanson's door.

The falling tide had deposited there the body of Abel Behenna stark upon the broken rocks. The rope trailing from its waist had been twisted by the current round the mooring post, and had held it back whilst the tide had ebbed away from it. The right elbow had fallen in a chink in the rock, leaving the hand outstretched toward Sarah, with the open palm upward as though it were extended to receive hers, the pale drooping fingers open to the clasp.

All that happened afterwards was never quite known to Sarah Sanson. Whenever she would try to recollect there would become a buzzing in her ears and a dimness in her eyes, and all would pass away. The only thing that she could remember of it all—and this she never forgot—was Eric's breathing heavily, with his face whiter than that of the dead man, as he muttered under his breath:

"Devil's help! Devil's faith! Devil's price!"

ARTHUR QUILLER-COUCH

The Roll-Call of the Reef

Sir Arthur Quiller-Couch (1863–1944) was a Cornish writer, literary critic and editor who often published under the pseudonym "Q". Quiller-Couch was born in Bodmin, son of Thomas Quiller-Couch, expert in Cornish folklore and history, who himself was the son of Jonathan Couch, naturalist and historian. Arthur's sister, Mabel, was herself a collector of strange tales of Cornwall, publishing *Cornwall's Wonderland* in 1914. He was educated at Clifton College then Oxford where he published his first Cornish Gothic novel, *Dead Man's Rock* (1887), a shipwreck narrative inspired by Robert Louis Stevenson's *Treasure Island* (1881–1882). He set many novels and short stories in Cornwall across his long and notable writing career, several of which drew upon the supernatural. He later completed Robert Louis Stevenson's unfinished novel, *St. Ives* (1898) and his own unfinished novel, *Castle Dor*, was completed by fellow Cornish Gothic author Daphne du Maurier in 1961. Quiller-Couch collected and published anthologies of verse, the most famous of which was the *Oxford Book of English Verse, 1250–1900* (1900), which remained the leading anthology of English verse until 1972. He was a Professor in English Literature at the University of Cambridge and a teacher of noted critic F. R. Leavis. 'The Roll-Call of the Reef' follows a longer tradition of the inevitable return of the spectral wreck, drawing upon older legends like the *Flying Dutchman*, the *Marie Celeste*, and *The Rime of the Ancient Mariner* to name but a few. The sea, and seafaring life, have long been sources of superstition and legends, and the Cornish coast, famous for its bountiful shipwrecks, has historically been a rich site for horrific narratives of the sea.

"es sir," said my host the quarryman, reaching down the relics from their hook in the wall over the chimney-piece; "they've hung here all my time, and most of my father's. The women won't touch 'em; they're afraid of the story. So here they'll dangle, and gather dust and smoke, till another tenant comes and tosses 'em out o' doors for rubbish. Whew! 'tis coarse weather, surely."

He went to the door, opened it, and stood studying the gale that beat upon his cottage-front, straight from the Manacle Reef. The rain drove past him into the kitchen, aslant like threads of gold silk in the shine of the wreck-wood fire. Meanwhile, by the same firelight, I examined the relics on my knee. The metal of each was tarnished out of knowledge. But the trumpet was evidently an old cavalry trumpet, and the threads of its parti-coloured sling, though frayed and dusty, still hung together. Around the side-drum, beneath its cracked brown varnish, I could hardly trace a royal coat-of-arms and a legend running, *Per Mare Per Terram*—the motto of the Marines. Its parchment, though black and scented with wood-smoke, was limp and mildewed; and I began to tighten up the straps—under which the drumsticks had been loosely thrust—with the idle purpose of trying if some music might be got out of the old drum yet.

But as I turned it on my knee, I found the drum attached to the trumpet-sling by a curious barrel-shaped padlock, and paused to examine this. The body of the lock was composed of half-a-dozen brass rings, set accurately edge to edge; and, rubbing the brass with my thumb, I saw that each of the six had a series of letters engraved around it.

I knew the trick of it, I thought. Here was one of those word padlocks, once so common; only to be opened by getting the rings to spell a certain word, which the dealer confides to you.

My host shut and barred the door, and came back to the hearth.

"'Twas just such a wind—east by south—that brought in what you've got between your hands. Back in the year 'nine, it was; my father has told me the tale a score o' times. You're twisting round the rings, I see. But you'll never guess the word. Parson Kendall, he made the word, and locked down a couple o' ghosts in their graves with it; and when his time came, he went to his own grave and took the word with him."

"Whose ghosts, Matthew?"

"You want the story, I see, sir. My father could tell it better than I can. He was a young man in the year 'nine, unmarried at the time, and living in this very cottage, just as I be. That's how he came to get mixed up with the tale."

He took a chair, lit a short pipe, and went on, with his eyes fixed on the dancing violet flames.

"Yes, he'd ha' been about thirty year old in January, eighteen 'nine. The storm got up in the night o' the twenty-first o' that month. My father was dressed and out long before daylight; he never was one to bide in bed, let be that the gale by this time was pretty near lifting the thatch over his head. Besides which, he'd fenced a small 'taty-patch that winter, down by Lowland Point, and he wanted to see if it stood the night's work. He took the path across Gunner's Meadow—where they buried most of the bodies afterwards. The wind was right in his teeth at the time, and once on the way (he's told me this often) a great strip of ore-weed came flying through the darkness and fetched him a slap on the cheek like a cold hand. But he made shift pretty well till he got to Lowland, and then had to drop upon hands and knees and crawl, digging his fingers every now and then into the shingle to hold on, for he declared to me that the stones, some of them as big as a man's head, kept rolling and driving past till it seemed the whole foreshore was moving westward under him. The fence was gone, of course; not a stick left to show where it stood; so that, when first he came to the place, he thought he must have missed his bearings. My father, sir, was a very religious man; and if he reckoned the end of the world was at hand—there in the great wind and night, among the moving stones—you may believe he was certain of it when he heard a gun fired, and, with the same, saw a flame shoot up out of the darkness to windward, making a sudden fierce light in all the place about. All he could find to think or say was, 'The Second Coming—The Second Coming! The Bridegroom cometh, and the wicked He will toss like a ball into a large country!' and being already upon his knees, he just bowed his head and 'bided, saying this over and over.

"But by'm-by, between two squalls, he made bold to lift his head and look, and then by the light—a bluish colour 'twas—he saw all the coast clear away to Manacle Point, and off the Manacles in the thick of the weather, a sloop-of-war with topgallants housed, driving stern foremost towards the reef. It was she, of course, that was burning the flare. My father could see the white streak and the ports of her quite plain as she rose to it, a little outside the breakers, and he guessed easy enough that her Captain had just managed to wear ship, and was trying to force her nose to the sea with the help of her small bower anchor and the scrap or two of canvas that hadn't yet been blown out of her. But while he looked, she fell off, giving her broadside to it foot by foot, and drifting back on the breakers around Carn dû and the Varses. The rocks lie so thick thereabouts, that 'twas a toss up which she struck first; at any rate, my father couldn't tell at the time, for just then the flare died down and went out.

"Well, sir, he turned then in the dark and started back for Coverack to cry the dismal tidings—though well knowing ship and crew to be past any hope; and as he turned, the wind lifted him and tossed him forward 'like a ball,' as he'd been saying, and homeward along the foreshore. As you know, 'tis ugly work, even by daylight, picking your way among the stones there, and my father was prettily knocked about at first in the dark. But by this 'twas nearer seven than six o'clock, and the day spreading. By the time he reached North Corner, a man could see to read print; hows'ever he looked neither out to sea nor towards Coverack, but headed straight for the first cottage—the same that stands above North Corner today. A man named Billy Ede lived there then, and when my father burst into the kitchen bawling, 'Wreck! wreck!' he saw Billy Ede's wife, Ann, standing there in her clogs, with a shawl over her head, and her clothes wringing wet.

"'Save the chap!' says Billy Ede's wife, Ann. 'What d'ee mean by crying stale fish at that rate?'

"'But 'tis a wreck, I tell 'ee. I've a-zeed 'n!'

"'Why, so 'tis,' says she, 'and I've a-zeed 'n, too; and so has everyone with an eye in his head.'

"And with that she pointed straight over my father's shoulder, and he turned; and there, close under Dolor Point, at the end of Coverack town, he saw another wreck washing, and the point black with people, like emmets, running to and fro in the morning light. While he stood staring at her, he heard a trumpet sounded on board, the notes coming in little jerks, like a bird rising against the wind; but faintly, of course, because of the distance and the gale blowing—though this had dropped a little.

"'She's a transport,' said Billy Ede's wife, Ann, 'and full of horse soldiers, fine long men. When she struck they must ha' pitched the hosses over first to lighten the ship, for a score of dead hosses had washed in afore I left, half-an-hour back. An' three or four soldiers, too—fine long corpses in white breeches and jackets of blue and gold. I held the lantern to one. Such a straight young man.'

"My father asked her about the trumpeting.

"'That's the queerest bit of all. She was burnin' a light when me an' my man joined the crowd down there. All her masts had gone; whether they carried away, or were cut away to ease her, I don't rightly know. Anyway, there she lay 'pon the rocks with her decks bare. Her keelson was broke under her and her bottom sagged and stove, and she had just settled down like a sitting hen—just the leastest list to starboard; but a man could stand there easy. They had rigged up ropes across her, from bulwark to bulwark, an' beside these the men were mustered, holding on like grim death whenever the sea made a clean breach over them, an' standing up like heroes as soon as it passed. The Captain an' the officers were clinging to the rail of the quarter-deck, all in their golden uniforms, waiting for the end as if 'twas King George they expected. There was no way to help, for she lay right beyond cast of line, though our folk tried it fifty times. And beside them clung a trumpeter, a whacking big man, an' between the heavy seas he would lift his trumpet with one hand, and blow a call; and every time he blew, the men gave a cheer. There (she says)—hark 'ee now—there he goes agen! But you won't hear no cheering any more, for few are left to cheer, and their voices weak. Bitter cold the wind is, and I reckon it numbs their grip o' the ropes, for they were dropping off fast with every sea when my man sent me home to get his breakfast. Another wreck, you say? Well, there's no hope for the tender dears, if 'tis the Manacles. You'd better run down and help yonder; though 'tis little help any man can give. Not one came in alive while I was there. The tide's flowing, an' she won't hold together another hour, they say.'

"Well, sure enough, the end was coming fast when my father got down to the point. Six men had been cast up alive, or just breathing—a seaman and five troopers. The seaman was the only one that had breath to speak; and while they were carrying him into the town, the word went round that the ship's name was the *Despatch*, transport, homeward bound from Corunna, with a detachment of the 7th Hussars, that had been fighting out there with Sir John Moore. The seas had rolled her further over by this time, and given her decks a pretty sharp slope; but a dozen men still held on, seven by the ropes near the ship's waist, a couple near the break of the poop, and three on the quarter-deck. Of these three my father made out one to be the skipper; close by him clung an officer in full regimentals—his name, they heard after, was Captain Duncanfield; and last came the tall trumpeter; and if you'll believe me, the fellow was making shift there, at the very last, to blow 'God save the King.' What's more, he got to 'Send us victorious,' before an extra big sea came bursting across and washed them off the deck—every man but one of the pair beneath the poop—and *he* dropped his hold before the next wave; being stunned, I reckon. The others went out of sight at once, but the trumpeter—being, as I said, a powerful man as well as a tough swimmer—rose like a duck, rode out a couple of breakers, and came in on the crest of the third. The folks looked to see him broke like an egg at their very feet; but when the smother cleared, there he was, lying face downward on a ledge below them;

256

and one of the men that happened to have a rope round him—I forget the fellow's name, if I ever heard it—jumped down and grabbed him by the ankle as he began to slip back. Before the next big sea, the pair were hauled high enough to be out of harm, and another heave brought them up to grass. Quick work, but master trumpeter wasn't quite dead; nothing worse than a cracked head and three staved ribs. In twenty minutes or so they had him in bed, with the doctor to tend him.

"Now was the time—nothing being left alive upon the transport—for my father to tell of the sloop he'd seen driving upon the Manacles. And when he got a hearing, though the most were set upon salvage, and believed a wreck in the hand, so to say, to be worth half-a-dozen they couldn't see, a good few volunteered to start off with him and have a look. They crossed Lowland Point; no ship to be seen on the Manacles, nor anywhere upon the sea. One or two was for calling my father a liar. 'Wait till we come to Dean Point,' said he. Sure enough on the far side of Dean Point they found the sloop's mainmast washing about with half-a-dozen men lashed to it, men in red jackets, every mother's son drowned and staring; and a little further on, just under the Dean, three or four bodies cast up on the shore, one of them a small drummer-boy, side-drum and all; and, near by, part of a ship's gig, with H.M.S. *Primrose* cut on the stern-board. From this point on, the shore was littered thick with wreckage and dead bodies—the most of them Marines in uniform; and in Godrevy Cove, in particular, a heap of furniture from the Captain's cabin, and amongst it a water-tight box, not much damaged, and full of papers, by which, when it came to be examined, next day, the wreck was easily made out to be the *Primrose*, of 18 guns, outward bound from Portsmouth, with a fleet of transports for the Spanish War, thirty sail, I've heard, but I've never heard what became of them. Being handled by merchant skippers, no doubt they rode out the gale, and reached the Tagus safe and sound. Not but what the Captain of the *Primrose* (Mein was his name) did quite right to try and club-haul his vessel when he found himself under the land; only he never ought to have got there, if he took proper soundings. But it's easy talking.

"The *Primrose*, sir, was a handsome vessel—for her size, one of the handsomest in the King's service—and newly fitted out at Plymouth Dock. So the boys had brave pickings from her in the way of brass-work, ship's instruments, and the like, let alone some barrels of stores not much spoiled. They loaded themselves with as much as they could carry, and started for home, meaning to make a second journey before the preventive men got wind of their doings, and came to spoil the fun. But as my father was passing back under the Dean, he happened to take a look over his shoulder at the bodies there. 'Hullo!' says he, and dropped his gear, 'I do believe there's a leg moving?' and running fore, he stooped over the small drummer-boy that I told you about. The poor little chap was lying there, with his face a mass of bruises, and his eyes closed: but he had shifted one leg an inch or two, and was still breathing. So my father pulled out a knife, and cut him free from his drum—that was lashed on to him with a double turn of Manilla rope—and took him up and carried him along here, to this very room that we're sitting in. He lost a good deal by this; for when he went back to fetch the bundle he'd dropped, the preventive men had got hold of it, and were thick as thieves along the foreshore; so that 'twas only by paying one or two to look the other way that he picked up anything worth carrying off: which you'll allow to be hard, seeing that he was the first man to give news of the wreck.

"Well, the inquiry was held, of course, and my father gave evidence, and for the rest they had to trust to the sloop's papers, for not a soul was saved besides the drummer-boy, and he was raving in a fever, brought on by the cold and the fright. And the seaman and the five troopers gave evidence about the loss of the *Despatch*. The tall trumpeter, too, whose ribs were healing, came forward and kissed the book; but somehow his head had been hurt in coming ashore, and he talked foolish-like, and 'twas easy seen he would never be a proper man again. The others were taken up to Plymouth, and so went their ways; but the trumpeter stayed on in Coverack; and King George, finding he was fit for nothing, sent him down a trifle of a pension after a while—enough to keep him in board and lodging, with a bit of tobacco over.

"Now the first time that this man—William Tallifer he called himself—met with the drummer-boy, was about a fortnight after the little chap had bettered enough to be allowed a short walk out of doors, which he took, if you please, in full regimentals. There never was a soldier so proud of his dress. His own suit had shrunk a brave bit with the salt water; but into ordinary frock an' corduroys he declared he would not get, not if he had to go naked the rest of his life; so my father—being a good-natured man, and handy with the needle—turned to and repaired damages with a piece or two of scarlet cloth cut from the jacket of one of the drowned Marines. Well, the poor little chap chanced to be standing, in this rig out, down by the gate of Gunner's Meadow, where they had buried two score and over of his comrades. The morning was a fine one, early in March month; and along came the cracked trumpeter, likewise taking a stroll.

"'Hullo!' says he; 'good mornin'! And what might you be doin' here?'

"'I was a-wishin',' says the boy, 'I had a pair o'drumsticks. Our lads were buried yonder without so much as a drum tapped or a musket fired; and that's not Christian burial for British soldiers.'

"'Phut!' says the trumpeter, and spat on the ground; 'a parcel of Marines!'

"The boy eyed him a second or so, and answered up. 'If I'd a tab of turf handy, I'd bung it at your mouth! you greasy cavalryman, and learn you to speak respectful of your betters. The Marines are the handiest body o' men in the service.'

"The trumpeter looked down on him from the height of six-foot two, and asked: 'Did they die well?'

"'They died very well. There was a lot of running to and fro at first, and some of the men began to cry, and a few to strip off their clothes. But when the ship fell off for the last time, Captain Mein turned and said something to Major Griffiths, the commanding officer on board, and the Major called out to me to beat to quarters. It might have been for a wedding, he sang it out so cheerful. We'd had word already that 'twas to be parade order; and the men fell in as trim and decent as if they were going to church. One or two even tried to shave at the last moment. The Major wore his medals. One of the seamen, seeing I had work to keep the drum steady—the sling being a bit loose for me, and the wind what you remember—lashed it tight with a piece of rope; and that saved my life afterwards, a drum being as good as a cork until it's stove. I kept beating away until every man was on deck; and then the Major formed them up and told them to die like British soldiers, and the chaplain read a prayer or two—the boys standin' all the while like rocks, each man's courage keeping up the other's. The chaplain was in the middle of a prayer when she struck. In ten minutes she was gone. That was how they died, cavalryman.'

"'And that was very well done, drummer of the Marines. What's your name?'

"'John Christian.'

"'Mine's William George Tallifer, trumpeter, of the 7th Light Dragoons—the Queen's Own. I played "God save the King" while our men were drowning. Captain Duncanfield told me to sound a call or two, to put them in heart; but that matter of "God save the King" was a notion of my own. I won't say anything to hurt the feelings of a Marine, even if he's not much over five-foot tall; but the Queen's Own Hussars is a tearin' fine regiment. As between horse and foot, 'tis a question o' which gets the chance. All the way from Sahagun to Corunna 'twas we that took and gave the knocks—at Mayorga and Rueda, and Bennyventy.' (The reason, sir, I can speak the names so pat, is that my father learnt 'em by heart afterwards. from the trumpeter, who was always talking about Mayorga and Rueda and Bennyventy.) 'We made the rear-guard, under General Paget; and drove the French every time; and all the infantry did was to sit about in wine-shops till we whipped 'em out, an' steal an' straggle an' play the tom-fool in general. And when it came to a stand-up fight at Corunna, 'twas we that had to stay sea-sick aboard the transports, an' watch the infantry in the thick o' the caper. Very well they behaved, too; 'specially the 4th Regiment, an' the 42nd Highlanders, an' the Dirty Half-Hundred. Oh, ay; they're decent regiments, all three. But the Queen's Own Hussars is a tearin' fine regiment. So you played on your drum when the ship was goin' down? Drummer John Christian, I'll have to get you a new pair o' drumsticks for that.'

"Well, sir, it appears that the very next day the trumpeter marched into Helston, and got a carpenter there to turn him a pair of box-wood drumsticks for the boy. And this was the beginning of one of the most curious friendships you ever heard tell of. Nothing delighted the pair more than to borrow a boat off my father and pull out to the rocks where the *Primrose* and the *Despatch* had struck and sunk; and on still days 'twas pretty to hear them out there off the Manacles, the drummer playing his tattoo—for they always took their music with them—and the trumpeter practising calls, and making his trumpet speak like an angel. But if the weather turned roughish, they'd be walking together and talking; leastwise, the youngster listened while the other discoursed about Sir John's campaign in Spain and Portugal, telling how each little skirmish befell; and of Sir John himself, and General Baird, and General Paget, and Colonel Vivian, his own commanding officer, and what kind of men they were; and of the last bloody stand-up at Corunna, and so forth, as if neither could have enough.

"But all this had to come to an end in the late summer, for the boy, John Christian, being now well and strong again, must go up to Plymouth to report himself. 'Twas his own wish (for I believe King George had forgotten all about him), but his friend wouldn't hold him back. As for the trumpeter, my father had made an arrangement to take him on as lodger, as soon as the boy left; and on the morning fixed for the start, he was up at the door here by five o'clock, with his trumpet slung by his side, and all the rest of his belongings in a small valise. A Monday morning it was, and after breakfast he had fixed to walk with the boy some way on the road towards Helston, where the coach started. My father left them at breakfast together, and went out to meat the pig, and do a few odd morning jobs of that sort. When he came back, the boy was still at table, and the trumpeter standing here by the chimney-place with the drum and trumpet in his hands, hitched together just as they be at this moment.

"'Look at this,' he says to my father, showing him the lock, 'I picked it up off a starving brass-worker in Lisbon, and it is not one of your common locks that one word of six letters will open at any time. There's *janius* in this lock; for you've only to make the rings spell any six-letter word you please and snap down the lock upon that, and never a soul can open it—not the maker, even—until somebody comes along that knows the word you snapped it on. Now, Johnny here's goin', and he leaves his drum behind him; for, though he can make pretty music on it, the parchment sags in wet weather, by reason of the sea-water getting at it; an' if he carries it to Plymouth, they'll only condemn it and give him another. And, as for me, I shan't have the heart to put lip to the trumpet any more when Johnny's gone. So we've chosen a word together, and locked 'em together upon that; and, by your leave, I'll hang 'em here together on the hook over your fireplace. Maybe Johnny'll come back; maybe not. Maybe, if he comes, I'll be dead an' gone, an' he'll take 'em apart an' try their music for old sake's sake. But if he never comes, nobody can separate 'em; for nobody beside knows the word. And if you marry and have sons, you can tell 'em that here are tied together the souls of Johnny Christian, drummer of the Marines, and William George Tallifer, once trumpeter of the Queen's Own Hussars. Amen.'

"With that he hung the two instruments 'pon the hook there; and the boy stood up and thanked my father and shook hands; and the pair went forth of the door, towards Helston.

"Somewhere on the road they took leave of one another; but nobody saw the parting, nor heard what was said between them. About three in the afternoon the trumpeter came walking back over the hill; and by the time my father came home from the fishing, the cottage was tidied up, and the tea ready, and the whole place shining like a new pin. From that time for five years he lodged here with my father, looking after the house and tilling the garden. And all the while he was steadily failing; the hurt in his head spreading, in a manner, to his limbs. My father watched the feebleness growing on him, but said nothing. And from first to last neither spake a word about the drummer, John Christian; nor did any letter reach them, nor word of his doings.

"The rest of the tale you'm free to believe, sir, or not, as you please. It stands upon my father's words, and he always declared he was ready to kiss the Book upon it, before judge and jury. He said, too, that he never had the wit to make up such a yarn; and he defied anyone to explain about the lock, in particular, by any other tale. But you shall judge for yourself.

"My father said that about three o'clock in the morning, April fourteenth, of the year 'fourteen, he and William Tallifer were sitting here, just as you and I, sir, are sitting now. My father had put on his clothes a few minutes before, and was mending his spiller by the light of the horn lantern, meaning to set off before daylight to haul the trammel. The trumpeter hadn't been to bed at all. Towards the last he mostly spent his nights (and his days, too) dozing in the elbow-chair where you sit at this minute. He was dozing then (my father said) with his chin dropped forward on his chest, when a knock sounded upon the door, and the door opened, and in walked an upright young man in scarlet regimentals.

"He had grown a brave bit, and his face was the colour of wood-ashes; but it was the drummer, John Christian. Only his uniform was different from the one he used to wear, and the figures '38' shone in brass upon his collar.

"The drummer walked past my father as if he never saw him, and stood by the elbow-chair and said:

"'Trumpeter, trumpeter, are you one with me?'

"And the trumpeter just lifted the lids of his eyes, and answered, 'How should I not be one with you, drummer Johnny—Johnny boy? If you come, I count: if you march, I mark time: until the discharge comes.'

"'The discharge has come tonight,' said the drummer; 'and the word is Corunna no longer.' And stepping to the chimney-place, he unhooked the drum and trumpet, and began to twist the brass rings of the lock, spelling the word aloud, so—C-O-R-U-N-A. When he had fixed the last letter, the padlock opened in his hand.

"'Did you know, trumpeter, that, when I came to Plymouth, they put me into a line regiment?'

"'The 38th is a good regiment,' answered the old Hussar, still in his dull voice; 'I went back with them from Sahagun to Corunna. At Corunna they stood in General Fraser's division, on the right. They behaved well.'

"'But I'd fain see the Marinys again,' says the drummer, handing him the trumpet; 'and you, you shall call once more for the Queen's Own. Matthew,' he says, suddenly, turning on my father—and when he turned, my father saw for the first time that his scarlet jacket had a round hole by the breast-bone, and that the blood was welling there—'Matthew, we shall want your boat.'

"Then my father rose on his legs like a man in a dream, while they two slung on, the one his drum, and t'other his trumpet. He took the lantern and went quaking before them down to the shore, and they breathed heavily behind him; and they stepped into his boat, and my father pushed off.

"'Row you first for Dolor Point,' says the drummer. So my father rowed them out past the white houses of Coverack to Dolor Point, and there, at a word, lay on his oars. And the trumpeter, William

Tallifer, put his trumpet to his mouth and sounded the *Revelly*. The music of it was like rivers running.

"'They will follow,' said the drummer. 'Matthew, pull you now for the Manacles.'

"So my father pulled for the Manacles, and came to an easy close outside Carn dû. And the drummer took his sticks and beat a tattoo, there by the edge of the reef: and the music of it was like a rolling chariot.

"'That will do,' says he, breaking off; 'they will follow. Pull now for the shore under Gunner's Meadow.'

"Then my father pulled for the shore and ran his boat in under Gunner's Meadow. And they stepped out, all three, and walked up to the meadow. By the gate the drummer halted, and began his tattoo again, looking out towards the darkness over the sea.

"And while the drum beat, and my father held his breath, there came up out of the sea and the darkness a troop of many men, horse and foot, and formed up among the graves; and others rose out of the graves and formed up—drowned Marines with bleached faces, and pale Hussars, riding their horses, all lean and shadowy. There was no clatter of hoofs or accoutrements, my father said, but a soft sound all the while like the beating of a bird's wing; and a black shadow lay like a pool about the feet of all. The drummer stood upon a little knoll just inside the gate, and beside him the tall trumpeter, with hand on hip, watching them gather; and behind them both my father, clinging to the gate. When no more came, the drummer stopped playing, and said, 'Call the roll.'

"Then the trumpeter stepped towards the end man of the rank and called, 'Troop Sergeant Major Thomas Irons,' and the man answered in a thin voice, 'Here!'

"'Troop Sergeant Major Thomas Irons, how is it with you?'

"The man answered, 'How should it be with me? When I was young, I betrayed a girl; and when I was grown, I betrayed a friend, and for these things I must pay. But I died as a man ought. God save the King!'

"The trumpeter called to the next man, 'Trooper Henry Buckingham!' and the next man answered, 'Here!'

"'Trooper Henry Buckingham, how is it with you?'

"'How should it be with me? I was a drunkard, and I stole, and in Lugo, in a wine-shop, I killed a man. But I died as a man should. God save the King!'

"So the trumpeter went down the line; and when he had finished, the drummer took it up, hailing the dead Marines in their order. Each man answered to his name, and each man ended with 'God save the King!' When all were hailed, the drummer stepped back to his mound, and called:

"'It is well. You are content, and we are content to join you. Wait, now, a little while.'

"With this he turned and ordered my father to pick up the lantern, and lead the way back. As my father picked it up, he heard the ranks of dead men cheer and call, 'God Save the King!' all together, and saw them waver and fade back into the dark, like a breath fading off a pane.

"But when they came back here to the kitchen, and my father set the lantern down, it seemed they'd both forgot about him. For the drummer turned in the lantern-light—and my father could see the blood still welling out of the hole in his breast—and took the trumpet-sling from around the other's neck, and locked drum and trumpet together again, choosing the letters on the lock very carefully. While he did this, he said:

"'The word is no more Corunna, but Bayonne. As you left out an "n" in Corunna, so must I leave out an "n" in Bayonne.' And before snapping the padlock, he spelt out the word slowly—'B-A-Y-O-N-E.' After that, he used no more speech; but turned and hung the two instruments back on the hook; and then took the trumpeter by the arm; and the pair walked out into the darkness, glancing neither to right nor left.

"My father was on the point of following, when he heard a sort of sigh behind him; and there, sitting in the elbow-chair, was the very trumpeter he had just seen walk out by the door! If my father's heart jumped before, you may believe it jumped quicker now. But after a bit, he went up to the man asleep in the chair and put a hand upon him. It was the trumpeter in flesh and blood that he touched; but though the flesh was warm, the trumpeter was dead.

"Well, sir, they buried him three days after; and at first my father was minded to say nothing about his dream (as he thought it). But the day after the funeral, he met Parson Kendall coming from Helston market; and the parson called out: 'Have'ee heard the news the coach brought down this mornin'?' 'What news?' says my father. 'Why, that peace is agreed upon.' 'None too soon,' says my father. 'Not soon enough for our poor lads at Bayonne,' the parson answered. 'Bayonne!' cries my father, with a jump. 'Why, yes'; and the parson told him all about a great sally the French had made on the night of April 13th. 'Do you happen to know if the 38th Regiment was engaged?' my father asked. 'Come, now,' said Parson Kendall, 'I didn't know you was so well up in the campaign. But, as it happens, I *do* know that the 38th was engaged, for 'twas they that held a cottage and stopped the French advance.'

"Still my father held his tongue; and when, a week later, he walked into Helston and bought a *Mercury* off the Sherborne rider, and got the landlord of the 'Angel' to spell out the list of killed and wounded, sure enough, there among the killed was Drummer John Christian, of the 38th Foot.

"After this, there was nothing for a religious man but to make a clean breast. So my father went up to Parson Kendall, and told the whole story. The parson listened, and put a question or two, and then asked:

"'Have you tried to open the lock since that night?'

"'I han't dared to touch it,' says my father.

"'Then come along and try.' When the parson came to the cottage here, he took the things off the hook and tried the lock. 'Did he say "*Bayonne?*" The word has seven letters.'

"'Not if you spell it with one "n" as *he* did,' says my father.

"The parson spelt it out—B-A-Y-O-N-E. 'Whew!' says he, for the lock had fallen open in his hand.

"He stood considering it a moment, and then he says, 'I tell you what. I shouldn't blab this all round the parish, if I was you. You won't get no credit for truth-telling, and a miracle's wasted on a set of fools. But if you like, I'll shut down the lock, again upon a holy word that no one but me shall know, and neither drummer nor trumpeter, dead nor alive, shall frighten the secret out of me.'

"'I wish to heaven you would, parson,' said my father.

"The parson chose the holy word there and then, and shut the lock back upon it, and hung the drum and trumpet back in their place. He is gone long since, taking the word with him. And till the lock is broken by force, nobody will ever separate those two."

ELLIOTT O'DONNELL

The Haunted Spinney

Elliott O'Donnell (1872–1965) was born in Clifton to an Irish father and an English mother. When O'Donnell was a child his father was murdered while travelling through Abyssinia (the former name for Ethiopia). Through his father, O'Donnell claimed to be the ancestor of ancient Celtic chieftains and dedicated his life to studying the Celtic world and investigating the paranormal. He enjoyed a diverse career, working as a rancher in Oregon, as a police officer in Chicago, and a schoolmaster in England before training as an actor in London. He served in the army in World War I then returned to the stage and screen. He mainly wrote in his spare time, publishing both popular fiction and serious investigations into the occult, its history, and paranormal events. He became such an authority on the supernatural that in the States he was referred to as "Mr. Ghosts", publishing over 50 books and appearing as an expert on television and radio. He published for many celebrated magazines, including *The Idler* and *Weird Tales* at the height of its success. We can think of O'Donnell as the first "celebrity ghost hunter", laying the foundations for *Most Haunted* and Derek Acorah. His interest in the paranormal, Celtic myths and legends, and his own experiences being raised in the South West collide in several of his short horror stories set in Cornwall. 'The Haunted Spinney' is explicitly inspired by his own research into hauntings and psychical phenomena and relies upon the geographical and cultural distance between

London and Cornwall. For the protagonist London is a site of safety, rationality, and civilisation, whereas Cornwall brings out the primitive barbarism of man. The narrative relies upon the outsider, the Londoner, being seen as more civilised and thus more trustworthy than the local people.

I

t was a cold night. Rain had been falling steadily not only for hours but days—the ground was saturated. As I walked along the country lane, the slush splashed over my boots and trousers. To my left was a huge stone wall, behind which I could see the nodding heads of firs, and through them the wind was rushing, making a curious whistling sound—now loud, now soft, roaring and gently murmuring. The sound fascinated me. I fancied it might be the angry voice of a man and the plaintive pleading of a woman, and then a weird chorus of unearthly beings, of grotesque things that stalked along the Cornish moors, and crept from behind huge boulders.

Nothing but the wind was to be heard. I stood and listened to it. I could have listened for hours, for I felt in harmony with my surroundings—lonely. The moon showed itself at intervals from behind the scudding clouds and lighted up the open landscape to my left. A gaunt hill covered with rocks, some piled up pyramidically, others strewn here and there; a few trees with naked arms tossing about and looking distressfully slim beside the more stalwart boulders; a sloping field or two, a couple of level ones, crossed by a tiny path, and the lane where I stood. The scenery was desolate—not actually wild, but sad and forlorn, and the spinney by my side lent an additional weird aspect to the place which was pleasing to me.

Suddenly I heard a sound—a familiar sound enough at other times, but at this hour and in this place everything seemed different.

A woman was coming along the road—a woman in a dark cloak with a basket under her arm, and the wind was blowing her skirts about her legs.

I looked at the trees. One singularly gaunt and fantastic one appalled me. It had long, gnarled arms, and two of them ended in bunches of twigs like hands—yes, they were exactly like hands—huge, murderous looking hands, with bony fingers. The moonlight played over and around me—I was bathed in it—I had no business to be on the earth—my proper place was in the moon—I no longer thought it—I knew it. The woman was close at hand. She stopped at a little wicket gate leading into the lane skirting the north walls of the spinney. I felt angry; what right had she to be there, interrupting my musings with the moon? The tree with the human hands appeared to agree with it. I saw anger in the movements of its branches—anger which soon blazed into fury as they gave a mighty bend towards her as if longing to rend her in pieces.

I followed the woman, and the wind howled louder and louder through those rustling leaves.

How long I scrambled on I do not know. As soon as the moonlight left me, I fell into a kind of slumber—a delicious trance—broken by nothing save the murmurings of the wind and the sighing and groaning of the winds—sweeter music I never heard. Then came a terrible change—the charm of my thoughts was broken, I awoke from my reverie.

A terrific roar broke on my ears and a perfect hurricane of rain swept through the woods. I crept cold and shivering beneath the shelter of the trees. To my surprise a hand fell on my shoulder; it was a man, and like myself he shivered.

"Who are you?" he whispered in a strangely hoarse voice. "Who are you? Why are you here?"

"You wouldn't believe me if I told you," I replied, shaking off his grasp.

"Well—tell me, for God's sake, man!" he was frightened, trembling with fright. Could it be the storm, or was it—was it those trees? I told him then and there why I had trespassed—I was fascinated—the wind, and the trees had led me thither.

"So am I," he whispered, "I am fascinated! It is a long word but it describes my sentiments. What did the wind sound like?"

I told him. He was a poor, common man, and had no poetical ideas—the wildly romantic had never interested him—he was but an ignorant labouring man.

"Sounded like sighing, groaning and so on?" he asked, shifting uneasily from one foot to another. He was cold, horribly cold. "Was that all?"

"Yes, of course! Why ask?" I replied. Then I laughed. This stupid, sturdy son of toil had been scared; to him the sounds had been those of his Cornish bogies—things he had dreaded in his infancy. I told him so. He didn't like to hear me make fun of him; he didn't like my laugh, and he persisted: "Was that all you heard?"

Then I grew impatient and asked him to explain what he meant.

"Well," he said, "I thought I heard a scream—a cry! Just as if someone had jumped out on someone else and taken them unawares! Maybe it was the wind—only the wind! but it had an eerie sound."

The man was nervous. The storm had frightened away whatever wits he may have possessed.

"Come, let us be going," I said, moving away in the direction of the wall. I wanted to find a new exit, I was tired of paths.

The man kept close to me. I could hear his teeth chatter. Accidentally I felt his hand brush against mine; his flesh was icy cold. He gave a cry as if a snake had bitten him. Then the truth flashed through me—the man was mad; his terror, his strange manner of showing it, and now this sudden shrinking from me, revealed it all—he was mad: the moon and trees had done their work.

"I'm not going that way," he said. "Come along with me; I want to see which of the trees it was that cried!"

His voice was changed, he seemed suddenly to have grown stranger. There was no insanity in his tone now, but I knew the cunning of the insane, and I feared to anger him, so I acquiesced. What an idea! One of the trees had cried; did he mean the wind? He grew sullen when I jeered at him. He led me to a little hollow in the ground, and I noticed the prints of several feet in the wet mud; then I saw something which sent the cold blood to my heart—a woman bathed in blood lay before me. Somehow she was familiar to me. I looked again—then again. Yes! there was the dark shawl, the basket, broken it was true, with the contents scattered, but it was the same basket; it was the woman I had seen coming down the road.

"My God! Whatever is this?" the man by my side spoke. He swayed backwards and forwards on his feet, his face white and awful in the moonlight—he was sick with terror.

"Oh, God! it is horrible! horrible!" Then with a sudden earnestness and a crafty look in his eyes he bent over her.

"Who is it?" he cried. "Who is the poor wretch?" I saw him peer into her face, but he didn't touch her—he dreaded the blood. Then he started back, his eyes filled with such savageness as I had never seen in any man's before; he looked a devil—he was a devil. "It's my wife!" he shrieked. "My wife!" His voice fell and turned into what sounded like a sob. "It's Mary! She was coming back to St. Ives. It was her cry! There—see it—confound you! You have it on your arm—your coat—it is all over you!" He raised his hand to strike me; the moonlight fell on it—a great coarse hand, and I noticed with a thrill of horror a red splash on it—it was blood! The man was a murderer! He had killed her, and with all the cunning of the madman was trying to throw the guilt on me.

I sprang at him with a cry of despair. He kicked, hit, and tried to tear my arms from his neck; but somehow I seemed to have ten times my usual strength. And all the while we struggled a sea of faces waved to and fro, peering down at us from the gaunt trees above.

He gave in at length; and I held him no longer with the iron grip, and help came in the shape of a policeman.

The man seemed to grasp the situation easily. There had been a murder, the man whom I had secured was known to him. He was a labouring man, of unsteady habits; he had been drinking, had met and quarrelled with his wife. The rest was to be seen in the ghastly heap before us.

The wretch had no defence, he seemed dazed, and eyed the bloodstains on his face and clothes in a stupid kind of way.

I slipped five shillings into the policeman's hand when we parted. He thanked me and pocketed the money; he knew his position and mine too—I was a gentleman and a very plucky one at that. So I thought as I walked back to my rooms, yet I lay awake and shuddered as visions of the nodding heads of trees rose before me, and from without, across the silent rows of houses, lanes and fields, there rose and fell again the wailing of a woman—of a woman in distress.

II

The murder in the spinney was an event in St. Ives; the people were unused to such tragedies, and it afforded them conversation for many weeks. The evidence against the husband was conclusive, he had been caught red-handed, he was an habitual drunkard, and he paid the penalty for his crime in the usual manner. I left St. Ives; I had seen enough of Cornwall, and thirsted for life in London once more, yet often at night, the sighing of the wind in the trees sounded in my ears and bid me visit them once more. One day as I was sitting by my fire with a pile of magazines by my side, taking life easily, for I had nothing to do but kill time, my old friend Frank Wedmore looked me up. We had been at Clifton together in the far off eighties, and he was the only friend of the old set of whom I had lost sight.

He had not altered so much, in spite of a moustache and a fair sprinkling of white hairs. I should have known him had I met him anywhere. He was wearing a Chesterfield coat, very spruce and smart, and his face was red with healthy exercise.

"How are you, old chap?" he exclaimed, shaking hands in the hearty fashion of true friendship. I winced, for he had strong hands.

"Oh, fit enough," I said, "but a bit bored. But you—well, you look just the same, and fresh as a daisy." I gave him the easy chair.

"Oh, I'm first rate—plenty of work. I'm a journalist, you know. Plenty of grind, but I'm taking a bit of holiday. You look pale. Your eyes are bad?"

I told him they got strained if I read much.

"I daresay you will think me mad," he went on, "but I'm going to ask you rather a curious question. I remember you used to be fond of ghosts and all sorts of queer things."

I nodded. We had many such discussions in my study at school.

"Well, I am a member of the Psychical Research Society."

I smiled doubtfully. "Well, you can't say they have discovered much. The name is high-sounding, but nothing beyond."

"Never mind. Some day, perhaps, we shall show the public that at present it is only in the early stages of investigation."

Wedmore lit a cigarette, puffed away in silence for a few seconds, and then went on:—

"I am undertaking a little work for the Society now."

"Where?"

"In Cornwall. Ever been there?" I nodded. Wedmore was very much at his ease.

"Been to St. Ives?"

I knew by instinct he would mention the place. He thought I looked ill, and told me I had been overdoing it.

"It is merely a case of 'flu,'" I assured him. "I had it six weeks ago, and still feel the effects." The woman in the hollow was before me; I saw again her shabby shawl and the blood round her throat.

"There was a murder down there, a short time ago."

"I heard of it," I remarked casually, "It was a wife murder, I believe."

"Yes! just a common wife murder, and the fellow was caught and hanged."

"Then why the ghost?"

"Well, that is the odd part of it," Wedmore said slowly, leaning back in his chair, his long legs stretched out. "I have heard from two St. Ives artists—I beg their pardon, golfists—that screams have been heard in the spinney about twelve o'clock at night. Not the time for practical jokers, and the Cornish are too superstitious to try their pranks in unsavoury spots. And from what I heard, the spot is singularly uncanny."

"They haven't seen anything?" I asked.

"No. Only heard the cries, and they are so terribly realistic and appalling that no one cares to pass the place at night; indeed, it is utterly banned. I mentioned the case to old Potters—you may have heard of him, he is the author of 'When the Veil is Cleared Away'— and he pressed me to go down and investigate. I agreed—then I thought I would look you up. Do you recollect your pet aversion in the way of ghosts?"

I nodded. "Yes, and I still have the aversion. I think locality exercises strange influence over some minds. The peaceful meadow scenery holds no lurking horrors in its bosom, but in the lonesome moorlands, full of curiously moulded boulders, grotesque weakness must affect one there—creatures seem to come, odd and ill-defined as their surroundings. As a child I had a peculiar horror of those tall, odd-shaped boulders, with seeming faces—featureless, it is true, but sometimes strangely resembling humans and animals. I believe the spinney may be haunted by something of this nature—terrible as the trees!"

"You know the spinney?"

"I do. And I know the trees." Again in my ears the wind rushed, as it had on the night in question.

"Will you come with me?" Wedmore eyed me eagerly. The same old affection he had once entertained for me was ripening in his eyes; indeed, it had always remained there. Should I go? An irresistible impulse seized me, a morbid craving to look once more at the blood-stained hollow, to hear again the wind. I looked out of the window, the sky was cold and grey. There were rows and rows of chimneys everywhere, a sea of chimneys, an ocean of dull, uninviting smoke. I began to hate London and to long for the countless miles of blue sea, and the fresh air of the woods. I assented, when better judgment would have led me to refuse.

"Yes; I will go. As for the ghost, it may be there, but it is not as you think, it is not the apparition of a man, it may be in part like a man, but it is one of those cursed nightmares I have always had; I shall see it, hear it shriek, and if I drop dead from fright you, old man, will be to blame."

Wedmore was an enthusiast, psychical adventure always allured him, and he would run the risk of my weak heart, and have me with him.

A thousand times I prepared to go back on my word, a thousand tumultuous emotions of some impending disaster rushed through me. I felt on the border of an abyss, dark and hopeless; I was pushed on by invisible and unfriendly hands; I knew I must fall, knew that the black depths in front would engulf me eternally. I took the plunge. We talked over Clifton days, and arranged our train to the west. Wedmore looked very boyish I thought as he arose to go, and stood smiling his good-bye in the doorway.

He was all kindness, I liked him more than ever. I felt my heart go out to him, and yet, somehow, as we stood looking at one another, a grey shadow swept around him, and an icy pang shot through my heart.

III

It was night once more, and the moonlight poured in floods from over the summit of the knoll where the uncanny boulders lay. Every obstacle stood silhouetted against the dark background. A house with its white walls stood grim and silent, the paths running in various directions up and alongside the hill were made doubly clear in the whiteness of the beams that fell on them. There were no swift clouds, nothing to hide the brilliance of the stars, and it was nearly midnight. The air was cold—colder than is usual in St. Ives. The lights of many boats twinkled on the bay, and Godrevy stood out boldly away to the right, looking not more than a mile or so away. There were no lights to be seen in St. Ives itself. The town was absolutely still and dark; not a voice, not a sound, not even the baying of a dog.

It was very ghostly, and I shivered.

Wedmore stood by my side. I glanced apprehensively at him. Why did he stand in the moonlight? What business had he there? I laughed, but I fear there was but little mirth in the sound.

"I wish you would stop that infernal noise!" he said. "I am pretty nervous as it is."

"All right," I whispered. "I won't do it again." But I did, and he edged sharply away from me. I looked over his head; there was the gaunt tree with the great hands—I fancied the branches were once again fingers; I told him so.

"For God's sake, man, keep quiet," he replied. "You are enough to upset anyone's nerves." He pulled out his watch for the hundredth time. "It's close on the hour."

I again looked at the trees and listened. Suddenly, although there had been absolute silence before, I heard a faint breathing sound, a very gentle murmur. It came from over the distant knoll. Very soft and low, but gradually louder and louder, and then as it rushed past us into the spinney beyond, I saw once more the great trees rock beneath it, and again came those voices—those of the woman and the man.

Wedmore looked ill, very ill I thought. I touched him on the arm. "You are frightened," I said. "You, a member of the Research Society, you afraid?"

"Something is going to happen!" he gasped. "I felt it, I know it—we shall see the murder—we shall know the secret of death! What is that?"

Away in the distance the tapping of shoes came through the still night air. Tap—tap—tap—down the path from the knoll. I clutched Wedmore by the arm. "You think you will see the murder, do you? And the murderer?"

Wedmore didn't answer, his breath came in gasps; he looked about him like a man at bay.

"And the murderer! Ha! It comes from there! See, it is looking at us from those trees. It is all arms and legs, it has no human face. It will drop to the earth, and then we shall see what happens!"

Tap—tap—tap. The steps grew louder—nearer and nearer they came. The great shadows from the trees stole down one by one to meet them.

I looked again at Wedmore, he was fearfully expectant; so was I.

A woman came tripping along the path; I knew her in an instant—there was the shabby shawl, the basket on her arm—it was the same. She approached the wicket. I looked at Wedmore, he was spellbound with fear; I touched his arm. I dragged him with me.

"Come!" I whispered, "we shall see which of us is right. You think the ghostly murderer will resemble us—resemble men. It won't. Come!" I dragged him forward. Had it not been for me he would have fled, but I was firm. We passed through the gate; we followed the figure as it silently glided on. We turned to the left. The place grew very dark as the trees met overhead.

I heard the trickling of water and knew we were close to the ditch.

I gazed intently at the trees; when would the horror drop from them? A sickly terror laid hold of me. I turned to fly.

To my surprise Wedmore stopped me; he was all excitement. "Wait!" he hissed, "wait! It is you who are afraid. Hark! It is twelve o'clock!"

And as he spoke, the clock of the parish church slowly tolled midnight.

Then the end came.

An awful scream rang out, so piercing and so full of terror that I felt the blood in my heart stand still. But no figure dropped from the trees. Not from the trees, but from behind the woman a form darted forward, and seized her round the neck; it tore at her throat with its hands, it dragged and hurried her into the moonlight, and then, oh! damning horror, I saw its face—it was my own.

The world in general laughed at the strange tale of Francis Wedmore.

The madman he had led at midnight, gibbering into St. Ives, did not convince the sceptical readers of the London dailies with his corroboration. But the St. Ives people knew and understood. It is on account of that the spinney so soon lost its ghosts, though the wind whistles as dismally there as ever.

E. M. BRAY

A Ghostly Visitation
A True Incident

This very short, strange story builds upon an existing tradition of Gothic tourist fiction set in Cornwall. Gothic tourism or dark tourism refers to travellers seeking out frightening places, such as former prisons and asylums, death sites, cemeteries, and even scary or morbid theme park attractions, like London Dungeons. Travellers have a long history of specifically seeking out places that scare and threaten them in a safe and exciting way, either because the darkness of the tourist site is historical or because mechanisms are in place to protect the tourist. The history of dark tourism is inextricable from Cornwall's own history. One of the first "package holidays" offered by the travel agent Thomas Cook was a rail journey to Bodmin jail in Cornwall where travellers could witness the hangings of criminals from the safety of their carriage. 'A Ghostly Visitation' features a woman on holiday, though importantly she is travelling alone. Women travelling alone is a recurrent theme in these narratives, and often ends in death, or worse—social judgment and moral degradation. The fear of increased mobility threatening social order motivates many stories throughout the nineteenth century.

April 11. —— Hotel, ——, Cornwall.

Such a lovely spring day. We arrive at length at the private hotel, where I am quite effusively received by the stout landlady.

She tells me that her brother has given her many instructions for my welfare, and she then proceeds to show me her two vacant bedrooms. One is on the first floor, a rather miserable little room, so small in fact that it seems to be entirely occupied by the huge double bed. The other room is on a higher floor and is very spacious and better furnished, but too large for any feeling of homeliness. This room, however, my landlady is very anxious I should occupy. I note, curiously enough, that it is the less expensive despite its size.

Explaining what a disadvantage so many stairs would be to me we return to the small room, and I desire to take it, but I can plainly see that the landlady is not pleased with my decision.

Now I am back again on my perch on the cliff, and I have been sitting and thinking of tomorrow night. I know so well how I shall be missing the howl of the wind and the shrill mew of the sea birds as they wing their way close under the cliff.

April 13. —— Private Hotel, ——, Cornwall.

I was so busy unpacking and getting settled in my new quarters that I had no time for an entry in my diary yesterday. But now as I take up my pen my hand shakes with the thought of what I am about to write.

Last night, feeling very tired, I went early to my room, and was soon ready for sleep. I had just put out my light when I became conscious that there was Someone standing between my bed and the dressing table.

I felt very annoyed, but not in the least frightened. *It* remained in the same spot until three o'clock that morning. I was conscious of *its* departure, and the moment it had gone I was able to sleep.

I have said nothing to anyone, but have noted that my landlady was careful in her inquiries as to how I had slept.

April 14. —— Private Hotel, ——, Cornwall.

Last night I again retired early to bed. Having put out my light I was at once conscious of a presence in the room. Unluckily great nervousness took hold on me so that I was unable to reach out my hand to get the matchbox.

Then I flounced round as a child will in anger and turned my back on the *thing*, which stood exactly in the same position as on the previous night.

Then I said aloud, "I don't care! You can stay there as long as ever you like; whoever you are, I'm going to sleep." As I uttered the last word I knew to my horror that *it* had come close to my bedside, and before I could move had struck me a stinging blow on the side of the temple with two of *its* fingers. It then left me...

My landlady looked quite anxious this morning when I came down, but I assured her that I had slept well.

April 15. —— Private Hotel, ——, Cornwall.

This evening I lighted my candle before entering my room. As I came into the room I saw that Someone was standing there. It was a tall, dark, very handsome woman; her eyes were black and piercing, and she was dressed in deep mourning with a mantilla over her head, which was neatly crossed on her bosom; the arms, which were well shaped and very white, were bare to the elbow.

At that moment all feeling of nervousness left me, especially as I could hear other people moving in the house.

I walked up to her and said:—

"Is there anything I can do for you? Perhaps there is some message I can take to someone for you?"

Without looking at me she replied:—

"There may be; I can't tell. There may be." And her voice was the most sorrowful I have ever heard.

"Is it a name you have forgotten; perhaps the name of Christ?" I ventured to ask. But she did not reply and appeared to be thinking very deeply.

"Why did you strike me the other night?" I asked. She replied very quickly:—

"You would not take any notice of me and I thought that you might be able to help me. I was very angry at the time. I suffer." This with a deep sigh.

"Do you think it would help you if I prayed for you?" I said; and then without waiting for a reply I dropped on to my knees by the bedside. No prayer came to my lips, and in my distress I could only remember the opening sentences of the Litany. I repeated the first sentences over three times, thinking that something must happen at the third, when as I began to say the well-known words she sank on her knees at my side and repeated each word after me. Then she sprang from her knees and was gone before I had uncovered my eyes.

April 18. —— Private Hotel, ——, Cornwall.

There has been nothing to record these last few days. My dark ghost lady has not visited me again, consequently I have slept peacefully.

April 19. —— Private Hotel, ——, Cornwall.

This afternoon just as it was beginning to get dusk I was sitting before my window looking out over the sea.

Suddenly there sailed across the sky a huge figure bearing something dark in its arms.

It came nearer and then paused between sea and sky, and once again I saw my ghost lady, now lying in the arms of this monster figure.

She looked at me and smiling said:—

"It is well; all is well, and there are many of us." Then she was borne away, and I saw as through a veil that there were many shadowy figures in her wake.

These too passed away, and I was left alone bewildered and wondering.

F. MARION CRAWFORD

The Screaming Skull

Francis Marion Crawford (1854–1909) was a novelist specialising in weird fiction. He was born in Italy to an American sculptor and studied around the world, in New Hampshire, Cambridge University, the University of Heidelberg, the University of Rome, and Harvard University. He studied Sanskrit in India and as a scholar researched his novels and short stories extensively. From 1897–1898 he travelled America and delivered lectures while researching his latest historical novel, *Marietta* (1901), set in a glass-making workshop in Venice. While visiting a glass works he suffered a severe lung injury which led to his death a decade later in 1909. Few of his works would be familiar to readers today, but they were extensively adapted into films, leading to a lawsuit from his widow. *The White Sister* (1909) was adapted many times, including a 1933 version starring Clark Gable. It draws heavily from an earlier Gothic tradition, featuring star-crossed lovers, aristocrats, freak deaths, a kidnapping and nuns in Italy, reminiscent of Ann Radcliffe and Horace Walpole. Many of Crawford's works were set in Italy, and Cornwall was not too much of a stretch—in the nineteenth century it was advertised as the Cornish Riviera, with Mediterranean waters and climate, and maps of Italy and Cornwall were often sat beside each other in tourist promotional materials to exaggerate the similarities of the peninsulas. 'The Screaming Skull' follows the tradition of old mariner's tales, and like many of Crawford's works was adapted into a pulp horror film in 1958. The sea captain is replaced by an anxious housewife and the story is transplanted from Cornwall to the United States. Crawford's narrative, however, is dependent upon Cornwall's cultural connections to its seascape and abundance of legends of haunted shores.

have often heard it scream. No, I am not nervous, I am not imaginative, and I never believed in ghosts, unless that thing is one. Whatever it is, it hates me almost as much as it hated Luke Pratt, and it screams at me.

If I were you, I would never tell ugly stories about ingenious ways of killing people, for you never can tell but that some one at the table may be tired of his or her nearest and dearest. I have always blamed myself for Mrs. Pratt's death, and I suppose I was responsible for it in a way, though heaven knows I never wished her anything but long life and happiness. If I had not told that story she might be alive yet. That is why the thing screams at me, I fancy.

She was a good little woman, with a sweet temper, all things considered, and a nice gentle voice; but I remember hearing her shriek once when she thought her little boy was killed by a pistol that went off, though every one was sure that it was not loaded. It was the same scream; exactly the same, with a sort of rising quaver at the end; do you know what I mean? Unmistakable.

The truth is, I had not realised that the doctor and his wife were not on good terms. They used to bicker a bit now and then when I was here, and I often noticed that little Mrs. Pratt got very red and bit her lip hard to keep her temper, while Luke grew pale and said the most offensive things. He was that sort when he was in the nursery, I remember, and afterward at school. He was my cousin, you know; that is how I came by this house; after he died, and his boy Charley was killed in South Africa, there were no relations left.

Yes, it's a pretty little property, just the sort of thing for an old sailor like me who has taken to gardening.

One always remembers one's mistakes much more vividly than one's cleverest things, doesn't one? I've often noticed it. I was dining with the Pratts one night, when I told them the story that afterwards made so much difference. It was a wet night in November, and the sea was moaning. Hush!—if you don't speak you will hear it now...

Do you hear the tide? Gloomy sound, isn't it? Sometimes, about this time of year—hallo!—there it is! Don't be frightened, man—it won't eat you—it's only a noise, after all! But I'm glad you've heard it, because there are always people who think it's the wind, or my imagination, or something. You won't hear it again tonight, I fancy, for it doesn't often come more than once. Yes—that's right. Put another stick on the fire, and a little more stuff into that weak mixture you're so fond of. Do you remember old Blauklot the carpenter, on that German ship that picked us up when the *Clontarf* went to the bottom? We were hove to in a howling gale one night, as snug as you please, with no land within five hundred miles, and the ship coming up and falling off as regularly as clockwork—"Biddy te boor beebles ashore tis night, poys!" old Blauklot sang out, as he went off to his quarters with the sail-maker. I often think of that, now that I'm ashore for good and all.

Yes, it was on a night like this, when I was at home for a spell, waiting to take the *Olympia* out on her first trip—it was on the next voyage that she broke the record, you remember—but that dates it. Ninety-two was the year, early in November.

The weather was dirty, Pratt was out of temper, and the dinner was bad, very bad indeed, which didn't improve matters, and cold, which made it worse. The poor little lady was very unhappy about it, and insisted on making a Welsh rarebit on the table to counteract the raw turnips and the half-boiled mutton. Pratt must have had a hard day. Perhaps he had lost a patient. At all events, he was in a nasty temper.

"My wife is trying to poison me, you see!" he said. "She'll succeed some day." I saw that she was hurt, and I made believe to laugh, and said that Mrs. Pratt was much too clever to get rid of her husband in such a simple way; and then I began to tell them about Japanese tricks with spun glass and chopped horsehair and the like.

Pratt was a doctor, and knew a lot more than I did about such things, but that only put me on my mettle, and I told a story about a woman in Ireland who did for three husbands before any one suspected foul play.

Did you never hear that tale? The fourth husband managed to keep awake and caught her, and she was hanged. How did she do it? She drugged them, and poured melted lead into their ears through a little horn funnel when they were asleep... No—that's the wind whistling. It's backing up to the southward again. I can tell by the sound. Besides, the other thing doesn't often come more than once in an evening even at this time of year—when it happened. Yes, it was in November. Poor Mrs. Pratt died suddenly in her bed not long after I dined here. I can fix the date, because I got the news in New York by the steamer that followed the *Olympia* when I took her out on her first trip. You had the *Leofric* the same year? Yes, I remember. What a pair of old buffers we are coming to be, you and I. Nearly fifty years since we were apprentices together on the *Clontarf.* Shall you ever forget old Blauklot? "Biddy te boor beebles ashore, poys!" Ha, ha! Take a little more, with all that water. It's the old Hulstkamp I found in the cellar when this house came to me, the same I brought Luke from Amsterdam five-and-twenty years ago. He had never touched a drop of it. Perhaps he's sorry now, poor fellow.

Where did I leave off? I told you that Mrs. Pratt died suddenly—yes. Luke must have been lonely here after she was dead, I should think; I came to see him now and then, and he looked worn and nervous, and told me that his practice was growing too heavy for him, though he wouldn't take an assistant on any account. Years went on, and his son was killed in South Africa, and after that he began to be queer. There was something about him not like other people. I believe he kept his senses in his profession to the end; there was no complaint of his having made bad mistakes in cases, or anything of that sort, but he had a look about him—

Luke was a red-headed man with a pale face when he was young, and he was never stout; in middle age he turned a sandy grey, and after his son died he grew thinner and thinner, till his head looked like a skull with parchment stretched over it very tight, and his eyes had a sort of glare in them that was very disagreeable to look at.

He had an old dog that poor Mrs. Pratt had been fond of, and that used to follow her everywhere. He was a bull-dog, and the sweetest tempered beast you ever saw, though he had a way of hitching his upper lip behind one of his fangs that frightened strangers a good deal. Sometimes, of an evening, Pratt and Bumble—that was the dog's name—used to sit and look at each other a long time, thinking about old times, I suppose, when Luke's wife used to sit in that chair you've got. That was always her place, and this was the doctor's, where I'm sitting. Bumble used to climb up by the footstool—he was old and fat by that time, and could not jump much, and his teeth were getting shaky. He would look steadily at Luke, and Luke looked steadily at the dog, his face growing more and more like a skull with two little coals for eyes; and after about five minutes or so, though it may have been less, old Bumble would suddenly begin to shake all over, and all on a sudden he would set up an awful howl, as if he had been shot, and tumble out of the easy-chair and trot away, and hide himself under the sideboard, and lie there making odd noises.

Considering Pratt's looks in those last months, the thing is not surprising, you know. I'm not nervous or imaginative, but I can quite believe he might have sent a sensitive woman into hysterics—his head looked so much like a skull in parchment.

At last I came down one day before Christmas, when my ship was in dock and I had three weeks off. Bumble was not about, and I said casually that I supposed the old dog was dead.

"Yes," Pratt answered, and I thought there was something odd in his tone even before he went on after a little pause. "I killed him," he said presently. "I could not stand it any longer."

I asked what it was that Luke could not stand, though I guessed well enough.

"He had a way of sitting in her chair and glaring at me, and then howling." Luke shivered a little. "He didn't suffer at all, poor old Bumble," he went on in a hurry, as if he thought I might imagine be had been cruel. "I put dionine into his drink to make him sleep soundly, and then I chloroformed him gradually, so that he could not have felt suffocated even if he was dreaming. It's been quieter since then."

I wondered what he meant, for the words slipped out as if he could not help saying them. I've understood since. He meant that he did not hear that noise so often after the dog was out of the way. Perhaps he thought at first that it was old Bumble in the yard howling at the moon, though it's not that kind of noise, is it? Besides, I know what it is, if Luke didn't. It's only a noise, after all, and a noise never hurt anybody yet. But he was much more imaginative than I am. No doubt there really is something about this place that I don't understand; but when I don't understand a thing, I call it a phenomenon, and I don't take it for granted that it's going to kill me, as he did. I don't understand everything, by long odds, nor do you, nor does any man who has been to sea. We used to talk of tidal waves, for instance, and we could not account for them; now we account for them by calling them submarine earthquakes, and we branch off into fifty theories, any one of which might make earthquakes quite comprehensible if we only knew what they are. I fell in with one of them once, and the ink-stand flew straight up from the table against the ceiling of my cabin. The same thing happened to Captain Lecky—I dare say you've read about it in his "Wrinkles." Very good. If that sort of thing took place ashore, in this room for instance, a nervous person would talk about spirits and levitation and fifty things that mean nothing, instead of just quietly setting it down as a "phenomenon" that has not been explained yet. My view of that voice, you see.

Besides, what is there to prove that Luke killed his wife? I would not even suggest such a thing to any one but you. After all, there was nothing but the coincidence that poor little Mrs. Pratt died suddenly in her bed a few days after I told that story at dinner. She was not the only woman who ever died like that. Luke got the doctor over from the next parish, and they agreed that she had died of something the matter with her heart. Why not? It's common enough.

Of course, there was the ladle. I never told anybody about that, and it made me start when I found it in the cupboard in the bedroom. It was new, too—a little tinned iron ladle that had not been in the fire more than once or twice, and there was some lead in it that had been melted, and stuck to the bottom of the bowl, all grey, with hardened dross on it. But that proves nothing. A country doctor is generally a handy man, who does everything for himself, and Luke may have had a dozen reasons for melting a little lead in a ladle. He was fond of sea-fishing, for instance, and he may have cast a sinker for a night-line; perhaps it was a weight for the hall clock, or some thing like that. All the same, when I found it I had a rather queer sensation, because it looked so much like the thing I had described when I told them the story. Do you understand? It affected me unpleasantly, and I threw it away; it's at the bottom of the sea a mile from the Spit, and it will be jolly well rusted beyond recognising if it's ever washed up by the tide.

You see, Luke must have bought it in the village, years ago, for the man sells just such ladles still. I suppose they are used in cooking. In any case, there was no reason why an inquisitive housemaid should find such a thing lying about, with lead in it, and wonder what it was, and perhaps talk to the maid who heard me tell the story at dinner—for that girl married the plumber's son in the village, and may remember the whole thing.

You understand me, don't you? Now that Luke Pratt is dead and gone, and lies buried beside his wife, with an honest man's tombstone at his head, I should not care to stir up anything that could hurt his memory. They are both dead, and their son, too. There was trouble enough about Luke's death, as it was.

How? He was found dead on the beach one morning, and there was a coroner's inquest. There were marks on his throat, but he had not been robbed. The verdict was that he had come to his end "by the hands or teeth of some person or animal unknown," for half the jury thought it might have been a big dog that had thrown him down and gripped his windpipe, though the skin of his throat was not broken. No one knew at what time he had gone out, nor where he had been. He was found lying on his back above high-water mark, and an old cardboard bandbox that had belonged to his wife lay under his hand, open. The lid had fallen off. He seemed to

299

have been carrying home a skull in the box—doctors are fond of collecting such things. It had rolled out and lay near his head, and it was a remarkably fine skull, rather small, beautifully shaped and very white, with perfect teeth. That is to say, the upper jaw was perfect, but there was no lower one at all, when I first saw it.

Yes, I found it here when I came. You see, it was very white and polished, like a thing meant to be kept under a glass case, and the people did not know where it came from, nor what to do with it; so they put it back into the bandbox and set it on the shelf of the cupboard in the best bedroom, and of course they showed it to me when I took possession. I was taken down to the beach, too, to be shown the place where Luke was found, and the old fisherman explained just how he was lying, and the skull beside him. The only point he could not explain was why the skull had rolled up the sloping sand toward Luke's head instead of rolling downhill to his feet. It did not seem odd to me at the time, but I have often thought of it since, for the place is rather steep. I'll take you there tomorrow if you like—I made a sort of cairn of stones there afterward.

When he fell down, or was thrown down—whichever happened—the bandbox struck the sand, and the lid came off, and the thing came out and ought to have rolled down. But it didn't. It was close to his head, almost touching it, and turned with the face toward it. I say it didn't strike me as odd when the man told me; but I could not help thinking about it afterward, again and again, till I saw a picture of it all when I closed my eyes; and then I began to ask myself why the plaguey thing had rolled up instead of down, and why it had stopped near Luke's head instead of anywhere else, a yard away, for instance.

You naturally want to know what conclusion I reached, don't you? None that at all explained the rolling, at all events. But I got something else into my head, after a time, that made me feel down-right uncomfortable.

Oh, I don't mean as to anything supernatural! There may be ghosts, or there may not be. If there are, I'm not inclined to believe that they can hurt living people except by frightening them, and, for my part, I would rather face any shape of ghost than a fog in the Channel when it's crowded. No. What bothered me was just a foolish idea, that's all, and I cannot tell how it began, nor what made it grow till it turned into a certainty.

I was thinking about Luke and his poor wife one evening over my pipe and a dull book, when it occurred to me that the skull might possibly be hers, and I have never got rid of the thought since. You'll tell me there's no sense in it, no doubt; that Mrs. Pratt was buried like a Christian and is lying in the churchyard where they put her, and that it's perfectly monstrous to suppose her husband kept her skull in her old bandbox in his bedroom. All the same, in the face of reason, and common sense, and probability, I'm convinced that he did. Doctors do all sorts of queer things that would make men like you and me feel creepy, and those are just the things that don't seem probable, nor logical, nor sensible to us.

Then, don't you see?—if it really was her skull, poor woman, the only way of accounting for his having it is that he really killed her, and did it in that way, as the woman killed her husbands in the story, and that he was afraid there might be an examination some day which would betray him. You see, I told that too, and I believe it had really happened some fifty or sixty years ago. They dug up the three skulls, you know, and there was a small lump of lead rattling about in each one. That was what hanged the woman. Luke remembered that, I'm sure. I don't want to know what he did when he thought of it; my taste never ran in the direction of horrors, and

I don't fancy you care for them either, do you? No. If you did, you might supply what is wanting to the story.

It must have been rather grim, eh? I wish I did not see the whole thing so distinctly, just as everything must have happened. He took it the night before she was buried, I'm sure, after the coffin had been shut, and when the servant girl was asleep. I would bet anything, that when he'd got it, he put something under the sheet in its place, to fill up and look like it. What do you suppose he put there, under the sheet?

I don't wonder you take me up on what I'm saying! First I tell you that I don't want to know what happened, and that I hate to think about horrors, and then I describe the whole thing to you as if I had seen it. I'm quite sure that it was her work-bag that he put there. I remember the bag very well, for she always used it of an evening; it was made of brown plush, and when it was stuffed full it was about the size of—you understand. Yes, there I am, at it again! You may laugh at me, but you don't live here alone, where it was done, and you didn't tell Luke the story about the melted lead. I'm not nervous, I tell you, but sometimes I begin to feel that I understand why some people are. I dwell on all this when I'm alone, and I dream of it, and when that thing screams—well, frankly, I don't like the noise any more than you do, though I should be used to it by this time.

I ought not to be nervous. I've sailed in a haunted ship. There was a Man in the Top, and two-thirds of the crew died of the West Coast fever inside of ten days after we anchored; but I was all right, then and afterward. I have seen some ugly sights, too, just as you have, and all the rest of us. But nothing ever stuck in my head in the way this does.

You see, I've tried to get rid of the thing, but it doesn't like that. It wants to be there in its place, in Mrs. Pratt's bandbox in the cupboard in the best bedroom. It's not happy anywhere else. How do I know that? Because I've tried it. You don't suppose that I've not tried, do you? As long as it's there it only screams now and then, generally at this time of year, but if I put it out of the house it goes on all night, and no servant will stay here twenty-four hours. As it is, I've often been left alone and have been obliged to shift for myself for a fortnight at a time. No one from the village would ever pass a night under the roof now, and as for selling the place, or even letting it, that's out of the question. The old women say that if I stay here I shall come to a bad end myself before long.

I'm not afraid of that. You smile at the mere idea that any one could take such nonsense seriously. Quite right. It's utterly blatant nonsense, I agree with you. Didn't I tell you that it's only a noise after all when you started and looked round as if you expected to see a ghost standing behind your chair?

I may be all wrong about the skull, and I like to think that I am—when I can. It may be just a fine specimen which Luke got somewhere long ago, and what rattles about inside when you shake it may be nothing but a pebble, or a bit of hard clay, or anything. Skulls that have lain long in the ground generally have something inside them that rattles, don't they? No, I've never tried to get it out, whatever it is; I'm afraid it might be lead, don't you see? And if it is, I don't want to know the fact, for I'd much rather not be sure. If it really is lead, I killed her quite as much as if I had done the deed myself. Anybody must see that, I should think. As long as I don't know for certain, I have the consolation of saying that it's all utterly ridiculous nonsense, that Mrs. Pratt died a natural death and that the beautiful skull belonged to Luke when he was a student in London. But if I were quite sure, I believe I should have to leave the house; indeed

I do, most certainly. As it is, I had to give up trying to sleep in the best bedroom where the cupboard is.

You ask me why I don't throw it into the pond—yes, but please don't call it a "confounded bugbear"—it doesn't like being called names.

There! Lord, what a shriek! I told you so! You're quite pale, man. Fill up your pipe and draw your chair nearer to the fire, and take some more drink. Old Hollands never hurt anybody yet. I've seen a Dutchman in Java drink half a jug of Hulstkamp in a morning without turning a hair. I don't take much rum myself, because it doesn't agree with my rheumatism, but you are not rheumatic and it won't damage you. Besides, it's a very damp night outside. The wind is howling again, and it will soon be in the south-west; do you hear how the windows rattle? The tide must have turned too, by the moaning.

We should not have heard the thing again if you had not said that. I'm pretty sure we should not. Oh yes, if you choose to describe it as a coincidence, you are quite welcome, but I would rather that you should not call the thing names again, if you don't mind. It may be that the poor little woman hears, and perhaps it hurts her, don't you know? Ghost? No! You don't call anything a ghost that you can take in your hands and look at in broad daylight, and that rattles when you shake it. Do you, now? But it's something that hears and understands; there's no doubt about that.

I tried sleeping in the best bedroom when I first came to the house, just because it was the best and the most comfortable, but I had to give it up. It was their room, and there's the big bed she died in, and the cupboard is in the thickness of the wall, near the head, on the left. That's where it likes to be kept, in its bandbox. I only used the room for a fortnight after I came, and then I turned out and took the little room downstairs, next to the surgery, where Luke used to sleep when he expected to be called to a patient during the night.

I was always a good sleeper ashore; eight hours is my dose, eleven to seven when I'm alone, twelve to eight when I have a friend with me. But I could not sleep after three o'clock in the morning in that room—a quarter past, to be accurate—as a matter of fact, I timed it with my old pocket chronometer, which still keeps good time, and it was always at exactly seventeen minutes past three. I wonder whether that was the hour when she died?

It was not what you have heard. If it had been that I could not have stood it two nights. It was just a start and a moan and hard breathing for a few seconds in the cupboard, and it could never have waked me under ordinary circumstances, I'm sure. I suppose you are like me in that, and we are just like other people who have been to sea. No natural sounds disturb us at all, not all the racket of a square-rigger hove to in a heavy gale, or rolling on her beam ends before the wind. But if a lead pencil gets adrift and rattles in the drawer of your cabin table you are awake in a moment. Just so—you always understand. Very well, the noise in the cupboard was no louder than that, but it waked me instantly.

I said it was like a "start." I know what I mean, but it's hard to explain without seeming to talk nonsense. Of course you cannot exactly "hear" a person "start"; at the most, you might hear the quick drawing of the breath between the parted lips and closed teeth, and the almost imperceptible sound of clothing that moved suddenly though very slightly. It was like that.

You know how one feels what a sailing vessel is going to do, two or three seconds before she does it, when one has the wheel. Riders say the same of a horse, but that's less strange, because the horse is a live animal with feelings of its own, and only poets and landsmen talk about a ship being alive, and all that. But I have always felt somehow that besides being a steaming machine or a sailing machine for carrying weights, a vessel at sea is a sensitive instrument, and a means of communication between nature and man, and most particularly the man at the wheel, if she is steered by hand. She takes her impressions directly from wind and sea, tide and stream, and transmits them to the man's hand, just as the wireless telegraph picks up the interrupted currents aloft and turns them out below in the form of a message.

You see what I am driving at; I felt that something started in the cupboard, and I felt it so vividly that I heard it, though there may have been nothing to hear, and the sound inside my head waked me suddenly. But I really heard the other noise. It was as if it were muffled inside a box, as far away as if it came through a long-distance telephone; and yet I knew that it was inside the cupboard near the head of my bed. My hair did not bristle and my blood did not run cold that time. I simply resented being waked up by something that had no business to make a noise, any more than a pencil should rattle in the drawer of my cabin table on board ship. For I did not understand; I just supposed that the cupboard had some communication with the outside air, and that the wind had got in and was moaning through it with a sort of very faint screech. I struck a light and looked at my watch, and it was seventeen minutes past three. Then I turned over and went to sleep on my right ear. That's my good one; I'm pretty deaf with the other, for I struck the water with it when I was a lad in diving from the foretopsail yard. Silly thing to do, it was, but the result is very convenient when I want to go to sleep when there's a noise.

That was the first night, and the same thing happened again and several times afterward, but not regularly, though it was always at the same time, to a second; perhaps I was sometimes sleeping on my good ear, and sometimes not. I overhauled the cupboard and there was no way by which the wind could get in, or anything else, for the door makes a good fit, having been meant to keep out moths, I suppose; Mrs. Pratt must have kept her winter things in it, for it still smells of camphor and turpentine.

After about a fortnight I had had enough of the noises. So far I had said to myself that it would be silly to yield to it and take the skull out of the room. Things always look differently by daylight, don't they? But the voice grew louder—I suppose one may call it a voice—and it got inside my deaf ear, too, one night. I realised that when I was wide awake, for my good ear was jammed down on the pillow, and I ought not to have heard a fog-horn in that position. But I heard that, and it made me lose my temper, unless it scared me, for sometimes the two are not far apart. I struck a light and got up, and I opened the cupboard, grabbed the bandbox and threw it out of the window, as far as I could.

Then my hair stood on end. The thing screamed in the air, like a shell from a twelve-inch gun. It fell on the other side of the road. The night was very dark, and I could not see it fall, but I know it fell beyond the road. The window is just over the front door, it's fifteen yards to the fence, more or less, and the road is ten yards wide. There's a quickset hedge beyond, along the glebe that belongs to the vicarage.

I did not sleep much more that night. It was not more than half an hour after I had thrown the bandbox out when I heard a shriek outside—like what we've had tonight, but worse, more despairing, I should call it; and it may have been my imagination, but I could have sworn that the screams came nearer and nearer each time. I lit a pipe, and walked up and down for a bit, and then took a book and sat up reading, but I'll be hanged if I can remember what I read nor even what the book was, for every now and then a shriek came up that would have made a dead man turn in his coffin.

A little before dawn some one knocked at the front door. There was no mistaking that for anything else, and I opened my window and looked down, for I guessed that some one wanted the doctor, supposing that the new man had taken Luke's house. It was rather a relief to hear a human knock after that awful noise.

You cannot see the door from above, owing to the little porch. The knocking came again, and I called out, asking who was there, but nobody answered, though the knock was repeated. I sang out again, and said that the doctor did not live here any longer. There was no answer, but it occurred to me that it might be some old countryman who was stone deaf. So I took my candle and went down to open the door. Upon my word, I was not thinking of the thing yet, and I had almost forgotten the other noises. I went down convinced that I should find somebody outside, on the doorstep, with a message. I set the candle on the hall table, so that the wind should not blow it out when I opened. While I was drawing the old-fashioned bolt I heard the knocking again. It was not loud, and it had a queer, hollow sound, now that I was close to it, I remember, but I certainly thought it was made by some person who wanted to get in.

It wasn't. There was nobody there, but as I opened the door inward, standing a little on one side, so as to see out at once, something rolled across the threshold and stopped against my foot.

I drew back as I felt it, for I knew what it was before I looked down. I cannot tell you how I knew, and it seemed unreasonable, for I am still quite sure that I had thrown it across the road. It's a French window, that opens wide, and I got a good swing when I flung it out. Besides, when I went out early in the morning, I found the bandbox beyond the thickset hedge.

You may think it opened when I threw it, and that the skull dropped out; but that's impossible, for nobody could throw an empty cardboard box so far. It's out of the question; you might as well try to fling a ball of paper twenty-five yards, or a blown bird's egg.

To go back, I shut and bolted the hall door, picked the thing up carefully, and put it on the table beside the candle. I did that mechanically, as one instinctively does the right thing in danger without thinking at all—unless one does the opposite. It may seem odd, but I believe my first thought had been that somebody might come and find me there on the threshold while it was resting against my foot, lying a little on its side, and turning one hollow eye up at my face, as if it meant to accuse me. And the light and shadow from the candle played in the hollows of the eyes as it stood on the table, so that they seemed to open and shut at me. Then the candle went out quite unexpectedly, though the door was fastened and there was not the least draught; and I used up at least half a dozen matches before it would burn again.

I sat down rather suddenly, without quite knowing why. Probably I had been badly frightened, and perhaps you will admit there was no great shame in being scared. The thing had come home, and it wanted to go upstairs, back to its cupboard. I sat still and stared at it for a bit, till I began to feel very cold; then I took it and carried it up and set it in its place, and I remember that I spoke to it, and promised that it should have its bandbox again in the morning.

You want to know whether I stayed in the room till daybreak? Yes, but I kept a light burning, and sat up smoking and reading, most likely out of fright; plain, undeniable fear, and you need not call it cowardice either, for that's not the same thing. I could not have stayed alone with that thing in the cupboard; I should have been scared to death, though I'm not more timid than other people. Confound it all, man, it had crossed the road alone, and had got up the doorstep and had knocked to be let in.

When the dawn came, I put on my boots and went out to find the bandbox. I had to go a good way round, by the gate near the highroad, and I found the box open and hanging on the other side of the hedge. It had caught on the twigs by the string, and the lid had fallen off and was lying on the ground below it. That shows that it did not open till it was well over; and if it had not opened as soon as it left my hand, what was inside it must have gone beyond the road too.

That's all. I took the box upstairs to the cupboard, and put the skull back and locked it up. When the girl brought me my breakfast she said she was sorry, but that she must go, and she did not care if she lost her month's wages. I looked at her, and her face was a sort of greenish, yellowish white. I pretended to be surprised, and asked what was the matter; but that was of no use, for she just turned on me and wanted to know whether I meant to stay in a haunted house, and how long I expected to live if I did, for though she noticed I was sometimes a little hard of hearing, she did not believe that even I could sleep through those screams again—and if I could, why had I been moving about the house and opening and shutting the front door, between three and four in the morning? There was no answering that, since she had heard me, so off she went, and I was left to myself. I went down to the village during the morning and found a woman who was willing to come and do the little work there is and cook my dinner, on condition that she might go home every night. As for me, I moved downstairs that day, and I have never tried to sleep in the best bedroom since. After a little while I got a brace of middle-aged Scotch servants from London, and things were quiet enough for a long time. I began by telling them that the house was in a very exposed position, and that the wind whistled round it a good deal in the autumn and winter, which had given it a bad name in the village, the Cornish people being inclined to superstition and telling ghost stories. The two hard-faced, sandy-haired sisters almost smiled, and they answered with great contempt that they had no great opinion of any Southern bogey whatever, having been in service in two English haunted houses, where they had never seen so much as the Boy in Gray, whom they reckoned no very particular rarity in Forfarshire.

They stayed with me several months, and while they were in the house we had peace and quiet. One of them is here again now, but she went away with her sister within the year. This one—she was the cook—married the sexton, who works in my garden. That's the way of it. It's a small village and he has not much to do, and he knows enough about flowers to help me nicely, besides doing most of the hard work; for though I'm fond of exercise, I'm getting a little stiff in the hinges. He's a sober, silent sort of fellow, who minds his own business, and he was a widower when I came here—Trehearn is his name, James Trehearn. The Scotch sisters would not admit that there was anything wrong about the house, but when November came they gave me warning that they were going, on the ground that the chapel was such a long walk from here, being in the next parish, and that they could not possibly go to our church. But the younger one came back in the spring, and as soon as the banns could be published she was married to James Trehearn by the vicar, and she seems to have had no scruples about hearing him preach since then. I'm quite satisfied, if she is! The couple live in a small cottage that looks over the churchyard.

I suppose you are wondering what all this has to do with what I was talking about. I'm alone so much that when an old friend comes to see me, I sometimes go on talking just for the sake of hearing my own voice. But in this case there is really a connection of ideas. It was James Trehearn who buried poor Mrs. Pratt, and her husband after her in the same grave, and it's not far from the back of his cottage. That's the connection in my mind, you see. It's plain enough. He knows something; I'm quite sure that he does, by his manner, though he's such a reticent beggar.

Yes, I'm alone in the house at night now, for Mrs. Trehearn does everything herself, and when I have a friend the sexton's niece comes in to wait on the table. He takes his wife home every evening in winter, but in summer, when there's light, she goes by herself. She's not a nervous woman, but she's less sure than she used to be that there are no bogies in England worth a Scotchwoman's notice. Isn't it amusing, the idea that Scotland has a monopoly of the supernatural? Odd sort of national pride, I call that, don't you?

That's a good fire, isn't it? When driftwood gets started at last there's nothing like it, I think. Yes, we get lots of it, for I'm sorry to say there are still a great many wrecks about here. It's a lonely coast, and you may have all the wood you want for the trouble of bringing it in. Trehearn and I borrow a cart now and then, and load it between here and the Spit. I hate a coal fire when I can get wood of any sort. A log is company, even if it's only a piece of a deck-beam or timber sawn off, and the salt in it makes pretty sparks. See how they fly, like Japanese hand-fireworks! Upon my word, with an old friend and a good fire and a pipe, one forgets all about that thing upstairs, especially now that the wind has moderated. It's only a lull, though, and it will blow a gale before morning.

You think you would like to see the skull? I've no objection. There's no reason why you shouldn't have a look at it, and you never saw a more perfect one in your life, except that there are two front teeth missing in the lower jaw.

Oh yes—I had not told you about the jaw yet. Trehearn found it in the garden last spring when he was digging a pit for a new asparagus bed. You know we make asparagus beds six or eight feet deep here. Yes, yes—I had forgotten to tell you that. He was digging straight down, just as he digs a grave; if you want a good asparagus bed made, I advise you to get a sexton to make it for you. Those fellows have a wonderful knack at that sort of digging.

Trehearn had got down about three feet when he cut into a mass of white lime in the side of the trench. He had noticed that the earth was a little looser there, though he says it had not been disturbed for a number of years. I suppose he thought that even old lime might not be good for asparagus, so he broke it out and threw it up. It was pretty hard, he says, in biggish lumps, and out of sheer force of habit he cracked the lumps with his spade as they lay outside the pit beside him; the jawbone of a skull dropped out of one of the pieces. He thinks he must have knocked out the two front teeth in breaking up the lime, but he did not see them anywhere. He's a very experienced man in such things, as you may imagine, and he said at once that the jaw had probably belonged to a young woman, and that the teeth had been complete when she died. He brought it to me, and asked me if I wanted to keep it; if I did not, he said he would drop it into the next grave he made in the churchyard, as he supposed it was a Christian jaw, and ought to have decent burial, wherever the rest of the body might be. I told him that doctors often put bones into quicklime to whiten them nicely, and that I supposed Dr. Pratt had once had a little lime pit in the garden for that purpose, and had forgotten the jaw. Trehearn looked at me quietly.

"Maybe it fitted that skull that used to be in the cupboard upstairs, sir," he said. "Maybe Dr. Pratt had put the skull into the lime to clean it, or something, and when he took it out he left the lower jaw behind. There's some human hair sticking in the lime, sir."

I saw there was, and that was what Trehearn said. If he did not suspect something, why in the world should he have suggested that the jaw might fit the skull? Besides, it did. That's proof that he knows more than he cares to tell. Do you suppose he looked before she was buried? Or perhaps—when he buried Luke in the same grave—

Well, well, it's of no use to go over that, is it? I said I would keep the jaw with the skull, and I took it upstairs and fitted it into its place. There's not the slightest doubt about the two belonging together, and together they are.

Trehearn knows several things. We were talking about plastering the kitchen a while ago, and he happened to remember that it had not been done since the very week when Mrs. Pratt died. He did not say that the mason must have left some lime on the place, but he thought it, and that it was the very same lime he had found in the asparagus pit. He knows a lot. Trehearn is one of your silent beggars who can put two and two together. That grave is very near the back of his cottage, too, and he's one of the quickest men with a spade I ever saw. If he wanted to know the truth, he could, and no one else would ever be the wiser unless he chose to tell. In a quiet village like ours, people don't go and spend the night in the churchyard to see whether the sexton potters about by himself between ten o'clock and daylight.

What is awful to think of, is Luke's deliberation, if he did it; his cool certainty that no one would find him out; above all, his nerve, for that must have been extraordinary. I sometimes think it's bad enough to live in the place where it was done, if it really was done. I always put in the condition, you see, for the sake of his memory, and a little bit for my own sake, too.

I'll go upstairs and fetch the box in a minute. Let me light my pipe; there's no hurry! We had supper early, and it's only half-past nine o'clock. I never let a friend go to bed before twelve, or with less than three glasses—you may have as many more as you like, but you shan't have less, for the sake of old times.

It's breezing up again, do you hear? That was only a lull just now, and we are going to have a bad night.

A thing happened that made me start a little when I found that the jaw fitted exactly. I'm not very easily startled in that way myself, but I have seen people make a quick movement, drawing their breath sharply, when they had thought they were alone and suddenly turned and saw some one very near them. Nobody can call that fear. You wouldn't, would you? No. Well, just when I had set the jaw in its place under the skull, the teeth closed sharply on my finger. It felt exactly as if it were biting me hard, and I confess that I jumped before I realised that I had been pressing the jaw and the skull together with my other hand. I assure you I was not at all nervous. It was broad daylight, too, and a fine day, and the sun was streaming into the best bedroom. It would have been absurd to be nervous, and it was only a quick mistaken impression, but it really made me feel queer. Somehow it made me think of the funny verdict of the coroner's jury on Luke's death, "by the hand or teeth of some person or animal unknown." Ever since that I've wished I had seen those marks on his throat, though the lower jaw was missing then.

I have often seen a man do insane things with his hands that he does not realise at all. I once saw a man hanging on by an old

315

awning stop with one hand, leaning backward, outboard, with all his weight on it, and he was just cutting the stop with the knife in his other hand when I got my arms round him. We were in mid-ocean, going twenty knots. He had not the smallest idea what he was doing; neither had I when I managed to pinch my finger between the teeth of that thing. I can feel it now. It was exactly as if it were alive and were trying to bite me. It would if it could, for I know it hates me, poor thing! Do you suppose that what rattles about inside is really a bit of lead? Well, I'll get the box down presently, and if whatever it is happens to drop out into your hands that's your affair. If it's only a clod of earth or a pebble, the whole matter would be off my mind, and I don't believe I should ever think of the skull again; but somehow I cannot bring myself to shake out the bit of hard stuff myself. The mere idea that it may be lead makes me confoundedly uncomfortable, yet I've got the conviction that I shall know before long. I shall certainly know. I'm sure Trehearn knows, but he's such a silent beggar.

I'll go upstairs now and get it. What? You had better go with me? Ha, ha! do you think I'm afraid of a bandbox and a noise? Nonsense!

Bother the candle, it won't light! As if the ridiculous thing understood what it's wanted for! Look at that—the third match. They light fast enough for my pipe. There, do you see? It's a fresh box, just out of the tin safe where I keep the supply on account of the dampness. Oh, you think the wick of the candle may be damp, do you? All right, I'll light the beastly thing in the fire. That won't go out, at all events. Yes, it sputters a bit, but it will keep lighted now. It burns just like any other candle, doesn't it? The fact is, candles are not very good about here. I don't know where they come from, but they have a way of burning low occasionally, with a greenish flame that spits tiny sparks, and I'm often annoyed by their going out of themselves. It cannot be helped, for it will be long before we have electricity in our village. It really is rather a poor light, isn't it?

You think I had better leave you the candle and take the lamp, do you? I don't like to carry lamps about, that's the truth. I never dropped one in my life, but I have always thought I might, and it's so confoundedly dangerous if you do. Besides, I am pretty well used to these rotten candles by this time.

You may as well finish that glass while I'm getting it, for I don't mean to let you off with less than three before you go to bed. You won't have to go upstairs, either, for I've put you in the old study next to the surgery—that's where I live myself. The fact is, I never ask a friend to sleep upstairs now. The last man who did was Crackenthorpe, and he said he was kept awake all night. You remember old Crack, don't you? He stuck to the Service, and they've just made him an admiral. Yes, I'm off now—unless the candle goes out. I couldn't help asking if you remembered Crackenthorpe. If any one had told us that the skinny little idiot he used to be was to turn out the most successful of the lot of us, we should have laughed at the idea, shouldn't we? You and I did not do badly, it's true—but I'm really going now. I don't mean to let you think that I've been putting it off by talking! As if there were anything to be afraid of! If I were scared, I should tell you so quite frankly, and get you to go upstairs with me.

Here's the box. I brought it down very carefully, so as not to disturb it, poor thing. You see, if it were shaken, the jaw might get separated from it again, and I'm sure it wouldn't like that. Yes, the candle went out as I was coming downstairs, but that was the draught from the leaky window on the landing. Did you hear anything? Yes, there was another scream. Am I pale, do you say? That's nothing. My heart is a little queer sometimes, and I went upstairs too fast. In fact, that's one reason why I really prefer to live altogether on the ground floor.

Wherever that shriek came from, it was not from the skull, for I had the box in my hand when I heard the noise, and here it is now; so we have proved definitely that the screams are produced by something else. I've no doubt I shall find out some day what makes them. Some crevice in the wall, of course, or a crack in a chimney, or a chink in the frame of a window. That's the way all ghost stories end in real life. Do you know, I'm jolly glad I thought of going up and bringing it down for you to see, for that last shriek settles the question. To think that I should have been so weak is to fancy that the poor skull could really cry out like a living thing!

Now I'll open the box, and we'll take it out and look at it under the bright light. It's rather awful to think that the poor lady used to sit there, in your chair, evening after evening, in just the same light, isn't it? But then—I've made up my mind that it's all rubbish from beginning to end, and that it's just an old skull that Luke had when he was a student; and perhaps he put it into the lime merely to whiten it, and could not find the jaw.

I made a seal on the string, you see, after I had put the jaw in its place, and I wrote on the cover. There's the old white label on it still, from the milliner's, addressed to Mrs. Pratt when the hat was sent to her, and as there was room I wrote on the edge: "A skull, once the property of the late Luke Pratt, M.D." I don't quite know why I wrote that, unless it was with the idea of explaining how the thing happened to be in my possession. I cannot help wondering sometimes what sort of hat it was that came in the bandbox. What colour was it, do you think? Was it a gay spring hat with a bobbing feather and pretty ribands? Strange that the very same box should hold the head that wore the finery—perhaps. No—we made up our minds that it just came from the hospital in London where Luke did his time. It's far better to look at it in that light, isn't it? There's no more connection between that skull and poor Mrs. Pratt than there was between my story about the lead and—

Good Lord! Take the lamp—don't let it go out, if you can help it—I'll have the window fastened again in a second—I say, what a gale! There, it's out! I told you so! Never mind, there's the firelight— I've got the window shut—the bolt was only half down. Was the box blown off the table? Where the deuce is it? There! That won't open again, for I've put up the bar. Good dodge, an old-fashioned bar—there's nothing like it. Now, you find the bandbox while I light the lamp. Confound those wretched matches! Yes, a pipe spill is better—it must light in the fire—I hadn't thought of it—thank you—there we are again. Now, where's the box? Yes, put it back on the table, and we'll open it.

That's the first time I have ever known the wind to burst that window open; but it was partly carelessness on my part when I last shut it. Yes, of course I heard the scream. It seemed to go all round the house before it broke in at the window. That proves that it's always been the wind and nothing else, doesn't it? When it was not the wind, it was my imagination. I've always been a very imaginative man: I must have been, though I did not know it. As we grow older we understand ourselves better, don't you know?

I'll have a drop of the Hulstkamp neat, by way of an exception, since you are filling up your glass. That damp gust chilled me, and with my rheumatic tendency I'm very much afraid of a chill, for the cold sometimes seems to stick in my joints all winter when it once gets in.

By George, that's good stuff! I'll just light a fresh pipe, now that everything is snug again, and then we'll open the box. I'm so glad we heard that last scream together, with the skull here on the table between us, for a thing cannot possibly be in two places at the same time, and the noise most certainly came from outside, as any noise the wind makes must. You thought you heard it scream through the room after the window was burst open? Oh yes, so did I, but that was natural enough when everything was open. Of course we heard the wind. What could one expect?

Look here, please. I want you to see that the seal is intact before we open the box together. Will you take my glasses? No, you have your own. All right. The seal is sound, you see, and you can read the words of the motto easily. "Sweet and low"—that's it—because the poem goes on "Wind of the Western sea," and says, "blow him again to me," and all that. Here is the seal on my watch-chain, where it's hung for more than forty years. My poor little wife gave it to me when I was courting, and I never had any other. It was just like her to think of those words—she was always fond of Tennyson.

It's of no use to cut the string, for it's fastened to the box, so I'll just break the wax and untie the knot, and afterward we'll seal it up again. You see, I like to feel that the thing is safe in its place, and that nobody can take it out. Not that I should suspect Trehearn of meddling with it, but I always feel that he knows a lot more than he tells.

You see, I've managed it without breaking the string, though when I fastened it I never expected to open the bandbox again. The lid comes off easily enough. There! Now look!

What? Nothing in it? Empty? It's gone, man, the skull is gone!

No, there's nothing the matter with me. I'm only trying to collect my thoughts. It's so strange. I'm positively certain that it was inside when I put on the seal last spring. I can't have imagined that: it's utterly impossible. If I ever took a stiff glass with a friend now and then, I would admit that I might have made some idiotic mistake when I had taken too much. But I don't, and I never did. A pint of ale at supper and half a go of rum at bedtime was the most I ever took in my good days. I believe it's always we sober fellows who get rheumatism and gout! Yet there was my seal, and there is the empty bandbox. That's plain enough.

I say, I don't half like this. It's not right. There's something wrong about it, in my opinion. You needn't talk to me about supernatural manifestations, for I don't believe in them, not a little bit! Somebody must have tampered with the seal and stolen the skull. Sometimes, when I go out to work in the garden in summer, I leave my watch and chain on the table. Trehearn must have taken the seal then, and used it, for he would be quite sure that I should not come in for at least an hour.

If it was not Trehearn—oh, don't talk to me about the possibility that the thing has got out by itself! If it has, it must be somewhere about the house, in some out-of-the-way corner, waiting. We may come upon it anywhere, waiting for us, don't you know?—just waiting in the dark. Then it will scream at me; it will shriek at me in the dark, for it hates me, I tell you!

The bandbox is quite empty. We are not dreaming, either of us. There, I turn it upside down.

What's that? Something fell out as I turned it over. It's on the floor, it's near your feet, I know it is, and we must find it. Help me to find it, man. Have you got it? For God's sake, give it to me, quickly!

Lead! I knew it when I heard it fall. I knew it couldn't be anything else by the little thud it made on the hearth-rug. So it was lead after all, and Luke did it.

I feel a little bit shaken up—not exactly nervous, you know, but badly shaken up, that's the fact. Anybody would, I should think.

After all, you cannot say that it's fear of the thing, for I went up and brought it down—at least, I believed I was bringing it down, and that's the same thing, and by George, rather than give in to such silly nonsense, I'll take the box upstairs again and put it back in its place. It's not that. It's the certainty that the poor little woman came to her end in that way, by my fault, because I told the story. That's what is so dreadful. Somehow, I had always hoped that I should never be quite sure of it, but there is no doubting it now. Look at that!

Look at it! That little lump of lead with no particular shape. Think of what it did, man! Doesn't it make you shiver? He gave her something to make her sleep, of course, but there must have been one moment of awful agony. Think of having boiling lead poured into your brain. Think of it. She was dead before she could scream, but only think of—oh! there it is again—it's just outside—I know it's just outside—I can't keep it out of my head!—oh!—oh!

You thought I had fainted? No, I wish I had, for it would have stopped sooner. It's all very well to say that it's only a noise, and that a noise never hurt anybody—you're as white as a shroud yourself. There's only one thing to be done, if we hope to close an eye tonight. We must find it and put it back into its bandbox and shut it up in the cupboard, where it likes to be. I don't know how it got out, but it wants to get in again. That's why it screams so awfully tonight—it was never so bad as this—never since I first—

Bury it? Yes, if we can find it, we'll bury it, if it takes us all night. We'll bury it six feet deep and ram down the earth over it, so that it shall never get out again, and if it screams, we shall hardly hear it so deep down. Quick, we'll get the lantern and look for it. It cannot be far away; I'm sure it's just outside—it was coming in when I shut the window, I know it.

Yes, you're quite right. I'm losing my senses, and I must get hold of myself. Don't speak to me for a minute or two; I'll sit quite still and keep my eyes shut and repeat something I know. That's the best way.

"Add together the altitude, the latitude, and the polar distance, divide by two and subtract the altitude from the half-sum; then add the logarithm of the secant of the latitude, the cosecant of the polar distance, the cosine of the half-sum and the sine of the half-sum minus the altitude"—there! Don't say that I'm out of my senses, for my memory is all right, isn't it?

Of course, you may say that it's mechanical, and that we never forget the things we learned when we were boys and have used almost every day for a lifetime. But that's the very point. When a man is going crazy, it's the mechanical part of his mind that gets out of order and won't work right; he remembers things that never happened, or he sees things that aren't real, or he hears noises when there is perfect silence. That's not what is the matter with either of us, is it?

Come, we'll get the lantern and go round the house. It's not raining—only blowing like old boots, as we used to say. The lantern is in the cupboard under the stairs in the hall, and I always keep it trimmed in case of a wreck.

No use to look for the thing? I don't see how you can say that. It was nonsense to talk of burying it, of course, for it doesn't want to be buried; it wants to go back into its bandbox and be taken upstairs, poor thing! Trehearn took it out, I know, and made the seal over again. Perhaps he took it to the churchyard, and he may have meant well. I daresay he thought that it would not scream any more if it were quietly laid in consecrated ground, near where it belongs. But it has come home. Yes, that's it. He's not half a bad fellow, Trehearn, and rather religiously inclined, I think. Does not that sound natural, and reasonable, and well meant? He supposed it screamed because it was not decently buried—with the rest. But he was wrong. How should he know that it screams at me because it hates me, and because it's my fault that there was that little lump of lead in it?

No use to look for it, anyhow? Nonsense! I tell you it wants to be found—Hark! what's that knocking? Do you hear it? Knock—knock—knock—three times, then a pause, and then again. It has a hollow sound, hasn't it?

It has come home. I've heard that knock before. It wants to come in and be taken upstairs, in its box. It's at the front door.

Will you come with me? We'll take it in. Yes, I own that I don't like to go alone and open the door. The thing will roll in and stop against my foot, just as it did before, and the light will go out. I'm a good deal shaken by finding that bit of lead, and, besides, my heart isn't quite right—too much strong tobacco, perhaps. Besides, I'm quite willing to own that I'm a bit nervous tonight, if I never was before in my life.

That's right, come along! I'll take the box with me, so as not to come back. Do you hear the knocking? It's not like any other knocking I ever heard. If you will hold this door open, I can find the lantern under the stairs by the light from this room without bringing the lamp into the hall—it would only go out.

The thing knows we are coming—hark! It's impatient to get in. Don't shut the door till the lantern is ready, whatever you do. There will be the usual trouble with the matches, I suppose—no, the first one, by Jove! I tell you it wants to get in, so there's no trouble. All right with that door now; shut it, please. Now come and hold the lantern, for it's blowing so hard outside that I shall have to use both hands. That's it, hold the light low. Do you hear the knocking still?

Here goes—I'll open just enough with my foot against the bottom of the door—now!

Catch it! it's only the wind that blows it across the floor, that's all—there's half a hurricane outside, I tell you! Have you got it? The bandbox is on the table. One minute, and I'll have the bar up. There!

Why did you throw it into the box so roughly? It doesn't like that, you know.

What do you say? Bitten your hand? Nonsense, man! You did just what I did. You pressed the jaws together with your other hand and pinched yourself. Let me see. You don't mean to say you have drawn blood? You must have squeezed hard, by Jove, for the skin is certainly torn. I'll give you some carbolic solution for it before we go to bed, for they say a scratch from a skull's tooth may go bad and give trouble.

Come inside again and let me see it by the lamp. I'll bring the bandbox—never mind the lantern, it may just as well burn in the hall, for I shall need it presently when I go up the stairs. Yes, shut the door if you will; it makes it more cheerful and bright. Is your finger still bleeding? I'll get you the carbolic in an instant; just let me see the thing.

Ugh! There's a drop of blood on the upper jaw. It's on the eye-tooth. Ghastly, isn't it? When I saw it running along the floor of the hall, the strength almost went out of my hands, and I felt my knees bending; then I understood that it was the gale, driving it over the smooth boards. You don't blame me? No, I should think not! We were boys together, and we've seen a thing or two, and we may just as well own to each other that we were both in a beastly funk when it slid across the floor at you. No wonder you pinched your finger picking it up, after that, if I did the same thing out of sheer nervousness, in broad daylight, with the sun streaming in on me.

Strange that the jaw should stick to it so closely, isn't it? I suppose it's the dampness, for it shuts like a vice—I have wiped off the drop of blood, for it was not nice to look at. I'm not going to try to open the jaws, don't be afraid! I shall not play any tricks with the poor thing, but I'll just seal the box again, and we'll take it upstairs and put it away where it wants to be. The wax is on the writing-table by the window. Thank you. It will be long before I leave my seal lying about again, for Trehearn to use, I can tell you. Explain? I don't explain natural phenomena, but if you choose to think that Trehearn had hidden it somewhere in the bushes, and that the gale blew it to the house against the door, and made it knock, as if it wanted to be let in, you're not thinking the impossible, and I'm quite ready to agree with you.

Do you see that? You can swear that you've actually seen me seal it this time, in case anything of the kind should occur again. The wax fastens the strings to the lid, which cannot possibly be lifted, even enough to get in one finger. You're quite satisfied, aren't you? Yes. Besides, I shall lock the cupboard and keep the key in my pocket hereafter.

Now we can take the lantern and go upstairs. Do you know? I'm very much inclined to agree with your theory that the wind blew it against the house. I'll go ahead, for I know the stairs; just hold the lantern near my feet as we go up. How the wind howls and whistles! Did you feel the sand on the floor under your shoes as we crossed the hall?

Yes—this is the door of the best bedroom. Hold up the lantern, please. This side, by the head of the bed. I left the cupboard open when I got the box. Isn't it queer how the faint odour of women's dresses will hang about an old closet for years? This is the shelf. You've seen me set the box there, and now you see me turn the key and put it into my pocket. So that's done!

*

Good-night. Are you sure you're quite comfortable? It's not much of a room, but I daresay you would as soon sleep here as upstairs tonight. If you want anything, sing out; there's only a lath and plaster partition between us. There's not so much wind on this side by half. There's the Hollands on the table, if you'll have one more nightcap. No? Well, do as you please. Good-night again, and don't dream about that thing, if you can.

The following paragraph appeared in the *Penraddon News*, 23rd November, 1906:

"MYSTERIOUS DEATH OF A RETIRED SEA CAPTAIN

"The village of Tredcombe is much disturbed by the strange death of Captain Charles Braddock, and all sorts of impossible stories are circulating with regard to the circumstances, which certainly seem difficult of explanation. The retired captain, who had successfully commanded in his time the largest and fastest liners belonging to one of the principal transatlantic steamship companies, was found dead in his bed on Tuesday morning in his own cottage, a quarter of a mile from the village. An examination was made at once by the local practitioner, which revealed the horrible fact that the deceased had been bitten in the throat by a human assailant, with such amazing force as to crush the windpipe and cause death. The marks of the teeth of both jaws were so plainly visible on the skin that they could be counted, but the perpetrator of the deed had evidently lost the two lower middle incisors. It is hoped that this peculiarity may help to identify the murderer, who can only be a dangerous escaped maniac. The deceased, though over sixty-five years of age, is said to have been a hale man of considerable physical strength, and it is remarkable that no signs of any struggle were visible in the room, nor could it be ascertained how the murderer had entered the house. Warning has been sent to all the insane asylums in the United Kingdom, but as yet no information has been received regarding the escape of any dangerous patient.

"The coroner's jury returned the somewhat singular verdict that Captain Braddock came to his death 'by the hands or teeth of some person unknown.' The local surgeon is said to have expressed privately the opinion that the maniac is a woman, a view he deduces from the small size of the jaws, as shown by the marks of the teeth. The whole affair is shrouded in mystery. Captain Braddock was a widower, and lived alone. He leaves no children."

[*Note*.—Students of ghost lore and haunted houses will find the foundation of the foregoing story in the legends about a skull which is still preserved in the farm-house called Bettiscombe Manor, situated, I believe, on the Dorsetshire coast.]

ARTHUR CONAN DOYLE

The Adventure of the Devil's Foot

Arthur Conan Doyle (1859–1930) was an author and doctor, most famous for creating the character Sherlock Holmes who debuted in *A Study in Scarlet* in 1887. By the end of his life Doyle had written four novels and fifty-six short stories starring Holmes and his partner in solving crime, Dr. John Watson. He also wrote fantasy, science fiction, comedy, plays, historical fiction, and poetry. He was born in Edinburgh and later educated in England and Austria before returning to Edinburgh for medical school. He spent some of his life in the South West of England, attempted to establish a medical practice in Plymouth, and even played football for the Portsmouth Association Football Club. Cornwall is not the first county to come to mind when thinking of Holmes—we are likely more drawn just over the Tamar to Dartmoor in Devon, the setting of Doyle's *The Hound of the Baskervilles* (1901–1902). Yet, Doyle's hound may take inspiration from the Beast of Bodmin Moor, the Cornish variant. Cornwall is essential to the machinations of the narrative in 'The Adventure of the Devil's Foot'. It relies upon a mining fortune, Holmes's interest in the county's ancient history, Watson's desire for a restful, leisurely break, and the quality of the air in particular. Without spoiling the plot, it is a tale reliant upon contemporary worries surrounding industry and air quality, where Cornwall provides an ideal case study, being seen as both rural and industrial.

n recording from time to time some of the curious experiences and interesting recollections which I associate with my long and intimate friendship with Mr. Sherlock Holmes, I have continually been faced by difficulties caused by his own aversion to publicity. To his sombre and cynical spirit all popular applause was always abhorrent, and nothing amused him more at the end of a successful case than to hand over the actual exposure to some orthodox official, and to listen with a mocking smile to the general chorus of misplaced congratulation. It was indeed, this attitude upon the part of my friend, and certainly not any lack of interesting material which has caused me of late years to lay very few of my records before the public. My participation in some of his adventures was always a privilege which entailed discretion and reticence upon me.

It was, then, with considerable surprise that I received a telegram from Holmes last Tuesday—he has never been known to write where a telegram would serve—in the following terms: "Why not tell them of the Cornish horror—strangest case I have handled." I have no idea what backward sweep of memory had brought the matter fresh to his mind, or what freak had caused him to desire that I should recount it; but I hasten, before another cancelling telegram may arrive, to hunt out the notes which give me the exact details of the case, and to lay the narrative before my readers.

It was, then, in the spring of the year 1897 that Holmes's iron constitution showed some symptoms of giving way in the face of constant hard work of a most exacting kind, aggravated, perhaps, by occasional indiscretions of his own. In March of that year Dr. Moore Agar, of Harley Street, whose dramatic introduction to Holmes I may some day recount, gave positive injunctions that the famous private agent would lay aside all his cases and surrender himself to complete rest if he wished to avert an absolute break-down. The state of his health was not a matter in which he himself took the faintest interest, for his mental detachment was absolute, but he was induced at last, on the threat of being permanently disqualified from work, to give himself a complete change of scene and air. Thus it was that in the early spring of that year we found ourselves together in a small cottage near Poldhu Bay, at the further extremity of the Cornish peninsula.

It was a singular spot, and one peculiarly well suited to the grim humour of my patient. From the windows of our little whitewashed house, which stood high upon a grassy headland, we looked down upon the whole sinister semicircle of Mounts Bay, that old death trap of sailing vessels, with its fringe of black cliffs and surge-swept reefs on which innumerable seamen have met their end. With a northerly breeze it lies placid and sheltered, inviting the storm-tossed craft to tack into it for rest and protection.

Then comes the sudden swirl round of the wind, the blustering gale from the south-west, the dragging anchor, the lee shore, and the last battle in the creaming breakers. The wise mariner stands far out from that evil place.

On the land side our surroundings were as sombre as on the sea. It was a country of rolling moors, lonely and dun-coloured, with an occasional church tower to mark the site of some old-world village. In every direction upon these moors there were traces of some vanished race which had passed utterly away, and left as its sole record strange monuments of stone, irregular mounds which contained the burned ashes of the dead, and curious earthworks which hinted at prehistoric strife. The glamour and mystery of the place, with its sinister atmosphere of forgotten nations, appealed to the imagination of my friend, and he spent much of his time in long walks and solitary meditations upon the moor. The ancient Cornish language had also arrested his attention, and he had, I remember, conceived the idea that it was akin to the Chaldean, and had been largely derived from the Phoenician traders in tin. He had received a consignment of books upon philology and was settling down to develop this thesis, when suddenly, to my sorrow and to his unfeigned delight, we found ourselves, even in that land of dreams, plunged into a problem at our very doors which was more intense, more engrossing, and infinitely more mysterious than any of those which had driven us from London. Our simple life and peaceful, healthy routine were violently interrupted, and we were precipitated into the midst of a series of events which caused the utmost excitement not only in Cornwall, but throughout the whole West of England. Many of my readers may retain some recollection of what was called at the time "The Cornish Horror," though a most imperfect account of the matter reached the London Press. Now, after thirteen years I will give the true details of this inconceivable affair to the public.

I have said that scattered towers marked the villages which dotted this part of Cornwall. The nearest of these was the hamlet of Tredannick Wollas, where the cottages of a couple of hundred inhabitants clustered round an ancient, moss-grown church. The vicar of the parish, Mr. Roundhay, was something of an archæologist, and as such Holmes had made his acquaintance. He was a middle-aged man, portly and affable, with a considerable fund of local lore. At his invitation we had taken tea at the vicarage, and had come to know, also, Mr. Mortimer Tregennis, an independent gentleman, who increased the clergyman's scanty resources by taking rooms in his large, straggling house. The vicar, being a bachelor, was glad to come to such an arrangement, though he had little in common with his lodger, who was a thin, dark, spectacled man, with a stoop which gave the impression of actual, physical deformity. I remember that during our short visit we found the vicar garrulous, but his lodger strangely reticent, a sad-faced, introspective man, sitting with averted eyes, brooding apparently upon his own affairs.

These were the two men who entered abruptly into our little sitting-room on Tuesday, March the 16th, shortly after our breakfast hour, as we were smoking together, preparatory to our daily excursion upon the moors.

"Mr. Holmes," said the vicar, in an agitated voice, "the most extraordinary and tragic affair has occurred during the night. It is the most unheard-of business. We can only regard it as a special Providence that you should chance to be here at the time, for in all England you are the one man we need."

I glared at the intrusive vicar with no very friendly eyes; but Holmes took his pipe from his lips and sat up in his chair like an old hound who hears the view-holloa. He waved his hand to the sofa, and our palpitating visitor with his agitated companion sat side by side upon it. Mr. Mortimer Tregennis was more self-contained than the clergyman, but the twitching of his thin hands and the brightness of his dark eyes showed that they shared a common emotion.

"Shall I speak or you?" he asked of the vicar.

"Well, as you seem to have made the discovery, whatever it may be, and the vicar to have had it second-hand, perhaps you had better do the speaking," said Holmes.

I glanced at the hastily-clad clergyman, with the formally-dressed lodger seated beside him, and was amused at the surprise which Holmes's simple deduction had brought to their faces.

"Perhaps I had best say a few words first," said the vicar, "and then you can judge if you will listen to the details from Mr. Tregennis, or whether we should not hasten at once to the scene of this mysterious affair. I may explain, then, that our friend here spent last evening in the company of his two brothers, Owen and George, and of his sister Brenda, at their house of Tredannick Wartha, which is near the old stone cross upon the moor. He left them shortly after ten o'clock, playing cards round the dining-room table, in excellent health and spirits. This morning, being an early riser, he walked in that direction before breakfast, and was overtaken by the carriage of Dr. Richards, who explained that he had just been sent for on a most urgent call to Tredannick Wartha. Mr. Mortimer Tregennis naturally went with him. When he arrived at Tredannick Wartha he found an extraordinary state of things. His two brothers and his sister were seated round the table exactly as he had left them, the cards still spread in front of them and the candles burned down to their sockets. The sister lay back stone-dead in her chair, while the two brothers sat on each side of her laughing, shouting, and singing, the senses stricken clean out of them. All three of them, the dead woman and the two demented men, retained upon their faces an expression of the utmost horror—a convulsion of terror which was dreadful to look upon. There was no sign of the presence of anyone in the house, except Mrs. Porter, the old cook and housekeeper, who declared that she had slept deeply and heard no sound during the night. Nothing had been stolen or disarranged, and there is absolutely no explanation of what the horror can be which has frightened a woman to death and two strong men out of their senses. There is the situation, Mr. Holmes, in a nutshell, and if you can help us to clear it up you will have done a great work."

I had hoped that in some way I could coax my companion back into the quiet which had been the object of our journey; but one glance at his intense face and contracted eyebrows told me how vain was now the expectation. He sat for some little time in silence, absorbed in the strange drama which had broken in upon our peace.

"I will look into this matter," he said at last. "On the face of it, it would appear to be a case of a very exceptional nature. Have you been there yourself, Mr. Roundhay?"

"No, Mr. Holmes. Mr. Tregennis brought back the account to the vicarage, and I at once hurried over with him to consult you."

"How far is it to the house where this singular tragedy occurred?"

"About a mile inland."

"Then we shall walk over together. But, before we start, I must ask you a few questions, Mr. Mortimer Tregennis."

The other had been silent all this time, but I had observed that his more controlled excitement was even greater than the obtrusive emotion of the clergyman. He sat with a pale, drawn face, his anxious gaze fixed upon Holmes, and his thin hands clasped convulsively together. His pale lips quivered as he listened to the dreadful experience which had befallen his family, and his dark eyes seemed to reflect something of the horror of the scene.

"Ask what you like, Mr. Holmes," said he eagerly. "It is a bad thing to speak of, but I will answer you the truth."

"Tell me about last night."

"Well, Mr. Holmes, I supped there, as the vicar has said, and my elder brother George proposed a game of whist afterwards. We sat down about nine o'clock. It was a quarter-past ten when I moved to go. I left them all round the table, as merry as could be."

"Who let you out?"

"Mrs. Porter had gone to bed, so I let myself out. I shut the hall door behind me. The window of the room in which they sat was closed, but the blind was not drawn down. There was no change in door or window this morning, nor any reason to think that any stranger had been to the house. Yet there they sat, driven clean mad with terror, and Brenda lying dead of fright, with her head hanging over the arm of the chair. I'll never get the sight of that room out of my mind so long as I live."

"The facts, as you state them, are certainly most remarkable," said Holmes. "I take it that you have no theory yourself which can in any way account for them?"

"It's devilish, Mr. Holmes; devilish!" cried Mortimer Tregennis. "It is not of this world. Something has come into that room which has dashed the light of reason from their minds. What human contrivance could do that?"

"I fear," said Holmes, "that if the matter is beyond humanity it is certainly beyond me. Yet we must exhaust all natural explanations before we fall back upon such a theory as this. As to yourself, Mr. Tregennis, I take it you were divided in some way from your family, since they lived together and you had rooms apart?"

"That is so, Mr. Holmes, though the matter is past and done with. We were a family of tin-miners at Redruth, but we sold out our venture to a company, and so retired with enough to keep us. I won't deny that there was some feeling about the division of the money and it stood between us for a time, but it was all forgiven and forgotten, and we were the best of friends together."

"Looking back at the evening which you spent together, does anything stand out in your memory as throwing any possible light upon the tragedy? Think carefully, Mr. Tregennis, for any clue which can help me."

"There is nothing at all, sir."

"Your people were in their usual spirits?"

"Never better."

"Were they nervous people? Did they ever show any apprehension of coming danger?"

"Nothing of the kind."

"You have nothing to add then, which could assist me?"

Mortimer Tregennis considered earnestly for a moment.

"There is one thing occurs to me," said he at last. "As we sat at the table my back was to the window, and my brother George, he being my partner at cards, was facing it. I saw him once look hard over my shoulder, so I turned round and looked also. The blind was up and the window shut, but I could just make out the bushes on the lawn, and it seemed to me for a moment that I saw something moving among them. I couldn't even say if it were man or animal, but I just thought there was something there. When I asked him what he was looking at, he told me that he had the same feeling. That is all that I can say."

"Did you not investigate?"

"No; the matter passed as unimportant."

"You left them, then, without any premonition of evil?"

"None at all."

"I am not clear how you came to hear the news so early this morning."

"I am an early riser, and generally take a walk before breakfast. This morning I had hardly started when the doctor in his carriage overtook me. He told me that old Mrs. Porter had sent a boy down with an urgent message. I sprang in beside him and we drove on.

When we got there we looked into that dreadful room. The candles and the fire must have burned out hours before, and they had been sitting there in the dark until dawn had broken. The doctor said Brenda must have been dead at least six hours. There were no signs of violence. She just lay across the arm of the chair with that look on her face. George and Owen were singing snatches of songs and gibbering like two great apes. Oh, it was awful to see! I couldn't stand it, and the doctor was as white as a sheet. Indeed, he fell into a chair in a sort of faint, and we nearly had him on our hands as well."

"Remarkable—most remarkable!" said Holmes, rising and taking his hat. "I think, perhaps, we had better go down to Tredannick Wartha without further delay. I confess that I have seldom known a case which at first sight presented a more singular problem."

Our proceedings of that first morning did little to advance the investigation. It was marked, however, at the outset by an incident which left the most sinister impression upon my mind. The approach to the spot at which the tragedy occurred is down a narrow, winding, country lane. While we made our way along it we heard the rattle of a carriage coming towards us, and stood aside to let it pass. As it drove by us I caught a glimpse through the closed window of a horribly contorted, grinning face glaring out at us. Those staring eyes and gnashing teeth flashed past us like a dreadful vision.

"My brothers!" cried Mortimer Tregennis, white to his lips. "They are taking them to Helston."

We looked with horror after the black carriage, lumbering upon its way. Then we turned our steps towards this ill-omened house in which they had met their strange fate.

It was a large and bright dwelling, rather a villa than a cottage, with a considerable garden which was already, in that Cornish air, well filled with spring flowers. Towards this garden the window of the sitting-room fronted, and from it, according to Mortimer Tregennis, must have come that thing of evil which had by sheer horror in a single instant blasted their minds. Holmes walked slowly and thoughtfully among the flower-plots and along the path before we entered the porch. So absorbed was he in his thoughts, I remember, that he stumbled over the watering-pot, upset its contents, and deluged both our feet and the garden path. Inside the house we were met by the elderly Cornish housekeeper, Mrs. Porter, who, with the aid of a young girl, looked after the wants of the family. She readily answered all Holmes's questions. She had heard nothing in the night. Her employers had all been in excellent spirits lately, and she had never known them more cheerful and prosperous. She had fainted with horror upon entering the room in the morning and seeing that dreadful company round the table. She had, when she recovered, thrown open the window to let the morning air in, and had run down to the lane, whence she sent a farm-lad for the doctor. The lady was on her bed upstairs, if we cared to see her. It took four strong men to get the brothers into the asylum carriage. She would not herself stay in the house another day, and was starting that very afternoon to rejoin her family at St. Ives.

We ascended the stairs and viewed the body. Miss Brenda Tregennis had been a very beautiful girl, though now verging upon middle age. Her dark, clear-cut face was handsome, even in death, but there still lingered upon it something of that convulsion of horror which had been her last human emotion. From her bedroom we descended to the sitting-room where this strange tragedy had actually occurred. The charred ashes of the overnight fire lay in the grate. On the table were the four guttered and burned-out candles, with the cards scattered over its surface. The chairs had been moved back against the walls, but all else was as it had been the night before. Holmes paced with light, swift steps about the room; he sat in the various chairs, drawing them up and reconstructing their positions. He tested how much of the garden was visible; he examined the floor, the ceiling, and the fireplace; but never once did I see that sudden brightening of his eyes and tightening of his lips which would have told me that he saw some gleam of light in this utter darkness.

"Why a fire?" he asked once. "Had they always a fire in this small room on a spring evening?"

Mortimer Tregennis explained that the night was cold and damp. For that reason, after his arrival, the fire was lit. "What are you going to do now, Mr. Holmes?" he asked.

My friend smiled and laid his hand upon my arm. "I think, Watson, that I shall resume that course of tobacco-poisoning which you have so often and so justly condemned," said he. "With your permission, gentlemen, we will now return to our cottage, for I am not aware than any new factor is likely to come to our notice here. I will turn the facts over in my mind, Mr. Tregennis, and should anything occur to me I will certainly communicate with you and the vicar. In the meantime I wish you both good morning."

It was not until long after we were back in Poldhu Cottage that Holmes broke his complete and absorbed silence. He sat coiled in his armchair, his haggard and ascetic face hardly visible amid the blue swirl of his tobacco smoke, his black brows drawn down, his forehead contracted, his eyes vacant and far away. Finally, he laid down his pipe and sprang to his feet.

"It won't do, Watson!" said he, with a laugh. "Let us walk along the cliffs together and search for flint arrows. We are more likely to find them than clues to this problem. To let the brain work without sufficient material is like racing an engine. It racks itself to pieces. The sea air, sunshine, and patience, Watson—all else will come.

"Now, let us calmly define our position, Watson," he continued, as we skirted the cliffs together. "Let us get a firm grip of the very little which we *do* know, so that when fresh facts arise we may be ready to fit them into their places. I take it, in the first place, that neither of us is prepared to admit diabolical intrusions into the affairs of men. Let us begin by ruling that entirely out of our minds. Very good. There remain three persons who have been grievously stricken by some conscious or unconscious human agency. That is firm ground. Now, when did this occur? Evidently, assuming his narrative to be true, it was immediately after Mr. Mortimer Tregennis had left the room. That is a very important point. The presumption is that it was within a few minutes afterwards. The cards still lay upon the table. It was already past their usual hour for bed. Yet they had not changed their position or pushed back their chairs. I repeat, then, that the occurrence was immediately after his departure, and not later than eleven o'clock last night.

"Our next obvious step is to check, so far as we can, the movements of Mortimer Tregennis after he left the room. In this there is no difficulty, and they seem to be above suspicion. Knowing my methods as you do, you were, of course, conscious of the somewhat clumsy water-pot expedient by which I obtained a clearer impress of his foot than might otherwise have been possible. The wet, sandy path took it admirably. Last night was also wet, you will remember, and it was not difficult—having obtained a sample print—to pick out his track among others and to follow his movements. He appears to have walked away swiftly in the direction of the vicarage.

"If, then, Mortimer Tregennis disappeared from the scene, and yet some outside person affected the card-players, how can we reconstruct that person, and how was such an impression of horror conveyed? Mrs. Porter may be eliminated. She is evidently harmless. Is there any evidence that someone crept up to the garden window and in some manner produced so terrific an effect that he drove those who saw it out of their senses? The only suggestion in this direction comes from Mortimer Tregennis himself, who says that his brother spoke about some movement in the garden. That is certainly remarkable, as the night was rainy, cloudy, and dark. Anyone who had the design to alarm these people would be compelled to place his very face against the glass before he could be seen. There is a three-foot flower-border outside this window, but no indication of a footmark. It is difficult to imagine, then, how an outsider could have made so terrible an impression upon the company, nor have we found any possible motive for so strange and elaborate an attempt. You perceive our difficulties, Watson?"

"They are only too clear," I answered, with conviction.

"And yet, with a little more material, we may prove that they are not insurmountable," said Holmes. "I fancy that among your extensive archives, Watson, you may find some which were nearly as obscure. Meanwhile, we shall put the case aside until more accurate data are available, and devote the rest of our morning to the pursuit of neolithic man."

I may have commented upon my friend's power of mental detachment, but never have I wondered at it more than upon that spring morning in Cornwall when for two hours he discoursed upon Celts, arrowheads, and shards, as lightly as if no sinister mystery was waiting for his solution. It was not until we had returned in the afternoon to our cottage that we found a visitor awaiting us, who soon brought our minds back to the matter in hand. Neither of us needed to be told who that visitor was. The huge body, the craggy and deeply-seamed face with the fierce eyes and hawk-like nose, the grizzled hair which nearly brushed our cottage ceiling, the beard—golden at the fringes and white near the lips, save for the nicotine stain from his perpetual cigar—all these were as well known in London as in Africa, and could only be associated with the tremendous personality of Dr. Leon Sterndale, the great lion-hunter and explorer.

We had heard of his presence in the district, and had once or twice caught sight of his tall figure upon the moorland paths. He made no advances to us, however, nor would we have dreamed of doing so to him, as it was well known that it was his love of seclusion which caused him to spend the greater part of the intervals between his journeys in a small bungalow buried in the lonely wood of Beauchamp Arriance. Here, amid his books and his maps, he lived an absolutely lonely life, attending to his own simple wants, and paying little apparent heed to the affairs of his neighbours. It was a surprise to me, therefore, to hear him asking Holmes in an eager voice, whether he had made any advance in his reconstruction of this mysterious episode. "The county police are utterly at fault," said he; "but perhaps your wider experience has suggested some conceivable explanation. My only claim to being taken into your confidence is that during my many residences here I have come to know this family of Tregennis very well—indeed, upon my Cornish mother's side I could call them cousins—and their strange fate has naturally been a great shock to me. I may tell you that I had got as far as Plymouth upon my way to Africa, but the news reached me this morning, and I came straight back again to help in the inquiry."

Holmes raised his eyebrows.

"Did you lose your boat through it?"

"I will take the next."

"Dear me! that is friendship indeed."

"I tell you they were relatives."

"Quite so—cousins of your mother. Was your baggage aboard the ship?"

"Some of it, but the main part at the hotel."

"I see. But surely this event could not have found its way into the Plymouth morning papers?"

"No, sir; I had a telegram."

"Might I ask from whom?"

A shadow passed over the gaunt face of the explorer.

"You are very inquisitive, Mr. Holmes."

"It is my business."

With an effort, Dr. Sterndale recovered his ruffled composure.

"I have no objection to telling you," he said. "It was Mr. Roundhay, the vicar, who sent me the telegram which recalled me."

"Thank you," said Holmes. "I may say in answer to your original question, that I have not cleared my mind entirely on the subject of this case, but that I have every hope of reaching some conclusion. It would be premature to say more."

"Perhaps you would not mind telling me if your suspicions point in any particular direction?"

"No, I can hardly answer that."

"Then I have wasted my time, and need not prolong my visit." The famous doctor strode out of our cottage in considerable ill-humour, and within five minutes Holmes had followed him. I saw him no more until the evening, when he returned with a slow step and haggard face which assured me that he had made no great progress with his investigation. He glanced at a telegram which awaited him, and threw it into the grate.

"From the Plymouth hotel, Watson," he said. "I learned the name of it from the vicar, and I wired to make certain that Dr. Leon Sterndale's account was true. It appears that he did indeed spend last night there, and that he has actually allowed some of his baggage to go on to Africa, while he returned to be present at this investigation. What do you make of that, Watson?"

"He is deeply interested."

"Deeply interested—yes. There is a thread here which we have not yet grasped, and which might lead us through the tangle. Cheer up, Watson, for I am very sure that our material has not yet all come to hand. When it does, we may soon leave our difficulties behind us."

Little did I think how soon the words of Holmes would be realised, or how strange and sinister would be that new development which opened up an entirely fresh line of investigation. I was shaving at my window in the morning when I heard the rattle of hoofs, and, looking up, saw a dog-cart coming at a gallop down the road. It pulled up at our door, and our friend the vicar sprang from it and rushed up our garden path. Holmes was already dressed, and we hastened down to meet him.

Our visitor was so excited that he could hardly articulate, but at last in gasps and bursts his tragic story came out of him.

"We are devil-ridden, Mr. Holmes! My poor parish is devil-ridden!" he cried. "Satan himself is loose in it! We are given over into his hands!" He danced about in his agitation, a ludicrous object if it were not for his ashy face and startled eyes. Finally he shot out his terrible news.

"Mr. Mortimer Tregennis died during the night, and with exactly the same symptoms as the rest of his family."

Holmes sprang to his feet, all energy in an instant.

"Can you fit us both into your dog-cart?"

"Yes I can."

"Then, Watson, we will postpone our breakfast. Mr. Roundhay, we are entirely at your disposal. Hurry—hurry, before things get disarranged."

The lodger occupied two rooms at the vicarage, which were in an angle by themselves, the one above the other. Below was a large sitting-room; above, his bedroom. They looked out upon a croquet lawn which came up to the windows. We had arrived before the doctor or the police, so that everything was absolutely undisturbed. Let me describe exactly the scene as we saw it upon that misty March morning. It has left an impression which can never be effaced from my mind.

The atmosphere of the room was of a horrible and depressing stuffiness. The servant who had first entered had thrown up the window, or it would have been even more intolerable. This might partly be due to the fact that a lamp stood flaring and smoking on the centre table. Beside it sat the dead man, leaning back in his chair, his thin beard projecting, his spectacles pushed up on to his forehead, and his lean, dark face turned towards the window and twisted into the same distortion of terror which had marked the features of his dead sister. His limbs were convulsed and his fingers contorted as though he had died in a very paroxysm of fear. He was fully clothed, though there were signs that his dressing had been done in a hurry. We had already learned that his bed had been slept in, and that the tragic end had come to him in the early morning.

One realised the red-hot energy which underlay Holmes's phlegmatic exterior when one saw the sudden change which came over him from the moment that he entered the fatal apartment. In an instant he was tense and alert, his eyes shining, his face set, his limbs

347

quivering with eager activity. He was out on the lawn, in through the window, round the room, and up into the bedroom, for all the world like a dashing foxhound drawing a cover. In the bedroom he made a rapid cast around, and ended by throwing open the window, which appeared to give him some fresh cause for excitement, for he leaned out of it with loud ejaculations of interest and delight. Then he rushed down the stair, out through the open window, threw himself upon his face on the lawn, sprang up and into the room once more, all with the energy of the hunter who is at the very heels of his quarry. The lamp, which was an ordinary standard, he examined with minute care, making certain measurements upon its bowl. He carefully scrutinised with his lens the talc shield which covered the top of the chimney, and scraped off some ashes which adhered to its upper surface, putting some of them into an envelope, which he placed in his pocket-book. Finally, just as the doctor and the official police put in an appearance, he beckoned to the vicar and we all three went out upon the lawn.

"I am glad to say that my investigation has not been entirely barren," he remarked. "I cannot remain to discuss the matter with the police, but I should be exceedingly obliged, Mr. Roundhay, if you would give the inspector my compliments and direct his attention to the bedroom window and to the sitting-room lamp. Each is suggestive, and together they are almost conclusive. If the police would desire further information I shall be happy to see any of them at the cottage. And now, Watson, I think that, perhaps, we shall be better employed elsewhere."

It may be that the police resented the intrusion of an amateur, or that they imagined themselves to be upon some hopeful line of investigation; but it is certain that we heard nothing from them for the next two days. During this time Holmes spent some of his time smoking and dreaming in the cottage; but a greater portion in country walks which he undertook alone, returning after many hours without remark as to where he had been. One experiment served to show me the line of his investigation. He had bought a lamp which was the duplicate of the one which had burned in the room of Mortimer Tregennis on the morning of the tragedy. This he filled with the same oil as that used at the vicarage, and he carefully timed the period which it would take to be exhausted. Another experiment which he made was of a more unpleasant nature, and one which I am not likely ever to forget.

"You will remember, Watson," he remarked one afternoon, "that there is a single common point of resemblance in the varying reports which have reached us. This concerns the effect of the atmosphere of the room in each case upon those who had first entered it. You will recollect that Mortimer Tregennis, in describing the episode of his last visit to his brother's house, remarked that the doctor on entering the room fell into a chair? You had forgotten? Well, I can answer for it that it was so. Now, you will remember also that Mrs. Porter, the housekeeper, told us that she herself fainted upon entering the room and had afterwards opened the window. In the second case—that of Mortimer Tregennis himself—you cannot have forgotten the horrible stuffiness of the room when we arrived, though the servant had thrown open the window. That servant, I found upon inquiry, was so ill that she had gone to her bed. You will admit, Watson, that these facts are very suggestive. In each case there is evidence of a poisonous atmosphere. In each case, also, there is combustion going on in the room—in the one case a fire, in the other a lamp. The fire was needed, but the lamp was lit—as a comparison of the oil consumed will show—long after it was broad daylight. Why? Surely because there is some connection between three things—the

349

burning, the stuffy atmosphere, and, finally, the madness or death of those unfortunate people. That is clear, is it not?"

"It would appear so."

"At least we may accept it as a working hypothesis. We will suppose, then, that something was burned in each case which produced an atmosphere causing strange toxic effects. Very good. In the first instance—that of the Tregennis family—this substance was placed in the fire. Now the window was shut, but the fire would naturally carry fumes to some extent up the chimney. Hence one would expect the effects of the poison to be less than in the second case, where there was less escape for the vapour. The result seems to indicate that it was so, since in the first case only the woman, who had presumably the more sensitive organism, was killed, the others exhibiting that temporary or permanent lunacy which is evidently the first effect of the drug. In the second case the result was complete. The facts, therefore, seem to bear out the theory of a poison which worked by combustion.

"With this train of reasoning in my head I naturally looked about in Mortimer Tregennis's room to find some remains of this substance. The obvious place to look was the talc shield or smoke-guard of the lamp. There, sure enough, I perceived a number of flaky ashes, and round the edges a fringe of brownish powder, which had not yet been consumed. Half of this I took, as you saw, and I placed it in an envelope."

"Why half, Holmes?"

"It is not for me, my dear Watson, to stand in the way of the official police force. I leave them all the evidence which I found. The poison still remained upon the talc, had they the wit to find it. Now, Watson, we will light our lamp; we will, however, take the precaution to open our window to avoid the premature decease of two deserving members of society, and you will seat yourself near that open window in an armchair, unless, like a sensible man, you determine to have nothing to do with the affair. Oh, you will see it out, will you? I thought I knew my Watson. This chair I will place opposite yours, so that we may be the same distance from the poison, and face to face. The door we will leave ajar. Each is now in a position to watch the other and to bring the experiment to an end should the symptoms seem alarming. Is that all clear? Well, then, I take our powder—or what remains of it—from the envelope, and I lay it above the burning lamp. So! Now, Watson, let us sit down and await developments."

They were not long in coming. I had hardly settled in my chair before I was conscious of a thick, musky odour, subtle and nauseous. At the very first whiff of it my brain and my imagination were beyond all control. A thick, black cloud swirled before my eyes, and my mind told me that in this cloud, unseen as yet, but about to spring out upon my appalled senses, lurked all that was vaguely horrible, all that was monstrous and inconceivably wicked in the universe. Vague shapes swirled and swam amid the dark cloud-bank, each a menace and a warning of something coming, the advent of some unspeakable dweller upon the threshold, whose very shadow would blast my soul. A freezing horror took possession of me. I felt that my hair was rising, that my eyes were protruding, that my mouth was opened, and my tongue like leather. The turmoil within my brain was such that something must surely snap. I tried to scream, and was vaguely aware of some hoarse croak which was my own voice, but distant and detached from myself. At the same moment, in some effort of escape, I broke through that cloud of despair, and had a glimpse of Holmes's face, white, rigid, and drawn with horror—the very look which I had seen upon the features of the dead. It was that vision which gave me an instant of sanity and of strength. I dashed from my chair, threw my arms round Holmes, and together we lurched through the door, and an instant afterwards had thrown ourselves down upon the grass plot and were lying side by side, conscious only of the glorious sunshine which was bursting its way through the hellish cloud of terror which had girt us in. Slowly it rose from our souls like the mists from a landscape, until peace and reason had returned, and we were sitting upon the grass, wiping our clammy foreheads, and looking with apprehension at each other to mark the last traces of that terrific experience which we had undergone.

"Upon my word, Watson!" said Holmes at last, with an unsteady voice, "I owe you both my thanks and an apology. It was an unjustifiable experiment even for oneself, and doubly so for a friend. I am really very sorry."

"You know," I answered, with some emotion, for I had never seen so much of Holmes's heart before, "that it is my greatest joy and privilege to help you."

He relapsed at once into the half-humorous, half-cynical vein which was his habitual attitude to those about him. "It would be superfluous to drive us mad, my dear Watson," said he. "A candid observer would certainly declare that we were so already before we embarked upon so wild an experiment. I confess that I never imagined that the effect could be so sudden and so severe." He dashed into the cottage, and reappearing with the burning lamp held at full arm's length, he threw it among a bank of brambles. "We must give the room a little time to clear. I take it, Watson, that you have no longer a shadow of a doubt as to how these tragedies were produced?"

"None whatever."

"But the cause remains as obscure as before. Come into the arbour here, and let us discuss it together. That villainous stuff seems still to linger round my throat. I think we must admit that all the evidence points to this man, Mortimer Tregennis, having been the criminal in the first tragedy, though he was the victim in the second one. We must remember, in the first place, that there is some story of a family quarrel, followed by a reconciliation. How bitter that quarrel may have been, or how hollow the reconciliation we cannot tell. When I think of Mortimer Tregennis, with the foxy face and the small shrewd, beady eyes, behind the spectacles, he is not a man whom I should judge to be of a particularly forgiving disposition. Well, in the next place, you will remember that this idea of someone moving in the garden, which took our attention for a moment from the real cause of the tragedy, emanated from him. He had a motive in misleading us. Finally, if he did not throw this substance into the fire at the moment of leaving the room, who did do so? The affair happened immediately after his departure. Had anyone else come in, the family would certainly have risen from the table. Besides, in peaceful Cornwall, visitors do not arrive after ten o'clock at night. We may take it, then, that all the evidence points to Mortimer Tregennis as the culprit."

"Then his own death was suicide!"

"Well, Watson, it is on the face of it a not impossible supposition. The man who had the guilt upon his soul of having brought such a fate upon his own family might well be driven by remorse to inflict it upon himself. There are, however, some cogent reasons against it. Fortunately, there is one man in England who knows all about it, and I have made arrangements by which we shall hear the facts this afternoon from his own lips. Ah! he is a little before his time. Perhaps you would kindly step this way, Dr. Leon Sterndale. We have been conducting a chemical experiment indoors which has left our little room hardly fit for the reception of so distinguished a visitor."

I had heard the click of the garden gate, and now the majestic figure of the great African explorer appeared upon the path. He turned in some surprise towards the rustic arbour in which we sat.

"You sent for me, Mr. Holmes. I had your note about an hour ago, and I have come, though I really do not know why I should obey your summons."

"Perhaps we can clear the point up before we separate," said Holmes. "Meanwhile, I am much obliged to you for your courteous acquiescence. You will excuse this informal reception in the open air, but my friend Watson and I have nearly furnished an additional chapter to what the papers call the Cornish Horror, and we prefer a clear atmosphere for the present. Perhaps, since the matters which we have to discuss will affect you personally in a very intimate fashion, it is as well that we should talk where there can be no eavesdropping."

The explorer took his cigar from his lips and gazed sternly at my companion.

"I am at a loss to know, sir," he said, "what you can have to speak about which affects me personally in a very intimate fashion."

"The killing of Mortimer Tregennis," said Holmes.

For a moment I wished that I were armed. Sterndale's fierce face turned to a dusky red, his eyes glared, and the knotted, passionate veins started out in his forehead, while he sprang forward with clenched hands towards my companion. Then he stopped, and with a violent effort he resumed a cold, rigid calmness which was, perhaps, more suggestive of danger than his hot-headed outburst.

"I have lived so long among savages and beyond the law," said he, "that I have got into the way of being a law to myself. You would do well, Mr. Holmes, not to forget it, for I have no desire to do you an injury."

"Nor have I any desire to do you an injury, Dr. Sterndale. Surely the clearest proof of it is that, knowing what I know, I have sent for you and not for the police."

Sterndale sat down with a gasp, overawed for, perhaps, the first time in his adventurous life. There was a calm assurance of power in Holmes's manner which could not be withstood. Our visitor stammered for a moment, his great hands opening and shutting in his agitation.

"What do you mean?" he asked, at last. "If this is bluff upon your part, Mr. Holmes, you have chosen a bad man for your experiment. Let us have no more beating about the bush. What *do* you mean?"

"I will tell you," said Holmes, "and the reason why I tell you is that I hope frankness may beget frankness. What my next step may be will depend entirely upon the nature of your own defence."

"My defence?"

"Yes, sir."

"My defence against what?"

"Against the charge of killing Mortimer Tregennis."

Sterndale mopped his forehead with his handkerchief. "Upon my word, you are getting on," said he. "Do all your successes depend upon this prodigious power of bluff?"

"The bluff," said Holmes, sternly, "is upon your side, Dr. Leon Sterndale, and not upon mine. As a proof I will tell you some of the facts upon which my conclusions are based. Of your return from Plymouth, allowing much of your property to go on to Africa, I will say nothing save that it first informed me that you were one of the factors which had to be taken into account in reconstructing this drama—"

"I came back—"

"I have heard your reasons and regard them as unconvincing and inadequate. We will pass that. You came down here to ask me whom I suspected. I refused to answer you. You then went to the vicarage, waited outside it for some time, and finally returned to your cottage."

"How do you know that?"

"I followed you."

"I saw no one."

"That is what you may expect to see when I follow you. You spent a restless night at your cottage, and you formed certain plans, which in the early morning you proceeded to put into execution. Leaving your door just as day was breaking, you filled your pocket with some reddish gravel that was lying heaped beside your gate."

Sterndale gave a violent start and looked at Holmes in amazement.

"You then walked swiftly for the mile which separated you from the vicarage. You were wearing, I may remark, the same pair of ribbed tennis shoes which are at the present moment upon your feet. At the vicarage you passed through the orchard and the side hedge, coming out under the window of the lodger Tregennis. It was now daylight, but the household was not yet stirring. You drew some of the gravel from your pocket, and you threw it up at the window above you."

Sterndale sprang to his feet.

"I believe that you are the devil himself!" he cried.

Holmes smiled at the compliment. "It took two, or possibly three, handfuls before the lodger came to the window. You beckoned him to come down. He dressed hurriedly and descended to his sitting-room. You entered by the window. There was an interview—a short one—during which you walked up and down the room. Then you passed out and closed the window, standing on the lawn outside smoking a cigar and watching what occurred. Finally, after the death of Tregennis, you withdrew as you had come. Now, Dr. Sterndale, how do you justify such conduct, and what were the motives for your actions? If you prevaricate or trifle with me, I give you my assurance that the matter will pass out of my hands for ever."

Our visitor's face had turned ashen grey as he listened to the words of his accuser. Now he sat for some time in thought with his face sunk in his hands. Then with a sudden impulsive gesture he plucked a photograph from his breast-pocket and threw it on the rustic table before us.

"That is why I have done it," said he.

It showed the bust and face of a very beautiful woman. Holmes stooped over it.

"Brenda Tregennis," said he.

"Yes, Brenda Tregennis," repeated our visitor. "For years I have loved her. For years she has loved me. There is the secret of that Cornish seclusion which people have marvelled at. It has brought me close to the one thing on earth that was dear to me. I could not marry her, for I have a wife who has left me for years and yet whom, by the deplorable laws of England, I could not divorce. For years Brenda waited. For years I waited. And this is what we have waited for." A terrible sob shook his great frame, and he clutched his throat under his brindled beard. Then with an effort he mastered himself and spoke on.

"The vicar knew. He was in our confidence. He would tell you that she was an angel upon earth. That was why he telegraphed to me and I returned. What was my baggage or Africa to me when I learned that such a fate had come upon my darling? There you have the missing clue to my action, Mr. Holmes."

"Proceed," said my friend.

Dr. Sterndale drew from his pocket a paper packet and laid it upon the table. On the outside was written, "*Radix pedis diaboli*" with a red poison label beneath it. He pushed it towards me. "I understand that you are a doctor, sir. Have you ever heard of this preparation?"

"Devil's-foot root! No, I have never heard of it."

"It is no reflection upon your professional knowledge," said he, "for I believe that, save for one sample in a laboratory at Buda, there is no other specimen in Europe. It has not yet found its way either into the pharmacopoeia or into the literature of toxicology. The root is shaped like a foot, half human, half goat-like; hence the fanciful name given by a botanical missionary. It is used as an ordeal poison by the medicine-men in certain districts of West Africa, and is kept as a secret among them. This particular specimen I obtained under very extraordinary circumstances in the Ubanghi country." He opened the paper as he spoke, and disclosed a heap of reddish-brown, snuff-like powder.

"Well, sir?" asked Holmes sternly.

"I am about to tell you, Mr. Holmes, all that actually occurred, for you already know so much that it is clearly to my interest that you should know all. I have already explained the relationship in which I stood to the Tregennis family. For the sake of the sister I was friendly with the brothers. There was a family quarrel about money which estranged this man Mortimer, but it was supposed to be made up, and I afterwards met him as I did the others. He was a sly, subtle, scheming man, and several things arose which gave me a suspicion of him, but I had no cause for any positive quarrel.

"One day, only a couple of weeks ago, he came down to my cottage and I showed him some of my African curiosities. Among other things I exhibited this powder, and I told him of its strange properties, how it stimulates those brain centres which control the emotion of fear, and how either madness or death is the fate of the unhappy native who is subjected to the ordeal by the priest of his tribe. I told him also how powerless European science would be to detect it. How he took it I cannot say, for I never left the room, but there is no doubt that it was then, while I was opening cabinets and stooping to boxes, that he managed to abstract some of the devil's-foot root. I well remember how he plied me with questions as to the amount and the time that was needed for its effect, but I little dreamed that he could have a personal reason for asking.

"I thought no more of the matter until the vicar's telegram reached me at Plymouth. This villain had thought that I would be at sea before the news could reach me, and that I should be lost for years in Africa. But I returned at once. Of course, I could not listen to the details without feeling assured that my poison had been used. I came round to see you on the chance that some other explanation had suggested itself to you. But there could be none. I was convinced that Mortimer Tregennis was the murderer; that for the sake of money, and with the idea, perhaps, that if the other members of his family were all insane he would be the sole guardian of their joint property, he had used the devil's-foot powder upon them, driven two of them out of their senses, and killed his sister Brenda, the one human being whom I have ever loved or who has ever loved me. There was his crime; what was to be his punishment?

"Should I appeal to the law? Where were my proofs? I knew that the facts were true, but could I help to make a jury of countrymen believe so fantastic a story? I might or I might not. But I could not afford to fail. My soul cried out for revenge. I have said to you once before, Mr. Holmes, that I have spent much of my life outside the law, and that I have come at last to be a law to myself. So it was now.

I determined that the fate which he had given to others should be shared by himself. Either that or I would do justice upon him with my own hand. In all England there can be no man who sets less value upon his own life than I do at the present moment.

"Now I have told you all. You have yourself supplied the rest. I did, as you say, after a restless night, set off early from my cottage. I foresaw the difficulty of arousing him, so I gathered some gravel from the pile which you have mentioned, and I used it to throw up to his window. He came down and admitted me through the window of the sitting-room. I laid his offence before him. I told him that I had come both as judge and executioner; The wretch sank into a chair paralysed at the sight of my revolver. I lit the lamp, put the powder above it, and stood outside the window, ready to carry out my threat to shoot him should he try to leave the room. In five minutes he died. My God! how he died! But my heart was flint, for he endured nothing which my innocent darling had not felt before him. There is my story, Mr. Holmes. Perhaps, if you loved a woman, you would have done as much yourself. At any rate, I am in your hands. You can take what steps you like. As I have already said, there is no man living who can fear death less than I do."

Holmes sat for some little time in silence.

"What were your plans?" he asked, at last.

"I had intended to bury myself in Central Africa. My work there is but half finished."

"Go and do the other half," said Holmes. "I, at least, am not prepared to prevent you."

Dr. Sterndale raised his giant figure, bowed gravely, and walked from the arbour. Holmes lit his pipe and handed me his pouch.

"Some fumes which are not poisonous would be a welcome change," said he. "I think you must agree, Watson, that it is not a case in which we are called upon to interfere. Our investigation has been independent, and our action shall be so also. You would not denounce the man?"

"Certainly not," I answered.

"I have never loved, Watson, but if I did and if the woman I loved had met such an end, I might act even as our lawless lion-hunter has done. Who knows? Well, Watson, I will not offend your intelligence by explaining what is obvious. The gravel upon the windowsill was, of course, the starting-point of my research. It was unlike anything in the vicarage garden. Only when my attention had been drawn to Dr. Sterndale and his cottage did I find its counterpart. The lamp shining in broad daylight and the remains of powder upon the shield were successive links in a fairly obvious chain. And now, my dear Watson, I think we may dismiss the matter from our mind, and go back with a clear conscience to the study of those Chaldean roots which are surely to be traced in the Cornish branch of the great Celtic speech."

F. TENNYSON JESSE

The Mask

Fryniwyd Tennyson Jesse Harwood, nee Wynifried Margaret Jesse
(1888–1958) was an author, journalist, and criminologist. Daughter
of Reverend Eustace Tennyson D'Eyncourt Jesse and Edith James,
she was a grand-niece of Alfred, Lord Tennyson, poet laureate.
Fryn's career was based upon true crime narratives. Her most
famous book, *A Pin to See the Peepshow* (1934), was a fictionalisa-
tion of the case of Edith Thompson and Frederick Bywaters, a
couple executed in 1923 for the murder of Thompson's husband
Percy. Jesse was also a reporter in the First World War, docu-
menting the German attacks on Belgium in *Collier's Weekly*. Her
grand uncle, Alfred Tennyson, shared her interest in Cornwall.
He travelled to the county on multiple occasions in the 1850s
to investigate the North coast and interview antiquarians while
researching King Arthur for his epic *Idylls of the King*. Jesse's story
is reflective of her interest in true crime cases. In *Murder & Its
Motives* (1924) she separated the motivation for murder into six
categories—Gain, Revenge, Elimination, Jealousy, Conviction,
and Lust of Killing, all of which can be seen in some degree in
'The Mask'. The story draws on the traditions of uncanny doubles
and Cornwall's mining history, and relies on the construction of a
heavily racially coded femme fatale—somehow both English and
homogeneously foreign. "Vashti", the protagonist, has a Persian
name, taken from the Old Testament, and her description draws

on Cornwall's ancient links to the Phoenicians and Jewish communities, as well as a reference to antisemitic and phrenological imagery awfully recurrent in the wider Victorian and Edwardian cultural imaginary.

hen Vashti Bath was "led out" by the two most eligible young men in the village, the other women spoke their minds pretty freely on the subject; and when she progressed to that further stage known as "arm-a-crook," and still refrained from making the fateful choice, comment waxed bitter. The privilege of proposal belongs in Cornwall to that sex commonly called "the weaker"—a girl goes through the various stages of courtship conducted out of doors, and if she decides to marry the young man, asks him to "step in" one evening when he has seen her home, after which the engagement is announced. Vashti, in the most brazen way, was sampling two suitors at a time, and those two the most coveted men in Perran-an-zenna, and therein lay the sting for the womenfolk.

"What is there tu her, I should like to knaw?" the Wesleyan minister's wife demanded of her friends at a somewhat informal prayer meeting. "She'm a blowsy, ontidy kind o' maid who don't knaw one end of needle from t'other. When her stockin' heels go into holes she just pulls them further under her foot, till sometimes she du have to garter half way down her leg!"

"She'm blowsy, sure 'nough," agreed a widow woman of years and experience, "but she'm a rare piece o' red and white, and menfolk are feeble vessels. If a maid's a fine armful they never think on whether she won't be a fine handful. And Vashti du have a way wi' her."

That was the whole secret—Vashti had a way with her. She was a splendid slattern—showing the ancient Phœnician strain in her coarse, abundant black hair, level brows, and narrow, green-blue eyes, with a trace of Jew in the hawk-like line of nose and the

365

prominent chin curved a little upwards from her throat. A few years, and she would be lean and haggard, but now she was a fine, buoyant creature, swift and tumultuous, with a mouth like a flower. For all the slovenliness of her clothes she had a trick of putting them on which an Englishwoman never has as a birthright, and rarely achieves. Vashti could tie a ribbon so that every man she passed turned to look after her.

Perran-an-zenna is a mining village, and some of the menfolk work in the tin mines close at hand, and some in the big silver mine four miles away. James Glasson, the elder and harsher-featured of Vashti's lovers, worked in the latter, and there was every prospect of his becoming a foreman, as he had a passion for mechanics and for chemistry, and was supposed to be experimenting with a new process that would cheapen the cost of extracting the silver. Willie Strick, the younger, handsomer, more happy-go-lucky of the two men, went to "bal" in the tin mines, and was disinclined to save, but then his aged grandmother, with whom he lived, had been busy saving for twenty years. Strick was an eager lover, quick to jealousy—Glasson was uncommunicative even to Vashti, and careless of her opinions. Though the jealousy irked her it flattered her too, but on the other hand, Glasson's carelessness, even while it piqued her, made her covet him all the more.

This was how matters stood one evening in late March when Vashti had gone up to the moors to fetch in the cows—not her own, no Bath had been thrifty enough for that, but belonging to the farm where she worked. As she walked along in the glowing light, the white road winking up at her through a hole in her swinging skirt, and a heavy coil of hair jerking a little lower on the nape of her neck with each vigorous stride, Vashti faced the fact that matters could continue as they were no longer. At bottom Vashti was as hard as granite, she meant to have what she wanted; her only trouble was she had not quite settled what it was she did want. Like all her race, she had a strain of fatalism in her, that prompted her to choose whichever of the two men she should next chance to meet—and the woman in her suggested that at least such a declaration on the part of fate would give her the necessary impetus towards deciding upon the other.

Lifting her eyes from the regular, pendulum-like swing of her skirt that had almost mesmerised her lulled vision, she saw, dark against the sunset, the figure of a man. She knew it to be either James or Willie because of the peculiar square set of the shoulders and the small head—for the two men were, like most people in that intermarrying district, cousins, with a superficial trick of likeness, and an almost exact similarity of voice. A prescience of impending fate weighed on Vashti; the gaunt shaft of the disused Wheal Zenna mine, that stood up between her and the approaching man, seemed like a menacing finger. The man reached it first and stood leaning up against it, one foot on the rubble of granite that was scattered around, his arm, with the miner's bag slung over it, resting across his raised knee. Vashti half thought of going back, even without the cows, but it was already time the poor beasts were milked, and curiosity lured her on. She went across the circle of greener grass surrounding the shaft, and found Glasson awaiting her.

To every woman comes a time in life when she is ripe for the decisive man; and it is often a barren hour when he fails to appear. For Vashti the hour and the man had come together, and she knew it as she met Glasson's look. Putting out his hands, ingrained with earth in the finest seams of them, he laid them heavily on her shoulders, like a yoke. His bag swung forward and hit her on the chest, but neither of them noticed it.

"Vashti, y'um got to make'n end," he said. "One way or t'other. Which es et to be?"

She shook under his gaze, her lids drooped, but she tried to pout out her full under-lip with a pretence of petulance. Suddenly his grip tightened.

"So 'ee won't tell me? Then by G—, I'll du the tellin'! Yu'm my woman, do 'ee hear? Mine, and neither Will Strick nor any other chap shall come between us two."

Wheeling her round, he held her against the rough side of the shaft and bent his face to hers; she felt his lips crush on her own till she could have cried out with pain if she had been able to draw breath. When he let her go her breast heaved, and she stood with lowered head, holding her hand across her mouth.

"Now we'll get the cows, my lass," said Glasson quietly, "and take'n home, and then yu shall ask me to step in."

During the short, fierce courtship that followed Vashti saw very little of Willie Strick, though she heard he talked much of emigrating, vowing he would disappear in the night and not come home until he had made a fortune. All of Vashti's nature was in abeyance save for one emotion—a stunned, yet pleasurable, submission. It was not until several months after her marriage that she began to feel again the more ordinary and yet more complex sensations of every-day life. If she had to the full a primitive woman's joy in being possessed, she had also the instinctive need for possessing her man utterly, and James Glasson was only partly hers. It was borne in on her that by far the larger side of him was his own, never to be given to any woman. Ambition and an uncanny secretiveness made up the real man; he had set himself to winning his wife chiefly because the want of her distracted him from his work and fretted him.

He bent the whole of life to his purposes, without any parade of power, but with a laborious care that gradually settled on Vashti like a blight. When she realised that no matter how rightly she wore her little bits of finery, he no longer noticed them, realised that she was merely a necessity to him as his woman—something to be there when she was wanted, she began to harden. He still had a fascination for her when he chose to exert it—his very carelessness and sureness of her were what made the fascination, but gradually it wore thinner and slacker, and a sullen resentment began to burn through her seeming submission.

The Glasson's cottage was tucked away in a hollow of the moor, only the chimney of it visible from Perran-an-zenna, and Vashti began to chafe under the isolation, and to regret she had never been at more pains to make friends among her own sex.

As summer drew to its full, Vashti watched the splendid pageant of it in the sky and moor with unappreciative eyes. If anyone had told her that her soul had been formed by the country of her birth and upbringing, she would have thought it sheer lunacy, but her parents were not more responsible for Vashti than the land itself. The hardness and bleakness of it, the inexpressible charm of it, the soft, indolent airs, scented with flowers, or pungent with salt, above all, that reticence that makes for lonely thoughts, these things had, generation by generation, moulded her forbears, and their influence was in her blood. Even the indifference with which she saw, arose from her oneness with her own country, and in this she was like all true Cornish folk before and since—they belong to Cornwall body and soul. The quality of reticence had become secretiveness in James Glasson—he took a childish pleasure in keeping any little happening from the world in general and Vashti in particular, and the consequence was that, in her, strength was hardening into relentlessness.

One market day she was returning from Penzance—a drive of some eight miles, accomplished in the cart of their nearest neighbour—with a paper parcel on her knee, which she kept on fingering under the rug as though to make sure it was still there. At the neighbour's farm she got out, thanked him, and started to walk the remaining mile over the moor, with the precious parcel laid carefully on the top of the basket of household goods. It had been one of those days when the air seems to have a liquid quality that makes it almost visible—a delicate effulgence that envelops every object far and near, blurring harsh outlines and giving an effect as though trees and plants stood up into an element too subtle for water and too insistent for ether. The cloud shadows gave a plum-like bloom to the miles of interfolding hills, and inset among the grey-green of the moor the patches of young bracken showed vivid as slabs of emerald. Lightly as balls of thistledown the larks hopped swiftly over the heather on their thin legs, the self-heal and bird's-foot trefoil made a carpet of purple and yellow; from the heavy-scented gorse came the staccato notes of the crickets, while in a distant copse a cuckoo called faintly on her changed, June note. As Vashti rounded the corner of the rutted track and the cottage came into view, she paused. The deeply sloping slate roof was iridescent as a pigeon's breast, and the whitewashed walls were burnished with gold by the late sunlight, while against the faded peacock blue of the fence the evening primroses seemed luminous. Even to Vashti it all looked different, transmuted. Her fingers pressed the shiny paper of the parcel till it crackled and a smile tugged at her lips. After all, it was not bad to be young and handsome on an evening in June, to be returning to a home of her own, with under her arm a parcel that, to her, was an event. Vashti had bought that thing dear to the heart of the country-woman, a length of rich black dress silk; she meant to make it up herself, and though her stitches were clumsy, she knew she could cut and drape a gown better than many a conscientious sempstress. And then—then she would take her place as wife to the most discussed man in all that part of Penwith and hold up her head at Meeting. Even James himself could not but treat her differently when she had black silk on her back.

She went through to the outhouse, which James used as a workshop, and tried the door. It was locked. "James!" she cried, rattling the latch, "James!"

She heard him swear swiftly, then came the sound of something hastily put down and a cupboard door being shut. Then Glasson opened the door a few inches, and stood looking down at her.

"Get into kitchen," he said briefly, "can't 'ee see I'm busy?"

Already Vashti's pleasure in her purchase was beginning to fade, but she stood her ground, though wrathfully.

"Yu needn' think yu'm the only person with secrets," she flashed: "I'd a fine thing to show 'ee here, if yu'd a mind to see it—now I shall keep'n to myself."

"Woman's gear!" gibed Glasson, "you've been buying fulishness over to market. Get the supper or I shan't have time for a bite before I go to see t' foreman."

"That's all yu think on," she retorted; "yu and your own business."

"That's all yu should think on, either," he said, pulling her towards him with a hand on the back of her neck, and kissing her on her unresponsive mouth. She stood sullenly; then, when he dropped his hand, went into the house. She heard him turn the key in the lock as she went. That night she cried hot tears of anger on to the new dress length, and next day she went across the moor and met Willie Strick on his way home to Perran-an-zenna.

That was the first of many meetings, for Willie's resentment faded away before the old charm of Vashti's presence. In spite of his handsome face, he was oddly like James. The backs of their heads were similar enough to give Vashti a little shock whenever she passed behind her husband as he sat at table, or each time that Willie lay beside her on the moor, his head on her lap. She would pull the curly rings of his hair out over her fingers, and even while she admired the glint of it, some little memory of a time when James' hair had glinted in the sun or candlelight, pricked at her—not with any feeling for him except resentment, but at first it rather spoiled her lover for her. They had to meet by stealth, but that was easy enough, as James was now on an afternoon core, and Willie on a morning one. To do the latter justice, he had tried, at the beginning, a feeble resistance to the allure that Vashti had for him, not from any scruple of conscience, but because his pleasure-loving nature shrank from anything that might lead to unpleasantness. And, careless as he seemed of his wife, James Glasson would be an ugly man to deal with if he discovered the truth. So far there had been nothing except the love-making of a limited though expressive vocabulary, and Vashti curbed him and herself for three whole weeks. She was set on possessing Willie's very soul—here, at least, was a man whom she could so work upon that he would always be hers even to the most reluctant outpost of his being. By the end of those weeks, her elusiveness, the hint of passion in her, and the steady force of her will, had enslaved Strick hopelessly: he was maddened, reckless, and timid all at once.

"Vashti, it's got to end," he said, desperately, as he walked with her one evening as near to the cottage as he dared, and as he spoke he slid an arm round her waist. To his surprise, she yielded and swayed towards him so that her shoulder touched his; in the sunset light her upturned face glimmered warm and bewilderingly full of colour.

"Wait a bit, lad," she breathed. "James goes up to London church town tomorrow to see one of the managers—happen he'll be gone a week or more…"

He felt her soft mouth on his cheek for a moment and his arms went round her—the next moment came a crash that seemed to split the sky, and from the outhouse leapt a whistling column of flame.

Stricken with a superstitious terror, Willie screamed—loudly and thinly, like a woman. Vashti recoiled, flung up her hands, then rushed towards the burning outhouse.

"James is in there!" she cried. "Oh, get'en out, get'en out!"

The flame had been caused by an exploded lamp, but there was not much inflammatory stuff for it to feed on, and a thick smoke, reeking of chemicals, hung above the outhouse. As Vashti, followed by the shaking Strick, reached the door, it swung open and a Thing stood swaying a moment on the step.

It seemed to the lovers' first horrified glimpse that all of Glasson's face had been blown away. The whole of one side of it was covered by an enormous blister, a nightmare thing, which, as the woman gazed at it, burst and fell into blackness. The same moment Glasson dropped his length across the threshold.

"The doctor, go for doctor," whispered Vashti with dry lips, "as quick as you can—I—I dursn't turn 'en over."

So Glasson lay with what had been his face against a patch of grass, while Willie ran, horror-ridden, to Perran-an-zenna, for the doctor.

Dry-eyed, Vashti watched by her husband for three nights, and all praised her for wifely devotion. She sat by the gleam of a flickering night-light, her eyes on the bandaged face—the linen was only slit just as much as was necessary for breathing.

"Well, Mrs. Glasson," said the doctor cheerily, as he finished his inspection on the third night, "I can give you good news. Your husband will live, and will keep the sight of one eye. But—though of course wonders can be done with modern surgery—we can't build up what's gone. He'll always have to wear a mask, Mrs. Glasson."

When he had gone Vashti went and stood by the bed, looking down on the unconscious man, who lay breathing heavily—how easy it would be to lay a hand over that slit in the linen—a few minutes, and this nightmare would be over. She half put out her hand, then drew it back. She was not yet capable of cold-blooded crime.

Lighting a candle, she took from a drawer a paper parcel, which she unfolded on the little table. As the still untouched folds of the black dress length, with a few little hard-edged blots on it that meant tears, came into view, Vashti's self-control broke down. She wept stormily, her head along her arms. Release had flaunted so near to her, and was withdrawn, and her horror of the Thing on the bed was mingled with a pity for it that ate into her mind. She dried her burning eyes, and picking up the scissors, began to cut a mask out of the tear-stained breadths; her invincible habit of considering herself forbade her, even at that moment, to use the good yards for such a purpose.

The candle-flame was showing wan in the grey of the dawning when Vashti put the last stitches to the mask—she had made it very deep, so that it would hang to just below the jawbone, and she had laboriously buttonhole-stitched round the one eye-hole, and sewn tape-strings firmly to the sides, top and bottom. The mask was finished.

James Glasson's figure, a trifle stooped and groping, with that sinister black curtain from cap to collar, soon ceased to be an object of fearful curiosity in Perran-an-zenna; even the children became so used to it that they left off calling out as he passed. He grew more silent and morose than ever, and his secretiveness showed itself in all sorts of ingenious petty ways.

Vashti had the imaginative streak of her race, and life in the lonely cottage with this masked personality took on the quality of nightmare. She felt his one eye watching her continually, and was tormented by the thought, "How much does he know?" Who could tell? Had he seen anything from the outhouse window when she had rashly let Willie come so near, or did he know who it was who had fetched the doctor? Sometimes a meaning word seemed to show that he knew everything, sometimes she argued that he could only guess. The black mask filled the whole of her life, the thought of it was never out of her mind, not even when she was working on her old farm, for she had to be breadwinner now. She found herself dwelling on what lay behind the mask, wondering whether it could be as bad as that black expanse, and once she woke herself at night, screaming: "Tear 'en down, Willie! Tear the black mask down!" and then lay trembling, wondering whether her husband had heard. For days he said nothing and she felt herself safe; then one night he turned to her. "There's no air," he complained. "Can't 'ee take down t' curtains? If 'ee can't do anything else, why—tear 'en down, tear 'en down!"

He had mimicked her very voice, and silent with fear, she took down the curtain, her fingers shaking so that the rings jingled together along the rod. One day, when he was working in the garden he turned to face the wind. She saw him sideways against the sky, and the black mask, held taut at brow and chin by the strings, was being blown inward. She never forgot the horror of that concave line against the sky.

She came to regard the mask with superstitious awe; it seemed James Glasson's character materialised—the outward expression of the inner man. Nervous and cowed to abjectness as she was, she felt near the end of her endurance. The perpetual scheming to meet Willie unknown to her husband—a difficulty now the latter was nearly always about the house-place, and the wearing uncertainty of "How much does he know?" were fraying her nerves. Some two months after the accident the crash came.

James had gone to Truro to see a surgeon there, and had announced his intention of spending the night with cousins. The utter bliss of being alone, and having the cottage free from the masked presence for even one day acted like a balm on Vashti. She forbade Willie to come near her till the evening, partly from motives of prudence, but chiefly because she craved for solitude. By the afternoon she was more her old, sufficient, well-poised self, and when evening drew on she busied herself about her little preparations in the kitchen with a colour burning in her cheeks and a softened light in her eyes. That evening Vashti Glasson was touched with a grace of womanliness she had never worn for her husband. Every harmless and tender instinct of the lover was at work in her, making her choose her nicest tablecloth, arrange a cluster of chrysanthemums in an ornate glass vase, put a long-discarded ribbon of gaudy pink in her hair. Then she took off her working frock of dirty, ill-mended serge, and shook out in triumph the folds of the black silk, now made up in all its glory, and hideous with cheap jet. It converted her from a goddess of the plough to a red-wristed, clumsy girl of the people; and when her hair was dressed in the fashionable lumps, with a fringe-net hardening the outlines, she looked like a shop-girl, but she herself admired the effect intensely.

When three taps at the window told that Strick was outside, the colour flew to her face, making her so beautiful that she triumphed even over her costume; she had become a high priestess of Love, and was not to be cheated of any of the ritual. She was decked out as for a bridal; no more rough-and-ready wooing and winning for her. But Strick's passion was somewhat daunted by all the preparations for his welcome; the kitchen looked unusual, and so did she, and he hung back for a moment on the threshold.

"What's come to 'ee?" he asked, foolishly agape.

"'Tes a weddin' gown made for yu," said Vashti simply.

"But 'tes black!" he stammered. "'Tes ill luck on a black bridal, Vassie."

"Ours is no white bridal, lad," she told him. "Come in and set down—yes, take that chair," and she pushed Glasson's accustomed seat forward for her lover.

Conversation languished during the meal—Willie Strick was bewildered by the oddness of everything, Vashti included—and his was no level head to plan any details or set a scene—Vashti won by stealth, anywhere and anyhow, was all he had thought of or wished for. Hers was the mastermind and he was helpless before it, and while she inflamed him she frightened him too.

A full moon swam up over the line of distant sea that showed in a dip of the moorland, and the lamp began to smell and burn low. They had finished supper, and Willie was drinking rather freely of the whisky she had set before him. Vashti turned out the lamp, and as she did so a sudden harsh noise sent the heart to her throat, while Willie sprang up fearfully. It was only the poker, that, caught by the full skirt of the black silk frock, had been sent clattering to the ground, but it made them stare at each other in a stricken panic for a speechless minute. The white light of the moon shone clearly into the room, throwing a black pattern of window-shadow over the disordered supper table, where the chrysanthemums, overturned by Willie's movement, lay across an empty dish, and in the silence

377

the two startled people could hear the rhythmic sound of the water as it drip-drip-dripped on to the floor.

Vashti was the first to recover herself. "Us be plum fulish, Willie!" she said, with an attempt at a laugh. "Do believe us both thought it was James, and him safe to Truro."

"If 'tes," said Strick madly, "he shan't take 'ee from me now. I'll have 'ee, I swear it."

Vashti did not answer,—with fascinated eyes she was watching the door slowly open—she could see the strip of moonlit brightness, barred by the darkness of an arm, grow wider and wider. She knew, before the form, so terribly like Willie's, now its masked face was against the light, appeared, that it was her husband.

Quite what happened next she could not have told. The little room seemed full and dark with fear—blind, unreasoning fear, that beat even about her head. The long-drawn-out crash of the overturned table added to her confusion—then quite suddenly the sounds of struggling ceased and one man rose to his feet. In the dimness of the room, seeing only the shape of him, she could not tell whether it were James or Willie, until he turned his face to the moonlight, and she saw, with a throb of relief, Strick's face.

"Get a light, Vassie," he whispered. "I fear he's dead."

She lit a candle and they knelt down by Glasson. In falling his head had hit the fender, and blood was trickling on to the floor. She ripped open his shirt and felt for his heart as well as her trembling fingers would allow. She lifted his arm and let it fall—it dropped a dead weight on to the tiled floor. It seemed to her excited fancy that already he was turning cold.

"Willie, you've killed 'en!" she whispered. They both spoke low, as though they thought the dead man could overhear.

"I didn't hit 'en," babbled Willie. "He stumbled and fell and hit his head—they'll make me swing for this—what shall us du, what shall us du?"

"Wait—I must think," commended the woman. She pressed her hands to her forehead, and sat very still.

"Have 'ee thought?" whispered Willie, anxiously.

"Yes—I've thought. Willie, yu'm rare and like—he—and that'll save us."

"What do 'ee mean?" asked Willie, thinking the shock had turned her brain.

"The mask!" replied Vashti, "the mask!"

Then, kneeling by the still body, they talked in whispers—she unfolding her plan—he recoiling from it, weakly protesting, and then giving way.

They were to take the dead man between them to the disused mine shaft and throw him down, then Willie was to wear the black mask, and take Glasson's place, until they could sail for America together. Like all simple plans, it had a touch of genius. Willie's constant talk of emigrating, his oft-heard boasts of slipping away in the night and not coming back till he had made a fortune, would all help to cover up his disappearance. And who was to connect it with Vashti and her silent, eccentric, black-masked husband—who would speak to him or her on the subject? And if they did—she could always invent a plausible answer, while he was safeguarded by the fact that the strongest point of likeness between the two men was their voices. The only dissimilar thing about them had been their faces.

"I won't wear his mask," said Willie, shuddering; "I couldn' put 'en against me. You must make me another."

"I'll make 'en now," said Vashti. She rose to her feet, and setting the candle on the seat of a chair, looked about her.

"You must put the room to rights," she commanded. "Make 'en look as though James and I had just had our bit o' supper. Mop up the water and sweep all the broken cloam together—and—and take him to the passage-way."

"Yu'm not going to lave me alone wi' he?" cried Willie, aghast.

"Edn room for me to work here. I'll be up overstairs making the mask. Keep t' curtain over the window."

Upstairs, she seized scissors and hacked a square out of the front of her gown. Then she sat and sewed as she had sewed once before, when her husband had lain motionless on the bed. Every now and then came small sounds of things being moved from down below, then a heavy fall and the sound of something being dragged.

"How's et goin', Willie?" she called out.

"'Tes all right," he called back. "I've put 'en in passage."

The moon was near setting when the mask was finished, and she went to the top of the stairs with it in her hand.

"There 'tes," she whispered. "I'll drop it down. Put it in your pocket and I'll change my gown. 'Tes time we were stirrin'."

The mask fluttered down in the darkness, and she went back to her room and changed swiftly into the old serge.

It was a ghastly journey to the old mine shaft, the heavy form of the dead man sagging between them. They dared have no light, and went stumbling over tussocks and ruts; but as both would have known the way blindfold, they found the shaft without difficulty. They scrambled up the sloping rubble of stones and tipped the body over the jagged hole in the side of the shaft, and after what seemed an interminable silence there came a thud from several hundred feet below them, then another, as though the body had rebounded, then all was stillness.

Vashti leant up against the side of the shaft, as she had leant when James kissed her there, and shut her eyes; the sweat running down her brow had matted her lashes together into thick points, and the drops tickled her neck so that she put up her hand to it. Both she and the man were drawing the deep, hoarse breaths of exhaustion, and for a few minutes they rested in silence—then he spoke. "Yu must be comin' back along o' me now," he told her, "the dawn'll be showin' soon."

"Yes, yes," cried Vashti, starting up, "us may meet someone going to bal, sure 'nough."

"Tes all right—I've got t' mask on. Come."

He closed his fingers over her arm so harshly that she winced, and together they made their way back in the cold, bleak hush that preceded the autumnal dawn. Gradually, as they went, some glimmerings of what her life would be henceforth appeared to the woman. The fear of neighbours, the efforts to appear natural, the memory of that slowly-opening door, and the still thing by the fender, the consciousness of what lay at the bottom of the disused shaft; and, above all, the terrible reminder of her husband in the masked Willie—it would be like living with a ghost...

Once back at the cottage, he drew her within and barred the door behind them. She moved away to find a light, but he caught her.

"Won't 'ee give me so much as a kiss, and me with red hands because of yu?" he asked.

She felt the mask brush her cheek, and broke away with a cry. She heard him laugh as she lit a candle, and turned towards him.

"A black bridal!" he cried wildly; "did I tell 'ee 'twas a black bridal? 'Tes a red one, do 'ee hear?"

"Willie," she begged him, "take off t'mask now we'm alone."

"Aren't 'ee afeared?" he asked.

"'Tes safe enough till mornin', and I du hate that mask more'n the devil. Take 'en off."

"I'll take 'en off—to please yu, lass."

He seized the mask violently by the hem and ripped it away—and she saw it was her husband.

"Yu fule!" he said slowly, following her as she backed away from him, her mouth slack with fear, her eyes glazed, her whole being showing her as almost bereft of her senses. "Yu fule to think to fule me! Yu was quick enough to say I was dead; I'm not so easy killed, Vassie. No so easy killed as your lover was—just the carven'-knife between his shoulders when he was stoopin' down, that's all. He was fearful of lookin' at the dead man; he never knew the dead man was lookin' at he. Yu heard him fall, Vassie, and thought it was him movin' me—"

"Put t'mask on," wailed Vashti, pressing her fingers against her eyes; "put t'mask on again, for the love o' God!"

"There's been enough o' masks," he retorted grimly. "You've got to bear to see me now; me, not your lover that you've helped to tip over Wheal Zenna shaft. Eh, yu fule, did 'ee think I didn' knaw? I've knawed all these months; I've seen 'ee meet 'en; I told 'ee I was going to stop the night over to Truro so as to catch 'ee together; I let 'ee think I was dead, and listened t' the plan yu thought to make. Only half a man am I, wi' no mouth left to kiss with? I've an eye left to see with, and an ear to hear with, and a hand to strike with, and a tongue to teach 'ee with."

"I'll tell on 'ee," said Vashti, "I'll tell the police on 'ee. Murderer, that's what yu are."

"I doan't think 'ee will, my dear. 'Tedn a tale as'll do yu any good—a woman who cheats her husband, and tries to kill 'en, and helps to carry a body two miles over moor and tip 'en down shaft. And what have 'ee to complain on, I should like to knaw? When I wear t'mask yu can pretend I'm Willie—handsome Willie. Willie who can kiss a maid and make a fine upstandin' husband. Willie was goin' to be me, why shudn' yu think I was Willie? Do 'ee, my dear, if 'tes any comfort to 'ee."

He slipped on the mask as he spoke and knotted the strings. The door had swung open, and the candle flame shook in the draught as though trying, in fear, to strain away from the wick. The steel-cold light of dawn grew in the sky and filtered into the room, showing all the sordid litter of it; the frightened woman, with a pink ribbon awry in her disordered hair, and the ominous figure of the masked man. He came towards her round the table.

"'Tes our bridal night, lass!" he said. "Why do 'ee shrink away? Mind yu that 'tes Willie speakin'! Don't let us think on James Glasson dead to the bottom 'o the shaft. I'm Willie—brave Willie who loves 'ee..."

As his arms came out to catch her, she saw his purpose in his eye, and remembered his words, "A red bridal, lass, a red bridal!"

At the last moment she woke out of her stupor, turned, and ran, he after her. Across the little garden, down the moorland road, over heather and slippery boulders and clinging bracken, startling the larks from their nests, scattering the globes of dew. Once she tried to make for a side-track that led to Perran-an-zenna, but he headed her off, and once again she was running, heavily now, towards Wheal Zenna mine-shaft. He was gaining on her, and her breath was nearly spent. Both were going slowly, hardly above a stumbling walk, as the shaft came in sight; the drawing of their breath sounded harsh as the rasping of a file through the still air. As she neared the shaft she turned her head and saw him almost on her, and saw the gleam of something in his uplifted hand. She gathered together all her will, concentrated in those few moments all the strength of her nature, determined to cheat him at the last. Up the rubble of stones she scrambled, one gave beneath her foot and sent her down, and abandoning the effort, she lay prone, awaiting the end.

But Vashti's luck held—it was the man who was to lose. A couple of miners who had been coming up the path from Perran-an-zenna had seen the chase and followed hot foot, unnoticed by the two straining, frantic creatures, who heard nothing but the roaring in their own ears. They caught Glasson as he ran across the patch of grass to the shaft, and he doubled up without a struggle in their arms. Physical and mental powers had failed together, and from that day James Glasson was a hopeless idiot—harmless and silent. Vashti had won indeed.

Admirable woman of affairs that she was, she took a good sleep before confronting the situation; then she made up her story and stuck to it. Willie's name was never mentioned, and his disappearance, so long threatened, passed as a minor event, swamped in the greater stir of Glasson's attempt to murder his wife. His madness had taken the one form that made Vashti safe—he had gone mad on secretiveness. How much he remembered not even she knew, but not a word could anyone drag from him. He would lay his finger where his nose should have been under the mask, and wag his head slyly. "Naw, naw, I was never one for tellin'," he would say. "James Glasson's no such fule that he can't keep 'enself to 'enself."

He lived on for several years in the asylum, and Vashti, after the free and easy fashion of the remote West, took to herself another husband. She went much to chapel, and there was no more religious Methodist to be found than she, and no one harder on the sins and vanities of young women. One thing in particular she held in what seemed an unreasoning abhorrence—and that was a black silk gown.